WHAT THE CRITICS ARE SAYING

"Eye opening and haunting…"

~Literary R&R: Charlene Reviews

Coming Out is a murder-mystery page-turner. I will admit, as a Conservative Christian, this is not a topic I read a lot of. Being that this novel is based around a transgender woman, I cautiously accepted it for review. I am pleasantly surprised to find that I enjoyed it immensely, and humbly admit that I learned a few things along the way. I read it straight through and found myself cheering Bobbi on, especially at the end, as she completely embraces her identity.

James writes with an honest, no-apologies style that grips you. Whether you have prejudices or not, the characters are engaging and believable, with true human emotion. A beautiful sincerity shines through the words and makes you identify with the struggles and horror Bobbi, and her friends, feel at being seen as less-than. The murder really plays a backseat to the identity struggles and, ultimately, to the ability of the human spirit to prevail. Eye opening and haunting, long after the last page. 5 out of 5 stars!

"…I HIGHLY recommend this book…"

~Bookingly Yours: Jenai

I do not remember EVER reading any GLBT (Gay Lesbian Bisexual Transsexual) book. When I was asked to review this book, I instantly liked the synopsis, it looked interesting, but I was afraid that there may be some scenes in the book that I may not like. True enough, there are scenes which I had to skip because I just didn't feel comfortable reading them, but I still continued reading. Why? Because honestly, the plot is great…. I HIGHLY recommend this book for those readers looking for a unique experience.

"You will find this a haunting, heartbreaking, and eye opening page-turner."

~Jackie Anton, Book Reviews by Jackie

"Needs to be read."

~Bleue Benton, Manager/Transgender Literature Collection
Collection Development Manager, Oak Park (IL) Public Library, www.oppl.org

Renee James has written a groundbreaking mystery. Her smart, perceptive, and engaging heroine leads us through gender identity issues as she seeks understanding, acceptance, and justice. This page-turner is important and needs to be read.

"Let's hope this fun book is the beginning of a long series."

~Rachel Pollack, Author, *The Secret Woman*

There are mysteries with transgender victims, and others with transgender villains (usually psychopathic serial killers). Much rarer—and sorely needed—are stories with genuine transgender heroines—"genuine" meaning really transgender and really heroic. Let's hope this fun book is the beginning of a long series.

"This book …goes to a place that only an insider would normally be privy."

~Honey West

Being a person who started their transition late in life. I ___ ___ ___ ___ ___ k like this when I was growing up I might have transitioned ___ ___ ___ nsgender experience you have to look beyond the make up ___ ___ ___ nside the individuals and those who admire them. This book ___ ___ ___ only an insider would normally be privy. If you want to have ___ ___ ___ ne in the shoes of a trans woman, from the inside out, pick up ___

Coming Out Can Be Murder

Windy City Publishers
2118 Plum Grove Rd., #349
Rolling Meadows, IL 60008
www.windycitypublishers.com

Published in the United States of America

First Edition: 2012

ISBN: 978-1-935766-28-5

Library of Congress Control Number: 2011941099

Cover Design by Quinn R. Pritchard | The Burroughs Group

COMING OUT
CAN BE
MURDER

RENEE JAMES

*The journey from male to female
is never easy. For Bobbi Logan,
it is pure murder.*

To Phyl
Appearance is
only a suggestion
of reality
—Renee
James

ACKNOWLEDGEMENTS

Thanks to Katie Thomas for being my mentor and for reading each draft of *Coming Out Can Be Murder*.

Thanks to Mary Whitledge for her wisdom, moderation, and professional counsel.

Thanks to June LaTrobe for sharing her intimacy with Boystown.

And thanks to my sisters and brothers in the Chicago transgender community—you make a difficult path so much easier to travel.

Prologue

SHE COOS THE WORDS IN HIS EAR, her voice oddly androgynous, neither fully feminine nor distinctly male.

"Johnnie, are we ever going to go out? Like in public? You know, maybe just to dinner or something?" His tranquility shatters. He becomes aware of where he is. Her breath is tinted with the smell of him. He feels the perspiration on his body and hers as she rubs against him. The feel of it is vile. Like they are painted in urine.

He feels the serenity evaporate, the rare calm that comes after an orgasm long denied, arriving like a bolt from a cloud of doubt. He tries to save it, tries to relive that glorious moment of eruption so violent it is followed by watery joints and a blank mind. A fat, sweet moment without guilt or doubt. Why does it work with this one? Why this…thing?

Their bodies slide against each other. He thinks of a snake sliding along his body, but suppresses the thought. When he lets his disgust take command of him, bad things happen. He blocks the serpent image but he can't check his revulsion. The tranquility is gone. The satisfaction is gone. The relief is gone. He feels crowded, suffocating. He pushes her off him.

"Get me some water," he says. It's a command. As he gives it he looks away. It is her principal virtue that she knows she is a thing and responds to him like a dim-witted servant. And the fact that, for some reason, she arouses him when real women can't.

She obediently rises quietly from the bed and pads off to the kitchen, naked. She looks back just before leaving the room to see if he's watching. He isn't.

He is staring blankly into space, his mind filled with fleeting images from an evening that started with such promise. A power date with the CEO of a new account. A hot, haughty bitch of a beautiful woman, eager to consummate a big business deal with dinner and a roll in the hay. She came on to him like a slut. She even got him hard, so hard he thought his body would work right this time. But the moment passed. He barely kept it together long enough to pleasure her and had to fake his own. He dashed into the bathroom as soon as they uncoupled so she couldn't see the empty condom. Trying to save face, trying to save the deal, maintain an image.

Yes, he told her, everything was okay. Just pressure at the office, a full bladder.

He left as soon as he could. His scrotum ached. His teeth were clenched. He wanted relief. He needed relief. He was bursting with shame and tension.

He drove straight to her place, parked a block away. Knocked on the door at just past midnight. She answered wearing a robe, still drowsy. He had wakened her from a deep sleep. "Johnnie!" she said with delight, her voice a whisper just like he trained her so the neighbors wouldn't hear. He was a stickler for privacy. That was one of their deals.

He stepped in and closed the door behind him. "Blow me," he said. That was the thing about her. She could always turn him on. Real women were always a problem, but this fake one, this tranny thing, this vile creature he would never be seen in public with could get him up and running in minutes.

She removed her robe and serviced him. When he was good and hard and into it, he gave her the signal and they went in the bedroom. She rolled a condom on him, spread it lightly with lube then helped him slide into her anus. He climaxed in minutes and stayed hard until she started talking.

She brings his water to him, stands beside the bed as he drinks it. The sight of her starts to turn him on again, the big soft breasts, the boyish ass, the queer voice.

She notices his swelling penis and goes for a second joust. "Are you ever going to do me in the pussy?" she asks. "I mean, you paid for it." She is trying to be seductive, hoisting one knee up on the bed to spread her legs and show him her vagina. She uses the fingers of one hand to open it, while the other hand rubs him.

The black rage comes from nowhere, just like the impulse to vomit. One moment he's staring at her crotch, disgusted with the sight of it but fascinated too. Then he hits the bitch in her puke-ugly thing. She tumbles backward, sprawling against her dresser, her legs splayed, shock on her face. She coddles her crotch with both hands and cries, big wet tears, quiet sobs.

"Why are you so mean to me?" she asks.

He ignores her. The room is silent except for her muffled sobs.

"My therapist says this isn't a healthy relationship for me," she says. "She thinks it's time for us to break it off."

Silence.

"I think so too," she continues, still oblivious to his mood.

He gets up from the bed and stands in front of her. She looks up at him with wet eyes, wiping the back of her hand across her nose like a child. He smiles benignly. Bends toward her. A smile plays on her lips in anticipation of the makeup kiss.

He reaches out with his left hand, touches her head softly, then quick, like a cat, he yanks her upright by her hair and before she can make a sound he hits her with his other hand, a hard fist. Her face splatters, blood covers her lips. He hits her again. A good shot. More blood. It feels good to him. She cries and holds up her hands, but he can't stop. The beast has risen and there's no holding it back now. He hits her again. And again. She tries to scream but he won't let that happen. Repulsive tranny queer! He grabs her throat and lifts her from the ground. Her bloody lips move but no sound comes out. She looks like a grotesque fish gasping for air and the sight enrages him more. How could such a gross, stupid thing turn him on?

He releases her throat and smashes her face again, then her stomach. She crumples to the floor, back against the bed. There are more punches. He lifts her upright again and aims a hard right hand for her face. It misses, hits her in the throat. Her eyes show panic, she makes a gurgling sound. She can't breathe. He has crushed her trachea.

As he watches the life ooze out of her, his rage subsides.

He waits for his pulse rate to return to normal, and clears his mind. This isn't the first time the beast has gotten out of control. He knows what to do.

He surveys the apartment. What had he touched? Her, the glass, the bed. Not the doorknob. Nothing in the bathroom or kitchen. He washes the blood off his hands and quietly goes room to room removing traces of himself. He wears his socks as gloves so he won't leave prints. He finds a garbage bag and fills it with the sheets and the condoms. He throws his drinking glass in the bag. He vacuums the floors and throws the bag in his garbage bag.

When he can't think of anything else to do, he leaves. He will dump the garbage bag where no one will notice it and he will sleep a deep, guiltless sleep.

May

MY FAVORITE TEACHER in cosmetology school had a placard on her workstation that read: "I believe in the curling iron as a higher power."

That was the most inspiring and spiritual revelation I have ever had. If you are a hairdresser, a real one, hair is beauty and hair is life. Painting is detached. Sculpting is artificial and cold. Music is one-dimensional. Hair is real. It's personal. It can be as sexy as an X-rated love scene and as beautiful as a Robert Frost poem.

To mark the fifth anniversary of my father's death, I laboriously handcrafted my own version of my teacher's placard in a flowery font and taped it to his tombstone. With apologies to those who think God is a woman, it read: "If there is a God, he is a hairdresser."

Dear old dad wouldn't have found it funny. He belittled male hairdressers as faggots and fairies and used them as the butt of jokes. Of course, the fact that his only son became a hairdresser was a mouthful of bitter irony that he just couldn't swallow. Dear old mom said it killed the poor guy, but I was just one more item on an endless list of disappointments in his life. My enduring recollection of him is of a man with clenched teeth, pursed lips and a permanent frown. I can't think of a time he smiled and he never laughed out loud in my presence. He was done in by his own anger and hate.

I don't think about my father very often, but just at this moment I'm working on a client whose open hostility reminds me of him. She's a large, unattractive redneck woman who is nearing morbid obesity. She is hyperactive in my chair so that foiling her bleach highlights is like trying to pin the tail on the donkey. And she talks non-stop. She has me pegged as a gay man, which most customers do, and she's been on a fifteen-minute harangue about how homosexuality is a sin and an abomination to God.

What she's doing in this salon is a mystery. Before launching into her Biblical diatribe, she gives me her life story. Born in some Kentucky backwoods. Escaped by marrying a boy who wanted to be a soldier. Got hit by a variety of ailments that caused her to put on weight and lose her youthful good looks.

Abandoned by hubby, she's alone, diabetic, and lives for evangelical TV shows.

This service is going to cost her $125 and it's not worth it. Her hair is trashed from endless bleach highlights done in speed salons where hair health takes a back seat to moving the client through. The best colorist in the city couldn't make this hair look good. She might just as well have gone to another econo-salon and had this done for $70 or so.

We're a very upscale salon on Chicago's near-north side, close enough to the Loop to pull in daytime business people, and right in the heart of the trendy neighborhoods rich yuppies call home. We're just as snotty as our clientele, too. This lady came in without an appointment wearing shapeless polyester clothes, bad makeup, and cheap accessories. No one wanted her. She'll be a crappy tipper because she can't afford to be here in the first place. But her appearance is equally off-putting to the stylists. This is an image business, especially in high-end salons, and we get blinded into thinking only the rich and beautiful are worthy clients. We shouldn't be like that, but we are. Me too, though I fight it. I should. After all, I have my own acceptance issues.

I took her because I take anyone if I have an open time slot. I mean, why sit on my butt in the break room when I could be making money, right? Plus sometimes these things work out.

But this won't be one of those times. She keeps trying to start a conversation with me about being gay. I keep telling her I don't talk about sex or politics with customers. She keeps telling me I'm going to hell for being a pervert. I want to tell her that an hour with her is enough to put anyone off women for a lifetime. But I don't. Part of being a hairdresser is never giving a client a reason to dislike you, even if you won't ever have them back in your chair again. Some clients will come up with reasons of their own to dislike you, usually completely unrelated to your work. They just want to vent their anger on someone and hairdressers are easy targets.

Especially fairies like me.

I wash out my brushes and bowls while she processes. When I come back to the chair she says, "Hey, are you a tranny? Is that why you look so gay?"

This woman is proof there is no benevolent God.

I issue my standard refusal to talk sex or politics. It doesn't daunt her.

"I read once that trannies hate having dicks," she says. She asks if I still have mine and sniggers. Her voice carries like a bad stink. Heads turn in the salon.

I stop working and make eye contact with her in the mirror. "Would you like someone else to finish this service? I'll find someone." My voice is grim. Not like me, but enough is enough.

She smirks. "I'll be good." Like it's funny.

I go back to work and she's off on a riff about moral decay in America, plotting Catholics and Jews, and a long chorus of Jesus loves you.

She pays with a gift certificate and gives me a religious brochure in lieu of a tip. I'm so happy the service is over I don't mind. I feel like a bad toothache has gone away and the timing is perfect. She's my last service of Saturday afternoon. My weekend starts now.

* * *

I DON'T KNOW if Miss Kentucky heard one of my colleagues call me a tranny or she made it up herself. In the break room, several of the girls refer to me as a queen sometimes, and so do I. I have long hair, and wear androgynous clothes and lots of jewelry. I like bright colors. There is a touch of femininity to my walk and diction. But I'm also six feet tall and have broad shoulders and masculine facial features, so the queen reference is a friendly way we can all acknowledge the fact that I'm a queer.

Of course, the funny thing is, I am a transsexual. It has taken me years to figure it out, but I'm transsexual. Nobody at work knows it yet, because, well, that's a long story. Suffice it to say, being a full-fledged transsexual is a much more serious offense against humanity than being a cross-dresser, which is just part time weird, or being gay, which is full time weird but you look okay to everyone.

And let's face it, here in America, how you look is a lot more important than who you are.

I bring this up now because my cab driver can't stop looking at me in his rear view mirror. He's staring because I am in full girl mode and he's made me but can't decide how he feels about it. I get this a lot.

When I'm away from the salon, I live as a woman. I'm 38 years old, six feet tall and weigh 170 pounds. Months of testosterone blockers and estrogen supplements have given me a set of shapely breasts and softer skin and caused my male genitalia to shrink. Electrolysis has eliminated my facial hair and what little body hair continued to grow after I started the hormones. My personality has changed, too. I am more prone to crying and have less of an edge to my temper.

Although I am what the smut websites refer to as a she-male, I'm not one of those seductresses featured on-line. I still look more masculine than feminine and would never pass as a woman even in Cinderella's ball gown and formal makeup. What I try to do is present myself as an attractive person, obviously transgendered, but nice to look at. That's what I *try* to do.

I haven't come out at work for lots of reasons. For one, I'm not sure I'm going to go all the way with this. Most people who have transgendered feelings don't actually change genders. I'm still trying to make sure who I really am.

The main reason for keeping my transsexuality a secret, however, is that I need my job and my clients. I might lose everything if I come out. It happens more often than not when transsexuals come out to co-workers, family, and friends. People who loved you just a minute ago now can't stand to look at you. Employers think you bring shame to the company and cause angst in the ranks.

So I haven't told anyone at work. I just let my body develop and share my little gender secret with the outside world very selectively. My trans friends know, of course. And my neighbors have figured it out because I started presenting as a woman all the time months ago. I have no plans for coming out at work but my breasts are becoming a problem. My mother's two great gifts to me were the miracle of life and a genetic predisposition to big breasts. About six months after I started hormones I was already nearly a B-cup. Even my doctor was impressed. I've been wearing a restraining undergarment to work for months, the kind used by female-to-male transsexuals to give them a male chest profile until they get a mastectomy. I'm almost a C-cup now and I'm starting to show, even with my breast-cover undergarment. The device is getting horribly uncomfortable. I feel like I'm mutilating myself.

I get a lot of stares as a transwoman, but this cabbie is making my skin crawl. I'm outside the safe cocoon of Boystown, the neighborhood where I live and where tolerance and acceptance are the universal language. I'm in the real world now. And I'm being eyeballed by an ethnic I associate with violence and a degree of intolerance that would make my last client seem like Mother Teresa. Thank goodness I'm wearing designer jeans and not a short skirt. It's bad enough that my blouse shows off the plumpness of my breasts.

"Did you want to ask me something?" I say finally, making eye contact in the rearview mirror.

Embarrassed, his eyes dart back to the road. He shakes his head no, but a few minutes later he starts staring at me again in the mirror.

When he pulls to the curb in front of my destination, he pivots to look at me directly. As I dig in my purse for money, he tries to peer down my top to see if my breasts are real. My lacy top reveals just enough cleavage to answer his question.

He says something I can't understand. I beg his pardon. He repeats it slowly, his lips moving in exaggerated fashion, like a kindergarten teacher working with a student on a new sound. He is asking me if I want to pleasure him sexually in lieu of the fare.

It's the only offer I've gotten today, so I guess in that respect it's the best offer I've had. But it still makes me want to vomit.

I shake my head politely and hand him the cash and tell him to keep the change. It includes a nice tip. His overture was crude and I suppose I should be insulted, but I'm not. He was just asking.

* * *

IT'S A BEAUTIFUL MAY DAY in Chicago, with temps in the seventies, a whisper of a breeze and clear skies. We only get a few spring days like this so you have to bathe in it while it's here. People are outside gardening, strolling, washing windows and cars, tossing footballs. A neighbor straightens up from his spading and takes a long look at me as I walk to the door. I start to get that creepy feeling I get when someone makes me. But then he smiles and waves. I wave back.

I'm heading up the walk of this bucolic, family-values tri-level house to attend a backyard barbeque. It will be cops and their wives. And me. I'm not looking forward to the experience. Most cops consider people like me an alien species, and I suspect most cop wives feel the same way. One doesn't. She's the one who invited me.

Marilee Sinowski isn't exactly your typical cop wife. She has a PhD in psychology, teaches at university and maintains a small practice. She's tough and smart and has a great heart. She's also beautiful and I've had a crush on her ever since we met. Yes, I find women attractive. Men too. If you're a church-going Christian conservative, I'm probably everything you hate.

I've been doing Marilee's hair for years. She has this fantastic, beautiful gray hair. It's almost white. And thick, with a nice wave. I fell in love with her hair before I fell in love with her.

She had come into the salon because she was sick of her life and wanted a change. Her husband had been involved with another woman. She had been feeling estranged anyway. He was a super-macho, tough guy type whose life revolved around police work and television sports. She was a refined woman with an intellectual life and an interest in the arts.

She might have just left him and started over, but there were children and marital equity involved. Hubby treated her well—no screaming or hitting, lots of respect, brought the paycheck home, took care of the house, cared about her. He even respected what she did, which is probably rare among cops. And he was repentant about his fling.

So Marilee came into a beauty salon for the first time in decades, and she came looking for a change. I had an open afternoon and I spent it working with her—a lovely cut, lots of styling tips, then a makeup session accompanied by a monologue on femininity and attraction.

That was almost eight years ago, back when I thought I was just a gay man, which seems like middle-American normalcy to me now. Anyway, she thought that was cute. She liked the cut. She stayed married and she has been coming to me for hair and makeup ever since. We also meet regularly for coffee. She is my friend so she can't be my shrink, not officially, but I have confided in her every step of the way in my strange journey. She has had a number of trans clients in recent years, most of them younger, thrown out on the streets by shocked parents, trying to understand themselves and how to cope, too broke to afford a shrink. Marilee sees them for nothing. She works with their minds and tries to get people from the community to work with their situations.

* * *

MARILEE'S HUSBAND answers the door, a beer in one hand. His big smile freezes for a fleeting moment when he sees me. It's a reflex, not malice. I get it all the time. I just don't match people's expectations and they get put off balance. Bill and I have met before, but he's never been comfortable around me. It was bad enough when he thought I was just gay and a little swishy. Now, as a transsexual, I'm sure I give him the total willies but I have to say he really works at it. He's painfully polite and respectful.

"Hello Bobbi." He reaches out for a handshake. I grasp his thick palm with my fingers. We press each other's flesh gently and he ushers me in the door.

"Most of the party is on the patio," Bill says. "Can I get you something to drink?"

I opt for a glass of white wine, the perfect yuppie selection. Not that anyone here is going to think of me as a yuppie.

As Bill pours I survey the milling group on the patio, an imposing gathering of testosterone freaks and the women who love them, soon to be invaded by a one-person freak show.

Bill hands me the wine and delivers the bad news. "Marilee had an emergency session with a client," he says, "and she's running a little late. She'll be here in a half hour or so. Meanwhile, I'd like to introduce you to some people."

Nausea and panic flare in my body. I thought I would have Marilee to cling to as I run the gauntlet of super-straight cops and ultra-orthodox wives. Being introduced by Marilee as her hairdresser somehow makes it seem easier to be so flamboyantly strange looking, a man with toned arm muscles and full breasts, wearing women's clothing and makeup.

I follow Bill out to the patio and go through introductions with a dozen or so people.

It goes better than I thought. The cops might not have expected a transsexual at a cop gathering, but they have no problem with me. One after another they shake hands, ask me how I am, try to keep the conversational ball rolling. Enjoying this weather? What a day for a barbeque, huh? Where do you live? Chicago is a city of neighborhoods, and cops know pretty much all of them, so one-liners about Boystown come easy. Oh yeah, nice place. Wish all our neighborhoods were so safe. And so on.

One, I don't catch his name, actually engages me in a short conversation. Asks about my activity in the GLBT community, what my neighborhood is like, how valuable the Center is. It turns out Boystown is his beat. His job is to build bridges between the Chicago Police Department and the city's gay-lesbian-trans population, the nerve center of which is Boystown. He asks if he can look me up. I agree, but mostly to get rid of him. Cops have always made me nervous, even though I'm not a criminal.

The wives are a different proposition. Several gape at me as we are introduced, while others stare at me from afar. I shouldn't be sensitive to these reactions, but I am. I feel ten feet tall. My breasts feel like watermelons. My body feels like it's sprouting forests of male body hair. My official shrink, who has to sign off on me getting a sex change operation some day, says I have to overcome this or it will cast doubt on my suitability for gender reassignment surgery.

As this painful round of introductions continues, one wife regards my outstretched hand with open disgust as if it were dog poop on her front porch. Unable to overcome the barrier, all she can do is stare at me, mouth open slightly, without saying anything or offering to shake hands. The woman next to her grasps my hand, a gracious act to help me save face. The others are less traumatized, but not sure how to speak to someone so clearly on the fringes of society. No one is rude, but the conversations don't go beyond the "nice to meet you" stage.

This is my life when I go out in the real world. In some ways, the polite awkwardness of many genetic women when they see me is as painful as outright bigotry would be. Bigots remind me that I'll never be accepted by everyone; polite ladies like these remind me that I'm strange and will be for the rest of my life.

Many of my transgendered sisters have overcome this sensitivity. The best of them have outgoing personalities and blithely work crowds like this as though they are in the mainstream of society. It puts people at ease and helps acceptance. I've seen it. I just can't do that myself. That's not who I am.

As I try to bolster my sagging ego, we approach two women chatting at the edge of the patio. They are overtly friendly as Bill and I approach. The nearest is a large black lady, as tall as me and heavier. Her face lights up with a big warm smile.

"I know who this is," she says, before Bill can introduce me. "You have to be Bobbi! I've heard so much about you, honey. I'm Barb." She engulfs me in a hug, a real one with some muscle to it. Her huge breasts press against mine, and her warm arms wrap around my torso. I feel a little like a child again, when my grandmother would embrace me just this way. And I feel like a sister. I'm warm all over. I hug back.

"Aren't you just beautiful!" she says as we break the embrace. "Debbie and I were just talking." She stops. "Where are my manners! Honey, this is my good friend Debbie. She's married to that good-looking Daniel cop over there with the sideburns and baby blue eyes." She sighs. "I'm with the biggest, blackest guy at the party, Joe." Debbie is smiling and shaking my hand. Barb turns to Bill, "We'll get this girl around, honey. You get back to your cops and keep them out of trouble, okay?"

Bill leaves with a grin, no doubt as relieved as I am.

Barb and Debbie are friends with Marilee. They must be good friends, because they know where Marilee was emotionally when she came into my salon the first time. I don't know if they know everything, but they know enough. "Bobbi, honey, you saved a soul when you became her hairdresser. Do you know that?" Barb asks.

Before I can answer, she goes on. "We were worried about her. She had the weight of the world on her shoulders for the longest time. Then one day we get together for our coffee klatch and in walks this hot North Shore socialite. It's Marilee, with a new hair-do, new clothes, a bounce in her step and a twinkle in her eye! And she said it all started with Bobbi, her new hairdresser."

Debbie is just as warm, but in a quieter way. She is a creative director at an ad agency. Barb is an attorney. Most of the other wives are stay-at-home moms, so the three professional women often end up together at these functions because they have things in common. Debbie asks me where I got my jeans. She's interested in getting a pair like them. It's a compliment. Maybe the ultimate compliment a genetic woman can pay a transsexual—not only does she approve of my feminine attire, she'd be willing to follow my example.

We chat about clothes and hair and makeup. They make me feel special and my inhibitions evaporate. This is fun.

Twenty minutes later, Marilee arrives. She looks flushed, her hair is in disarray and her expensive business suit is just a little askew. In a woman who always looks just so, these little deviations are a sign. The emergency session has not gone well.

She makes her round of the guests, the gracious hostess, hugging, smiling, laughing, and exchanging witty repartees. She is especially warm and effusive when she gets to us.

"I'm not surprised to see you surrounded by these ladies! I've been telling them you're my secret weapon for years. Just don't give any of them my time, okay?"

She hugs me and whispers in my ear, "I need to talk to you for a minute. Can we break away for awhile?"

"Of course," I say. Worried.

* * *

MARILEE LEADS ME to her bedroom. It's the safest place for a quiet, private conversation, and Bill knows I'm no rival for Marilee's affections. If Marilee weren't so clearly upset I would have made a joke about it.

Marilee sits in one of two stuffed chairs in the corner of their bedroom. I take the cue to sit in the other chair. A small tea table separates us. I cross my legs and wait silently as Marilee breathes deeply, looks up, looks away, begins to speak several times and halts. I have never seen her so anxious.

"Bobbi, I have to talk to someone," she says finally. "I have to talk to someone I can trust completely. Not a word of this can ever be spoken to anyone. Ever."

I nod.

"Not ever!" she repeats. She is making her point, but she's also telling me to speak. She needs reassurance.

"Your secrets are safe with me," I say soberly. I want to say something funny about my whole life being about secrets. I mean really, you wouldn't believe what you pick up as a hairdresser. But this is not the time or the place.

"I've been counseling a very special transwoman for several years." Marilee pauses, considering what to say, what to leave unsaid.

"She has always had doubts about her worth as a human being. As a woman." Another pause. "She measured her value according to the men in her life. She went for big breasts, tiny skirts, elaborate makeup. Anything-goes sex. She was a prostitute when I first met her.

"For the last year or so, she's been seeing someone and trying to get a grip on her life. At first, it seemed like a breakthrough. Mr. Wonderful was a professional man, an executive with a big company downtown. He gave her presents. Brought her flowers. Helped her pay for her transition, helped with the rent.

"But it wasn't a normal relationship. It was secretive.

"Seems like…George…let's call him George…anyway, seems like he wasn't ready to settle down. He wanted to see other women. And he wanted her to service his friends when he brought them around. He said it turned him on and that she liked it too.

"My client found this both exciting and abhorrent. The sex was exciting, but she knew that George was rejecting her, too. He had come to think of her as just his whore. She's been trying to get herself ready to break it off with him for the past month or two. It wasn't an easy decision for her. Part of her considered herself George's property because he's been so generous. And part of her was afraid to go back out on her own.

"I got a call from 'George' this morning. He wanted to be seen, as a patient, as soon as possible. Today. I knew something was wrong. My patient had been trying to get him to come in with her for months and he wouldn't do it. In fact, I'd never talked to him before. I asked him if everything was okay and he said yes, this was something he needed to do for his girlfriend. So I met him at my office. He was very careful to frame it as a psychologist-client meeting. As soon as we finished the formalities, he told me he had killed my client and he wanted me to know that nobody walks out on him, that whatever I did to convince her to leave him had gotten her killed. It was my fault, not his.

"And he knew I couldn't tell anyone. If he had told me he was going to kill her, I could have gone to the police. But when someone confesses a crime to a psychologist or a priest after the fact, it's confidential information. He knew this. It was fun for him, telling me this. Thrilling to know he was getting away with it and someone else knew."

She breaks into tears. "What can I do, Bobbi?" she repeats over and over again, crying and wailing into a pillow on her lap so the sound won't carry. What a mind-fuck! She can't share this with her husband because he's a cop. It would make him crazy. So she unloads to her hairdresser.

I move to her side and hug her. There is nothing for me to say. All I can do is let her know I am there with her. And for her.

When she gets control of herself, she takes a deep breath. "I want so badly to tell Bill, or make an anonymous tip. Or throw my career away and just come forward. But I've heard all the stories about how these things can go wrong and the murderer ends up getting a not guilty verdict and a lifelong pass.

"And," she adds. "I took an oath. I actually thought about exactly this circumstance before I took it, too. So…I need to live with it."

We are quiet for a while.

"You can't tell anyone about this, right?" she says at last.

"Right," I respond. Tears are streaming down her face. Mine too. She stands and we wrap our arms around one another and hug as if the world was going to end in the next minute.

"I will keep your secret," I whisper. "When you need to talk about it, I will be there, wherever you need me."

* * *

THE SUNDAY AND MONDAY newspapers have nothing about a murdered t-girl, which isn't as surprising as it is disappointing. Only a fraction of Chicago's murders get reported in the newspapers, fewer still on television. Coverage favors big names, horrific circumstances. The loss of a transwoman only gets a paragraph on a slow news day, and nothing on an average day. At least, that's the word in our community.

My Monday drags, as it often does. On this day, my appointment book is dominated by a succession of elderly ladies who come to me for perms. Many of the other stylists won't do this work. Neither perms nor little old ladies are considered hip. But I love perms and I love being busy, so Monday is a good billing day for me, even if the conversation drags sometimes.

I survive the workday and dash home to change into a cute new party dress, do my hair and put on makeup. One of my clients gave me a big tip because, she said, she wanted to buy my dinner for being so sweet. I feel honor-bound to dine out. Instead of dining in the safety of a Boystown eatery, I choose a mid-level café on the northwest side of the city, near the meeting I am attending tonight.

The neighborhood is a white middle-class enclave, with a mix of young professionals and older, second and third generation ethnics. Definitely not a magnet for gays or transgenders. Definitely not an area where I blend in.

That's why I'm here. I've decided to make myself come out in the real world more and get used to it. Making the decision was easy, but acting it out is terrifying. Even though I'm very comfortable in the straight world as a somewhat effeminate male, I feel completely conspicuous as soon as I go fully femme.

The hostess at Café Lorenzo greets me with an automatic smile and hello before I step out of the shadows of the entry and into the dim light of the greeting area. When I am fully visible, her eyes register surprise. She glances away and her smile disappears. She is unable to look at me. This is how polite people express disgust at inappropriate people like me. I feel like a hairy giant in a tutu.

"One, please," I say, without waiting for her to speak again. It simplifies things. No awkward silence, no grasping for words. She'll either seat me or ask me to leave. She is young, transparent, still speaking with pseudo Valley Girl intonations. Her makeup is too red for her complexion, but not bad. She has chunky blond highlights in her level-6 brown hair and wears it below the shoulder. Her hair tells me this is her career, at least for now. A student's color would have been homemade, from a drugstore bottle if she was poor enough to be waitressing at night. This color is a step up from home color. The makeup shows a lack of sophistication...maybe a high school dropout, definitely not a college girl. I'm fully aware that I am scrutinizing others just as they do me. It's part of being human, maybe. Or maybe in my case it's just the hairdresser mentality.

The café is almost empty—I've come early so there would be no waiting for tables. It's not being asked to leave I fear; Chicago is pretty serious about civil rights for everyone. What worries me is waiting for a table at a crowded bar counter or having to stand in the reception area with all those disapproving eyes boring into me.

"Of course," she says, and leads me into the dining area. She seats me at a small table for two in a corner, out of the way. Good. I won't be the center of attention. And there is a lamp on the table that emits just enough light to read by. I will bury my head in the book I've brought along as soon as I have ordered so as to be oblivious of how those around me are reacting.

By the time I order, my bladder is killing me. It's nerves, I know, but there's no dismissing the urge. I have to go to the ladies room. Naturally, the café has begun filling up. Five or six tables are occupied; about half the customers are women.

Most transgenders have at least one nightmare story about being humiliated over their use of a women's bathroom or a dressing room in a public place. I rise with real dread. I make myself concentrate on moving like a woman, even though I feel like an NFL lineman. My wedges add two inches to my height so I tower over most of the people I see in this place, even the men. I focus on my walk. Casual pace, placing my forward foot almost directly in front of my navel with each step, letting my hips rotate just a little. My right arm swings, my hand bent up so the palm faces the floor. I carry my purse over my left arm.

There is no one in the place when I enter. I hustle into the far stall and do my business, hoping to get out before anyone else comes in. I hope that everyone who saw me come this way is waiting for me to leave before using the facilities themselves.

No such luck.

As I go to the sink to wash my hands, two women walk in. One goes into a stall, the other to the sinks to work on her makeup. We exchange glances in the mirror. She does that subtle kind of double take, where her eyes widen a notch in surprise then she suppresses it. I smile a little. She smiles a little back. It's a humorless smile, but at least she isn't screaming.

* * *

THOSE TEPID ACTS of tolerance in the restaurant are enough to put me in a light mood as I walk into the monthly meeting of the Chicago TransGender Alliance. It's pathetic that I am so sensitive about these things, but that's just how it is.

Chicago's TransGender Alliance was established back in the seventies, when cross-dressers dwelled in closets and transsexualism was a dark science. The membership today takes in the whole transgender spectrum: hetero male cross-dressers, flamboyant gay queens, transsexuals, and transsexual wannabees, and a smattering of fetishists. Plus spouses, lovers, partners, friends, and the occasional tranny chaser—guys who have a thing for transwomen. Female-to-male transsexuals are rare in TGA. They don't need a support group as much as those of us flying the other way do. After a few months on testosterone and maybe a mastectomy, they pass easily as males and move into the mainstream of society.

Our group is made up of mostly older transgenders—most members are somewhere over forty and some are in their sixties and seventies. Younger trans people who are out no longer really need a support group, I suppose. They can feminize themselves with internet-purchased hormones, and they live the club life in Boystown, or take refuge on trans-friendly college campuses.

The average TGA member is a male-to-female transgender who denied her feminine identity for decades, until some incident or just the rising pressure of life made her come out. Most of us were the male in a male-female marriage at some point; around half have children. Most are divorced, and most divorces came within a year or two of coming out as a cross-dresser.

Our group has a preponderance of transsexuals. The classic story is the individual comes out to his spouse as a cross-dresser. The spouse struggles for a year or two trying to understand, while the cross-dresser pursues his feminine self like a teenage boy chasing his first sexual encounter. The spouse freaks and leaves. The cross-dresser is left with nothing but his femme side, comes out to the rest of the family, friends, maybe even work associates and ends up being disowned by most of them. Women he dates drop him when he comes out to them. He gets more into the femme life, starts hormones, and lives as a transsexual.

Of the transsexuals I know, only half have gone all the way with reassignment surgery, where they trade in their penis for a vagina. Many have no intention of going all the way with it, some aren't sure, and some just don't have the tens of thousands of dollars it takes.

* * *

HE WATCHES THE TRANNIES drift into the banquet hall. They're older. Not his cup of tea. But he feels the need for arousal and this is a much safer venue for him than the clubs where the young stuff lurks. Or searching for new meat on the Internet.

He idly evaluates each one from a window seat in the deli across the street. Not the best vantage point but the material isn't that great anyway. Older. Bigger. Lots of fatties. He shudders. He hates fat. It makes him nauseous. It drives him to keep his own body lean and trim, even in his early fifties. It's a big turn-on for women, an older man with a little gray in his hair having a hard body.

A trans man passes by. There's an idea, he thinks. What would that be like? Catch him when he still has breasts, not too much body hair. He tries to picture that in an erotic way. It doesn't work.

A tall masculine looking tranny passes right in front of his window and crosses the street to the banquet hall. She has broad shoulders and a strong male jaw, but she looks sexy anyway. Her boobs jiggle. Her arms flail a little as she trots across the street, short steps, just a little awkward in summer wedges. He wonders how far along she is, what she'd be like in bed. A big girl might be fun.

He pictures her with bared breasts and a little tranny penis and starts to get aroused. Time to think about something else. The beast can't come out today.

* * *

I DRIFT INTO THE ROOM and make my way to the bar. There are maybe twenty ladies in the room and one transman so far. The crowd won't be big tonight—there's no special event scheduled, and no free food.

I find a stool next to Cecilia and place my drink order, crossing my legs, checking my posture. Part of transitioning is learning to do these things naturally, but it takes practice. Leg crossing is especially difficult when you have the male appendages to deal with.

Cecilia gives me a faint nod as I sit down. She is one of the longest-tenured members of the group and has been fully transitioned for many years. Still, she is as loud and gross as a redneck laborer, and as arrogant as a millionaire stockbroker. She has made sure no one is offended by her transsexuality by making the obnoxiousness of her person the most obvious thing about herself.

But Cecelia knows everything that's going on in the community, every rumor, every tryst, every bust, everything. So I violate one of my cardinal rules and sit next to her with the intent of conversing, which usually consists of listening to her.

"Good evening, Cecilia," I coo. "I heard a rumor that one of our girls got beat up last weekend. Have you heard anything about that?"

"Not beat up, honey," she answers in her raspy voice. She turns to look at me through hooded eyes, like a socialite. "She was beaten to death. A real mess, from what I hear."

"Do we know her?" I ask.

"I do. I don't know about you." Cecilia is boasting and putting me down at the same time. "Mandy Marvin is the victim. There are no suspects."

My mind goes numb. I can't speak, but in my head I can hear a terrible scream straining to be heard. As the shock sinks in, it becomes unbearable but all I can do is cradle my glass of wine and look at it. My eyes tear up.

Mandy was a friend and a client, sweet and beautiful. She had dreams.

* * *

MURDER IS AN ABSTRACT concept to most of us. Violent crime is something that happens to people who live in bad neighborhoods, or to sex workers. Oh most of us in the trans world get verbally abused, even physically intimidated. But mostly these acts are blows to our pride. They make us feel like freaks, unwelcome, unwanted members of polite society.

Mandy's death is a shock on many levels. She was my friend and I am grieving for her. I had no idea Marilee and Mandy knew each other but she must be the client Marilee was talking about on Saturday. And her death is a message to all us trannies: no matter where you are, who you are or how good you look, you are not safe. You will never be safe.

Mandy was one of the most beautiful women I've ever seen, trans or genetic. She was beautiful even before she transitioned and afterward she was beyond stunning. She was 5-5 with a willowy build, thick lush hair, an oval face, and shapely legs. Hormones gave her a nice set of perky breasts and gradually feminized her facial features even more. Her voice was androgynous, a hint of smoky resonance at the octave where men's and women's ranges meet. She cultivated a breathless quality to go with it, and she had always formed words like a girl. I would have given anything to be her. Physically at least.

She came to Boystown as a teen. Knew she was trans all her life and was thrown out by her family. She started living full-time femme right away and made a living turning tricks. She had been a hooker and a dancer in a tranny club for a couple years by the time she started coming to TransGender Alliance functions, which is where I met her. Even though we were a generation apart in age, she liked the way I did my hair and I ended up doing hers and I have ever since.

We ugly girls think pretty girls have it made, but it's not true. Mandy's beauty gave her a doorway to life that wasn't available to me and she took it. It meant good money and it was mostly easy. And when you've lived half your life taking abuse from men for being effeminate, having them finally lust for you seems like a fantasy come true. But once you start down that path, it's very hard to go anywhere else.

Mandy wasn't especially bright, but after a couple years in the sex trade she could see the limits of her career. By then she was starting to think of herself as a woman. She didn't want to be a prostitute any more. When I met her she was trying to get off the streets. She did waitressing and worked retail. The money was awful, but she got by. She got help from boyfriends and some in the community said she still did tricks, but for bigger bucks for an escort service. She got her gender reassignment surgery a year ago.

We weren't best friends. We were too different for that. But I was her hairdresser and a sort of older sister for her, and I thought she was one of the sweetest people I've ever met, so we quite naturally drifted into a warm friendship.

For the past year or so she mentioned a special guy she was seeing. Handsome, rich, and great in bed, he even had her thinking about happily ever-after.

Maybe Mr. Wonderful had some issues.

My thoughts are short-circuited by Cecelia's loud voice. Two other girls have joined us. She's holding court.

"I'm guessing she was with a john," says Cecilia. "She never bothered to work on a career..." Cecilia launches into a monologue on the younger trans generation, preoccupied with sex, drugs, and rock and roll. She can be the transwoman incarnation of a right wing talk-radio host—an opinion on everything, untiringly judgmental, malformed physically and emotionally, yet somehow charismatic for those who lack self-esteem or any trace of intelligence.

Cecilia's jabber oozes off to the corners of my consciousness then slips into the ether. Mandy's image fills my mind. I always think of her as smiling and laughing. She had an infectious laugh. She livened up every room she ever entered.

She had a good heart, too. With her looks, she could have been arrogant, but I never heard her say anything nasty about anyone.

"You're full of shit about Mandy," I blurt out. The others are stunned at my brazen challenge to Cecelia's authority. "She had a day job. She quit tricking a long time ago."

I stare into Cecelia's eyes. "Mandy was my friend. She never mentioned you."

I move away from the group and find a seat at an empty table. I am beginning the mourning process. This has hit me hard. I need to find a private place to think. And weep.

* * *

THERE IS STILL NO PRESS COVERAGE of Mandy's death on Tuesday. Retail clerks don't have the status for such coverage, I guess, and prostitutes, her former profession, are even less remarkable in death.

Tuesday night I get a call at home from a cop, a Phil someone. My pulse picks up a few beats. Why is a cop calling me?

"Hi Bobbi," he says. "We met at Marilee and Bill's party on Saturday. I mentioned that my beat is the GLBT community...?"

"Oh, yes!" Relief. I'm not sure why I thought I might be in trouble with the law, but contact with the police has always made me nervous. His image comes into my mind—nice looking, late thirties, maybe forty, in good shape. Kind eyes. I remember that especially. I find kind eyes very attractive in a person.

"How are you?" I'm speaking in my femme voice and feeling very self-conscious about it. I'm sure Officer Phil perceives me more as a beer-drinking buddy than a woman.

"I'm fine," he says. "I was hoping to talk with you at the party, but you got away too fast." Pause. I wait for him to move on to another subject so I don't have to explain myself, but he's a trained listener and waits.

"Yes, well, I had some other obligations that night," I say.

He doesn't respond right away. I think he is trying to decide whether or not to draw me out.

"What I had hoped to ask you is if we might meet once in a while so you could tell me a little about the trans community and what I can do to connect with people. We want trans people to feel they can trust us."

I don't draw the attention of tranny chasers—they go for the cuter, younger girls—so I know this isn't a veiled pass. Plus, something about Officer Phil seemed very sincere and human, even in that brief moment we met.

"I think all of us will appreciate that, officer," I reply. "What did you have in mind?"

"Well, I was hoping we could meet for a drink or a meal or a coffee tomorrow—whatever works for you."

An image floats into my mind of me walking into my favorite Boystown café on the arm of a nice looking cop. I actually blush at the thought. I have forbidden myself to engage in carnal activities during my transition so that whatever I end up doing, it's based on the real me, and not fulfilling the fantasy of some lover I've taken along the way. It can get complicated. I've heard of one girl who went all the way so she could keep her heart-throb, and of course, he left her eventually. And I know a pre-op girl who has put off her gender reassignment surgery because her boyfriend is only interested in pre-op transwomen, not post-ops and not genetic women. Go figure, huh?

"Okay," I say, drawing out the word while I get my mind back on the question. "I get off at six tomorrow."

"That works," he says. "I'll be off duty so I can imbibe. Let's have a drink somewhere convenient for you at, say, six-thirty or so."

So we make a date for six-thirty at Side Winders, a trans-friendly gay bar near my apartment. After I hang up I realize I will have no time to go home and change into my femme self. Ordinarily, this wouldn't bother me at all. I'd just go in my androgynous work get up. But things are changing for me. I'm very intent on expressing my female self. And the news about Mandy is eating at me. It's one thing for the straight world to call us names and recoil at our looks, it's quite another for a transwoman to be murdered and for the murder to be ignored.

***

I SLEPT POORLY last night. Mandy's face kept popping into view. I would see her in my chair on one of her visits, laughing, gesturing. I kept recalling one particular appointment where she worked on her vocal inflections the whole time, keeping both of us in stitches.

She was a free spirit and a party girl, but she had a very nice human side, too. Even though her family disowned her when she came out she never held it against them. It broke her heart, but it didn't make her bitter in any way that I could see. After her father died, her mother suffered a debilitating stroke. Mandy's only sibling, a sister, lived far away. There was an aunt in the area, but she had her own problems. So it was Mandy who looked in on Mom several times a week, did her shopping, helped clean the house, and negotiated the caretaker services that mom received from the state. Mom was increasingly unpleasant to Mandy and never acknowledged her as a woman, but Mandy never missed a visit.

Maybe this is why Mandy was so active sexually. She was looking for affirmation.

Mandy occupies my thoughts as I get ready for work, and the more I think about her goodness and the complete indifference of the media to her murder, the angrier I get.

My anger boils over as I pack my girl clothes for tonight's date in a bag. My plan is to change at work. Do it surreptitiously, in the john, and sneak out the back door. If someone sees me, so be it.

But as I fold my clothes I begin seething about how this society treats trans people. Culminating in the murder of a sweet, good-hearted girl that doesn't even get covered in the newspaper. And that makes me really resent having to lie about who I am. It pisses me off that my cute outfit is going to get wrinkled sitting in a bag all day and that I'll have to do my makeup on the run and I won't be able to do anything pretty with my hair.

All because I'm not supposed to be who I am. Because I can pay taxes, obey the law, be good to everyone and still get murdered because it's okay to kill trannies.

As I think about these things, my hands tremble with rage and the tears begin to flow. Fury and torment fill my soul to bursting. I hold my breath with all my might so that I don't scream. When my lungs shriek for air, I exhale and vent my rage by ripping my clothes from the bag and throwing the bag against the wall.

I'm going to work as a woman today. It's the only action I can think of that quells the storm inside me enough to go on. From this day forth I'm going to be who I am, no matter what. I'm Bobbi Logan, transwoman, hairdresser, friend to any who will have me, enemy of none. I'm a good citizen and a good person and I'm a woman. All of you who disapprove can go fuck yourselves.

* * *

THIS ISN'T HOW you are supposed to come out at work. In fact, it's exactly how they tell you NOT to do it. You should let everyone know what's happening, face to face, but in your male persona. I actually have a canned speech that I've been working on ever since I started hormones and started thinking about coming out at work.

"Most people are born with a male or female body and that's the gender they identify with. But a few of us aren't so lucky. I was born a boy but in my heart, I've always been a girl ..."

I rehearsed this in a mirror once, and when I got to that part I could see people reacting as vividly as if it were real. One person gets that ashen green complexion that comes with nausea, another groans and says "Oh shit!" Several just get sour looks on their faces. One pukes spontaneously.

I'm walking in the salon door wearing white jeans, a white cotton top, and white sandals with a low heel. My hair is brushed back at the temples and full. My dangling white and black earrings match my necklace, a white choker with a black amulet. I'm wearing light makeup in subtle tones, carefully blended so the final affect minimizes my flaws and plays up my strengths and looks completely natural. I drew a lot of looks on the El coming to work, and a few double takes on the street, so I'm not fooling anyone. But I look pretty good. Or at least I thought so when I did my last mirror check before coming to work.

The clients in the waiting area don't really notice me. They wouldn't—none of them are my clients. But as soon as I step into the field of vision of the receptionist, I start drawing stares. She notices right away: the sandals and the breasts.

The receptionist's mouth gapes. She is staring at me in shock.

One by one, other stylists notice me as I set up my station. A couple of them just arch their eyebrows a little and go back to work. You see a little of everything in this business, so having the gay hairdresser show up in girlie mode doesn't exactly stop the earth from rotating.

On the other hand, some other stylists are more demonstrative. One silently mouths "Oh my God" as she stares at me; another recoils in disgust. Reality slaps me in the face. If this were some hip, youth-oriented salon, the debut of a trans hairdresser might not be such a big deal. But we're a little older and we cater to a cross section of high-powered business people and young professionals. They don't come here to see wild hair and piercings, and they have never seen a drag queen or a transwoman in here doing hair.

I feel like an utter freak. Part of me is standing outside myself, looking at me, seeing a man with tits, a twisted, ugly subhuman.

I retreat to the bathroom and check myself in the mirror.

It helps. I may be a bit of an ungainly female, but I'm not so bad. My makeup is perfect. It makes my face more oval, my eyes bluer, and my high cheekbones subtler. My hair is nice. Not ultra-femme, but cute and professional. I like it. My breasts are slightly showy, because my nipples are making a very visible impression in my blouse. I should have worn a sports bra, or at least something with a little padding, but I was so focused on being me, on expressing myself, I wore a sexy lacy thing that would be perfect for a wedding night, but not so great for a first day at work as a girl.

When I go back into the salon, my colleagues who never noticed my breasts before can't keep from staring at them now. Every time I talk to someone, sooner or later their eyes stray from my face to my chest.

The girl at the station next to mine, a playful, cheerleader type, catches me in the break room. "Are those yours?" she asks, nodding her head at my chest. I nod in the affirmative. "What's going on?" she asks. "Are you, you know…?"

"Yes," I say, confirming the obvious. "I'm transitioning. I'm a transsexual."

"Well," she says. Her voice trails off as she tries to think of something to say. "Well, good luck with that."

No one else says anything about my appearance, but Roger, the salon owner, has taken several very long looks at me. Just before my first service, Roger calls me into his office.

"What's going on here, Bobbi?" he asks.

I look at him questioningly.

"You know what I mean." I do, but I don't want to be the one to say it. "What's with the outfit and the…the…are those real?" He nods in the direction of my chest.

I nod yes.

"Is this…permanent?"

Roger is very direct. He's an okay guy—fair, respectful, honest—but not especially warm. His voice has a bit of an edge to it now. Conflicting thoughts race through my mind: he's going to fire me; he's not going to fire me and all I have to do is say yes and the next part of my transition can begin. This is the moment I've been dreading and wanting for months. All I have to do is say yes and I'm Bobbi the girl, all day every day.

Or I say yes and Roger fires me in disgust, and I become an unemployed transwoman with bleak prospects of picking up another job any time soon.

I try to respond to him but I can't talk. Tears well up in my eyes.

Roger has seen lots of hairdressers cry. We're a high-strung lot, even the straight ones. But despite all his experience, he's not sure what to do.

"It's okay, Bobbi. It's okay. I just want to know. I would have appreciated a heads up, that's all. I mean, I knew you were kind of effeminate, but I didn't know you were transsexual. You could have said something, you know."

"I'm sorry, Roger." I say. My voice is high and tinny. I'm still crying, trying not to sob. This is not the Bob Logan I knew for so many years. He was stoic, controlled. He could take abuse from football coaches and murderous hits from violent linebackers without flinching. Without showing his anger, even. Part of me is standing to the side, taking all this in, while the other part is crying and sniffling.

"Yes," I sob. "I'm trans. I've been on hormones for months. I need to start living as a woman full time." I cry some more. "I'll do it gradually. I'll come in like this for awhile."

"What do you mean 'like this'?" Roger asks. His tone is businesslike.

"Slacks and jeans and shirt-type tops. Not too much makeup. Nothing super-girlie…?" I end in a question, wondering what he'll say.

He looks at me in silence for a beat or two, his eyes wandering down to my chest, then back up to my eyes. I feel like my boobs are the size of watermelons.

"Okay," he says. "You know more about this than I do. I just don't want to lose a lot of customers over this. I know you're going to lose some. A lot. That's fine, however it works out. But I don't want the other chairs losing customers, okay?"

I nod.

"If it gets bad, I may have to let you go."

I nod again.

"For what it's worth," he says as he starts to leave the room, "You look fine. It's just a shock to the rest of us. Be tasteful, do your job, be friendly to everyone and this might all work out. Okay?"

"Okay," I say.

I feel like a teenager who has just been forgiven by her father for wrecking the family car.

* * *

MY FIRST CLIENT is a businesswoman who works nearby, a textbook type A personality. I've been doing her hair for several years. We've never really talked about personal things before. I don't know how this is going to go down with her.

I get my answer quickly. As I greet her in the reception area, she looks at me and her eyes widen. She reaches my chair, sits down and takes a long look at me in the mirror. "Well," she says, "I was going to ask you how you've been, but... wow! What's going on?"

She smiles a little as she says it.

"I'm in a gender reassignment program," I answer.

"You make it sound like a night school course," she responds. "You're having a sex change?"

I stammer and stutter for a moment, then try to explain that the process is more nuanced than that and I'm still early in the journey.

"My, my, my," she says. "I've always thought of you as my gay hairdresser. This is going to take some getting used to."

We talk more than we usually do during her service. Usually she's on the phone constantly, calling or texting. But apparently finding out your hairdresser is changing genders can push selling and buying to the backburner for an hour or so.

When I finish her cut and color, she gives me the same generous tip she always does and books her next appointment six weeks in advance, just like always.

My next few clients are less committal, basically, pretending not to notice. It occurs to me finally that they didn't know how to ask. Sort of like when a large woman looks like she's pregnant. You don't want to ask her if she's pregnant only to find out you've deeply hurt someone who is dealing with a terrible weight problem.

I ponder whether I should just tell people up front, or maybe send out a personal letter explaining things. Or just shut up and do hair. I decide to try the upfront treatment. I sit my next client in my chair, and come around in front so we are looking directly at each other.

"Sharon," I say, "I want you to know I am in a gender reassignment program and I'm going to be working as a woman from now on. I know that some people are very, very uncomfortable being around transsexuals. I really value you as a customer and a friend, but if my transition is going to be a problem for you, I'd like to refer you to one of our other stylists so we don't lose you as a customer."

I sound like a low-budget tour guide.

Sharon looks away, ill at ease. "No, that's fine. I like the way you do my hair."

I do her color touch up in near silence. She foregoes the blow-dry and leaves. The whole time she looked as though she was sucking on a lemon. I won't be seeing her again.

I'm nervous and self-conscious now. I feel like I'm the muscle-bound strong man in the circus wearing an itsy bitsy bikini, being stared at by everyone around me.

Still, I do the same thing with my last client. He's a tall, heavyset muckety-muck with a big CPA firm. Rich. Conservative. I expect the worst, but it doesn't happen. "Ah what the heck," he says, when I finish my spiel. "I always wondered if I shouldn't be having a woman cut my hair, but I liked the way you did it. So now I'll have a woman cutting my hair just the way I like it."

He makes his next appointment before leaving, but that doesn't mean he won't call in later and cancel it. Or just not show up.

I wonder if I'll be able to pay my bills in the coming months without dipping into savings.

* * *

AFTER A TENSE DAY of constant scrutiny, Boystown beckons like a warm, glowing Oz, a place of colors and characters and acceptance. It is a small triangle-shaped island in Chicago's Lakeview community, maybe two miles long and about a mile wide at its widest point. Gays started congregating there in the seventies and eighties, long before it was a fashionable neighborhood, long before it was designated "Boystown" by the city in the nineties.

Most of the buildings date back to the thirties or forties and they're just one or two stories in height. If you were on an architectural tour of Chicago, you wouldn't come here. If you were sightseeing, you'd probably move quickly from the lakefront just east of here to Wrigleyville, home of the Cubs' ivy-wall ballpark and thousands of upwardly mobile young professionals, just to the west.

But for those who take the time to stroll our streets and look around, Boystown is a miracle of diversity. It is home to a half-dozen coffee shops, several wine shops, gay-themed book stores, gourmet food restaurants and stores, art shops, pulsating clubs, and a panoply of stores serving the needs of drag queen performers and other transgenders.

Acceptance is a way of life here. We are a community built on society's rejects. As long as you respect others, no one messes with you, no matter how many piercings or tattoos you have, no matter how odd you look or who you love. Even the straight people who live here are accepting and there are a lot of them. This is a good place to live. You can breathe here. It's my refuge and my hope, and tonight, as I wind my way through the clogged sidewalks of Halsted Street to meet Officer Phil, it is my salvation. It's good to be home.

In a neighborhood famous for its variety of wild and crazy bars and clubs, Side Winders is special. It has a genteel, mannerly ambience. It caters to an older crowd, middle aged and up. No television sets, no deafening sound system. It's quiet and filled with comfortable, stuffy chairs and old wooden tables and a dark, intimate bar.

It reminds me of some of the exclusive gentleman-only clubs I visited as someone else's guest back in my days as an accepted member of society. Except that Side Winders' clientele is almost exclusively gay men. Gay women pop in occasionally, so do transgenders, and even straight men and women now and then. But it's a high-end gay bar where you can carry on a conversation without shouting and without having to fight off amorous advances.

Officer Phil is at the bar, deep in conversation with several other patrons, when I walk in. He is very gregarious and obviously at ease in the place. He seems like the kind of person who would be at ease anywhere. In fact, in an hour he would know dozens more people in this room than I would meet in a month.

So, as he stands and smiles a greeting to me, I wonder, what can he learn from me?

We shake hands. He looks at me from top to bottom and says, "Bobbi, you look great tonight. Thank you for coming."

I feel like a wrestler in a dress. I'm not used to straight men complimenting me on my girlish charms.

We get a table. I dash off to the ladies room to pee and do my makeup. I don't have any anxieties about using the ladies room here. Female visitors to a gay bar should be ready for anything. Plus, I have the place to myself. I'm the only person in the joint professing to be a woman.

When I get back, Officer Phil has ordered two glasses of red wine. We toast to each other's health. Then Phil sits back in his overstuffed chair, looks at me, and smiles. "So, Bobbi, I'd like to know more about you—how long you've been trans, when you first knew, what it's like being transgendered in Chicago, all that stuff."

"Okay," I say, "But I'd like to know a little about you, first. Starting with, why are we meeting? You can't possibly find me attractive"—he starts to correct me but I wave him silent—"no, no, don't object, I'll lose respect for you. And you don't need me to introduce you to people. Half the men in this bar would trade state secrets for a chance to go out with you. So what's the deal?"

Officer Phil gives me an amused smile. "The smile and shoeshine stuff only gets you so far. I need to really know some of the people in this community if I'm going to do my job right. I have to know what it's like to live here, what it's like to be gay or transgendered, what kind of obstacles you face, what kind of dreams you have, what kind of trouble you have. You personally and you collectively."

"Why?" I ask.

"Because I can't be a good cop if I don't understand the culture. That's why we have black cops and Latino cops and Asian cops as well as us Anglos. I'm not gay or trans, but I think I'll do better if I know more about what it's like to be gay or trans.

"And, frankly, I'm hoping that the people I get to know will be my friends and help me understand things that happen that I don't understand."

"Like what?" I wrinkle my nose as I ask.

"Well, let's say a transgender woman gets rolled. What do you know about her that might help us find the perp and make a case? What kind of person are we looking for? Did you see anything suspicious at that time? What are you hearing on the street? Like that…"

"If I can help, I will," I say. "One thing you should know up front is that a lot of the crimes against transwomen involve a john and a trans hooker, but that doesn't mean the girl isn't human. Our girls, especially the young ones, do what they have to do to survive. It's not like they can join the plumber's union or something."

He nods and waits for me to talk some more. I take the bait.

"But it's not all hookers and johns," I say. "Violent breakups aren't unusual in the trans world. Emotions run really high. You have transwomen themselves on hormones, going from birth to puberty to womanhood in a matter of months." I think of my sobbing spree in the salon earlier as a case in point. "And the men who are attracted to trannies often have some major issues themselves."

"Such as?" he asks.

"I think some of them are having sexual orientation issues. Some are closet gays and can't deal with it, so they try to satisfy their lust with someone in between genders. I think a lot of them are straight but they're bored by their sex lives and they're looking for an exotic high. And some just like the power they have over a transwoman."

Officer Phil arches his eyebrows, asking for an explanation.

"They are control freaks. There are movies about them taking over the lives of genetic women. Certain types of women are vulnerable to people like that—low self-esteem is a big theme. And if you think genetic women have self-esteem issues, you can multiply that by a hundred for transwomen. So yeah, some of the guys that seek out transwomen have a creepy dominance thing going on."

Officer Phil ponders this for a moment.

"How common are these types?" he asks.

"Truthfully, I don't know. I've heard a story or two, but I don't have any experience with them. In fact, I haven't actually dated as a transwoman."

He gets that questioning look on his face again. "Any reason?"

I sip my wine. "Lots of them. But let's face it, a girl like me doesn't exactly have to fight off suitors."

"I'm not buying that for a minute," says Officer Phil.

I smile. Gosh. A compliment. He has brown eyes and a nice smile. I tell him it's part of my transition strategy. We get into a question and answer session about transsexual motivations.

He asks about my history. I give him the Cliff's Notes version.

We talk for about an hour. As we stand to leave, I ask, "So, do you have any suspects in Mandy Marvin's murder?"

Officer Phil blinks. He wasn't expecting the question. He has a lot to learn about the trans community. The investigation of Mandy's murder will be the main topic of conversation among us for months, and until it is solved, we will wonder if the cops are really trying. We're used to being marginalized. Officer Phil shakes his head. "I can't talk about an on-going investigation. I wish I could. I hope you understand." But his tone of voice doesn't match his words. He doesn't wish he could. He isn't hoping I understand. He's telling me this is none of my business and he's not going to talk about it.

Officer Phil didn't just say no, he said hell no. And it makes me wonder why.

* * *

"HEY TIGER," she says. "Nice ride!"

They are lying side by side on the bed in her hotel room. She has put her panties back on but remains bare-chested.

Her breasts are firm for a mature woman. She's had some work done on her body, he realizes. No problem here, he thinks. She's the hottest real woman he's known since his teen years. A Type-A businesswoman. Knows what she wants and gets it. Amen. A-fucking-men. He likes that she just wants to get laid. Talks dirty. No romantic games, no flowers, no deeper meaning, no probing each other's psyche.

Still, she reads him like a book. Putting on the panties after sex. How did she know he doesn't like to see it or touch it? How did she know he likes seeing tits?

For that matter, how did she get him to make love twice? Once is a minor miracle most nights with a regular woman, even women twenty years younger than her.

"What are you thinking, Tiger-man?" she asks.

"I'm thinking that you are the greatest fuck of all time," he says. It's a compliment and she takes it as one, beaming. "I haven't had a double orgasm in years. How do you do it?"

Her eyes twinkle. "It's just like business. You decide what you want, then you figure out how to get it."

He cocks his head at her quizzically.

"Honey, when we get older our bodies sometimes need some help. Me, I have a surgeon." She touches a breast, runs her fingers along her jawline. "You? You just needed some pixie dust."

He still doesn't follow.

"Remember the cheese and crackers?" she asks.

He nods. He had a half dozen of them when he got there. They were all made up.

"Remember the sprinkles on top?"

He nods his head yes, understanding where this was going.

"Well sweetie pie, I took the liberty of drugging you and you're going to be getting boners for hours. And if one pops up before you leave, you don't have to ask where to park it. Just pop it in. No questions asked."

He smiles, even chuckles. But inside he's thinking how he never needed chemical help when his boy bitch was around. He can feel the fire rising in his head. He's getting very, very needy and no mere woman, not even this one, will be able to satisfy his hunger.

* * *

THE AIR IS THICK in my tiny bathroom from the steam coming off my bath water. I can feel beads of water running down my face and neck. My hair is soaking wet, clinging to my skin. I am dreamily relaxed. I have cleaned off all my makeup, flossed and brushed, taken my meds and generally fulfilled all my obligations for the day. It is a relaxing thought. The hot water is relaxing, too. The smallness of the room is relaxing. The privacy…

My mind wanders. I contemplate my male organ and try, for the millionth time, to imagine what it will look like to see nothing there someday. I wonder what it will feel like. I know I will be much more comfortable crossing my legs, though the shrinking that the hormones have caused already makes that easier. My doctor tells me that eventually my testicles will be the size of peas. I wonder if that makes castration easier. I wonder if there will be enough skin from the scrotum to make a vagina. I wonder if I will ever make love to a man as a woman. I wonder what that would be like. My experiences as a gay lover were sometimes exciting, but never really tender or intimate.

As I wander through this now-familiar maze of thoughts, I have been subconsciously rubbing my breasts. They are tender and will remain tender until they quit growing. I rub them lightly to relieve the tenderness, but it's also arousing. I don't get erections anymore but I feel erotic sensations in my crotch. My body tingles. My nipples harden. My mind becomes a kaleidoscope of faces and forms. Nice smiles. Pretty eyes. Beautiful hair. Officer Phil leaning over the table to talk to me, his face so sincere and warm, his light brown eyes...

I cut it off. I am aroused. Really aroused. By a straight man. I wonder, does this mean I really am a woman in waiting, or is this just what happens when you put a gay man on hormones and deny him sex for a year or two? Is this how women masturbate? I am intrigued and frightened at the same time.

To keep from driving myself crazy, I focus my concentration on what I learned after Officer Phil and I went our separate ways.

I went to the GLBT Center, the focal point of gay, lesbian and trans life in the city. Word had already spread about Mandy's murder and community mourning was in progress. A wall with a large bulletin board had been set aside for the purpose. People were leaving notes, teddy bears, dolls, and flowers.

The notes told an interesting story about Mandy. People remembered her beauty, her vivacity, her party-girl spirit. People loved things about her, but somehow, I had the feeling that no one knew the real, deep-down-inside her. Even me. Maybe that's the ultimate challenge of being pretty, finding a way to get people to notice the rest of you.

Against my better judgment, I accepted an invitation to join Cecelia and her friends for dinner. I felt bad about how I had left things with her, otherwise I would have given her an excuse and been on my way. Dining with Cecilia in a public place is one of the most painful experiences I've ever had. In addition to being loud, she is calculatingly audacious. She calls frequently and loudly for waiters, broadcasts her table conversation to the tables around her, and complains non-stop about the service and the food.

For all that, she's tapped in to everything.

We went to an informal diner near the Center. I asked if anyone has heard about any progress in the investigation of Mandy's murder. Rebecca scoffed, a reaction that was supposed to show her deep knowledge and educated cynicism all at the same time. She blows it by looking to Cecelia for approval. Cecelia ignores her and puts on her own sour face.

I ask if the others have talked to Officer Phil yet. Cecelia smirks. Tina tries to do the same. Rebecca emits a falsetto chuckle.

"I doubt if Officer Phil could find a Catholic in the Vatican," she says.

Cecelia waits for the chatter to die down, then issues one of her queenly proclamations. "It doesn't matter how good he is," she says. "This one's not going to get solved." She says it in a low voice, which is very unlike her.

We all look at her, waiting for an explanation. Cecilia has an endless list of personal shortcomings, but falsifying information isn't one of them.

"Why?" I ask.

Cecelia gets this priggish look on her face. "The fix is in. That's all I can say."

"You mean they don't care about a t-girl getting murdered?" asks Tina.

"Probably more like they don't want to find out Mandy was balling some city hall big shot—or two or three," says Cecelia. "That kind of thing can ruin careers. For the big shot and the cops who out him."

"You make it sound like she was a hooker with a big database," I say. I'm wondering if it was possible that Mandy was doing some johns on the side without her friends' knowledge.

"She was a party girl. She liked to have a good time. People liked to have her at parties. From what I hear, she got invited to parties that big names in politics and business went to, and she was known to go home with a big shot on occasion." Cecilia smiles slightly.

Mandy had never mentioned such things to me, but she wouldn't have. I knew she partied a lot, and even as a pre-op she dated straight men. It wouldn't be a stretch to think of her going home with a department chief or an executive. In fact, as I thought about it, it seemed likely she did, especially back when she was tricking. I couldn't help wondering if her Mr. Wonderful was a city higher-up. On the other hand, our community goes overboard with conspiracy theories sometimes and Cecelia's proposition sounds a little farfetched.

"How would they keep the investigator from pursuing the case?" I ask.

"It's easy. They only assign one detective to the case and they load him up with other cases and pressure him to focus on them. Bingo, no detective."

"What about Officer Phil?" I ask.

"He's a beat cop. He spends his time in the neighborhood, doing police relations and dealing with street crime. He doesn't have the time or the training to investigate a murder."

I ask how Cecelia knows this. She smiles. "Don't ask, don't tell." She must have a cop friend. I look at her. No, not a lover. Not even the most desperate tranny chaser would pursue a night with Cecelia. Not so much because of her looks, but more her persona. She is a cross between a professional wrestler and a drag queen.

As I recall this conversation, one other remarkable thing occurs to me: Cecelia spoke in a conversational voice almost the whole time and didn't heckle the waiter once. And she treated me like her best friend.

What is the world coming to?

June
———

WHEN TRANSSEXUALS COME OUT, the ground shakes, the heavens cloud and the throats of the faithful erupt in screeches and screams.

Parents are repulsed, then guilt-ridden, then angry that their child is no longer "normal."

Wives think their partner is gay, then wonder if they themselves are too butch, then come to realize that it's not them, it's that their partner is a degenerate and they want a divorce before the stigma attaches to them the way a skunk scent clings indefinitely to its victims.

Employers show their surprise but usually don't panic; they control their disgust, make all the right noises, and find a reason to get rid of the embarrassment in a few months.

And that's when the transwoman does it the right way. When you do it the wrong way, like me, the same things happen, but faster.

I have nothing to complain about. My boss didn't fire me on the spot, and I got the family rejection crap over with long ago. After I was caught wearing my sister's clothes at age five, dear old dad never wanted anything to do with me. I never repeated the sin, and he never mentioned the original transgression, but I think deep down inside he knew I was a fairy. He never went to my Little League games, or my high school football games, or the plays I was in, or anything else. He went to my high school graduation ceremony because mom insisted and mom insisted because it would have looked just awful if they didn't. He put up most of the money for college on three conditions. I had to maintain a 3-point-something grade point average, I had to major in business (no commie pinko liberal arts majors in THIS family!), and I had to promise to not come home when I graduated. I didn't, and he didn't bother coming to my college graduation, which was fine with me.

As for my mother, she was on this earth to do whatever my father said, to think what he wanted her to think, and to say whatever made him happy. Her life was a job and she accepted it with quiet resignation. She had kids because she was supposed to. She kept house, made dinner, sat mutely through PTA meetings. She wasn't mean, but she wasn't warm, either. She never tucked me in at night. We didn't do prayers or hugs or bedtime stories.

My parents were there to set rules for performance and behavior, and make me pay the consequences if I failed to comply. It wasn't a bad set up. They weren't cruel or abusive, they just didn't like me much. And as time went on, I didn't think much of them, either. But we got along fine and I learned to stand on my own two feet early.

My family life was a good preparation for coming out at work. In the two weeks since I went fully femme in the salon, the other stylists mostly indulge me like a leper who insists she's still human. Only a couple of them give me outright hateful stares, but everyone else goes through their days trying not to acknowledge my presence.

Yes, it hurts. I've thought about trying to hire on at a younger, hipper salon where a trans stylist would be no big deal, but I'm not a tattoos and piercings kind of hairdresser. And let's face it: I'm no kid, either. I'm too old for those places.

My clients receive the news of my transition with varied responses. Some take it in stride, some are shocked. Some are just surprised. Mild revulsion is a recurring theme. One lady was outright hostile. She gaped when I came to get her in the waiting area then shrunk back in horror when we got to my chair and I explained about my transition. She shook her head emotionally, as if I were a demon from hell, and said she couldn't have me touch her. She cancelled her service on the spot. She stopped at the front desk on her way out just to tell the receptionist in a loud voice that she was never coming back as long as they would let a "thing" like me work here. She said "thing" like I was something that stank and was ugly to look at.

In my dictionary of life, that scene will always define humiliation. Any sense of human spirit I brought to work that day was crushed. She was shrill and demonstrative. Every eye in the salon was on us. I could feel them, the clients and the hairdressers. They all felt what my client felt. Communal disgust. As the woman left the shop I was left standing alone in the middle of the floor, holding a cape, a shocked, blank look on my face. Tears of frustration and hurt welled up. When I could finally will myself to move, I put the cape on my chair and walked silently to the ladies room, tears streaming down my cheeks.

She has been the worst but even many of the ones who have been pleasant or civil have left without booking their next appointment. I'm losing so many people I'm terrified that I will not be able to support myself much longer. I have no safety net. No parents to run home to, no boyfriend, no understanding sibling. If I can't pay the rent, I live on the street.

As awful as this has been, going back to my male presentation is something I won't even consider. In fact, I didn't even think about it until last night, and even then I wasn't thinking about un-transitioning, I was trying to figure out why I wasn't tempted to do it.

The answer is, for better or worse, this is who I am. I'm not a man. I'm a transwoman. Ugly, disliked, rejected, whatever, this is who I am.

Over many sleepless nights and tense, ego-bruising days, I have pieced together a plan. My goal is to keep half my clients. To get there, I have to get a quarter of them to pre-book the next service and somehow get one-third of the rest of them to come back.

My strategy is to do something special, something a little edgy—or even a lot edgy—for every service. I'm trying to give them a reason to use me even if they think I'm a freak. You can kind of imagine someone at a cocktail party getting a compliment on her hair, saying, yeah, my hairdresser is a she-male (slight facial recoil to show disgust) but he/she is so-o-o creative! It's her excuse to keep coming back without endorsing my lowlife gender orientation.

I might get some business from people who think a transgender stylist is exotic.

Whatever. I can't do any worse than if I did nothing at all, and I might do better.

* * *

I'VE BEEN SO CAUGHT UP in my own trials and tribulations I actually went several days without thinking about Mandy. That ended today when I had my regular sit down with Marilee.

I tell her I'm out at work now, and the reaction has been pretty awful. She draws out of me the story of the woman who humiliated me, and the others who barely disguised their disgust. Her soft, full lips quiver as I speak. Wetness fills her soft brown eyes. Her pain is somehow reassuring. No one has ever felt my pain before, or even asked about it.

"Oh Bobbi," she says, dabbing a tissue at her eyes and shaking her head with enormous sadness. "I'm so sorry that happened to you. I know it hurts.

But as much as it hurts, you need to talk about it." She embraces me for a long, warm moment, then sits me down again, and gestures with her hands for me to talk.

I confess my range of responses: desperate loneliness and isolation; feeling like a hairy ape freak; premonitions of being homeless and starving; trying not to cry in the salon; crying my eyes out at home; anger toward the nasty women. Replaying the scenario with the horrible woman who called me a "thing," where I ask her why she can't keep a husband. She is newly divorced. It would be a really hurtful thing to say.

Marilee asks if it would have made me feel better to say that. Yes, and no. Making someone else feel bad wouldn't make me feel better about myself, but it would be fun to see a bully get a face-full of herself. In a poetic-justice sort of way. I wouldn't have felt so pathetic right then and there, but when I thought about it later, I'd be ashamed of myself.

"What would make you feel better?" she asks.

"Being 5-7 and a size 6," I say.

She laughs and shakes her head with a wry mom smile, like I was a precocious six-year-old who just said something funny. "What else?" she pushes.

I blush, and she can see it even through my makeup. "I don't know," I say, wanting to change the subject.

"Come on," she coaxes. "We don't get anywhere if you keep it all inside."

I fidget and try to find the words. I don't want to say exactly what I'm thinking because it's too embarrassing. It's embarrassing to admit to myself, let alone to Marilee. Finally, I say, "I've been having erotic dreams."

She smiles. She is happy for me. "Good!" she says. "Tell me about them."

"They involve Officer Phil."

Mildly awkward silence. "Okay. Keep going."

"Uh, well, he turns me on. I've had several dreams about going on dates with him, him coming into the shop to see me, going to dinner…"

Marilee waits to see if I'll finish the image. I don't. She says, "What happens in these dreams?"

In my mind I feel Officer Phil's lips on mine, our hands caressing each other's erogenous zones. My heart pumps faster.

"We make love," I confess, hoping to leave it there.

"Do you make love as a woman?" she asks.

My heart flips again. Do I? Do I feel him slipping between my legs in the dream?

"I don't know," I tell Marilee, "But he tells me I'm beautiful and sexy and it feels wonderful."

"Close enough," she says.

* * *

"WHAT DO YOU KNOW about Mandy's murder?" Cecelia asks me, leaning across the table and speaking in a conspiratorial voice just above a whisper.

We're at dinner in a trendy restaurant, a California wine country cuisine kind of place. Very expensive. Very straight. People at several tables cast furtive glances at us, followed by suddenly hushed conversations. I feel like a spectacle. Someone will surely be coming by to exercise their God-given right to humiliate and embarrass us. Or me, anyway.

"All I know is what you told me." I respond. "Why? Is something going on?"

Cecelia grimaces. "If you mean, is the investigation making progress, no. I told you, that's a dead issue. No pun intended."

She sits back in her chair for a moment, contemplative, then leans forward again. "We'll talk about that again later. Let's order and talk about pleasanter things," she says.

Cecelia compliments me on my attire and my presentation. "How is your transition going?" she asks.

I tell her about coming out at work. The animosity and rejection. The cool distance even the friendlier stylists have taken. Worries about client retention. As I speak, my emotions well up, my voice trembles as I'm caught unawares by how troubled I still am. I thought I had moved beyond these things.

Cecelia asks more questions, almost like a shrink. I describe my recurring feeling of being a giant hairy sumo wrestler in a dress.

"Oh God," she says, gesturing broadly with one hand. I fear she is going to respond in her characteristic volume. But when she talks again she reduces her voice for one-to-one communication.

"We all go through that. You know who you are. If someone else has a problem with that, it's their problem, not yours. And quit worrying about how you look. Just be."

She continues in this vein for a while. I'm trying to imagine myself doing that.

"I know that's good advice," I say, "but it's so much easier said than done. I mean, what if the man at the next table stands up and comes over here and starts yelling at us, that we're perverts and faggots and all that. What do you do?"

Cecelia fumbles with her purse. "Well, personally, I either tell him to suck on his own limp dick or I nail him with a shot of this…" She produces a can of pepper spray.

She snickers. "Look honey, everyone deals with it a different way. I've always been a big mouth and I decided early on I wasn't going to apologize to anyone for who I am. I figured if I was the loudest, most brazen idiot in the room no one would mess with me. It works. Of course, lots of people don't like me. You're one, I know."

I start to object but she cuts me off. "No, Bobbi, you don't need to deny it. I don't take offense. I really do know who I am and what I am.

"I'll just say that being loud and brash isn't all that I am. I really do try to give back to the community and every once in a while I do something kind of nice that goes unnoticed."

I believe her and say so. She beams.

We order. She pulls her chair closer to mine.

"A few general hints," she says. "First of all, don't worry about your colleagues in the salon. In a few weeks, they will be used to you. People who you were friendly with before will be friendly again. The others won't be friendly, but they probably won't be antagonistic, either. It takes too much energy.

"I also don't think you should lose any sleep over your client retention. I don't know any hairdressers who have transitioned, but I have known several girls who were in sales. The ones who conducted themselves professionally did fine."

Cecelia lets this sink in for a moment.

"For what it's worth," she says, "I think you're going to do very well. You have a quiet, dignified way about you. It makes people like you and trust you. And even though it's true that you don't look like a genetic woman, you have an attractive, kind of exotic appearance. I think for every person who leaves you because of your appearance there will be two who seek you out."

Knock me over with a feather! I really had no idea Cecelia could be so charming. Other than Marilee, she is the only person who has offered any real hope and encouragement to me since I came out.

We talk about other things during dinner—TransGender Alliance issues and people, Chicago politics, men. Officer Phil, it turns out, has caught the fancy of many of our sisters. "What about you?" she asks.

I feel myself blush. "Yes, he's hot," I finally concede.

"Oh come now, Bobbi," Cecelia chides me. "Confess, you'd love to be in a dark room with soft music with him, right?" She gets more graphic, asks me why I'm squirming. I explain about my determination to remain chaste during my transition, and why.

She arches her eyebrows thoughtfully. "Well, Bobbi, you really are different. I had no such restraints. In fact, I couldn't move fast enough into my new skin."

Cecelia tells her story. A high-powered bank executive, a trophy wife, two high-achieving kids. Big stock portfolio. Nice side business as a financial consultant to individuals. The country club, company limo. High profile player in the state's Republican Party. Flew first class. Gave orders, talked loud, apologized to no one. Made a fortune.

"Then one day Mrs. Swenson, wife to Robert Swenson, who was me in a former life tells me she's been having an affair. She tells me this not because she wants a divorce, but because she doesn't want to be sneaky and she doesn't think I'll care.

"She says we never have sex anymore and it can only mean one of two things—that I don't find her attractive, or that I'm gay."

Cecelia pauses for dramatic effect, then shrugs. "You know, she made me deal with it. It was true, I hadn't been interested in her sexually for years, even though she was beautiful and provocative and a willing bed partner. I never really had dealt with why I lost interest in her sexually, even though I was aware of it.

"When she told me, I was jealous. But not the kind of jealous a man would be. I didn't want to make love with her or shoot her lover or hit her or any of those things. I didn't know what to think or do or say. I didn't know how I felt. And I knew that wasn't right."

Cecelia looks away for a moment.

"So I start seeing a shrink and a couple weeks later, I have a pretty good idea of who I am. I had buried memories of how much I liked my sister's and mother's clothes because I had been scolded for trying sis' wardrobe once. After that, I denied that whole part of me. I buried it because I was also competitive, and you couldn't win in business or in life if people thought you were a sissy.

"A month after my wife told me about her affair, I told her I was a transsexual and I was going to transition. I've never been more certain of anything in my life."

Cecelia stops talking. Her silence breaks my ruminations on how different our revelations were, Cecelia's and mine, she struck by a lightning bolt of certainty later in life, me shadowed by a reality from childhood that I still have doubts about.

"How did your wife take that?" I ask.

A sad smile plays at her lips. "She was disappointed. She had hoped I was gay because we could make an accommodation—she'd have her plaything, I'd have mine and we'd carry on. Me prancing around in a dress, borrowing her makeup, playing golf with her and her friends…well, that wasn't going to cut it. Plus, she wasn't gay, she said. She couldn't live with another woman. She was horrified what everyone would think, how much grief the kids would get at school, all that.

"We divorced quickly, before I began living as a woman. No word to anyone about my secret—just, we've grown apart, it's time for an amicable separation, the kids are taking it well, blah, blah, blah. I got to keep some of the family fortune.

"I haven't seen her since the divorce and I've only seen one of my kids—my daughter. I'm an embarrassment to them."

For all her bluster, Cecelia is deeply hurt by this. Just like the rest of us. Even though the people in our lives feel like the person they knew no longer exists, for us, we're still the same person. We love who we loved before, and we want our friends to still be our friends. Our gender has changed, but not our essence.

I start to ask Cecelia another question, but she holds up one hand in a "stop" motion. "Hold on Bobbi," she says in a low voice. "I want you to keep watching me while I say something. Don't turn until I tell you to. Bobbi, directly behind you is a handsome man in a silver gray suit with a blue tie, fiftyish, silver-gray hair. He's at the bar with another man and a woman in her thirties, long blond hair, big boobs."

"In a moment, I want you to stand up and look that way as if you're looking at the bar, then go to the ladies' room. When you come back you can get another good look at him. Do that, and then we'll talk."

I am only partly mystified by Cecelia's cloak and dagger. I'm mainly concerned with going into the ladies' room in a nice straight place like this.

47

I can just feel some society matron screaming that there's a man in the ladies room, followed by me coming out in handcuffs.

Fearful as I am, I am also under Cecelia's spell, at least for tonight. Trying to be as bold and self-assured as she would be, I rise on cue and pivot slightly, looking to the bar as I smooth my skirt and straighten my blouse. I see the gentleman Cecelia described right away in my peripheral vision. He looks like a mafia don, or maybe a senator. The two people with him listen raptly as he talks. He glances at me as I stand, looks back to his audience then looks at me again for several beats.

As I walk to the ladies' room, I focus on walking in a feminine manner and not tripping over anyone. He made me, of course, that's what the second look was about.

Another woman is in the ladies' room when I enter. She has just finished drying her hands. As we pass closely by each other in the narrow entrance way she glances up at me. I am nearly a foot taller than she in my heels. She reads me instantly, swallows the surprise, looks grimly straight ahead and is gone. I face a roomful of the same encounters when I go back to my table.

When I return, Cecelia looks at me with her sly smile. "So, what do you think?"

"He's very handsome," I say. She gestures with her hands to say more. "He looks like he's wealthy and powerful."

"Very good!" says Cecelia. "He is wealthy and powerful, and he is good looking and knows it."

"He's also the bastard who killed Mandy."

* * *

HE'S HOLDING COURT with his wit and charm. It is so easy. They are so simple. He is so powerful. This one is too easy.

The Cocker Spaniel. Strand has already named him. He rolls into town with his slut of a wife, full of fake anger about a billing, ready to get the fee reduced and show the silly MBAs back home what an asset he is. As if a company lawyer like him would have any sense of what it takes to go to court. As if a real meat-eating litigator would be intimidated by a jelly-spined bureaucrat like him.

The fool is overwhelmed in minutes. It takes a few numbers and a little attitude. Winning is cheap. Losing is expensive. Other firms do their best. We win.

The Spaniel has been eating out of his hands ever since.

Now, in the bar, Strand lays on the charm, reciting his courtroom war stories. Funny, interesting. A little self-deprecating humor to sharpen the focus of the picture he is painting: we always win. That's what you pay for. Other law firms do their best for you, we win. The Spaniel hangs on every word, laughs at every punch line, giddy that his company can't lose, having the time of his life. Mrs. Spaniel is locked in too, face flushed, lips parted. Phony, snotty bitch. All store-bought airs with her designer clothes, gaudy jewelry, surgically enhanced skin, bulbous plastic tits. Arrogant on the outside, hungry on the inside. Coming on to him. He can feel her heat. She is imagining herself with him. He has this affect on women. She disgusts him even more than her simple husband. It would be fun to fuck her hard in the ass. Until she squealed. Until she bled.

The thought doesn't make him horny. It makes him angry.

"Balance," he reminds himself.

As he begins another story, a movement in his peripheral vision causes him to glance away from the Spaniel and his bitch. A tall woman dressed almost entirely in white has just risen from her table. She is trim, unusually athletic. She glances at him while she straightens her skirt and top, then walks toward the restrooms. He turns back to his guests and begins to speak when he realizes the tall woman isn't a woman. He glances back at her. Yes, a tranny. And familiar looking, too.

He tells his story without a hitch, but part of his mind is working on a mental picture of the tall tranny. It comes to him. She's the one he saw going to the trans meeting.

She returns to her table as he is finishing a story and he gets a good look at her. Handsome face, masculine, but hot. Nice cleavage. Plump breasts that jiggle as she negotiates the restaurant tables in short strides. Nice legs. Nice ass. Boyish but shapely. He feels heat in his loins. Pictures pop into his mind of the tall tranny servicing him. His body parts can feel her touch. He feels himself mounting her.

He knows he will lose control if he doesn't stop, so he blocks her out and focuses on the Spaniel and his pathetic bitch. Only a master can do that, he thinks.

* * *

IF THE POPE HIMSELF had just invited me over for Mass, I couldn't be more stunned. Cecelia's revelation comes out of nowhere, a shock that robs me of the power of speech. Without looking at the man again, I have called up his face in my memory. I'm good at this. It comes with doing hair. You think about the face and how different hairstyles would complement it.

Part of me is dubious. Cecelia identified him with great relish, not with horror, which would have seemed more appropriate. It makes me wonder if this is just gossip. Part of me is thinking that this face is vaguely familiar, like someone I might have met somewhere.

"How can you be so certain?" I ask.

"They were an item," says Cecelia. "Not a public item. Not opening night at the theater. Very clandestine. I actually forgot about it until our conversation the other day, about Mandy having a beau, getting off the streets. I only saw them together once, really drunk, in the Paradise Club. They were sitting at the bar and she started turning him on, right there in front of God and everyone. They went into the alley. He never came back in but she did, and she told me she was in love. True love. After that she got a job in the Loop, got a nice apartment, got her sex-change surgery and told everyone she had a lover. No more tricking, she said. I didn't believe it, but I never saw her with another man.

"His name is John Strand, as in Strand, Benson and Hayes. Big downtown law firm. They handle a lot of city and state business. Strand is connected to everyone and everything. Major contributor to both political parties. A-list invitee to big events. First-name basis with the mayor and governor, the power people in the city council and the state assembly."

"Quite a catch for Mandy," I say. I'm somewhat impressed by the money and power, but I'm mostly caught up in how good-looking he is.

"Not really," says Cecelia. "He's a big shot. He could never be seen in public with a transwoman. Not among the hoi polloi anyway. That night in the club was a mistake. As far as I know, he never went out in public with her again. He helped her get a place, set her up. Stopped in when he needed something. I heard he brought friends sometimes, but I don't know about that. Either way, it wasn't going anywhere."

"So what happened?" I ask.

Cecelia shrugs. "Who knows? No one saw it. Maybe she pushed him for a commitment, or threatened to out him if she didn't get what she wanted. Or maybe they just had an argument and once he hit her he couldn't stop." She shrugs as if to say "it happens."

It does.

"But how can you be sure it was him?" I ask. "It could have been some other john, or maybe just someone who made her on the street and followed her home."

"Maybe," Cecelia nods. "But not likely. You were right before. I checked with some younger girls she partied with and they said what you said. Mandy hadn't been hooking, she wasn't seeing anyone else. Mr. Wonderful bankrolled her rent and groceries, bought her nice clothes, you name it. She was working at a day job. She did a little clubbing, but just with girlfriends.

"Plus, our Mr. Strand likes to beat up women." Cecelia draws this out a little for dramatic effect.

"How do you know this?"

"Bobbi, I just know. I can tell you for sure that he is a mean bastard. And I know there have been complaints over the years. Nothing on the record. Kind of like this investigation, eh?"

We talk awhile longer, going over the same points. I'm not convinced, but keep my doubts to myself.

After Cecelia pays the tab and we rise to go, she delivers her biggest surprise. "Oh, by the way, I'd like to introduce you to Mr. Strand on our way out." she says lightly.

She reads the shock in my face and smiles sweetly. "I guess I forgot to mention, John and I were business associates back in the day. I think you'll enjoy this." She slides her arm through mine and guides me to the bar.

"John Strand!" she exclaims. "I just couldn't pass by without saying hello to one of my oldest and dearest colleagues!" She turns to the couple with Strand and explains, "John and I worked together years ago. He's a wonderful attorney."

Strand is momentarily taken aback when we approach, but you can only see it in his eyes. The man has a lot of poise.

"How have you been?" he says with great familiarity and warmth. "Please forgive me, but I've forgotten your name."

Cecelia extends her hand in greeting. "Oh come on John, no need for apologies. It's Cecelia Swenson." She actually enjoys his fleeting embarrassment. "But you knew me as Robert." A wave of recognition comes over Strand's face and he smiles. It's a politician's smile. Automatic. Not friendly, but not unfriendly either.

Cecelia shakes hands with the man and woman, again introducing herself. Even without Cecelia's reference to her former male identity they would have made her as trans. Cecelia looks like a tall older woman with somewhat puffy features, but her voice gives her away. Cecelia sees the recognition on their faces, and seems to enjoy it.

"You have to understand that I was a different person when John and I worked together. I'm sure he'll tell you about it."

She turns back to Strand. "I just wanted to say hi and introduce you to my good friend Bobbi."

On cue, he extends a hand. I swallow and extend my own hand, bejeweled with several rings and a large bracelet. I feel like I am exposing myself.

"Hi, Bobbi," he says. His eyes are focused hard on me and he is smiling. He embraces our handshake with his left hand, which is warm and intimate. I'm flushing like a school girl.

"Hello, John," I respond. "Nice to meet you." I try to sound feminine but I'm not even close. He takes it in stride and introduces me to his friends, somebody and somebody Wilson. I can feel him looking at me while the introductions are going on.

Cecelia catches this too. And, being Cecelia, decides to have fun with it.

"Bobbi is the hottest hairdresser in the city," Cecelia tells Strand. "She does men's hair, too. You should try her some time."

I blush so hard I can feel the heat on my face. Strand smiles. "Sounds like a good idea. Bobbi, do you have a card?"

I fumble in my purse like a ten-year-old girl playing dress up. Finally I find one and hand it over. Strand's fingers brush against mine as he takes it. Mrs. Wilson asks for a card, too. I fumble less this time, and get a smile from her as I deliver it. I force myself to speak. "It would be a treat to do either or both of you." My voice is too soft. I really need to be more confident. Or at least sound that way.

Cecelia's last words to me as we parted were a warning. "I'm a little worried about how interesting Strand found you," she says. "Don't be fooled by his good looks and public demeanor. I've known him for a long time. He is a dangerous, despicable man and if he feels like hurting you, he'll do it. Keep your distance."

Cecelia is noticeably tense when she says this. Another first. There is something in this world that actually intimidates Cecelia. Who would have guessed?

***

THE BAR AT ERNIE'S IS PACKED with Rush Street revelers, an intimidating army of straight people. One of them is a hetero male, my first date as a transwoman. The rest will be gawking strangers as soon as I open the door and cross the threshold.

I'm already wishing I hadn't made this date. It's not a romantic meeting. The guy is a client, a nice guy who wanted to talk about something. He picked the place, a straight bar on Rush Street, well outside my safety zone.

Well, I'm committed now. I take a deep breath and enter. The first face I see is Ray's. He greets me at the door. I am relieved. The thought of working my way through the milling crowd is scary. It's one thing to be made as a transwoman, it's another to be nose-to-nose with someone when it happens.

Ray hugs me. It's a greeting hug, but nice. I hug back. He takes my hand and leads me back to the lounge area. We slither between groups of people. One merrily inebriated middle-aged man feels my body brush against his as I try to squirm by. He smiles and feels me up. "Very nice!" he says. I should be furious, but I'm caught up in the fact he didn't make me. He was being inappropriate, but I'm thrilled he thought he was being inappropriate with a woman. I just can't get angry about it. Besides, that's the first time I've been felt up and to be honest, I liked it.

Ray finds an empty table and we sit down. Magically, a waitress appears to take our order. "So!" says Ray, looking at me after the waitress is gone. "You look lovely tonight, Bobbi. Is it okay for me to say that?"

I smile. "Of course. And don't stop now. You're lying, but it's for a good cause."

"I'm not lying," he answers. "You look great. How are you?"

As we go through the usual conversation-starting ritual, I take in Ray from a new perspective. In the salon, my interactions with clients are almost all through a mirror. It's very different actually looking at someone face-to-face.

Ray is a big, nice-looking guy in a cuddly way. Scandinavian features, light complexion, dark blond hair. Nice smile. White teeth. I notice a little redness between his eyebrows. He's been tweezing. I make a note to offer him an eyebrow wax next time he comes in for a haircut.

"How is your transition going?" he asks.

I fidget. "As well as can be expected, I guess. Most of the hairdressers in the salon are still trying to deal with it. They don't like it but they aren't giving me a hard time. They just leave me alone. My clients? I don't know. Some seem to accept it, but my bookings are down quite a bit, so we'll see."

"Ahhh!" Ray gestures with one hand, as if wiping away what I said. "You'll do fine. Before you know it, people will be lined up to have you do their hair. But I'm surprised about the other stylists. I thought hairdressers were the most accepting people in the world."

"Some are. We're really open to gays for obvious reasons. But transitioning is different. The salon world is all about looks and appearances. And a lot of t-girls don't look right. I certainly don't."

Ray debates the point. I wish I had the feeling he was being gratuitous. I wouldn't mind a friendly drink with some harmless ego stroking. But I'm afraid Ray is going to say he has the hots for me. I'm definitely not ready for that. Even if he were the man of my fantasies, which he is not.

It passes. The wine comes. I ask Ray what's going on in his life. Marilee says that question is an invitation to someone to unburden themselves. "Don't ask it unless you're prepared to do a lot of listening," she advises.

Ray starts with what I know—he had a brief marriage, shotgun type, about ten years ago, before extra-marital pregnancies became fashionable. He's always paid child support, but had limited contact with the mom and his son. Mom wanted him to stay, took it personally when he didn't. Too many ugly scenes that couldn't be good for the boy, so he just showed up for birthdays, Christmas, Saturdays once a month.

It's been obvious for years that the boy is gay, Ray says, finally getting into it. The boy is effeminate, gets bullied, does poorly in school.

"When you told me your story, it got me to thinking about Jon," Ray explains. "It fits. Gail says he has always liked to play dress up in her clothes. The one time I took him out to buy clothes he told me he didn't like boy's clothes. Very matter of fact about it. And when I can get him to talk at all about school and stuff, he talks about the girls in his class or in his neighborhood. But it's not like a boy would talk about girls. He talks about what they wear, what they look best in. He tells me about one girl who got pink highlights in her hair and he says it like he's jealous."

I give him a campy smile and exaggerated hand gesture. "He sounds like my kind of boy."

"I think my son is a transsexual, Bobbi," Ray says, smiling at my humor, but earnest. "So, what do I do?"

What indeed? I didn't see this coming. All I really know about transsexuality is what it's like to be me, and even that's a little vague at times.

"Are you asking me for parenting advice?" I ask, finally.

"I'm hoping you know something about it. Gail actually asked me to give her some advice. I'm trying."

I marvel silently at what an awful choice I am for parenting advice. Not only am I not one, I don't even have good parental role models to draw on.

"I'm looking for information. Advice. Contacts." he says. "I mean, we don't know anything about this. Do kids ever grow out of it?"

As I respond I'm overwhelmed by how little certainty there is about anything in this nook of the human race. "Ray, lots of kids cross-dress as children. Most of them move on to other things. It's just one of many life experiments that kids do as they grow up.

"But for some kids, it's not something you outgrow. Some of us hide it so our parents don't get hysterical and we don't have to deal with neighborhood bullies, but it's still there when we turn ten and twenty and fifty-five. If you're one of us, you don't outgrow it. Some keep it hidden all their lives. They make a life in the body they were born with. But some of us do something about it.

"Your son might be trans, based on what you say. You definitely shouldn't take my word for it. In fact, I'll give you the name of a shrink to contact. There are only a few in Chicago who have any notion at all of what transgenderism is, let alone how to deal with it."

I jot down Marilee's name and number. Then I tell him about an article I read a few months ago. The parents of a transsexual child, born male but identifying from her earliest days as female, decided to raise her as a girl.

It worked well in early childhood. She looked and talked and acted like a girl, got along well with the others, did well in school, enjoyed her life. But things got complicated when she approached puberty. The parents realized their daughter would be traumatized by male puberty, and by the alienation it would cause her from her friends and classmates and neighbors.

They consulted with physicians and psychologists and finally opted to use testosterone blockers to postpone her puberty until she was old enough to make a gender decision.

"Ray," I said, "I have no idea if that's a workable solution. It happened in Europe. I'm not sure it's even legal here, and I have no idea what side affects it might have. But I think that story gives you an idea of how profound this is going to get."

Not that Ray needed convincing.

We spend another twenty minutes on the easy stuff. Love your child without condition. Most transsexuals are disowned or icily distanced by their families as soon as they come out. It adds to depression, failure in other life struggles, suicide, drugs. This is not a glamorous life choice, especially when your own family reviles you.

Ray is visibly relieved as we say goodbye. He has a course to pursue. It's better than just treading water in the middle of the ocean. I remember when I read that article I wondered what it would have been like for me if I had been raised as a girl, by supportive parents. If I had never been a boy. If I had never teased a girl, never had body hair or erections. Physically, it is an attractive thought. I would never have become so big and so muscular; a near lifetime of hormones would have feminized my skin and my features, too.

On the other hand, this person that I am would never have existed.

Funny, really. As much as I fantasize about being a normal-looking woman and passing for one, the thought that I might have grown up just that way and avoided being who I am today is not attractive. It is chilling, in fact.

Still, if I had a trans child, I would want to do for her or him what those parents did for their child.

Outside, when my cab comes, I turn to shake Ray's hand. He hugs me and kisses me on the cheek. I drive off into the night wondering if my coming out is going to lead to more of these kinds of sessions.

* * *

SHE TUGS OPEN HIS PANTS and sets to work on him. He watches, fascinated by her blend of girly and boyish features. Nimble fingers, full lips, large soft breasts. Masculine nose. Male-sized feet and hands. She is hungry. She's been eager to go down on him all night. He could feel it. And it turned him on. He teased her for a while, letting the urge build. Clever repartee, little jokes here and there, compliments. It was driving her crazy.

Her mouth is fantastic. Better than the last one, really. Too good. He can feel himself on the verge. He stops her. He puts his hands on her face and gently lifts until she is looking at him. He motions to the couch. He hands her the condom and they strip. He smiles. She still has a tiny penis and testicles. She rolls the condom on him, applies the gel, enjoying it. He turns her over. He smiles again. She moans and talks to him but he ignores her. He is living in his mind now, reliving real and imagined couplings from his life, from movies. She is the briefest blip in the succession. As he nears climax, that big tranny hairdresser takes center stage. So butch, but so femme. He imagines her in lewd, animalistic ways. It arouses him to a fever pitch. She is chanting to him, urging him, praising his manhood, asking for more, more, more. She worships him. He tries to recall her name for a moment then submits to a wild orgasm that makes him blind and breathless.

When it's over he can barely mask his contempt for the silly boy-bitch at his side. She thinks she has given him the ride of his life. Stupid freak. But she did get him started, she got him turned on initially. He controls his contempt. He'll get her number because he knows the beast will be back, and this one can feed the beast. And if the beast consumes her some night, no one will care.

***

TODAY IS MY DAY off, but I have been dreading it for some time. I'm having lunch with my ex-wife, Betsy. We set this up before I decided to go full-time femme. She has a document I have to sign so she can sell the house we bought together. It's hers, but we never got around to finishing all the paper work. We could have done this by mail, but it seemed important to her to get together in person. I still love her, in my strange way, and I think she loves me, too.

I haven't told her I'm transitioning. It was bad enough when I told her I was gay. Still, I can't bring myself to cancel because I know it would disappoint her, and I've done too much of that already.

I finally summon the courage to call her cell and give her fair warning. I go directly to voice mail. Of course. She's at work. I leave a jumbled message, a forewarning that I'm living as a woman and she might want to cancel. I leave my phone number.

I get caught up in the day and don't think about it again until I'm fighting mid-day traffic on my way to meet Betsy. I realize she never called back, which probably means she didn't get my message. Which means she's going to get the shock of her life when I show up.

I enter Northtown Deli hoping to slip into the ladies' room to dry off my perspiration and touch up my makeup before Betsy sees me. But this is not a day for lucky breaks. Or gentle introductions. She spots me immediately and I see her, too. She's in the back booth—very considerate of her—and even from there, I'm easy to see. I'm taller than most of the customers, even the men.

Betsy is a slim, graceful woman of thirty-six. She wears a conservative, understated business suit over a white blouse, a modern-art brooch on one lapel. Fine gold chains fall from her neck. Dangling gold earrings swing lightly from her lobes. She wears her hair in a mid-length bob. It's symmetrical and perfectly graduated. It has been blown-dry with a round brush for fullness.

She gets more beautiful with maturity, and she was always a looker. She has great, wide eyes with Mediterranean darkness and an almost erotic almond shape. She has full lips with natural color, so perfect it's a sin to put lip gloss on them. She isn't wearing any today, perhaps because she knows I like her better without. Her bone structure is the stuff of photographic models—high cheek bones, slight hollows just beneath them, and a chin that manages to be both strong and petite at the same time.

Her overall appearance speaks of openness and humanity while also communicating that she is a no-nonsense woman of the world. Usually. Not right now, though. Right now, she is gaping at what used to be her husband. She is clearly stunned at the sight of me and the harder she tries not to be, the worse it gets. Her mouth is open, her eyes are rolling up as she stares at me getting ever closer to her.

I feel like a bad joke. Even though I don't want to, I am seeing me through her eyes. The man she once made love to is in heels, an above-the-knee black dress, carrying a purse. My hair is bouncing up and down with each step and my breasts are jiggling. Several heads turn as I walk the aisle to her booth. I pause for a fleeting moment to see if she will stand to exchange hugs. She doesn't. I slide into the booth opposite her as gracefully as I can. She stares in silence for another several seconds. I use the moment to try to get my heartbeat under control.

Our waiter appears. "Can I get you something to drink?" he asks. He almost addresses me as "sir," which would have been just perfect. I order water with a slice of lemon. I try to sound feminine but it's hopeless.

Betsy is still staring at me.

"Bob," she says finally, "What is going on?"

"I'm transsexual. I'm becoming a woman. I go by 'Bobbi' now." I try to say it almost automatically, as I have in breaking the news to friends and acquaintances. But this is much harder. The pain on Betsy's face brings tears to my eyes.

Betsy is speechless. Her mouth is still open, her lips trying to form a word.

"I'm a transsexual, Betsy," I say finally. I can anticipate her initial questions. "I always have been. It just took a lot of years to understand it. When I was five I tried to wear my sister's dresses. I thought they were beautiful and they felt wonderful. My parents screamed at me for it. Told me that wasn't how a boy should play. My father never looked at me the same again. So I didn't do it again until after you and I split up and I came out. As gay." I'm rambling now, trying to fill the dead air as she remains transfixed by the spectacle that I am. "Oh, I had pangs now and then, but I buried them. Never told anyone. Not you, not my parents, not my sister, not my best friend, not even my first boyfriend."

I keep babbling, unable to stop. I give her the whole sorry story in obituary-like brevity. Got to know some trans people. Tried it out. Knew it was me from the get-go. Thought I was a cross-dresser, but as time went on I never wanted to cross back to male. "I'm a transsexual," I say, one more time. My lips quiver a little when I say it.

I wait for her to say something, but she can't. I can't stand the silence. I have to fill it. "I'm very sorry this came as such a shock," I say, my voice husky and cracking. I really want to cry. "I left you a voice mail message this morning to give you a heads up and give you a chance to back out on this, but I guess you didn't get it."

Betsy shakes her head slowly. "No," she says. "I forgot my cell phone this morning."

She stares at me. A river of silence flows between us…

"My god, Bob—Bobbi—are you sure about this?" she asks. "How far along are you?"

"I'm sure," I say. It's a white lie. I may never be sure. But the full truth would get us into a conversation I don't want to have.

"I see you have breasts," Betsy says, nodding at my cleavage. "Have you… you know."

"No," I answer. "Next summer." The polite expression is gender reassignment surgery. Clinicians call it castration. It makes you think. And I'm not sure I'll ever do it, let alone next summer. But I don't want her to know my doubts.

The waiter brings my water. We order light lunches. It gives her a chance to regain her composure.

"So," she says, "How do you like it? Being a woman?" She wipes away a tear as she asks.

"If I was a real woman, I would love it," I answer honestly. "But I'm a transwoman and just starting out, really, and that's different. A lot of people will never accept me as a woman. I have to live with that. It can be challenging.

"The other thing that's really tough is sitting down to pee. It seems like such a production."

She laughs, still dabbing at tears. "You'll learn to make it quick."

She takes a deep breath and exhales, relaxing herself, then asks a series of questions about me, my transition program, the shrink, the hormones, how it makes me feel, am I dating. By the time we finish our lunches, we are chatting almost like old friends. Almost. There is a lull in the conversation.

"Was it awful for you when we made love?" There's an edge to her voice. A hurt maybe.

"No, never." I answer. "The sex was better than anything I've ever experienced and the intimacy was...better. Because I really loved you and because I always thought you were an incredibly sexy woman. I still do. But my true confession is that there were times when I was trying to imagine what it was like to be you, to have me touching you, to have me inside you, to hear me gasping in your ear when I came, to feel what you feel when you came. It was wildly erotic."

"Why didn't you tell me?" she asks.

"How could you have understood? I didn't understand it myself until..." My voice trails off. Until when? When did I know?

"It's taken forever to figure out who I am, Betsy. I didn't want this to be the answer."

Tears trickle down her face. She reaches across the table to grasp my hands in hers. We exchange teary smiles.

The one person in the world who has every right to hate me actually loves me.

We finally get around to the documents then talk about her. She has remarried. Don is his name. She produces the mandatory photo of a nice looking man, middle aged, fairly trim, nice smile. He has a daughter, little Belinda, from his first marriage. Betsy and Belinda get along fine. The ex is nice enough. They hope to have another child while Betsy still can. There's also a dog and, soon, a house in the suburbs.

"Do you love him?" I ask. Her recitation of his fine qualities seems just a little mechanical.

"Oh yes," she says, smiling. "I didn't want to dwell too much on that since we were once ...you know..."

We both laugh a little. It can be awkward talking to a girlfriend who used to be your husband. She gets a wistful look on her face. "Yes, I love him," she says. "Very much. But I'll always love you too, Bobbi. And Bob. I'll always love Bob. You were my first and you'll always be there in my heart."

I can no longer hold back my tears. We touch hands in the middle of the table and hold each other in silence for a long moment. It has been years since someone has made me feel loved like this. I can hardly bear it.

"I want you to come out for dinner when we get settled," Betsy says when the moment passes.

I smile politely. That isn't going to happen. Think of what the neighbors would say! But it is a nice gesture, and I reciprocate with an open invitation for a cut and color. Lunch ends happily. We hug. Hard. There is still love between us. And I still think she's hot.

As I stroll home I think how close we came to me fathering Betsy's child. She was just starting to talk about a baby when we split up. I had become a less interested lover. I realize now that my Bobbi persona was starting to force its way out of the dark place I put it in so many years ago.

By then I had quit my marketing job. Partly because I was sick of the infighting in the company and the breathtaking stupidity of some of our executives. But partly because I wanted to go to beauty school. I had always been interested in doing hair, but I had kept it a secret because it wasn't a masculine ambition. What brought me out in the open was meeting a hairdresser at a party one night. Ronald had longish, wavy hair, perfectly plucked eyebrows, a white smile. He smelled good and wore a lot of jewelry. He was slightly effeminate, but he was very masculine in his overtures to me.

To my shock and horror, he fascinated me. I was entranced as he talked about hairdos and clients, and before long I was imagining what it would be like to make love with him. I managed to control myself, but I had erotic dreams about Ronald for weeks. Somewhere in there, I told Betsy I'd like to go to beauty school. I had always had a secret desire to do hair, even as a child, and Ronald re-awakened that in me. Betsy was surprised, but okay with the idea.

Working as a hairdresser let me express myself in ways I couldn't before. I went with tight-fitting shirts and slacks, pierced ears, colored hair. I developed a soft, slightly effeminate lisp, especially at work. Little by little, Bob was becoming Bobbi. I would look at hairdo books and picture the styles on my customers and on me, too. I would meet gay hairdressers and the occasional gay customer and start to evaluate them as lovers. My interest in lovemaking with

Betsy ebbed and eventually died.

One night Betsy demanded to know why I wasn't interested in her any more. She thought I was having an affair. I told her I was gay. I told her about being attracted to Ronald. We started planning our divorce. We were both humiliated and embarrassed by my new reality, but we were considerate of each other and there were no hard feelings at the end.

Since then, we communicate occasionally—a Christmas card, a phone call. I knew when she got engaged. She knew about my hairdressing career, my fling with Ronald, and my move to Boystown.

The torrid affair I dreamed about with Ronald didn't really happen. We groped for a few weeks then Ronald went on to other lovers, a whole string of them.

Ronald was a much better mentor than lover. He took an interest in my hairdressing career and gave me great advice. He steered me to the best teaching seminars and introduced me to Roger, a brilliant hairdresser opening an upscale salon in a trendy near-north neighborhood. I've been with Roger's salon ever since. And I've never stopped loving what I do.

I'm glad Betsy and I didn't have children. It wouldn't have been fair to her or the child. I don't suppose I'll ever see her again. But if she ever did invite me to dinner at their new place, I think I'd go. I love her. I would love her as a sister. And I think she could love me as a sister.

* * *

July

YOU'D THINK SOMEONE whose life is going up in flames would stick to solving their own problems, but I just can't let this thing with Mandy go. There's absolutely no indication that the police are conducting any kind of serious investigation and it's driving everyone to distraction. My trans sisters protest loudly to one another, but that just frustrates me more. I need to do something.

I'm in the Michigan Avenue cosmetics store where Mandy worked, waiting for a salesgirl named Annie to go on break so she can talk to me. I ponder the miracle skin remedies that sell for prices that make cocaine and heroin look cheap, then the foundations, powders and blushes. I'm serious about my cosmetics, but not this serious.

At last Annie takes her break. We move briskly down the street to a coffee shop, making small talk as we go. Annie says the store's products are okay but way overpriced, the customers can be a royal pain, and the pay is not bad for retail. She is a pretty girl. More than pretty, really. Early twenties. Dark mid-length hair framing a pixie face, soft, sexy eyes, dusky skin without a single flaw. Full lips, beautifully tinted in a sheer lip gloss that adds a touch of pink and a hint of red. Her eyeliner is especially elegant, a strong line with perfect symmetry on top; a finer line under the lower lash; both meeting in an upward arc at the far corner of each eye to give her an even more exotic look.

We both order coffees, Annie adds a croissant with butter and jam. Her food choice calls attention to the fact that she is a little pudgy. A product of her gene pool, perhaps, but especially eating a fatty fast-food diet, I suspect. At her age, her slight pudginess is cute, cuddly. In ten years, she will probably look matronly, or worse.

Inwardly, I sigh. I would make any sacrifice in diet and gym work to keep that body together if it were mine. Of course, I'm sure there are people who would have loved to have my male body, too. Such is life.

"So, how well did you know Mandy?" I ask, when we get settled.

Annie averts her gaze from me as she answers. "I knew she was transsexual.

I knew her parents disowned her. I know she did some hustling. She knew a lot about me, too. We were friends."

"Do you have any idea why someone would want to kill her?" I ask.

Annie is looking down at the table now. A tear trickles down her cheek. She dabs at it with her napkin. "Not any good reason."

I consider this answer for a moment. Annie is telling me to ask my question in a different way.

"Do you know a bad reason to hurt her?"

Annie looks up at me. "Because she was, you know…"

"Trans?" I finish for her.

"Yes." She nods and sobs slightly. "And she was involved with a weird guy."

I arch my eyebrows in question.

"He bought her stuff, lots of things, even her operation. But he was using her. I don't think he ever treated her right. If he did, she never talked about it. She told me a couple times he brought home friends and had her fuck them."

Annie looks up again. "She never talked about him taking her somewhere nice. Not even a movie."

It comes pouring out of Annie, now. Mandy thought this man was her sugar daddy. He helped with the rent, paid for her surgery. Bought her clothes and jewelry. But he also smacked her around sometimes. So did his friends, Annie thinks.

"I wanted her to get away from him, but she was having a hard time with that. You don't make enough in retail to have your own big apartment in a nice neighborhood, and she had the nice clothes, cool stereo, good food. She'd have had to go from that to sharing a place with someone and shopping at Target, you know? She was coming around to that decision, but it took time. That was the big thing. But also, she really got off on sex with him. Maybe even with some of the friends. I think she liked the danger. It could have been any of them."

Annie sips her coffee and looks at her watch. Our time is almost over.

"What was his name?" I ask.

"She never mentioned his name," she says. "It was some deep dark secret because the guy was rich and famous or something."

* * *

AS I HURRY TO the salon, deep in thought, a young man, possibly in his late teens, stands beside me at a stop light, looking me up and down.

"You're really stupid looking, do you know that?" he says. Out of the blue. I hadn't even looked at him.

"Of course I do." I'm shocked that I can speak at all. My self-esteem has just been pulverized. "If a dim wit like you can see it, I certainly can."

I am startled at what I've said. And he is stunned into a moment of silence, staring at me. I expect him to hit me, then and there, or scream at me. His face is a study in anger and hatred.

"You fuckin' queer!" he says, finally. He clears his throat and spits in my face, a great wad of goo splattering against one cheek, ringed by droplets of spittle covering a broader area. He stomps off.

Several other people at the crosswalk take this in. When the light changes, they walk on without comment. Though I try not to, I have mental flashes of what they see. A pathetic man in a dress being cursed and spat upon by a brainless punk. I remove a tissue from my purse and dab the spit from my forehead and cheeks, and from my black silk T-shirt. I am humiliated, but I'm also angry. No one should be treated the way I was just treated. And no one should do what that punk just did and get away with it.

As I walk I think about what I might have done physically to defend myself. Cecelia favors pepper spray, but I am much less evolved than she is. I'm thinking of a karate fist to the Adam's apple, or a quick shot to the solar plexus, or the old standard, a well-placed knee to the groin.

My thoughts bounce back and forth between my humiliation and John Strand. There was a man who vented his anger with his fists. In lethal doses. I try to convince myself that being spit on by a stranger is nothing compared to being beaten to death. But it's not working. They are kindred acts of violence and disrespect, perpetrated by people who feel they have the right to violently disrespect other people. One was murder. The other was a prelude to murder or something like it.

* * *

MAYBE FOR SOME PEOPLE the spitting incident would just be a bad day, something you shrug off after a bad night's sleep, or maybe sooner. For me, it strikes much deeper. It has been three days since the incident. Everywhere

I go I feel like an assault from a stranger is imminent. I have to force myself to leave my apartment and every moment I'm out I feel like a misfit and a fair target for every thug and right-wing whack job on the street. I admitted as much to one of my colleagues in the salon. Kelly isn't much of a talker and isn't really friendly with anyone, so I was surprised when she asked me how I was doing in my new skin.

I told her about the spitting incident, and how I'm still obsessing about it. She patted my hand in a sort of understanding, caring way, then asked, "Have you considered going back?"

It took me a moment to realize she meant back to being a male. "No," I said.

Funny, even though I still wonder if I am really a woman, I realized at that moment that I haven't ever thought about "going back." Maybe I will in the future, but right now, I can't change what I am any more than Kelly can make herself into a warm, slim woman instead of the plump, taciturn person she has always been.

In the middle of my musings, I seat my third client of the day. She's a late-twenties/early thirties lady wearing conservative business attire. Top-buttoned blouse with ruffled button line, summery cotton skirt below the knees, matching jacket, comfortable shoes. She has minimal makeup—mascara, a hint of blush not well-placed, a touch of eye shadow, no lipstick, no foundation. She has thick hair, pulled back in a bun, granny glasses. She could be attractive but she's going for plain.

I seat her, loosen her hair and let it fall. "Tell me what you'd like to accomplish today," I say as I lift and drop tresses of hair to get an idea of its texture and weight.

She looks at me in the mirror. "Well, I need to trim the ends. I want to keep the basic length. I need to pull it back. Beyond that, I don't know."

Something in her tone tells me she wants to say more.

"How long have you worn your hair in this style?" I ask. She has a very basic, one-length haircut. No layers. No face framing. Simple. Plain.

"Oh, God. Forever. But the few times I've ever gone for something different I felt like a fool. This seems to be me. Or at least the me I'm comfortable with."

We go back and forth for a while. I want to give her a style she can wear straight and simple or glam up a little and get out for a party or a night on the town. She's okay with layers and texturizing, but I have to sell her on my face-framing concept, which is basically a long, swept bang that tapers down to her full length. It would open up her face so much more and reveal it as the face of an attractive, complex woman. I hold the hair back in the angle I'm suggesting. What looks back at me is an independent, mature person whose bemused expression does not hide an inner need for affirmation of her desirability.

"Okay," she says, finally. "When Mandy told me to have you do my hair, she said to trust you. So I'm trusting you."

"Oh," I say, more than a little surprised at the coincidence of her showing up at a time when I am obsessing on Mandy's death. "Are you a friend of Mandy's?"

"I'm her sister," the lady says.

I stop dead and study her face in the mirror. Then I come around in front of her and look directly at her. Yes, I can see some faint resemblances to Mandy. Her face is more oval than Mandy's, but they shared strong bone structure. They also share level-7 blond hair, medium texture, moderate wave. Blue eyes. Medium skin tone that browns in the summer sun.

After a long pause, I collect my wits. "I'm so very sorry for your loss. I can't tell you how much all of us in the community loved her, me especially."

"Thank you," she answers. "I was hoping we could talk about her while you do my hair."

We talk constantly from that point on, through the shampoo, the cut, the blow dry. She doesn't have to get back to work, and I don't have another service for an hour, so I continue working on her long after the cut, setting her hair in hot rollers, teasing and roughing it.

I ask her about Mandy as a boy and a sibling. They were close, Melissa says. She knew about "Mandy" from the beginning, let Mandy wear her clothes when their parents weren't around. Marvin was always effeminate. Her father could barely tolerate the boy, was embarrassed that he was "queer." Mom tried to keep him within the bounds of middle class normalcy for the sake of peace in the family, but when Marvin was a senior in high school he rebelled once and for all. He came to the dinner table one night with his somewhat shaggy boy's hair done in a feminine spike, tight jeans, tank-top, dangling earrings, a touch of blush and lipstick.

"From now on, I'm Mandy," she said, as the family, even Melissa, stared at her.

When dad recovered his ability to speak, he issued the age-old proclamation: not in my house you won't. Then the ultimatum—dress and act like a boy or get out.

Mandy got out. She came to Boystown, crashed with whoever would take her in, worked as a waitress and a hooker. Melissa stayed in contact, gave her money and essentials as best she could, until the prostitution started.

"I just couldn't watch it," Melissa says.

Sometime after that Mandy reached out to TGA for some support. Not many young trans girls do that, especially ones as pretty and passable as Mandy. But Mandy needed acceptance. Not from hungry johns. Not even from admirers. She needed some sense of family. I tell this to Melissa. She nods, sad-eyed.

Melissa was away when Mandy had her gender reassignment surgery. She was living in Pennsylvania, where her husband had been transferred. Her husband forbade her to have anything to do with her degenerate brother. To try to save a failing marriage, she didn't see Mandy through that terrifying phase of her transition. That had proved to be the final straw in her marriage; soon after, she divorced and moved back to Chicago and tried to patch things up with Mandy.

There is not much for me to say. Mandy's story is a familiar one.

In the end, Melissa feels better for having talked about it. She says so, and she looks like she feels better. She looks great, too, but that doesn't mean much to her. She's not in the mating game anymore. Has heavier things on her mind. I like her. I think she likes me, too. But I doubt we'll ever see each other again. We live in different worlds. We connected this once over someone we both loved, but there's not much more for us to say. Still, I tell her I'd love to have her in again, and next time I'd like to do her makeup. She smiles but stays non-committal. She won't be calling. She's numb from the compound tragedies of her life, an unworthy husband, a failed marriage, a beloved sibling dead. I feel her pain as if it were a hot tear on my own cheek. She is a victim of Mandy's murder, too. When she leaves we just shake hands. Melissa is not a hugging person at this stage of her life.

As I start on my next client, I am haunted by the image of Mandy as a child going out as a girl for the first time with her sister, flushed and excited. The sweet innocence of youth. This image stays with me all day, and I mourn quietly on my walk home.

My grief is fueling a glowing ember of anger deep inside. It started with the bigot on the street corner. His meanness. His face twisted in hate, a sneering bully assaulting someone for no reason other than he could. He somehow made what happened to Mandy personal.

A genetic woman would want to talk about it, but I'm not there yet. I may never get there.

I want revenge.

* * *

CECELIA TOLD ME her party would be a small gathering of friends for a buffet dinner and cocktails. There are fifteen or twenty people in her sumptuous apartment when I arrive. Most are in the living room, nibbling and sipping and gazing out her floor-to-ceiling window. Hundreds of feet below, the Chicago River wends like a jewel through the Loop, dark blue in the shadows, almost turquoise in the direct sun. A canyon of breathtaking architecture towers around it, in its own way as majestic as the Grand Canyon.

I can't help but pause to gape, too. This is a million-dollar view of the continent's most beautiful city.

There are a few TGA girls in the gathering, but most are straight people Cecelia knows from business or her volunteer activities outside the community. Cecelia is directing servers in formal attire, trays of hors d'oeuvres in hand.

Delicious vapors of garlic and butter and bread float over the room like clouds of temptation, sheer torture for a weight-conscious girl on hormone therapy.

I bypass the guests and the food and drift quietly through Cecelia's pad. It's elegant and tasteful. The décor is soft earth tones with bright white moldings at the top and bottom of each wall, and white wainscoting in the dining area. Her furniture is comfortable modern—a rust-colored couch and matching recliner, four wing chairs in browns and teak wood tones, teak coffee table and end tables, a teak dining set.

Her bedroom is done in cheery yellow and white. The four-poster bed looks like something from a little girl's dream book, with its yellow and white checked canopy and thick mattress. The childhood Cecelia never had. A floor-to-ceiling bookcase facing the foot of the bed is packed with hardcover and large format books. I move closer. It is a transgender library, with a full compendium of the most respected journals of early transsexuals, psychology texts, biographies, and obscure titles, some in foreign languages.

The second bedroom is a sort of office/den/library. Bestseller titles fill the bookshelves and a heavy oak desk with computer paraphernalia takes up most of one wall. A reading chair and footstool sit next to a floor lamp and face an overstuffed visitor's chair.

As loud and vulgar as Cecelia can be in her public behavior, she is clearly a woman of taste in her private life.

I'm browsing the titles in the bookshelf when someone else enters the room. I turn.

"Hi Bobbi!" he smiles. It's Officer Phil. My breath gets shorter, like a teenage girl standing in Elvis' shadow. There's no denying it, I have the hots for this man.

"Hi Officer," I answer, smiling back.

"Please, please, it's Phil," he says. "How have you been?"

We make small talk. I can feel my face flush the whole time, and I can't think of anything intelligent to say. I am a middle-aged adult with a lot of life experience behind me, yet I'm acting like a schoolgirl. Marilee is right. I may be thirty-eight years old, but right now I'm an adolescent girl hormonally.

Phil asks if I'd like a glass of wine.

"Yes," I say. "And I need to start introducing myself to the other guests. I'm afraid I started exploring Cecilia's place before any of that. I'm not much for meeting new people, especially straight ones."

Phil raises his eyebrows in surprise. "Really? You seemed so comfortable at Marilee and Bill's party. Personally, I would have been shaking in my shoes meeting all those cops at one time."

"I'll take that as a compliment, but please don't think it's true. Deep down inside, I was wetting my pants."

I can hardly believe I used the wet pants analogy. But when I start working the room, it turns out to be an apt metaphor: when I'm among strangers and feeling self-conscious my bladder shrinks to thimble size. After meeting a half dozen people I can hardly walk for how badly I have to pee. I break away from the clusters of people and wend my way to the hall bathroom. It's in use. Of course.

Desperately, I go to Cecelia's private bath, adjacent to her bedroom. The door is locked, but a voice inside calls "just a minute" as I try the door. I wait in agony, wishing I could grab myself. The doorknob turns, and I ready myself to dash into the bathroom. A man's form fills the doorway and blocks my access. I want to push past.

"Oh, hello!" says a familiar voice. "We've met, I think."

I look up from the floor, from his Alan Edmond shoes and wool worsted slacks to his custom-tailored shirt to the face of John Strand.

"Yes, that's right. You're Cecelia's friend from the restaurant. Let's see. . . Bobbi, right? You're a hairdresser?"

When I recover my poise, I answer. "Yes. And I'd love to hear more about you and Cecelia in the old days. But first, I really, really need to go."

He stands aside but doesn't apologize for delaying me. "Need some help?"

My eyes swivel from the toilet to his face. Did I hear right? He has a playful smile on his face. Good god! He's flirting with me. With ME!

"I think I can handle it." I start to close the door.

"So to speak. . ." he quips just as the door closes.

It's a boy joke. This does not fit the suave, debonair image he projected at the restaurant. I wonder which John Strand is the act.

When I rejoin the party, Cecelia is orchestrating a conversation between Officer Phil and John Strand. Now I know why she invited the man she suspects of murdering a sister. She wants to get Phil on Strand's trail. Personally, I don't see how that can happen. Strand isn't going to talk about his involvement with Mandy. He's a smart guy and no one is that dumb anyway.

Cecelia's guests are a pleasant lot. I converse easily with them. They are the guests of a trans sister, so acceptance isn't an issue.

After nearly two hours, I find Cecelia and say my thank-yous and goodbyes. I'm hungry for my kind of food and, as much as I love my little black dress, I long to take it off and get out of my heels and just kick back and relax.

John Strand intercepts me at the door. He holds my elbow in one hand and escorts me into the hallway to the elevator alcove. It is set off from the hallway to Cecelia's flat, silent and secluded. He pivots in front of me to press the down button, pinning me against the wall. He does not move back after pressing the button. He stands very close to me. Very close. Our faces are inches apart. I can feel his breath on my skin. Warm and moist. I detect the aroma of white wine as I breathe in. The intimacy of the moment has an aphrodisiac affect on me. I should be uncomfortable with how close he is. Especially him. And yet, looking into his gray eyes, feeling his closeness and masculinity, I'm dizzy with arousal. I half expect him to kiss me because his lips are so close to my face. God help me, I want him to.

"I'm booking an appointment with you next week." His voice is as soft as a sunbeam, his lips so close to my skin I can feel the heat of them. I remember handing him my business card when we met in the restaurant.

"I'm really looking forward to it," he says. "And by the way, you look really hot tonight." With that, he puts his tongue in my ear and softly cups my breast with one hand and pulls my lower body to his with the other. I will myself to act horrified but he's gone before I complete the thought. No matter. I can't muster any indignation. I can barely keep enough strength in my knees to remain upright.

I breathe deeply in the elevator, trying to get control of myself. I'm disgusted that I'm turned on by a monster. An alleged monster. I want to be livid that he would take such liberties with me. I clearly remember how girls responded to my groping passes as a teenage boy. Real anger. Real indignation. But my overwhelming feeling is arousal. Can a man that sexy be the monster Cecelia says he is? My middle-aged mind says yes, but my adolescent body says, who cares?

By the time I reach the lobby I have recovered partial control of my senses. Still, images flash through my mind—his gray eyes, chillingly cold yet hotly seductive. His warm, wet tongue in my ear. I know he is trifling with me, so I am leery. But I cannot deny that my whole body is aroused. Nor can I ignore my fear.

Good heavens, do genetic women go through this?

* * *

HE OPENS THE BATHROOM DOOR and she's standing there, like a wet dream. The hairdresser tranny. Tall, powerful looking but with big soft boobs and a girly-boy face with that chiseled bone structure and the soft mouth that swallowed him in his fantasies. He feels swelling in his loins and uses his mental willpower to suppress it.

As he says hello, he looks her up and down. The combination of male and female features is tantalizing. Her short dress reveals shapely legs and her nice boy ass, curvy but tight. This one likes to show herself off. She wants it.

He tries to start a conversation with her, but she needs to use the bathroom. He steps aside, catches her glancing at him as she enters the facility. He can feel the heat as she passes him. She wants him.

"Need some help?" he asks. He's teasing to see how she'll react. One of his great courtroom talents is the ability to read people, to tell what they're thinking, and to instantly respond. It's like extra-sensory perception, but better. The ESP fruitcakes

bend forks, he bends wills. He's hung dozens of juries by finding the fractured souls on the panel and connecting with them. The same thing works on winning clients, where the real money is, and he's used it to build one of the city's greatest law firms. The entire world is populated by weak-willed fools. The rich and powerful have no more resistance to him than drug-addicted hookers and transsexual girly boys.

The tall tranny brushes aside his juvenile suggestion, but she glances at him when she does it and her face tells him everything. She is wary, aloof, but smitten. She is also big and strong. She is as tall as him. Dangerous. In a fight she would be a handful. The sight of her raises the beast in him. He visualizes mounting her and humping, her squealing. Would she cry if he slapped her? He starts to get erect and stops the thought.

He rejoins the party, conversing lightly with other guests while unobtrusively tracking the tall tranny's movements. The sight of her keeps him stimulated, makes a dull party fun.

His former client laces her arm through his and says she wants to introduce him to some people. His public self smiles, his inner self shudders with disgust. She was an ugly man and now she's an ugly woman. Disgusting. Who would ever have thought that such a big, overbearing, unpleasant man wanted to wear dresses and have his cock whacked off?

He calls her Cecelia repeatedly so he can get adjusted to her gender. He is about to ask her why she invited him to this soiree when she introduces him to Phil someone. As they chat, it turns out Phil-someone is a cop and his beat is Boystown.

He goes into litigator mode, like he's just gotten an unexpected answer from a witness. His public face, the part of him people see, doesn't change at all, but inside, a faint alarm bell starts ringing. Did this bitch know about him and that stupid cow? Could they have run into Cecelia at a club and he didn't recognize her? You'd never miss her as a tranny, giant that she is, but she doesn't look like Robert Swenson, either. He didn't recognize her as Swenson's alter ego until she introduced herself.

He controls his anxiety. If she could place him with the cow he would have been questioned by now. But even if she could link him to the dead tranny, there's no evidence they've been together for months, no physical evidence he was at the crime scene. Years of litigation experience tell him to relax. If you don't help the prosecution make a case, most of the time they won't.

The moment fades. He moves on to other clusters of people. He sees the tall tranny getting ready to leave and rushes to meet her. He escorts her to the elevators, out of sight of the partygoers. She has trouble looking at him. She feels unworthy. He knows it as surely as he knows how that turns him on. She will do anything when the time comes, anything to please him. He teases them both by speaking softly to her with his lips almost touching her face. When she finally looks him in the eye she can't stop. Her eyes are round and blue and they plead for understanding and love. Oh yes, bitch, he thinks, you will get everything you want and more. Her strength seems massive standing so close, her worried, pouty face so helpless. His senses spark and flare.

When the elevator door opens, he makes one last advance. Not enough to scare her, just enough to leave her hot and bothered. He walks away from her before she can object. When he hears the elevator doors close, he leans against the wall and takes a moment—just a moment—to collect himself, get his pulse and his penis under control. Yes, this bitch is food for the beast. Maybe super-bitch, the best ever.

***

"BE CAREFUL, HONEY," Cecelia warns me. It is the morning after, and I have the morning off. She calls as my coffee finishes dripping into the pot, dark and bitter.

"When John Strand sets his sights on someone, he is relentless."

"Why on earth would he be interested in me?" I ask. "He can have his choice of beautiful women, trans or otherwise. Why me? I don't even look like a woman."

"Bobbi!" Cecelia says my name like an exasperated teacher talking to a pupil. "You are so self-conscious you are blind. No, you don't look like a genetic woman. But you are feminine and you have an exotic aura.

"But understand something else with John Strand. He doesn't want to love anyone. It's dominance with him. And it gets mean. You be careful!"

We talk awhile longer and make a date to go shopping together.

***

"SO, BOBBI, HOW'S YOUR LOVE LIFE?"

John Strand is in my chair for a lunch hour haircut.

"John, I never discuss sex, politics or my love life with customers," I answer.

He smiles his good-natured smile. "Of course. Bad for business, right?"

I conduct a brief consultation with him. He just wants a trim. His hair is freshly cut, not more than three weeks. It's excellent work. There is no reason for him to be here.

Naturally, the assistant is on break so I have to shampoo him myself. It is strangely quiet in the shampoo room as I seat him and warm the water. As I move to one side to rinse him, he runs one of his hands up my thigh to my crotch. I'm sure he thinks I will flinch and draw back. I don't. In my years as a gay man, I fielded overtures likes this many times.

"Get your hand off me right now or I will shove this hose down your throat," I tell him.

He smiles.

I sit him up and towel his hair. "John, this isn't going to work. I'm a hairdresser, not a hooker."

"I'm sorry," he says. "I meant it as a compliment. Please, cut my hair."

He's back to being a smooth, big-time lawyer. He's a very good-looking man and he is elegantly dressed. He came in wearing an $800 suit, perfectly fit to show off his narrow waist and wide shoulders. Beneath the coat is a perfectly tapered cotton shirt with crisp blue stripes, and a tie that looks like it's being worn for the first time, a swarm of blues, golds and reds.

Having a man this hot saying you're sexy is heady stuff for anyone, and it's off the charts for a masculine-looking t-girl like me. Even knowing he's just toying with me, I feel my face glow.

He is good to his word for the rest of the service. I concentrate on my work and don't talk much. He's glad to fill the dead air space with rambling narratives. He talks about a divorce case a friend of his is handling in which both marital partners have turned out to be gay and they're fighting over whether a gay male couple or a gay female couple would be the better parents for the children. He talks about sports. He talks about his favorite bars and clubs. He talks about a charity he's involved in, and the work he's doing on their upcoming dinner-dance.

I glance at him as little as possible during the cut, not wanting to encourage any more passes. I finally realize this is silly—he is not influenced one way or another by what I do. He does whatever he feels like doing, whenever he feels like doing it.

What I see in my glances is confirmation of my first up-close impression of him. There is a coldness about him that's hard to define. There is no empathy in him. He tries to fake it, but he can't. Even his sense of humor has a meanness to it. He laughs at the frailties and shortcomings of others and not at anything else, at least, not in my brief time with him. It shows in his eyes. Even when he smiles, even looking at him through the filter of a mirror, his eyes lack humanity. They are reptile eyes.

Before he leaves he asks me if I'll go clubbing with him on Saturday night. He says it like he knows I will decline. I do. Even though I lose control when he gets close to me, I know he's a creepy, nasty man and he may very well be a psychopathic killer.

* * *

ROBERTA IS SIPPING TEA and glancing at me contemplatively. Against my better judgment, I have been unloading about my transition tensions. The stares. The fears. The doubts. I don't like being this open with her. I keep thinking she'll use this crap to postpone my gender reassignment surgery someday.

"Are you seeing anyone? Romantically?" The question comes out of nowhere. I want to dodge it but can't think of a way.

"No," I answer. She waits, wanting me to fill the silent space. I know better, but I do. "But I'm getting very turned on by some of the men I meet. Straight men." I fidget as I say the words.

"That seems to bother you, but why?"

"Because I don't think wanting to make love with men is a good reason to transition." The words pour out even though I don't want to say them, don't want to get into this with her.

Roberta looks at me with real surprise. This is new ground for us, even though I've talked about it with Marilee in our girl chats. She waits for me to continue. Despite myself, I do.

"I'm just afraid I'm going to get involved with some straight man and fall in love with him and transition just so he won't throw me out. Then of course, he'll throw me out anyway and then I'll suddenly realize I'm not a woman, I'm just a miserable gay boy who got himself castrated."

Roberta leans forward. "Do you think of yourself as a gay man? Do you miss it?"

I shake my head in the negative. My throat is constricted, tears are forming. There is nothing about being male I miss. "But what if I'm living a lie?"

She smiles. More like a big sister than a shrink.

"It happens, Roberta. You know it happens!"

"Yes. It can," she concedes. "But somehow, I just don't see you as the type to lie to yourself or anyone else."

"You don't?"

"Well, let's see. You told your wife when you thought you were gay. You told your friends when you thought you were trans. You told your co-workers, even though you risked rejection from people who accepted you. All in all, Bobbi, I can't see you pretending to be someone you aren't, not for anyone."

I consider this for a while and Roberta lets the silence lay there.

"It's just that I'm obsessed with sex all of a sudden. I'm constantly looking at my breasts and feeling myself up. I put my hand on my crotch and pretend like I have a vagina. I fantasize about men mounting me…"

"Men?" says Roberta. "Many men or just one?"

"Both," I answer, blushing.

"Well good!" she says. "Why wouldn't you? Did you think teenage girls don't explore their bodies as they change? Tell me about the men. We're getting to the good part."

"When it's just one, it's a man I met a few weeks ago. When it's a group, there's one man I know and the rest are just faceless forms." I blush crimson. Without saying it outright I've just told my transition shrink I have gang-bang fantasies. I don't think that's a normal girl thing.

She asks me more questions about what the men are like and what we do.

"The other thing that bothers me is the man in the gang bang dream. . . he's not a nice man."

"In your dreams he's not nice?" she asks.

"No, in real life." I squirm. "People say he treats his girlfriends badly. He hits them sometimes, and I guess there's other things, too."

"Like what, for example?"

"S&M, group sex, porno movies." I don't want Roberta to know who I'm talking about. It's enough she knows I'm fantasizing about someone who treats women badly.

"Okay, he's not a nice man, but why is this so troubling, Bobbi?"

"It's that he turns me on. It's like a vampire movie. I know he's bad. More than bad. Evil. But when he touches me I want to…to…" My voice trails off. I don't want her to know the wild fantasies I've had about this man. It's too embarrassing.

"And why does this worry you?" she asks.

"Well, it just seems like I'm so over-sexed I can't think straight. And that makes me wonder if I'm really a woman or just a very neurotic man."

Roberta allows another long silence. "Honey," she says finally, "Women have been attracted to dangerous men since the dawn of time. Especially adolescent girls. And on the female evolutionary scale, you are very much in your adolescence."

I spontaneously begin crying. I'm overwhelmed with emotions, so many I can't sort them out. I feel like a whore and a baby girl and a simpering, hulking gay man all rolled into one.

Roberta moves to my side on the couch and puts her arms around me. I bury my face on her shoulder. My body is racked by sobs.

After awhile, I stop crying and sit up. She looks at me, a small smile on her face, warmth in her eyes.

"It's going to be fine, honey," she says. "You're doing fine. These are things you go through. You're facing them the way I wish everyone did. You're a sweet, sensitive woman and you question everything. Good! You're a stronger person for it."

Her voice trails off.

"You could go a little easier on yourself on the fantasies, though. Everyone has fantasies and some of them are weird."

"What kind of fantasies do you have?" I ask, trying to make my voice work.

"Well, that's a topic for another time," she says.

* * *

WHAT I DIDN'T SHARE with Roberta—and can't share with her, or Marilee or anyone, for that matter—is that my dreams are also plagued with nightmares about John Strand.

It seems when I'm not servicing lovers in my dreams, I am watching Strand beat Mandy to death, or rough up a t-girl, or rape a hooker. These are horrifying visions. Violent. Bloody. Strand is coldly unaffected by the carnage, while I scream, then cry, then feel my horror turn to anger. Cold-blooded anger. Lately, as I watch, my own misshapen female persona invades the scene. At first, I just ripped Strand away from his victim and the dream ended. Then one night after I ripped him off the girl and he sprawled on the ground, I heel-stomped his face. I was wearing spiked heels and I could feel the spike crunch through his eye socket, see the blood spurt, hear his otherworldly screams.

I awoke at that point, shaking. I felt fear, horror, disgust.

I've had that dream several times since, and others like it. I still feel the horror, fear, and disgust, but I feel something else, too. As I hold my heel solidly on his face and the life drains gradually out of his body, I feel a sort of relief. Like the world is a better place for what I've done. Like, lives that would otherwise be lost to the predator or shattered by him will now have a chance to be lived and enjoyed. A rational person would feel horror at what they had done, but I do not. Not a shred.

Good lord, how I wish I could talk about this with someone.

* * *

August

IT HAS BEEN STEAMING hot for several weeks and that has created a general lethargy in the city and certainly in my life. Work is slow. This month's TransGender Alliance meeting was poorly attended because lots of girls just stayed home, out of the heat. And nothing seems to be happening in the investigation of Mandy Marvin's murder, even though people from the community keep pressuring Officer Phil about it, especially Cecelia who latches on to him like a pit bull whenever she sees him.

We've had lots of daytime highs in the mid-nineties, and several days hit a scorching hundred degrees. When I walk to work, I go early and don't put on makeup until I get there. When I walk home, it's later, after six or seven when the sun is lower on the horizon and cooling breezes start rolling in from Lake Michigan. Otherwise, I take the El and try to ignore the stares from other passengers and the oven-like heat in the packed cars.

My little apartment is barely habitable. I have one window air conditioning unit, a working antique that is just one step up from a window fan. It's in the living room/kitchen area and I've slept out there several nights.

My days off have been the hardest. I don't know how to explain it, but I am morbidly self-conscious about going out in the skimpy girl clothes that are comfortable in this heat. I have halter tops and short shorts and tennis skirts. I love how they feel and I even think they look cute on me. But I also feel like people passing me on the street would think I look ridiculous. So I huddle in my hot-house apartment or go out in jeans and long sleeve tees or throw a button-front blouse over a tank top. And boil.

The unending days of discomfort have driven me to a desperate act today. I am going to a public beach to lie in the sun.

I am making my way across North Avenue beach, looking for Cecelia.

She has made me her personal project. She wants to help me get more comfortable in my female identity and not even I can resist her constant efforts to make me try new things. And I appreciate her intentions. She's right about me—I lack courage.

I thought Cecelia was completely daft when she suggested the beach outing, but she wouldn't let it die. Over a period of weeks, I saw her pale skin evolve to a healthy glow and realized that I should be getting a little sun, too. I'd prefer to do my sunbathing on a roof, in privacy, but my building doesn't allow roof access.

I find Cecelia. It's not hard. It's ten a.m. on Tuesday morning. There are only a few people scattered around the beach, and only one is a six-foot-something platinum blonde.

The early hour is a sort of practical compromise. We both know about the potential for skin cancer, so we don't want to be on the beach between noon and three. Cecelia prefers the late afternoon for sunning, but I would only agree to expose my she-male body to the public in the morning, when fewer people would be around.

"Good morning, Bobbi," Cecelia says, looking up at me from a sitting position on her beach towel. She is wearing a one-piece swimming suit that minimizes her heaviness, which is in her belly. The suit is modest, but it reveals her large breasts in a way her high-neckline dresses and tops don't. In spite of myself, I gawk at her cleavage for a moment then force myself to look away.

"Please tell me you aren't wearing a nun's habit underneath all that," Cecelia says. She's smiling. It's a good-natured ribbing. I'm wearing a flowing white sundress over my two-piece suit, and a loose cotton top over that. Everything is in white. I look like a snowstorm. But it feels wonderful. It's feminine and the morning air on the lakefront is just cool enough to make the overgarments comfortable.

"I couldn't find any nun's clothes at the resale shop," I answer back. "But I got this outfit for fifteen dollars, Ms. Smart Ass." I'm now the girl who can't afford anything, but I did splurge on this. I mean, you can't really have a monumentally new experience in an old outfit, right?

Cecelia smiles and launches into a monologue about sunbathing at the crack of dawn. I lay out my towel, place my bag, and take a deep breath. Time to expose my transgendered body to the world.

With Cecelia prattling on as though nothing important is happening, I take off the top. Gentle breezes flow across my bare shoulders like a cool shower. I feel naked and glance around to see if people are staring. They aren't.

Slowly, I peel off the sundress. I thought about doing this sitting down, so people wouldn't notice me. But my rational side insisted otherwise, and

Cecelia's presence sealed the deal. If I'm going to be a woman, I need to quit hiding.

As I step out of the dress I am bombarded by sensations. The overwhelming one is nakedness. My two-piece suit is pretty modest as beachwear goes, but it's a lot less than I've ever worn in public before. The morning air skims over every pore of my exposed skin. It moves like a chill fog around my bare legs, my tummy and back. I feel it on my feet and on the exposed parts of my breasts. It flows under my arms and over my bare shoulders. This must be how a stripper feels the first time she takes off her clothes in front of strangers. I have goose bumps all over, but it's not cold air that's causing them. My heart is pounding loud enough to wake the dead. I feel sexy and ridiculous at the same time.

I sneak another look around the beach. No one is looking.

* * *

AT ELEVEN, WE SIT UP and apply sunscreen, each helping the other cover her back. I have been drowsing for the past half hour, at peace with the world. Unaware of anyone else on the beach except Cecelia, who was also quietly napping.

As I apply her sunscreen I look around. There are a few more people on the beach and I can see more coming from the parking lot. A woman about thirty feet away is watching us; her girlfriend is still prone, basking in the sun. She has made us but isn't even talking about it to her friend.

A group of high-school boys passes by, laughing and carrying on. We draw some second looks, but they keep moving.

"What's the world coming to when a tranny girl can't even get a good insult on the beach," says Cecelia, reading my mind.

"No kidding," I agree. "If tits on a bull don't piss you off, what will?"

At noon we pack up and head for a café for lunch, Cecelia's treat. The heat of the day is building. I overrule my ingrained modesty and pack my jacket away, opting to dine in the comfort of a sundress no matter what those around me think.

We draw plenty of looks and second looks in the café, but Cecelia blithely ignores them and I follow her lead. By the time we place our orders, we are old news to the other patrons and no one pays much attention to us.

Our conversation is lazy, aimless, an extension of the beach conversation.

I've never seen this part of Cecelia. She has always been focused and intense. Serious. Here we are talking about odd news items, jokes, great lunch foods, Fifties music.

I'm having a wonderful time, I realize.

"Cecelia," I say, when the conversation wanes, "This has been a great time for me. Thank you very much."

She holds up her hands. "Now don't go getting all gooey on me," she says. "It's just a day at the beach."

I smile. "It's more than that for me," I say. "You got me to do something new. I never thought I'd say this back when we were arguing about TGA politics, but you're a really good influence on me."

Cecelia blushes. She actually blushes!

"Truth be told, Bobbi," she says, "You're a good influence on me, too."

* * *

SUMMERS TEND TO BE slow in the salon business, and this one is no exception. But my bookings are worse than slow. They are in the disaster zone. The only thing keeping me from tapping my savings account is a little spurt in my home business, and a lot of economizing.

Just before Labor Day, Roger calls me into his office. My heart pounds as soon as he asks me to join him. I've been dreading this for weeks.

"Well, Bobbi, we have some good news and we have some bad news," he starts. I wonder what the good news could possibly be and I hope that the bad news isn't a severance notice. I could hold out on savings for a while, but it would put my GRS operation way, way back.

"On the positive side," he says, "only a couple of the stylists complain about you anymore, and I haven't heard any complaints from your customers for at least a month."

He looks up from his notes and establishes eye contact with me. "You know the bad news. You've lost a lot of your regulars. If they don't re-book before they leave the shop, they don't come back. And most of them aren't rebooking before they leave. It looks like you'll bottom out at around 30 or 40 percent of the clients you had before you started transitioning."

Roger says this almost apologetically. He's rooting for me, I know he is. We've always gotten along. At first, everyone thought it was because we were both gay, but that had nothing to do with it. When you own a business like Roger does, the only important things are practical ones. It doesn't matter to him if you're cute or ugly, fat or thin, gay or straight, female or male. What matters is how well you attract and retain customers.

What Roger liked about me was that I work hard. I get to the shop early. I stay late. In the early days, when I only had a few clients, I kept busy sweeping floors, helping with shampoos, giving complimentary hand and scalp massages. Any scut work that needed to be done, I did. I soaked up our in-salon teaching classes, and I took dozens of others outside the salon at my own expense.

I got good at my craft, then really good, and still pursued knowledge. I stayed loyal. I didn't gossip and I didn't push him for a bigger commission and I didn't get into spats with my co-workers.

And my business grew. In my time here I have raised my rates four times. This happens when you start nearing your booking capacity at your current rate of charge. And I was getting close to another rate increase when I dropped my transsexual bomb on the world.

"Do you think I need to cut my rates?" I ask Roger.

"No," he says, shaking his head.

It gets very quiet in his tiny office. My god, he's going to fire me. My heart pounds. Would anyone ever hire me? I try not to imagine living as a homeless person in Chicago.

"I've thought about this a lot, Bobbi," he says, staring me in the eye again, his face very serious, sympathetic. Like he doesn't want to say what he has to say.

He hesitates a moment. He's going to fire me! I've never been fired from anything and my heart nearly stops at the thought that this might be it.

"I think we need a new strategy," he says, finally. "It's time for you to quit apologizing for being trans and just sort of tout it…let it all hang out."

Air flows into my lungs and my heart begins beating again as I realize he isn't firing me. It takes a moment to process what he said. I raise my eyebrows questioningly and cock my head slightly.

"You actually have a much, much better retention rate with walk-ins than with your regulars," he says. "I bet you don't give them the sex-change talk, do you?"

I nod. He's right. I never thought of it, but there's no reason for me to tell a stranger I was ever anything but what I am now.

"That's what I thought," Roger says. "So as of right now, this moment, stop with the little talk about your transition. That invites clients to judge you. Bullshit! You're a great hairdresser, Bobbi. They're lucky to have you doing their hair. You're going to give them a great cut and color, the best they've ever had, and whether you do it in a dress or a tuxedo isn't any of their business."

It makes sense. I nod in agreement.

"Next," says Roger, on a roll now, "instead of dressing androgynously and trying not to offend anyone, just get on with it! Do like the other girls and don't look back. Wear short skirts and fishnet stockings. Get some spiky heels and sexy boots. Show some cleavage. Wear more makeup. Change your hair color every month.

"I think people will eat it up," says Roger. "Even the ones who think they hate transwomen. They hate gays, too, but that never stopped them from having one of us do their hair."

My god, my boss is telling me to wear sexy clothes, show more skin. How often does that happen outside of a bordello? The elation is followed by doubt. Can I possibly pull that off? In the end, I kiss his cheek and cry.

He sits me down again. There's more. I need to send personal notes to each client who does not re-book with me before leaving the salon: it was great seeing you, I enjoyed doing your hair, I have some ideas for your next service, and don't forget to book another appointment in six to eight weeks to keep your hair looking great.

Roger is buying new business cards for me that show a photo of me as a woman. I pay for the photo shoot and he does the rest.

I have seen Roger coldly fire people on the spot and escort them to the door. And he has no trouble pulling one of us into his office for a dressing down when the situation calls for it. This is a businessman who has no trouble making tough personnel decisions. Which makes this day all the more special. It would be easier and cheaper for him to just get rid of me, but he's standing by me.

Someday, I will repay him in kind. I swear it.

***

ALONG WITH PAYING the rent, my other great challenge is sleeping. I have angry dreams or nightmares about Mandy almost every night. It is eating me up. I'm obsessing and time is making it worse, not better. I see John Strand's reptile eyes staring at me, his face coming closer. I close my eyes to kiss him back and I have an image of him beating Mandy with his fists, even as I feel his hands stroke my body, making me hot.

It is disgusting. I hate myself for it, still. I awaken with a sore jaw from clenching my teeth, still exhausted. I continue to think that I should get myself a lover, maybe even buy one, to try to blunt my physical attraction to this monster. If it worked, it would do wonders for my guilt and disgust. But I'm committed to celibacy until I am really sure about my gender identity.

And so I carry on.

* * *

HER HAIR SMELLS OF CIGARETTE SMOKE. Her breath reeks. He can smell it from here, even though her face is buried in his crotch. She is moaning as she works. Her fake ecstasy is as repulsive as her odor. He wretches and pushes her away.

She startles. "Is everything okay, Honey?" she asks.

Her breath hits him like a stink bomb. He covers his nose with one hand. He cocks a leg and drives his foot into her face, shoving her sprawling to the floor. She emits a shocked exclamation, but he doesn't hear her. The beast is talking. The beast is in a rage.

She looked perfect on the Internet. Sultry face, big tits, pre-op cock, thick lips, smooth skin. 'I want it all,' the ad said. Well, hallelujah. And the timing was perfect. Andive owed him for legal services. Andive set up the meet. Andive reserved the room. An untraceable encounter. A night to let the beast out.

"...Are you listening to me, goddammit? Who do you think you are?" The foul smelling bitch is yelling at him. She's rubbing her face and angry.

The beast roars in rage.

Suddenly she is sprawled on the floor again, her legs akimbo, her big tits heaving in sobs, her cock lying limp on the floor. Blood gushes from her nose and lips. He sees blood on his right hand, tries to remember the feeling of hitting her so he can savor it. One shot! The beast is hungry tonight. He can feel his fists on flesh, feel the stinking thing's bones break, hear her sobs and whines.

"Shut up," he says to her, just loud enough to penetrate her hysteria. The beast is flying tonight! It takes all his will power to resist hauling her into the bathroom and pounding her head on the tub until her skull breaks open and her brain leaks out. It

would be delicious. Much better than the last one. She was an accident. This one is disgusting. It would be fun to kill her, to kill her stink. But this isn't the right time or the right place. Too dangerous. Another time, he promises himself. He can control the beast. That's what makes him great.

He gets a wet cloth from the bath and drops it on her knees. She flinches, expecting another blow. He stands over her. "Clean yourself up," he says. "Don't get any blood on the carpet."

She uses the cloth to dab blood from her nose and lips. He sits in a chair a few feet from her. Breathes deeply. The beast is still hungry. The beast wants more, but the great one is in control now.

"I'm sorry," he says, peeling large bills from a roll. "It's a war thing. I have blackouts sometimes." There is no emotion in his voice. He doesn't try to hide the fact he's lying. It doesn't matter. She'll believe because she wants to believe.

"Nothing broken, right?"

She feels her nose, runs her tongue across her teeth. "Maybe my nose," she simpers.

"Look at me," he says. She does. He pretends to examine her nose.

"No," he says. "It's not broken."

He hands her a wad of bills. "There's $500 there. Will that cover everything?"

The bitch starts to count the money then sobs. She nods her head yes.

"Okay," he says. "You can get dressed and go now."

She struggles to her feet and dresses. With the money clutched in one hand, she reaches for the door with the other. He grabs her wrist.

"Put the money away," he says. She looks at him, scared. He takes the roll, opens her tiny purse, inserts the cash, snaps the purse closed.

"Like that," he says. "We can't have the neighbors talking, can we."

She nods. Shaky.

"Now, just so we understand each other, that means you don't say anything to the hotel or the cops, right?" His voice is falsely warm.

She nods.

"Okay. I'm taking you at your word. But just so we understand each other, if you betray me it will be the last thing you ever do. Understand?"

She takes a deep, convulsive breath and nods, eyes down.

"Good," he says. "You have a wonderful evening and enjoy the money you made tonight." It's his close-the-sale voice. Warm, mellow, inviting. The money and the send off will overcome her memory of the other stuff. She'll feel sorry for him in a day or two, a poor war veteran with violent flashbacks, so sweet and generous otherwise.

She'll come willingly when he calls the next time. Eager. And there won't be a time after that.

He smiles, pats her hand, and opens the door for her. She returns his smile uncertainly. It's working already. I own her.

September

MY ELEVEN O'CLOCK SHOWS UP thirty minutes late. She struts straight to my chair, ignoring the receptionist. Throws her purse on my station, plops in the chair, smoothes her clothing and looks at me, ready to give orders. Her mouth freezes in the open position, her command demeanor gives way to theatrical shock. "Oh my God!" She raises a hand to her face and makes her eyes round as if Lucifer himself were standing before her.

It doesn't occur to her to apologize for being late. Of course not. The nasty ones don't care. Of course, if you keep them waiting ten minutes they go postal.

If I were still gay Bobby I would have had another client coming in and I would have had the satisfaction of telling Vickie she'd need to re-book. But I'm not in a position to be proud. I'll be lucky to bill $200 today. My career is on the precipice. My life, too. Anyone who will consent to sit in my chair gets my best work and my feigned love and attention.

Vicky once referred to herself as a "hair whore." I'm not sure how she arrived at that designation, but she is as obsessed with hair as a hairdresser is. She comes to me for her cut, which currently is lots of layers, lots of volume, lots of texturizing. She goes to another salon and hairdresser for her color, which currently is an amazing panoply of blonds and reds that make her look like a palomino with the odd burgundy streak just to make sure everyone knows she dyes her hair. And she goes to several different hairdressers—including me—for styling in weeks between her cuts and colors.

She's married to some rich guy and they live in a multi-million-dollar condo in the sky. She spends a fortune on her appearance. Her skin has a perpetual tan. A dentist somewhere keeps her teeth so white you have to look away when she smiles or you'll go blind.

Then there's the cosmetic surgery. Her lips have a rubbery quality and they don't smile quite right. She has fantastic breasts, also silicone. Her skin has the smooth tightness of a teenager, but her lips are getting closer to her ears, and her smile is starting to look like a skeleton's grimace. It's hard to say how old she is. I'm guessing mid-fifties, but she could be a hard-living forty-something or a surgically preserved sixty-something.

And here she is in my chair, doing her very best to make me feel bad. She holds up a hand, gesturing me not to cape her. "Wait. Wait just a minute, Bobbi," she says. "I have to think about this for a minute. This is a big shock. I mean, I knew you were a light in the loafers, but this! This!"

She squints into the mirror, staring at me. I stare back. Yes, I feel like a freak on display at a circus, playing to a derisive crowd that entertains itself by throwing gooey refreshments at me and laughing.

"I mean, my God, Bobbi!" she continues. "You have boobs! My God! Are those real?"

My shame is turning to anger. I look at her in the mirror and see a person far more malformed than me, a skeleton with nice hair and too-blue eyes and lips that flop when she moves them. I want to say something pointedly nasty. Something that hurts her as much as she has hurt me. But I don't.

"I'm Bobbi. I cut hair better than anyone you know. I color hair better than your colorist. I style your hair better than anyone, you've said so many times. So make a decision, Victoria. Do you want me to do your hair or do you want to leave?"

I don't know where that came from. Even when I had a full appointment book and testosterone coursing through my veins, I would never give someone such an ultimatum. She found my soft spot. I hate bullies.

She sputters and fumes for a moment. "Well, let's try it and see how it goes," she says.

"Fine," I reply. "What are we doing?"

"Just trim it a little and style it the way you did last time."

I lead her to the shampoo bowl and shampoo and condition her hair in silence. I lead her back to my chair and do the cut, blow dry and curling iron set in total silence. I do the comb out, the teasing, the spraying and shaping in silence. I give her the hand mirror and turn the chair so she can see the back of her head. She nods her approval.

Victoria's hair makes her look like a cross between an aging madam and a high society matron who is desperate to get laid by a young buck. But it's the look she wants and it's usually fun to do. I assume it keeps her husband interested, or if not him, perhaps a paramour somewhere.

She pays at the reception desk and puts a $20 bill in my tip jar. She looks at me as she puts the bill in the jar. I'm not sure what her message is. The tip doesn't mean anything. She probably uses twenty-dollar bills for sanitary napkins.

After she leaves Christine comes by and puts a hand on my shoulder. "What a bitch," she says. "Don't let her get you down."

I watch Christine's retreating form in mute amazement. That's the nicest thing any of my colleagues have said to me since I started working as a transwoman.

I can use the moral support.

* * *

IT'S ALMOST FIVE and I'm ready to call it a day when the receptionist sticks her head in the break room.

"Oh Bobbi," she calls, in a teasing, sing-song voice. "You have flowers up front."

I frown in confusion. Marilee? Trying to cheer me up? No one has ever sent me flowers. Eyes follow me as I make my way to the reception counter where a virtual forest of yellow, gold, brown and orange flowers pose against a background of green leaves and lace and shoots. Some of the stylists are actually smiling as they watch me walk to the front. Not mean smiles either. Even as I wrestle with who might have sent the flowers, I am basking in the thought that a few of my colleagues are not only beginning to accept me, but even to wish me well.

The bouquet is stunningly beautiful. I reflexively take a deep breath and put my hands to my bosom as I behold the arrangement. I have never seen anything so beautiful.

The receptionist plucks a small envelope from the bouquet and hands it to me. "Come on! Tell us who they're from," she says.

As I open the envelope I tell her they are probably from a girlfriend of mine. I open the card.

Roses are red, violets are blue, why can't I keep my mind off you? It is signed "J." I realize who it is when I read the P.S.

We should be friends. How about a drink tonight? There is a phone number to call.

John Strand. He's expecting me to be honored by the expensive flowers, but what captures my attention is the fact he won't sign his name. What gall!

"So who sent them?" asks the receptionist. "You didn't tell us you had a hot romance going on." Several others have clustered around to admire the bouquet. It really is unusually stunning. It must have cost a fortune.

I put the card back in its envelope and the envelope in the pocket of my designer jeans. "Oh they're from a girlfriend of mine who knows I'm working through some things right now. She's trying to make me feel better."

"Boy, I wish I had a friend like that," says one. I nod in agreement, but I'm thinking this is not a gift from a well-wisher. It is an insult from an arrogant cur, who uses and abuses people, especially people like me.

My colleagues are shocked when I decide to leave the flowers in the salon. I have no space at home, I explain, and it would be a shame not to share this beauty with a lot of people instead of just me. They buy the explanation and one girl hugs me with appreciation. Truthfully, I'm relieved. I feel like I just got a bag of rotting garbage out of my home.

*　*　*

CECELIA IS WAITING FOR ME as I stroll into the TransGender Alliance meeting room.

"Have you heard?" she says.

"I don't think so." I can't think of anything I've heard that would make me as animated as she seems to be.

"They're trying to pin Mandy's murder on some guy they think was her john," says Cecelia in a conspiratorial whisper.

"Do they have an actual suspect, or is this the same stuff they've been telling us?" I ask.

"They're ready to make an arrest. I don't know the guy's name, but it isn't Strand." Cecelia is still speaking in a whisper, but she is getting agitated. A tiny drop of spittle flies from her mouth as she speaks, landing on my cheek. "Some of the girls here tonight are saying they already arrested the guy, but my sources say it hasn't happened yet."

"It sounds like they have proof," I say, thinking out loud.

Cecelia sneers. "Right. Proof. They have a trans hooker saying he beat her up and someone else saying they saw him pick up Mandy that night. Don't forget, these people plant guns so they can get away with murder. Getting some snitch to corroborate a story is child's play for them."

"But Cecelia, why would they frame someone for this?" I ask. "It makes no sense!"

"Of course it makes sense. They get to clear the murder and they protect one of the city's made men," she answers. "This is a hoax, Bobbi! A travesty! Mark my words. That bastard is getting away with murder!"

She fumes for another minute or two then circulates through the growing crowd. I consider her argument but just can't buy it.

I run into Katrina. She is buzzing about the rumor that the police have arrested someone. In fact, that's the main topic of conversation among the group.

"Do you think they have the right guy," I ask Katrina, "or is this just a cover-up?

"A cover-up? You've been talking to Cecelia." She laughs. "It's no cover-up. They might not have the guy who did it, but he beats up transwomen so he deserves anything he gets."

During the meeting the president opens the floor for members to comment about the ongoing investigation. Several take the opportunity to convey what they have heard about the suspect, the investigation, the proof. Most take the floor just to unburden themselves. One or two are eloquent. A couple more manage to make a point. Most just ramble. A sort of free-association flow of ill-formed or utterly unformed thoughts.

There is no resolution to anything. No one knows who killed Mandy. No one knows who she was dating, or if she was dating anyone. Except Cecelia, of course. But Cecelia doesn't name names, not in public. Not even Cecelia will risk the wrath of Strand. No one really knows if Mandy was tricking again, either. Most of those who ventured an opinion doubted it. I share that doubt.

Tears are shed liberally. We weep for Mandy. And we weep for us, for our class of despised outcasts of society.

I chat briefly with friends after the meeting then depart. It is a night for a long, quiet walk home. I begin heading south and east, pulling my form-fitting leather coat closed and tying the belt against the chill night winds. A car pulls to the curb beside me. A man calls my name through an open window.

"Bobbi!"

I flinch. This is not a place where you want a stranger in a car trying to grab you. I walk faster, looking for a place to run

"Bobbi, it's me. Johnnie!"

Johnnie? I peer into the window. It's John Strand. Good lord. I can't believe he actually uses that form of his name with me.

"Hi John," I say. "Thanks for the flowers, no thanks on everything else."

"Come on Bobbi, at least get to know me. I'm actually a nice guy. I like to have a good time. I love to party. I love to buy gifts for ladies. Come on. Just one drink. My club is just a few minutes from here."

I must look like I'm having second thoughts. God help me, I am. My life has been a succession of idle days in the salon and empty nights alone in my stuffy apartment. I need to get out more. In some irrational part of my brain I'm thinking this might be entertaining.

He smiles his roguish smile. Insincere, but fun. And sexy. He wants to use me, I know, but I don't sense any danger here. The police have the murderer and, besides, I'm too big for him to bully.

"C'mon, hop in Bobbi!" he says. "It'll be fun. I promise."

I stop. It's just one drink. Even if it isn't fun it might at least get him off my case. Impulsively, I get in his car. As soon as I close the door I realize how stupid this is, but I refuse to let him see my weakness. He leans over and kisses me on the cheek. I don't resist. Then he kisses me on the lips, quickly. He withdraws just as I raise my hands in protest but the truth is, my protest is an empty reflex. A show. My whole body is on fire. I feel stupid for being so easily aroused by such a transparently phony man, but mostly I feel aroused. He moves with the grace and power of a panther. I can almost feel his flat, muscular abdomen on mine, his arms around me, his lips on mine. I have been without sex for way too long.

I try to hide my arousal from him.

"What's with the 'Johnnie' routine?" I ask it sarcastically. I want to establish a tone here.

"I'm trying to show you my softer, gentler side," he says. He flashes me his sincere smile. It's a hustle but it works because I want to give him the benefit of the doubt.

"I don't believe you have a softer, gentler side, Strand," I say. "I think you are a ruthless man who uses people. What I can't figure out is why you have any interest in me."

"Well, let's talk about that in a minute," he says, pulling into a parking spot on the curb of a residential street. We are just around the corner from Boystown's biggest flesh market, a dance bar that throbs four nights a week with horny johns and hot hookers and sex-starved masses of every description. Young t-girls flock here on weekends along with young gays and a lot of tourists to dance and grope and get laid. But this is Tuesday night. There won't be anything going on there on Tuesday night.

He makes small talk as we walk to the club. He steers me down the alley to the back entry of the building. Strand steps in and tows me behind him. We walk down a dark hallway until he stops at a door and knocks. A voice within barks out a question I can't make out.

Strand grunts something unintelligible. He slides one arm around me. I decide not to resist for now. It's dark and spooky, like entering an opium den. The rational part of me wants to bolt, but this other part doesn't want to show him any fear.

The doorway opens and is filled by an ogre-like life form, part human, part bulldog. He looks like a walking muscle. No neck, thick legs and arms, a dark beard that shows through his skin even though he is clean shaven. His lips are thick and ugly. He has heavy jowls. He could be forty years old or sixty. He doesn't look at me or Strand. Strand puts a roll of bills in his palm and he slaps a key in Strand's hand then closes his door. Not a word spoken.

Strand looks at me, pulls me closer for an instant, and winks. "I told you it would be fun. What could be more fun than that?" He laughs and leads me further down the hall. It gets darker with each step. Just as the noise of the dance hall's sound system becomes audible, he stops at another door and uses the key to open it.

Inside, it's like the nightclub version of corporate skyboxes at athletic stadiums. There's a wet bar and refrigerator, several chairs that are light enough to be pushed to the walls to clear a dance floor, a couch that folds out into a bed, a flat-screen television set. Strand flips a switch and music from the club floods the room.

"Want to dance?" he yells above the music. I shake my head no.

He manipulates buttons on a control panel. The music goes off and the flat screen TV comes alive with images of naked and semi-naked men and women dancing and having an orgy. I turn away from the screen. This is beyond insulting.

"Let's get the drink out of the way," I say, walking to the bar. I'm pissed off. Men get turned on by raunchy movies, not women. He's telling me what he thinks I am. And it's even more insulting because he's right. What should absolutely anger and humiliate me is also turning me on. He will never know this, but I do.

He smiles, switches to soft jazz, and comes to the bar. The choice is beer or hard liquor. I opt for bourbon with a splash of water. He pours himself a scotch.

Of course. The booze of choice for bumbling idiots trying to pass themselves off as cool. I'm relieved, though. I cannot stand the smell of scotch, especially not on someone's breath. It is like a chastity belt for me. If he kissed me I would puke all over.

He serves the drinks. We sit facing each other on bar stools. I cross my legs and fold my arms. "So." I say.

"So, why do you dislike me, Bobbi? This could be a great thing!"

I wait a moment before answering.

"Strand, why are you interested in me? I'm not cute. I'm not pretty. I don't even pass for a woman. And I'm old enough to be the mother of your kind of girl."

"Bobbi!" he says, without missing a beat. "You're erotic! Kind of girly. Kind of butch. Big soft tits, cute tight ass. A look on your face like you could never get enough. You drive me crazy!"

I don't say anything.

"So what is it? Am I ugly? Do I have bad breath?"

I resist the temptation to comment on his scotch.

"Come on, Bobbi. Talk to me."

"Strand, did you murder Mandy?" It spills from my mouth before I even form the thought to say it. It is a bitch-slap for treating me like a sex-starved idiot, which I am, but that makes it even more insulting.

We face off in stunned silence. For once there is something other than coldness in his eyes. Intensity. Anger. I have insulted him. Good!

He recovers his poise. "Why would I kill Mandy?" His voice is low and much too calm. Seething anger bubbles just below the surface. A demon being held back. Barely. His rage powers visions in my mind. I see him hitting me with his fist, fluid pieces of me filling the air, igniting the release of all his demons. Another punch. Another. Another. I see him beating me to a pulp as I cower, a sniveling helpless wretch. I wish I could revert back to my pre-hormone male strength. Suddenly I feel thin and weak. I think he may kill me, just like he did Mandy. Yes, seeing him like this, I can visualize him killing someone.

"What makes you think I killed Mandy?" he asks. His eyes fade back to a reptilian setting. Piercing, cold.

"She was your girlfriend!"

"She was my hooker." He says it with an eerie calm.

"You abused her!"

"How? By buying her things? Paying her doctor bills? Putting her up in a nice apartment?" He looks at me casually.

"By having her fuck other guys."

"Bobbi, she was a hooker. Hookers fuck guys. She was well paid."

"You beat her up!"

Strand shakes his head from side to side. "Bobbi. Bobbi. I never hit her. Once in awhile one of her johns beat her up, that's all. Not me."

"Why did *she* say you beat her up?" Lying to a liar.

"Is that what she said?" he asks.

"Yes."

"Was that when she said I was her boyfriend?"

"Yes."

"Did she imply to you that she wasn't a hooker anymore?"

"She said it, she didn't imply it," I respond. "And she had a good job and worked hard at it."

"So when she got bruised up, she couldn't tell you it was some john who did it, right? Not without telling you there wasn't a boyfriend and she was still a hooker. Right?"

I don't answer. He could be telling the truth, but I don't want to think that Mandy was living a lie. Not for me.

"I didn't kill Mandy," he repeats. "I didn't hit her. We had sex together. Really, really hot sex. That's it."

It's the way he says it that bothers me. There is no emotion in his voice. He's like an athlete or a politician reading a prepared statement apologizing for cheating on his wife. And yet his argument is persuasive on a logical level.

He stands in front of me, putting his hands on the armrests of my barstool, leaning his face inches from mine. We lock eyes. I let mine tell him I have absolutely no fear of him and I'm not buying his bullshit for a minute.

"Come on, Bobbi, let's dance."

Suddenly my senses are blind to everything but his hot, hard body against mine. He's a liar and mean bastard but when he gets close like this I can't think of anything but how horny he makes me feel. I let my gaze flow over his face, his straight, masculine nose, his strong chin, his lips. I recall how his kiss felt. I want him to kiss me again, and caress my breasts and run his hand to my crotch. I want badly to take his tongue in my mouth and suck it. I want him to have his way with me in as many ways and as often as he wants.

We don't dance so much as shuffle our feet a few inches at a time, swaying slowly, out of rhythm with the music but in perfect time with each other. His hand on the small of my back pulls me flush against him. Our bodies are glued together from our loins to our faces. I can feel him become erect. I make it through the song on rubbery knees, but I can't hide my arousal. I am breathing deeply, like a woman approaching orgasm. When the song ends I am clinging to him with both arms. His hand rubs my bottom. I rub his. He brings a hand to my breast and cups it, rubbing my nipple between his thumb and forefinger. I inhale and gasp. Reflexively, my hand moves to the front of his pants. I feel his erection, run my hand up and down a few times, then open his zipper. We fall more than sit on the sofa.

And just like that I surrender my she-male chastity like an oversexed teenager.

* * *

I AM IN STRAND'S CAR. He is driving me home after our "drink." I have traded my virginity for thirty minutes of orgiastic lovemaking. The only smart thing I did all night was to use the condoms that were in ample supply in Strand's love nest.

To be honest, though, I'm not feeling used or guilty. I needed this. My body can still feel his. I'm still aroused. To be honest, if he wanted to do any of it again, or all of it, I'm ready. It's been too long. I haven't had sex with anyone in more than a year and even before that I had a crappy, fragmented sex life. I feel so good now. So relaxed. Fulfilled.

Strand has been quiet during the short drive. As we pull up to the curb in front of my apartment building it occurs to me that he didn't have to ask where I live.

The car stops. Strand puts it in drive and looks at me. I'm wondering if he will walk me to my door. I'd like that.

My question is quickly answered.

"Goodnight, Bobbi," he says. Dismissive. Curt.

I wait for the rest, a kiss, the line about great sex, "I hope it was as good for you as it was for me." It doesn't come. He's looking out the window, away from me. I realize he expects me to just get out and leave. He turns to me finally and slips a hand into my blouse. He grabs one of my breasts and squeezes it with all his strength. I try not to scream but it's a shock and the pain is blinding. Tears pour from my eyes. He twists it a little. I push his arm away and he finally relents. I hold myself and try to catch my breath. I look at him without comprehension. Why? I start to cry and try to stifle my sobs. He smiles that cold smile of his.

"The party's over," he says. "Time to go." He gestures to the door. Get out.

I stare at him in disbelief. His handsome face is silhouetted against the light from a street lamp. It is blank. Not angry, not sad, not happy. Nothing. He is waiting for me to get out so he can get on with the important things in his life.

I get out of the car quickly, trying not to let him see my tears. That would be further humiliation, to let him see me cry like an ugly she-male.

Men have used me before, that's not what's making me furious. They take you home, go through the motions with the "had-a-great-time" stuff. You know they won't call again, and they know they won't call again, but it's not the end of the world. Disappointing, yes. Maybe a little ego-bruising. But it was about sex and now the sex is over. I can deal with that.

This is different. He wants me to know he used me. Fucking me was fun, but this is the real John Strand. He wants me to feel like garbage because it makes him feel like God. It isn't about sex, it's about power. Twisted, perverted, mean power. Cecelia warned me, but I was stupid.

I walk to my building. Tears are streaming down my face. I can't hold them back any more. My breast and nipple are very sore. It hurts just having the fabric of my blouse brush across it. It will be sore for days. Just like he wanted.

Strand has sent me a message, but I have received two messages. He thinks I'm shit. That came through loud and clear. So did the other message: He is the son of a bitch who killed Mandy. It would have happened just like this. A kinky romp in the hay, followed by an irritation, followed by some abuse. Fatal this time, but nothing to lose sleep over.

If he had killed me tonight, he'd be sleeping like a baby in an hour. I should be scared by that thought, but mostly I'm angry. Not stomp-your-foot angry. Get even angry. Put a knife in his gut and turn it angry.

I peel off my dress and throw my panties away. I start a hot bath and inspect my breast in the bathroom mirror. It is discolored, streaked with angry purple. I recline into the hot tub and let the waters soothe me. I will contemplate my revenge as soon as I wash all traces of that sick bastard from my body. The stains on my soul are there forever, I fear.

***

HIS BODY STILL TINGLES. His loins still feel tight. The beast is glowing. A sumptuous feast. He glances at the tranny. She's looking out the window, a slight smile on her face. From his angle she looks like a man. His hands reflexively recall fondling her male parts. He grimaces. It was a turn-on then. It made him wild. Now it makes him sick. How could something so disgusting turn him on?

He concentrates on his driving. Don't want a ticket now, not with a tranny in the car. Especially not this one, so obviously a girly boy. It would be all over the police force in a few days. Then City Hall. He would be a laughing stock. A queer lover.

He pulls to the curb in front of the tranny's apartment building, tells her goodnight in a deliberately dismissive way, then looks out the window, wondering what it would be like to really rip loose on her, make her bawl like a baby and beg for mercy. Maybe jump her, tie her up, share her with Andive and his dimwitted buddy…a jump and hump. He likes the sound of that.

His serenity is interrupted by the realization the tranny is still sitting in his car. It irks him. The freak wants to be treated like a prom queen. Thinks it's a real person.

He turns to it, trying to hide his anger. He doesn't want to yell, doesn't want to hear the tranny's boy voice, doesn't want any crap about how great it was. The tranny's blouse is open on top and he can see a bare breast. It seemed sexy before but now it looks like a big zit. He snatches the repulsive growth with one hand and squeezes. Hard. The tranny squeals in pain and starts crying. Good! He squeezes harder and twists, trying to make it pop. The stupid freak scratches at his hand, crying. He starts to get erect, but in another part of his mind he doesn't want any scratches. Too hard to explain, too dangerous. He relents. "The party's over," he says. "Time to go." He gestures to the door then looks away. He can't bear to see the thing anymore.

The tranny struggles out of the car, sobbing like a pussy girl, but lurching like a big queer boy. He barely notices. He pauses to straighten his clothing and check his mirrors then pulls out, thinking about where to stop for a nightcap.

***

I HAVE FELT LIKE human scum all day. Not just my usual giant hairy ape in a dress freaky, but worthless, despised. Strand's final gesture last night makes me feel pathetic. An alien.

My client is a middle-aged businesswoman. Her furtive glances in the mirror and stony-faced expression tell me she is clearly uncomfortable with me. I sigh. Why should she be different? Every client I've had today has been a bore or a snot, or both. Color clients have been simple root touchups. Haircut services have been simple trims. They have been boring people, either incapable of conversation or unwilling to engage in it with a pervert like me.

It has been a very long day. I hardly slept at all last night. I'm sore. My breast is killing me whenever I move. And I feel violated by every real or imagined sidelong glance I attract, on the street, in the salon, riding the El.

Tonight is comfort night. Comfort food. Maybe a hamburger and greasy fries and a slice of chocolate cake. To hell with the diet. Comfort clothes. Comfort bath with perfume-scented oil and a soothing cleansing cream.

I hope it all leads to a dreamless sleep, or even pleasant dreams. Last night was all about Strand. I don't remember all the details, but whenever he had me aroused he would do something demeaning. Laugh in my face and call me a queer. Belt me with his closed fist, knocking out teeth and breaking my nose. Grabbing my breast and squeezing it with all his might until it popped, like a water balloon. Always followed by that scornful smirk as he looks away, done with the girly boy next to him, eager to get her out of his sight.

With each episode I would awaken, sometimes sobbing, sometimes screaming. Always feeling degraded. Always crying like the helpless sissy I am.

I have not been so low since…I don't know when. I wasn't hit this hard by my divorce. Or being disowned by my parents. When those things happened there was always something to at least partly counterbalance my heartbreak: I was at least going to be able to be me.

But the genius of Strand's abuse was that it showed me who I am. Who I really am. I'm not a woman. I'm not a man. I stood in front of the mirror last night and saw a ridiculous human form with breasts and a shriveled penis. Tears had made his makeup run in streaks down his face. One tit was obscenely black and blue. Pink lipstick was smeared around his mouth. He was crying. That image and that feeling are still with me now. I have expected everyone I see today to scream insults at me, to laugh, sneer, and point. I didn't want to wear girl clothes this morning. I had to force myself. I'm so weary of being the village oddity.

One thing that's changed as this day has worn on is that my shame is beginning to turn to anger. When this client, Dollie or Ditzy or whatever the hell her name is, glances at my image in the mirror and frowns, I'm not self-conscious. Yes, it's me, I think to myself. I'm a freak giving you a great haircut and when I'm done you'll still be a plain, dull woman. Save your judgments for someone who cares.

I'm just touching up her cut when Officer Phil walks in. He can see me from the door and waves as he goes to the receptionist. She listens to him for a moment then comes to my chair.

"Bobbi, the officer wants to know if you can fit him in for a trim? I told him you were done for the day."

"Tell him if he can wait a minute while I finish up I'll be glad to."

Ordinarily, I'd be tingling with arousal at the thought of being able to run my fingers through Officer Phil's hair for a half hour. Not tonight. Tonight, I'm just a pathetic hairdresser who needs the business.

The one nice thing about it is my snotty client gets a peek at Phil and her body language tells me he makes an impression on her. I enjoy her mind-fuck. She just spent thirty minutes being disgusted with me and now the best looking guy she's seen all day is waiting to spend quality time with me. Eat your heart out, honey.

The ice princess leaves, no tip, no pre-booking, no thanks. It's about me, but it's about her, too. Having a friend like her would be like drinking a glass of sand in the desert.

Officer Phil sits in my chair. I ask him what he wants done while I conduct my customary scalp and hair assessment. He has nice hair, thick with rich luster and some natural body that lets it hold a style well.

I cut his hair in silence. Yes, there are a couple of pangs of desire, but they are fleeting. I'm in a crappy mood and I just want to get on with my comfort night.

Near the end of the service he looks at me in the mirror and gets a questioning look on his face.

"Are you all right, Bobbi?" he asks. "You don't seem to be your usual self."

"I'm just having a bad day," I respond.

"Anything I can help with?" he asks.

I look around the room to see if anyone is listening. It's late. Only two other chairs are working and they are on the other side of the room. The receptionist is doing her cleaning rituals for closing. We are effectively alone.

"Yes, as a matter of fact there is something you can help with." My voice has a snotty edge to it that I'm too tired and too hurt to correct. "I'd like to know who you're investigating for Mandy's murder. It's like nothing is happening. Have you guys written her off?"

"You know I can't discuss an ongoing investigation," he says.

"What I know is the police have been hiding behind that lame excuse for months," I say. "Everyone in the community thinks you guys have just walked away from the whole thing because you don't want to bust anyone for killing a tranny. Is that the deal?"

Phil stares at me earnestly in the mirror. I pause to return the eye contact. "You know it's not, Bobbi," he says.

"I *don't* know that." His sincerity pisses me off for some reason. "I know there hasn't been any news out of the investigation in months. The cops dodge the question whenever it comes up.

"I also know that none of the investigators have asked any of us if Mandy had a boyfriend. Well, she did. And some of the girls think that's who did it. But you guys don't want to look under that rock, right?"

"Not true," says Officer Phil. "We're investigating several leads regarding men Mandy might have been seeing. I can't say more than that, but believe me, the case is getting a lot of attention."

I choke back any further comment. I want to tell him I know who did it and I know they know who did it and no one wants to touch the bastard. But saying it won't help anything. They either know about Strand or they don't. Me telling them won't change a thing. If they wanted to know what I know or think, they would have asked.

Besides, I'm not ready to tell anyone what I know about Strand. And especially not how I came by the knowledge. Not until I decide what to do about it.

Officer Phil interprets my silence as angry sulking. "Okay, confidentially, the detectives are looking at a guy who has a history of beating up transwomen, especially hookers. Please, don't pass this around, especially not that I'm saying it. It could really cost me."

"Mandy wasn't a hooker anymore," I say. "She was straight. She had a job and a boyfriend."

"Everything the investigators have turned up says she was still turning tricks," says Officer Phil. "Don't beat me up about it—it's not my investigation. I'm just telling you what I know. We could be close to an arrest."

This is what creates jaded perspectives from the trans community, I guess. We are all being caught up in a giant mudslide and we can't do anything about it. And the guy who should be getting buried is standing on the high ground watching it happen with a smirk on his face.

"What about the rumor that you guys have arrested someone?" I ask.

Phil looks at me in the mirror in surprise. "An arrest? Not to my knowledge. Who's saying that?"

"Pretty much everyone in the community, now," I respond. "I don't know where it started, but what everyone is saying is that you guys busted some guy who has a record of beating up trans hookers."

"Not so, Bobbi," he replies. "The investigators brought a guy in for questioning a couple days ago, but that's it. No charges."

"Who was the guy?" I ask.

He makes a face at me in the mirror rather than repeating the mantra about commenting on an on-going investigation.

"So, what brings you to my chair, Phil?" I ask, changing the subject. It is kind of strange that he all of a sudden shows up here.

"My barber retired and I need a haircut," says Officer Phil. "Everyone says you're a great stylist."

On a better day, that scant praise would make my soul glow, but today it's just a smile and small talk.

* * *

October

BACK WHEN I WAS A MALE, seemingly a normal hetero type, married, in the mainstream of society, when someone or something bruised my male ego, I would stew and fret endlessly over it. I would lose sleep, sometimes for many nights. I would replay the incident over and over and over again, imagining different things I could have done and how the outcome would have been more rewarding. Or at least less humiliating.

Many of the actions I imagined myself taking were violent, inspired by books and movies about tough cops and revenge. I came close to violence once or twice, but always choked back the impulse because the two most likely results were so unpleasant to contemplate, to wit: I beat the crap out of the other guy and get sued, or I get the crap beat out of me.

The conflict was very emasculating. I felt like a real man would leave his adversary in a puddle of defeat, walking off into the sunset.

I'm recalling this with some irony as I soak in my oil-scented bath, running my fingers over my breasts and my genitalia. It is the latter that make me recall my male days. After all these months on hormones, my male parts are very small. My doctor told me I'm nearing the point of no return as far as being a functioning male again. He said I was effectively castrating myself. He didn't say it unkindly. More like he wanted to make sure I heard him and understood what's happening. I do.

The funny thing is, I don't feel emasculated and I don't feel like I'm castrating myself. I feel like I'm becoming what I'm supposed to be.

These changes feel good to me right now. I don't hate my male genitalia, but I don't really have a use for them, either.

But I still have fears. Fears that I will awaken some day and wish I was still Bob, the testosterone-driven guy who lifted weights and played football.

But I don't need a penis and testosterone to feel the anger Bob felt. I feel it. I think of Strand with his evil smirk, inflicting pain on other people and enjoying it, getting away with it because he's rich and powerful and no one wants to tangle with him. I keep having involuntary images pop into my mind of how he killed Mandy, his fist driving into her face with the sickening *whack* of a Mike Tyson left hook, blood splattering through the air. I see him slap her and hit her. I see him kick her. I see him heel stomp her beautiful face. And in every scene I see him with that thin-lipped smirk, an expression of disgust for lower forms of life, and of supreme confidence in his innate superiority.

I feel the anger all right. I lose sleep over what he has done and his unworldly pride at having done it and gotten away with it.

I have begun to think about revenge. And my biggest fear isn't getting caught, or failing and facing retribution. It is the little voice in the back recesses of my brain that says a real woman wouldn't think this way, and neither would a real transwoman on hormones.

* * *

CECELIA AND I ARE IN A very snotty dress store on Michigan Avenue. A saleslady is dutifully showing Cecelia some of their latest styles in formal dressware. Cecelia is not the least bit concerned when the clerk icily comments that their sizes only go up to 12. She says it as an arrogant put-down. Cecelia is a Woman 2X at least and is ruining the image of the store.

"Don't worry, honey," Cecelia tells the lady, disregarding her veiled snottiness. "If I see something I want I'll have it made for me. I'm rich and I prefer originals to these mass-produced things."

That is the fun part. The haughty witch blushes and purses her lips and resigns herself to showing more styles to Cecelia.

But the other aspects of the outing are tedious. We are objects of great curiosity to the others in this shop, and I hate being stared at. Also, I'm not into gowns and formal dresses. The only good thing about them is that they usually call for updos. I love updos. I love doing them, and I love wearing them. Not the cutesy little Spring Virgin dos you see at middle class weddings and high school proms. I like the big, slinky, sexy romantic styles.

I suggest to Cecelia that I wait for her in the coffee shop down the street, but she waves me off.

"I'll just be a few more minutes," she says. "I already know I don't want anything—this is just to make the nasty bitch sweat. Then we'll do lunch, my treat, and I'll catch you up on the latest gossip."

* * *

AS WE WAIT FOR OUR delicate seafood salads, Cecelia leans in conspiratorially and puts one hand on mine.

"I found out who the main suspect is in Mandy's investigation," she says. "I know where he works and where he lives and we're going to get to know him this afternoon. That's our entertainment."

I start to object.

"It'll be fun," she says.

I'm dubious.

"Don't worry," she says. "We won't follow him very far. I know his after-work routine. We'll leave him when we get near my church."

Inwardly, I groan. Cecelia is active in a church that caters to the spiritual needs of gay and trans people. I was shocked at how serious she was about religion. She is so skeptical about everything else, who would ever have thought she would give her heart to a leading man who had died two millennia ago and whose biography was written by people who spent way too much time in the sun?

She reads my mind. "Don't worry, I'm not dragging you to a service," she says. "I want you to come to a Trans Advocates meeting."

I nod my head okay with more than a little resignation.

The Advocates spearhead our community's political action activities. They work on the local and state level and synchronize with a national headquarters on federal issues. It's thankless work and very few girls participate. Six is a big meeting.

For me Trans Advocates is a moral imperative that I've been ducking. I should do my part, but I have so little time as it is and, frankly, the work is brutal. It's not just time consuming. You end up visiting politicians' offices to tell our story, usually to twenty-two-year-old staffers who are absolutely mind-fucked by the presence of a man in a dress talking to them. Definitely not my forte. Or my calling.

* * *

WAYNE ICOTT IS A WIRY, smallish man, maybe 5-9, with an Errol Flynn mustache and sideburns. He looks something like the young Sonny Bono, but in today's clothing and not nearly as cute. His dark blond hair is neatly trimmed. He's wearing gray slacks and a navy blue blazer with a striped tie.

He's trying to dress like an up-and-coming corporate middle manager but it's not working. The tie is a little too wide and the knot is a big, old-fashioned one. The colors in his shirt and tie aren't crisp; he has a blue on blue on blue theme going and it's boring. He doesn't look like a rising corporate star, that's for sure. He looks nerdy.

He's an accountant, Cecelia tells me. He works for a bank. He has been there for nearly twenty years doing pretty much the same thing.

"From what I'm told," says Cecelia, "the boy has the personality of a tree stump. He just crunches numbers and goes home at night."

The way she says it, it's easy to picture him having an obsessive fantasy life, since he doesn't have a real life at all.

We follow him to the El, then north to Boystown.

"He's divorced. He was married for a few years and the two of them called it quits. I'm guessing they had to wake up wifey to tell her it was over," says Cecelia.

When he gets off the train he walks a few blocks to a popular bar that draws a mixed crowd of gays and straights. He stands at the bar and orders a drink, looks around a little. We take a corner booth, out of his line of sight. I stare. He's a little creepy, but I just can't imagine him as a violent type.

The longer I stare at him the more convinced I am that he's just your average john. He gets a prostitute to get laid because he's between lovers right now, or because he's got some kind of fetish only a hooker will go along with.

When Cecelia goes to the ladies room, I get up and go to the bar, like I want to order a drink. I stand next to the nerd. The bartender is working on an order. I look around, my eyes finally falling to rest on Wayne. He's looking at me.

"Hi" I say, smiling at him. "How are you today?"

His eyelids raise a fraction as he makes me as trans.

"I'm great. How about you?" he answers. He smiles, too. It's kind of a cute smile.

"I'm doing the best I can with what I've got," I say.

He blushes. I hadn't intended the double entendre but it's out there now, so I wait to see where it goes. There is a brief, awkward silence as he tries to think of something to say.

"Do you come here often?" he asks.

Maybe the worst pickup line in history.

"Oh, you know," I say. "I go to other places more. But I like to come here sometimes." I want to get him talking and get a sense of how he relates to trannies, not that there's much parallel between beautiful young Mandy and me.

He smiles and blushes, looks at me for a moment, then at his drink. If I didn't know about him, I'd bet what's left of my family jewels he is a computer geek. He can't think of anything to say.

"How about you?" I ask, trying to give him a conversation thread he can work with. "Are you a regular here?"

He shifts his gaze back and forth between me to his drink as he answers. "Well, I usually stop in here once or twice a week. I hit some other places too."

We prattle on in small talk until Cecelia returns. "Well, well, well," she says, looking at the two of us, "What have we here?"

"Hi Cecelia," I say. "This is…" I look at the nerd. "What did you say your name is?"

"Wayne," he says.

"Cecelia, this is Wayne. Wayne, Cecelia. I'm Bobbi." I smile brightly and he smiles back. Cecelia seems miffed that I'm talking to him. She nods at him without smiling.

"We need to get going, Bobbi." She turns abruptly to retrieve her things from our booth.

"Oh, too bad," I say to Wayne. "I think I'd really enjoy getting to know you."

He smiles and nods. He's definitely interested.

"I'll be at the Pink Baton and some of the other bars Friday night," I say. "Look for me."

He smiles and nods.

"Or just come in and let me give you your next haircut," I say as I hand him one of my cards.

Outside, Cecelia is frosty. "What was that about?"

"Just curiosity," I say. "I just couldn't picture that guy as a violent type."

"And now?" says Cecelia.

"Now I absolutely can't see him hitting anyone. He might get off on something kinky, but he's not violent. He didn't beat Mandy."

"You know this from a five-minute conversation at the bar?" Cecelia exclaims. "It takes psychologists months to find out something like that."

"It might take months to find out why they do it, but I'll bet most psychologists get a strong feeling pretty fast about whether or not someone is dangerous. This guy isn't dangerous. I'd bet on it," I say.

"You *have* bet on it, Bobbi," says Cecelia. "That murder suspect knows who you are and where to look for you. Oh yes, I saw you give that schmuck your card. What are you going to do if he starts following you home from work?"

"Ask him to buy me a drink...?" I smile, trying to take the edge off our conversation.

"Very funny," says Cecelia. "This is serious. These people aren't to be trifled with. Not Icott. And certainly not Strand."

I must have reacted to Strand's name without knowing it, because Cecelia stops and stares at me. "Please tell me you have not had contact with Strand," she says, staring a hole in my head.

"Well, you introduced us!" I say it defensively. "Since then he's sent me flowers, asked me out and even came in for a haircut once."

"So you went out with him?"

I nod yes.

"How was it?" she asks after a short silence.

"Awful. A colonoscopy would be more romantic."

"Bobbi, he is a bad man. Do you hear me? He is a bad, bad person. As in evil. Don't ever be alone with him ever again! He's a violent, dangerous, cruel man," says Cecelia. "This is not speculation, Bobbi. I know this. For an absolute fact, apart from anything to do with Mandy. I've known him for twenty years. Do not be alone with him!"

"No problem," I answer. "I can't stand the bastard anyway."

* * *

MY INNER RAGE ABOUT Mandy's murder is fueled by every snotty comment from a customer, every double take from a passer-by on the street, every sneer from a waiter or a salesperson.

And the memory of how Strand treated me is on a continuous loop in my mind, made even more painful by the realization that Strand was the only man who ever came on to me as a transwoman. I am so pitifully sex-starved, I gave myself to him like a star-struck groupie.

Some of my dreams are still violent, but a change is taking place in the violent scenarios. Increasingly, I'm moving from being the victim in these dreams to becoming the perpetrator, and my victim is Strand.

What bothers me about this is not that I have violent, vengeful thoughts, but that this is such a male reaction to things. It makes me wonder who I really am. Would a *real* woman dream of such personal, bloody vengeance? Would a real transwoman?

I am plagued by two obsessions, day and night. Getting even with Strand for Mandy and me. And doubts about my inner femininity. All of my transsexual friends are angry about Mandy's murder and the ineptitude of the police investigation, but none of them have violent obsessions about it. At least, none of them talk about it. I wonder once more if I am really trans, or it I'm just a pathetic mess of a male destined for even greater misery by becoming a woman.

And I worry that if Mandy's murder is never resolved, I will never sleep through the night again. As it is, I sleep for maybe two hours each night before my angry dreams waken me. I eventually get back to sleep, but I spend the night napping and waking, napping and waking. I get just enough sleep to make it through each day, but I never feel relaxed or refreshed.

Before my father disowned me he told me what it was like to be an infantryman in Vietnam. Long sweeps in the jungle. Constant tension. Ambushes and booby traps. Treacherous villagers. Enmity between career soldiers and draftees. Sleep deprivation. Bad food. Heat. Frustration. Fear. His tour was a year-long nightmare, he said.

He was explaining the My Lai Massacre to me, how a company of regular Americans could riotously murder dozens of unarmed civilians, mostly women and children and old men. It came up in a high school history class and I asked him about it. "I could have done it," he said, his voice just above a whisper, after he told me what it was like to be there. "We were in a nightmare. Always scared. Always tired. Always mad. It makes you crazy, living like that. Anyone could have done it. Don't let anyone tell you otherwise."

I was two years old when he shipped out. When he came home he was moody and withdrawn. He hardly talked to me even before he knew I was queer. In fact, that was probably the closest moment I had with him, that brief point in time when he told me about Vietnam.

I think about that now because I feel like I am having a parallel experience. I feel like I'm in a nightmare that I can't get out of.

***

BACK IN HIGH SCHOOL, when I was trying to be a straight, all-American male, a girl I was dating berated me for not defending her honor by fighting a guy who said he had been her lover.

It wasn't like he was lying. They had been lovers. She told me this, but even before she did, I knew it. The problem was that he was now talking about it in a way that made her feel put down.

I wanted to be angry about it, but for the life of me, I wasn't. And I didn't understand why she was angry, either.

I thought about it a lot. I thought maybe I should just go ahead and fight him. I probably could have held my own and maybe even prevailed as a sort of consensus winner. But I kept wondering what that would accomplish. I'd probably get kicked out of school if I won, or maybe go to the hospital if I lost badly. The guy wasn't misrepresenting anything, so I'd make an enemy out of someone who didn't need to be an enemy.

The only thing I'd get out of it was another month or so dating this girl. But did I really want to date someone who demanded that I draw blood from others for the privilege? In the end, I decided she wasn't worth it. I tried to tell her so in a nice way, but it made her mad and she ended up calling me a fairy and breaking up with me on the spot.

Little did she know.

Through early adulthood there were parallel experiences where I felt called upon occasionally to engage in violence to protect my honor…in all cases, the events involved bullying, which has always angered me terribly.

I lost many nights of sleep over these incidents because I never did respond violently, like a "real" man would.

What is different about the sleepless nights I've experienced after the Strand incident is that there is a victim. Or at least I think there is. Mandy is the victim and I think Strand is the person who murdered her. I saw his cold-blooded contempt for human life when I was with him that night after our "drink."

It still chills me how stone-cold cruel he was in the car. Thin lips twisted in a contemptuous sneer, looking away as if he didn't know who I was. Squeezing me to make me cry, to make sure I knew he considered me garbage.

I can see him doing the same things with Mandy, and her begging him for forgiveness, just one more chance. Maybe trying to go down on him. Strand hitting her with a vicious hook. I can hear her flesh splatter. I can see the faint look of satisfaction on his face as she sprawls on the floor, blood coming from her ear. She scrambles to her knees and pleads with him. This time he has more punching room. He brings a roundhouse hook that knocks her unconscious and drives her across the room. He kicks her, then props her up on a chair and hits her some more.

He breaks bones and ruptures skin and flesh until her pretty face looks like hamburger. Then he quietly washes his hands, dabs blood off his expensive clothing, and departs without a second thought, leaving her to die from a severe concussion and hemorrhaging.

I don't know that this is how it happened, but I know it must be close to the truth. I can feel it.

The question is, do I let him get away with it?

If I kill him, I go to jail. If I try and fail, he'll kill me and still be free. If I do nothing, I'll go on trying to rebuild my hairdressing business and survive to complete my transition to womanhood. Well, transwomanhood.

The choice is overwhelmingly clear to me. My goal in life right now is to become a woman and be a successful person.

So, why can't I get the thought of revenge out of my mind?

* * *

CECELIA AND I are having a late dinner at a place called Slim's, a near-north eatery with at least a hundred items on the menu, all prepared from canned and frozen goods. She picked the spot, but she picked a cheap place because I'm picking up the tab. I called the meeting.

I get my money's worth quickly. As the hostess leads us to a booth, I catch sight of a waitress staring at us. The look of disgust on her face is unmistakable. Her mouth opens, her lips curl, her eyes frown slightly. As we settle into our booth, the hostess pauses in front of the waitress, who curls the fingers of one hand into a fist and looks skyward. I can't hear what they are saying, but it's pretty clear that she's our waitress and she would rather stick nails in her eyes than make us happy to be here.

These are the confrontations I hate, although right now I'm fascinated to see how Cecelia handles the situation.

The waitress comes to our booth and hands us menus. "The special of the day is…" she mumbles something unintelligible. More mumbles ending in "drink?"

She is almost a parody of a waitress. Overweight, too much makeup and poorly applied. Decent hair cut, but colored a ridiculous shade of red. Pink lipstick that tries to be feminine but comes off as trailer park trash. And she's grossed out by us?

Cecelia looks up when the mumbling stops.

"Let's start over, honey," she says. "Do you have a name?"

"Jeri," says the waitress, her face all attitude.

"Jeri," repeats Cecelia. "I have a brother named Jerry. And we fought the Jerrys in World War Two. Nice name, Jeri.

"Now, Jeri, suppose you tell us what those specials are—in English, this time."

Jeri recites the specials, avoiding eye contact with either of us.

"Thank you Jeri," says Cecelia. "Now what you can do for us is go bring the manager."

Jeri pauses, gaping at Cecelia.

"Now, Jeri," Cecelia says. "Right now." She makes a dismissive, walking gesture with two fingers on one hand.

Jeri's face becomes a mask of anger and she spins around and leaves. Moments later, the hostess comes to our booth.

"I'm the night manager here," she says. "Is there a problem?"

"Yes," says Cecelia. "Your waitress is hostile to us. I do not trust her to serve us uncontaminated food." She pauses to pull a business card from her purse and offer it to the hostess. "I'm a member of the GLBT Advocates Committee. We inform management when company employees treat minorities badly and give them an opportunity to correct the situation."

Cecelia is surprisingly artful. She doesn't say legal action will follow, but anyone would assume that's the next step.

"Okay," says the hostess, uncertainly.

"I have two requests of you tonight," says Cecelia, all business. "First, I'd like you to serve our food yourself and make sure your waitress does not have access to it." The hostess nods her assent.

"Second, I would strongly encourage you to talk with the day boss and the owner about Jeri. We are in a new century in a great city and this is not the time or the place where a service business can afford to lose customers or incur lawsuits because of the petty bigotries of the hourly help."

The hostess nods. She would like to take our order, but Cecelia is just getting warmed up. She reminds the hostess of several big harassment lawsuits that have been litigated in recent years, and points out what a difference adding or losing even five percent of your customers can have on the business and its employees. The hostess nods repeatedly.

We finally order and the hostess departs. She sends the waitress on break.

"The GLBT Advocates committee?" I say to Cecelia.

She smiles. "It's my own invention. It actually exists. I filed papers with the state. I'm the only member, though you are certainly welcome to join. So is anyone else. But I get to stay Chairwoman, and I get to use my position and the stature of the committee to file complaints when I feel they are warranted."

We laugh. The hostess brings us our drinks and a plate of appetizers. The appetizers are on the house, she says, an apology for the restaurant's lapse in service. We thank her.

"So, what's the occasion?" Cecelia asks.

"I want to know why you were so sure Strand killed Mandy," I say. "And I want to know why you are so afraid of Strand."

Cecelia gets a very serious expression on her face and stares me in the eye. "Those two things are related, but I guess you understand that, right?"

I nod yes.

"Okay. I've already told you why I think he killed Mandy. He was seeing her and he's known to be violent with women. At some point, the girl needs to get out. Mandy wasn't that smart. She convinced herself that Strand was Mr. Right, and that she was going to be his princess."

"So you don't think Wayne Acott killed her, do you?"

"No." Cecelia raises a hand, signaling me to let her continue. "But that doesn't mean he might not be dangerous. You have to be careful, Bobbi."

"How do you know Strand's violent?" I ask.

"Years ago, he fired the attorney who managed my company's account. It came out of nowhere. I asked her what happened and she gave me the old crap about going in new directions and all that.

"Well, we were pretty good friends. She'd had our account for a good while, so there had been a lot of meetings and phone calls and dinners and lunches. No hanky panky, but friends based on mutual respect. She was very sharp.

"Naturally she wanted to stay in touch and use me as a reference, and I was glad to do that. I had her out to dinner one night to see how things were going. She put on a brave front, but we ended up getting smashed. And she ends up telling me how Strand started out as her mentor, bringing her up the ladder. Then how one day he seduces her and they have this affair, but as time goes on he gets rougher and rougher. She thinks it's the only way he can get it up. One night he hits her so hard he dislocates her jaw. He's all apologies and pays for everything, but she feels like she saw the dragon.

"After that, he leaves her alone in the office. She hears rumors now and then, but nothing solid. Then one day word breaks that a girl who worked part time as a receptionist for the firm had been beaten to death. Her secretary knew the girl, knew she had met a sugar daddy a few months earlier, moved into a nice new apartment, started wearing nice clothes.

"Wanna guess who she told the secretary her sugar daddy was?" Cecelia arches her eyebrows at me.

I shake my head in amazement.

"My friend was too smart to ever share that with anyone," says Cecelia. "If she had, she would have lost her life as well as her job. Of that I am sure.

"Here's the irony. A few years after that, I drop out of the banking world and start transitioning. A few years after that, Strand's name comes up again. He beat a t-girl I knew to within an inch of her life. I didn't know it was him. All I knew was, she had nowhere to go when she got out of the hospital, so I put her up. One night we're watching the news on television, and Strand's photo comes on the screen. She starts hyperventilating and shaking and points to the screen and says, 'That's him, that's the guy who tried to kill me.'

"Well, Vanessa was a hooker and a transwoman and no one was going to believe her if she brought charges against a suit like Strand, so she didn't bother. But it ruined her. She got into drugs and ended up OD-ing.

"Since then, every time I hear about a t-girl getting beaten up by an anonymous john, I think of Strand."

I sip my water.

"Did Mandy tell you specifically that it was Strand she was seeing?" I ask.

"She did better than that," says Cecelia. "She brought him over to me at a club one night and introduced him. I told you this, remember?"

I nod yes. "I just want to make sure."

"Bobbi, please tell me you aren't planning on doing anything dramatic," says Cecelia.

"A pansy like me?" I strike a campy drag queen pose. "What would I do?"

I purposely evade Cecelia's occasional questions about what I'm thinking.

We enjoy an awful meal together, dominated mostly by her advice about steering far clear of Strand. I listen, but part of me is asking why I don't share with Cecelia—or even my shrink—what I'm really thinking.

But I know the answer. I've known it for a while.

I don't want any witnesses.

* * *

WHAT I HATE MOST about this is lying to Marilee.

We are in her office at home. It's a meeting of friends, but one of the friends is a psychologist so it's not like lunch with Cecelia or whatever. It's more official. It's like having a heart-to-heart with your mom, but your mom's a shrink. And yes, I sometimes think of her as the mother I never had. The spiritual one. She's also a sister. And as I've already admitted, sometimes in my dreams she's my lover. It's complex and confusing, but the simple fact is, I love her.

"So," she says, "How is your sex life?"

"What sex life?" I say, hoping to get off the subject.

"Are you still celibate, Bobbi?" she asks, very directly. She must be reading my body language or something. She has a sixth sense about these things. It can be very unnerving.

"No. I had a, a…" I struggle for the right word, "I had a lapse. It won't happen again."

"Who was the man?" she asks.

"I don't want to talk about it." There is no way I will ever tell Marilee that I ever got involved with Strand, let alone that I had sex with him. It would tear her up to know how far this has come. And I still don't know where it's going.

"Why is that, Bobbi?" God I hate the circles shrinks take you in. No wonder half the population prefers to pour their hearts out to hairdressers. When you tell us you don't want to talk about it, we go on to another subject.

"It was stupid and it was awful," I say.

Marilee gestures with both hands—keep talking.

"He picked me up in a bar," I confess. "We fucked our brains out, then he dumped me on the curb at my apartment building. I'm stupid and I lack self-control. I spent a week feeling like a knothole in a fence that got violated by a pervert. Except I'm the perv. And I'm over it."

"How was the sex?" she asks. I knew she would.

"It was fantastic. While it lasted." The reality of my answer brings tears. I dab at them with a tissue. It comes away black from running mascara and eye shadow. I've been in a Goth mood since Strand had his way with me. That's undoubtedly one of the clues Marilee reads.

"So it was the being dumped part that bothers you?"

I nod my head yes.

"How was that different than other one-night stands?" she asks. This hurts a little. By gay lifestyle standards, I was never into indiscriminate sex. But let's face it, if you go clubbing there are going to be times when your judgment gets impaired by a cute face or a hot bod or too much to drink. Yes, it happened to me, too. Not often, but more than once. It left me feeling hollow.

"He had contempt for me. He hurt me."

"How did he hurt you, Bobbi?" Marilee asks.

I tell her about him squeezing my breast. I confess that I cried. I cry again.

"I'm so sorry, so very sorry Bobbi," she says. She hands me the box of tissues. It occurs to me I'm acting like a teenage girl who just got dumped by her boyfriend. Except this doesn't have anything to do with a teenage boy. This is about a psychopathic bully.

She puts her arms around me and lets me cry for a while. Her hug is like a wonderful warm womb where I am safe and loved.

She gets up and hands me my glass of water.

"Okay," she says. "So much for your sex life." We both laugh softly. "Just so you know, Bobbi, I'm not super enthusiastic about your abstinence from sex. I'm not advocating that you go out and get laid every night either. It's just that you're a normal, healthy human being and you are combining the urges of a teenage girl with the mind of an experienced adult, so the pressures are extraordinary."

As she qualifies her statement some more, I'm thinking she might be right. I might think a little more clearly if I was getting it on with some nice guy every once in a while. Or lady.

Marilee leads me through some of the other events of my week. We dwell on how slow my hair styling business is.

"I'm really worried that the world isn't ready for a transgendered hairdresser," I say. "At least, not one that looks like an ape in a mini dress."

"Bobbi, stop that right now! That's not what you look like and it's not funny. You're giving yourself an excuse to fail!"

She stands again and grabs my hand, pulls me up and leads me to the bathroom where we both stand in front of the mirror. I tower over her.

"Bobbi, look! You are an attractive human being! You should see this better than I do. I've heard you say it to your clients. You have great bone structure, beautiful hair, a slim body, nice boobs. Honey, you don't look like a Barbie Doll and maybe some people don't see you as a genetic woman, but Bobbi you are an attractive person. You are pretty in your own right.

"Now get all the appearance nonsense out of your mind and get on with your life. You are a sweet, warm, wonderful woman." She pauses for a beat or two. "Yes, woman. Just accept it and move on."

I regard her image in the mirror in stunned amazement. It may not seem like much to you, but in all the months I've labored to understand whether I'm a transsexual woman or just a neurotic man, not one of my friends ever offered an opinion on it. I understand why. You take on a lot of responsibility if your word becomes the reason someone ends up growing breasts and castrating themselves.

It's even bigger for a shrink to say it, even though she's my friend.

* * *

November

WINTER WINDS WHISTLE through the highrise caverns of the Chicago Loop, making my fingers numb and my head ache. I'm standing in front of a highrise office building in a cute little mini-dress with black hose and high-heel boots and a very chic short trench coat that looks great but provides almost no shelter from the cold. Fortunately, I'm wearing makeup, otherwise my skin would be blue and my lips purple.

It is five o'clock and office workers are pouring out of the place. I have been here for thirty minutes and I plan to stay another hour, if I can last that long. I'm handing out leaflets promoting my exquisite cosmetology services for a special introductory rate. I hand one to every person I can get to. Most of them try to avoid me. It's not personal. That's how we are in America. No one wants to get shaken down by a stranger passing out literature.

Still, I have a feeling I'm doing okay. My weird appearance repels some people, certainly. But it also attracts the curiosity of others. For every rude rebuff I'm finding someone who establishes eye contact and smiles. Perhaps a dozen so far have actually paused to look at what I'm handing out.

"Hi, I'm Bobbi and I'd love to be your new hairdresser," I say, when this happens. If they stop long enough, I tell them that I do great cuts and colors, updos, and even original styles. I try to personalize it. I told one lady I liked her color but I'd like to see her try something just a little younger and edgier. She liked that.

I'm doing this because my bookings are still shockingly low, especially for this time of year. Roger paid for the handouts, I put in the time. I want to distribute a thousand of them myself. I want the people who take them to know that I'm the hairdresser they'll be seeing. Me. Bobbi. The queen. That way there won't be any histrionics and if I give them a good service I figure I have a good chance of getting them back.

I also use the new business cards Roger ordered with my transwoman picture on them. They cost a small fortune compared to regular cards, but it's the same idea: let's focus on reaching people who don't have a problem with a transgendered hairdresser. Roger thinks some of my customers will pass my card around as part of their war story about hobnobbing with a transsexual. I think he's right, and it might bring in another client or two. Either way, Roger is going the extra mile to help. It means a lot to me. Not just because he's my boss, but because he's on my side. When I started to transition, the most I hoped for was that some people would be indifferent to me because so many others were antagonistic. Someone actually wanting to see me succeed? Wow.

Before I'm done, I'll cover all the office buildings within a mile or so of the salon. I do one in the morning, and another in the afternoon if I don't have appointments slated. For evenings when I can't make the office rush hour, I'm going to stake out apartment buildings when I get off. I won't hand out as many leaflets, but I might make better contacts. We'll see.

Whatever, when this night ends, a hot bath is going to feel fantastic. That thought keeps me going.

* * *

SO MUCH FOR THE HOT BATH. As I climb the stairs to my apartment I see Cecelia and a young man standing at my door. Cecelia waves. "It's about time you got here," she calls.

Cecelia's idea of humor. I try to smile but my face is frozen and I really don't have the energy anyway.

As I reach the top of the stairs, Cecelia does the introductions. "Bobbi, this is Jo-Jo. Jo-Jo, Bobbi. Can we come in for a minute?"

As if anyone could refuse Cecelia. Certainly not me.

As I unlock my apartment door I take a closer look at Jo-Jo. His name is obviously derived from the name Joe, and he looks a lot more like a Joe than a Jo-Jo. He looks like a young male, mid-twenties, about 5-10, medium build. He has pleasant features, masculine but with soft, smooth skin and a sort of roundness to his face rather than sharply defined bone structure. His hair falls just below the jaw, thick, medium-blond with a nice natural wave.

When we get in the apartment and take off our coats, I note that Jo-Jo has long, pointy nipples poking from his long-sleeve T-shirt. Estrogen. I mentally switch from thinking of Jo-Jo as a man to thinking of her as a transwoman. Her skin and breast development indicate she's on hormones. The long nipples combined with relatively undeveloped breasts make me think she hasn't been on hormones very long. I've heard some transsexuals say their initial reaction to estrogen was the formation of enormous nipples, with the fuller breast development coming later. The smoothness of her skin seems more like a long-term hormone program.

The answers come fast.

"Jo-Jo has been doing her own transition and has just come to us for help," Cecelia explains. "I've got her scheduled with Doctor McBride to get her hormone regimen straightened out. Her internist has no idea how to get breasts to go with those nipples, but McBride will take care of her."

Cecelia pauses in mid-thought and reaches over to pull my blouse taut against my breasts. "Jo-Jo, McBride got Bobbi to a B-cup in what, six or seven months?" She looks at me, eyebrows raised in question. I nod, yes, wondering if she's going to feel me up. She releases my blouse and sits back down.

"We're also going to help Jo-Jo find a counselor and we'll help her with her wardrobe," Cecelia continues. "We're here now because she needs a cut and style, and I told her that you're the greatest hairdresser in the city."

I smile. Cecelia could sell refrigerators to Eskimos if she thought it would be interesting.

"What kind of style are you thinking about, Jo-Jo?" I ask.

Jo-Jo maintains an almost bovine calmness throughout all this and answers me serenely, "I don't know. I want to grow it longer." That's it. She shrugs.

I sit her in the chair in my living room that I use when I do haircuts at home. It faces a mirror that extends five feet high on the wall. I flip on the track lights that light up the person in the chair as if they are royalty. I examine Jo-Jo's hair and scalp. It is clean, healthy hair. No evidence of color.

"You have very nice hair," I murmur. "We can do pretty much anything you want with it. We can cut it in a bob or a graduated bob if you want a classy, easy-to-maintain look. We can layer it and punk it up or go for big and sexy. We can do a kind of androgynous pompadour," I sweep her hair back on the sides to imitate the look of a fifties style inspired by Elvis Presley. It would look great on... her. I'm having trouble thinking of Jo-Jo as a "her" because she isn't presenting herself in a feminine way. Her clothing is gender neutral. Her jewelry is not even metrosexual. And her face is vacuous male despite a little shaping to the eyebrows.

Cecelia oohs and ahhs at the pompadour look. "That's the ticket, honey," she says. "It's sexy and athletic at the same time."

Jo-Jo smiles but says nothing. I ask if any of those styles sounds interesting. She smiles and says she doesn't really know.

I've known lots of transgenders who were uncertain about hairstyles, didn't know the nomenclature, weren't sure what would look good, couldn't make up their minds, whatever. But Jo-Jo is beginning to feel like an airhead to me. She doesn't look like she's on drugs, but she acts like she's on a trip a long way from home.

I lack patience for lost souls like this one, or the many T-girls in our community who get so obsessed with their gender issues and their appearances there isn't anything else to them. After a long night in the cold, I definitely am not in the mood to coax something out of Jo-Jo when I could be in a nice hot tub, sipping wine. Still, Cecelia's example towers over me. This often over-bearing woman who crushes arrogant bigots like so many bugs can't say no to even the most clueless transwoman. And neither can I.

"Okay, Jo-Jo. Tell me about your lifestyle." When in doubt, get to the basics.

"Well, I'm twenty-six, I live in the city, I work as a personal trainer. . . like that you mean?" she says, looking at me in the mirror. A veritable speech.

"That's a start," I say. "What do you do for fun?"

Jo-Jo rattles off a list of sports. . . soccer, handball, long distance running, softball, football. I ask about the arts. No. Nightlife? Going out to dinner. Going to parties. I point to her wedding ring. "Are you married?"

"Yeah," says Jo-Jo. Silence.

"How is your wife with your transition?" I ask.

Jo-Jo shrugs nonchalantly. "Fine." Like it's no big deal.

"Really?" I'm astonished. "Do you have any idea how rare that is?"

Jo-Jo shrugs again, same vacuous smile. "I guess."

I'm trying not to judge Jo-Jo, but it's hard. Very few wives stand by husbands who just get into cross-dressing. Wives who stay with a spouse who transitions are one in a thousand, maybe rarer. Jo-Jo acts like it's expected. She's in for a shock, though she's so dull she might not feel it when it comes.

"Have you come out at work yet?" I ask. I'm wondering how feminine to go with her cut.

"Oh yes," says Jo-Jo.

"How did they take it?"

"Fine," says Jo-Jo. Like it's no big deal.

We talk some more, me asking ten-word questions, her giving three-word answers. I'm wondering if Jo-Jo just has a low IQ or just lacks social awareness. Either way, it wouldn't break my heart if she decided to find a different hairdresser.

In the end, I recommend a basic layered cut that she can wear like a long pixie or sweep back into a cool pompadour, or just wear flat and look kind of masculine, like now. I pull out an old hairdo magazine and mark several styles.

"Why don't you think about it for awhile and give me a call when you're ready to do something," I say. "We can either do it here at night for $25 or in my shop during the day for $60. Let me know."

"Well, uh, uh," she responds, "I was hoping we could do it tonight." Punctuated with that vacuous face.

Shit. I'm tired and sore and cold and hungry. I wouldn't want to cut Oprah's hair right now, even if it would make me rich and famous and give me thirty minutes to chat with the greatest woman on earth. Doing Jo-Jo's hair is on a par with bobbing for apples in a toilet. But I could never turn down Cecelia, and I need the money anyway.

Cecelia chats away as I cut. It's a relief, really. Trying to carry on a conversation with Jo-Jo is way too hard. During a lull in the conversation I ask Jo-Jo what her wife does. I can't picture what kind of woman would settle for Joe the airhead as a man, let alone go along with the Jo-Jo transition.

Cecelia answers. "As a matter of fact, Sue is an attorney and she works at Strand, Benson and Hayes." Cecelia raises her eyebrows to punctuate the significance of that to me.

"I told her we have a dear friend at that firm who we can't talk about because she hasn't come out," says Cecelia. Jo-Jo is looking into space. I'm not sure she has even heard the conversation. Cecelia winks at me as she finishes her explanation. That's why they're interrupting my night: Cecelia is trying to get a contact in Strand's firm. She must collect sources like bug collectors search out butterflies.

They finally leave around ten o'clock. Jo-Jo actually looks cute. I puffed up her hair and applied some makeup and lipstick, gave her pointers on mascara and eyeliner and blending bases and powders. I don't think she got much of it, but she left here looking a lot prettier than I'll ever be.

No matter. It's after ten and I'm slipping my naked body into a hot tub at last. I will sip wine and feel myself up and try to imagine what it will feel like when I have a vagina. I will also wonder if Jo-Jo is really a transsexual or just a dimwitted party boy looking for another sexual adventure. And that will bring me back to Bobbi. Girl in a man's body? Or a gay boy who wants to try missionary-position sex? Or failed hetero man who can't get it up but still wants to get it on?

*　*　*

I'M STILL HANDING OUT PROMOS to rush-hour people morning and evening, and still freezing my tush off doing it.

Tonight has been particularly odious. A bunch of people, maybe a dozen, have rudely rejected my flyer. One man looked at me and said, "Jesus, get away from me." A middle-aged woman looked at me like I was a giant turd on the sidewalk and said, "Never. Not ever," as she walked away. Many others said the same kind things with their eyes and body language. Still, there is the occasional smile and a few people actually begin reading the pamphlet as they walk away. I have to keep reminding myself that that's what I'm after. Maybe eight or ten people each week who will give me a try. I have to block out the people who find me odious. I can't, really. Not entirely. But I don't let them keep me from doing what I have to do.

The traffic coming out the door of the building has slowed to a trickle. It's after six and I'm tired and cold. I decide to knock off and head for home. Even though it's really cold, I decide to walk. I need the exercise. I've been shedding weight since I started hormones. Part of it is trying to get thinner and more feminine looking, and part of it is that I'm losing muscle mass. I'd lose some muscle anyway, but I'm doing it by design, trying to alter my big, heavy male musculature into long, lean muscle that still has some athletic dynamism but looks more femme. That's the goal.

As I start north on State Street I see a familiar figure pass under a light on the other side of the street. It's Strand. I wonder why he's walking. I've seen him leave his building before and it's always in his black BMW, a suitably pretentious and aloof way to navigate the streets of the city he must figure he owns.

On a whim, I follow him. He makes his way to a high-end hotel on North Michigan. I stay behind him and on the opposite side of the street, tucked into the crowd of pedestrians. Moments after he enters the hotel, I take a deep breath. Should I try to follow him in? Chances are, the doorman will shoo me away like a skid row bum; the only trannies who come to a place like this are hookers and they look a lot better than me.

I dither for a minute then follow him in. The doorman gives me a long look. He's trying to decide whether or not to let me pass. I don't look like a hooker, but I surely don't look like their typical client, either. This place is for execs with big egos and bigger expense accounts. A middle-aged, six-foot transsexual? Not a likely customer, but in this day and age, who knows for sure? I flash him a smile and greeting, trying to act like a self-assured big shot, albeit trans. It works. He opens the door for me with a smile.

Inside, I make my way into the lobby, hugging the walls to be as invisible as possible. No sign of Strand. I work my way around the lobby and peek into the lobby bar. No luck. A waitress sees me and approaches.

"Can I get you something?" Professional. Courteous.

I order a glass of wine, trying to feign self-confidence in a hotel for millionaires. As she gets the wine, a small table with a view of the lobby opens up. I seat myself. When she returns, she serves the wine and asks if there will be anything else.

"Maybe," I say. "I'm meeting a friend here in the lobby tonight and I wonder if you've seen him." I describe Strand.

She shrugs. "I don't know," she says. "That describes half the men who come in here."

Point taken. But after I finish my drink I stop at the front desk and ask the same question. The clerk isn't sure. "What is the gentleman's name?" he asks.

I hesitate. Do I really want to do this? "Strand," I say. "John Strand."

The clerk punches a keyboard and looks at his screen, frowns, punches more keys, frowns again. "I don't show a guest with that name," he says. "Perhaps he hasn't checked in yet."

Of course he hasn't checked in yet. Not under his own name, anyway. I thank the clerk and find a seat in the corner of the lobby and wait another fifteen minutes. I don't see Strand. He is having a tryst of some sort. Probably a genetic woman since he's so private about his trannies. Could a shit like him actually love one person and brutalize everyone else? At seven-thirty I decide I will never know and make my exit.

* * *

THANKSGIVING IS THE WORST holiday for me. A long, cold weekend with not much to do. A little buzz at the salon on Friday and Saturday but nothing like Christmas or even Easter. And Thanksgiving Day itself is as lifeless as a cemetery. The GLBT Center serves a dinner, but it's a couple hundred strangers eating cafeteria-style. Decent food, but institutional. A jail with no walls.

All in all, it makes you feel like a bum taking charity, another face in a mass portrait of unwanted souls.

Whatever my mother's failings, she was an excellent cook and that made Thanksgiving Day special in my childhood. The house would fill with mouth-watering aromas and Mom was actually happy and energized, bustling around the kitchen. My moody sister lightened up too, flitting between helping Mom and talking on the phone. My father got deep into whatever football game was on. I'd sit in front of the TV with him and pretend we were pals. I hung on his every word, took even his curses to heart, shelled walnuts for us both, made crackers and cheese. He never treated me like a pal or a son, but he was civil to me at those moments, and that was as good as it got between us.

Dinner itself was usually quiet. Mom and Dad made small talk. My sister shared girlfriend gossip. I fantasized about all sorts of things. Sports. Saving someone's life. What I would do if I was my sister, how I'd wear my hair, who I would want for friends, what clothes I'd wear.

Thanksgiving gatherings ended for me after high school. Sis invited me for Thanksgiving once after our parents died. Nice gesture, but an awful experience. I was in my gay phase, and she stipulated that I couldn't bring a boyfriend or talk about gay life. She blamed it on her husband, but she was just as repulsed. It was awkward and boring. They never invited me again and if they had, I would have declined.

I think these thoughts as I finish my hair and makeup. Wouldn't Sis and hubby just love having me over now, eh? It's funny though. She looks at me and sees a pervert and I look at her and see a wasted life. She is fat, sloppy, bored with her job, angry at her life. Her husband is a self-absorbed moron, also fat, his life entirely devoted to televised sports. Their son was an obnoxious, mean little bastard by the age of five and will only be the same thing but bigger as he matures.

She would be so much happier today if she had ever been able to see the potential for herself that I saw when I so wanted to be her.

I shake the thought as I collect my coat and purse. Dinner at the Center is better than thinking these thoughts. And maybe someone will want to go out for a nightcap afterwards.

* * *

December

I HAVE GOOD DAYS AND BAD DAYS in dealing with the fact that I am an oddity wherever I go. I'm coping fairly well today, maybe because the news about Strand's affair has me focused on something more than myself.

It's a good thing, too, because one of the other stylists has a client who is breaking her neck to stare at me. Many times when this happens I have all kinds of self-esteem issues. For the rest of the day I'll feel like people are staring at me with overt disgust.

Carol, the stylist, is getting tired of the lady's act, too. Naturally, the bitch is here for highlights and a cut. It's hard enough doing highlights on a client who constantly moves her head. Doing a cut is beyond frustrating and even a little dangerous since our shears are razor-sharp.

I decide to save a life. As my next client is being shampooed I walk over to Carol's chair. Her client, a baggy-looking middle-aged lady with sagging features, abruptly looks away as I draw near. I stand in front of her.

"Excuse me," I say. "Was there something you wanted to ask me?"

The woman squirms, glances up at me for a mille-second, then away. "No" she says.

I glance at Carol, who has a slight smile on her face. Of my colleagues in the salon, Carol has been the most supportive and sympathetic to me.

"Okay," I say. "It seemed like you wanted to ask me something, so I thought I'd check. If you ever do want to, just say so. Carol will tell you I'm easy to talk to."

Carol smiles at the reference. I return to my chair. Her client stares a hole in the floor.

There are many different types of bullies in our society. Carol's client represents maybe the least damaging. They're the ones with no guts. You can face them down and it makes you feel sort of empowered when they shrivel up. Problem is, without actually having an encounter, I can't tell one of these from a screaming tyrant or a bone-breaking bully or one of those really nasty passive-aggressive twits.

And, sometimes people who stare really do have questions they're afraid to ask. I've broken down a few barriers by inviting them to ask whatever they want. I give them honest answers—it's usually about my plumbing or why I'm doing this or what it's like or who I date or all of those things. But in answering them, I establish human contact and they start to think of me as a person rather than a freak, at least a little bit, and it takes the edge off. All the girls in the salon have clients who now greet me when they come in.

My next client gets my mind off all this. It's Ray, the father of the transgendered child. We haven't talked since he asked my advice about how to help his son become a girl.

"What's new in your life?" I ask Ray after we go through the client consultation ritual.

"Well, thanks to you, we're actually working on a plan for Laurie," he says. "That's her name. She and her mom came up with it. They asked me if I was okay with it and I said yes, of course." Ray runs with it. I don't have to say another word for the whole service.

They all understand that it's going to be hard, but they're going to work together to get through it. "It's the damndest thing," he says. "Laurie's mother and I never agree on anything and we're actually okay on this."

Laurie is almost eleven. They are taking her to Marilee once a week and they have a family session every two weeks. Laurie is a girl at home but will finish out the school year as a boy at school. Next fall, they'll enroll her as a girl at another school. Ray is paying for everything. They're going to see about blocking her puberty until she's old enough to start female hormones—or decides she'd rather be a boy.

"You can't believe the change that's come over her, Bobbi," Ray exclaims. "She's happy. She smiles and laughs. She and her mom have been shopping for a wardrobe of girls' clothes. Laurie's in heaven and her mom seems like the weight of the world just slid off her shoulders."

I smile and nod slightly. Ray keeps going. It's like a dam has broken. When he takes a breath, I ask, "Am I hearing a little romance budding between you and your ex?"

I have to stop cutting as Ray shakes his head. "No. No, nothing like that. But I think we are becoming friends. I hope so. This other way takes so much energy."

"Why wouldn't you be friends?" I respond. "My goodness, you've never fought her on anything, have you?"

"Not really," he says. "I don't know anything about raising kids. And I have some money, so I can take good care of the two of them and all it means is I live in Wicker Park instead of a lakefront condo. Big deal.

"And I gotta say," he says after a moment's thought, "Gail's never really taken advantage of that. When she asks for more money, it's not for a fancy car or a new outfit or whatever. It's because the dryer went kaput or Laurie needs braces. I'm pretty lucky."

I can see why Molly took it so hard when Ray left her. He's one of the nicest guys I've met. I mean, what divorced husband gives up a fancy apartment and hip lifestyle to take care of his ex-wife. Heck, most of the divorced men I know don't even live up to their obligations to their kids. It must have been really hard on Molly. This man is so decent and so huggable. You could really do some happy ever-aftering with a guy like this. I bet she felt like her heart was broken when he left. I'd feel that way.

After Ray's service, I sit in my chair and update my card on him. It occurs to me that the feelings he aroused in me are new. I don't want to sound superficial, but whenever I have found someone sexually attractive in the past, it was based on physical characteristics that I noticed right away. This was different. It started with what a really good person this man is, then what it would be like to be held by him and loved by him. He would never be interested in me, and I'm not disappointed at that thought. I'm strangely refreshed to have felt these things about someone.

Is this just age? Hormones? Or am I starting to think like a woman?

***

MY FIRST CHRISTMAS as a transwoman.

When I was married and passing as a normal person, I always wondered how many people actually experienced the kind of holiday joy that's portrayed in popular movies and books and television shows about Christmas. I liked the music and the lights, but the whole run-up to Christmas seemed stressful for everyone and the harder people tried, the more their Christmas spirit seemed contrived. Except for kids of a certain age, and their parents.

As a gay man living alone, the holidays were just lonely. I had no family to dine with or buy gifts for, and none of my romances coincided with the holidays. There was plenty of merriment to be had in the clubs and bars, but

I'm not much of a drinker and I wasn't into the meat market part of clubbing either. So I read a lot of books, toured the city lights, visited museums and the like.

I thought my first holiday season as a transwoman might be different, but it hasn't been. Marilee and her husband are holidaying with one of their kids in Michigan, Cecelia has gone to Florida for a week, and Ray has his daughter and his ex at a resort in Arizona. I've taken in some events at the Center, but to be honest, my heart's just not in it.

It's okay. I don't get depressed or suicidal or anything. Maybe because I kept my true self hidden for so many years, this feels a lot like all the holidays of my life. Even as a child, Christmas seemed overblown. My mother went through the motions of being in the spirit of things, but my father didn't even try to fake it. I'd get a football or a shirt or whatever on Christmas day, we'd have the mandatory big dinner, then we'd all just try to make it through a long boring evening in our own respective ways. Thanksgiving was better, I guess because it came without expectations.

When I told my family I was gay I didn't have to think up excuses not to come for Christmas dinner any more. The invitations just stopped. They may have quit having Christmas, for all I know, or they may have just quit inviting me. When I think about my family—as I often do for a moment here or there during the holidays—what I find most remarkable about us is that four people who had absolutely no love for one another could treat each other reasonably well for so long.

* * *

I DON'T HAVE TO BE OUT HERE freezing my butt off.

My appointment book is getting a little better. The rush-hour handouts are working. I've picked up a rash of new customers who have already been in and a bunch more who have booked their first visit. Most of the ladies who have come in have rebooked and I'm running a two-for-one deal that's bringing in new customers, too—any client who gets someone else to book with me gets a half-off service and so does the new client.

Even though things are picking up, I'm still passing out leaflets one or two nights a week. I want the business, but I also have an ulterior motive. I'm keeping an eye out for Strand. Every once in a while I catch sight of him moving north and I follow him. He always heads for a four-star hotel, for a tryst. I don't know if the sex is any good, but they don't spare the expense on the hotels.

As for why I'm following this jerk, I'm not sure. Maybe I'm just jealous that he treats someone else like a human being and me like garbage. All I know is, I'm not going to let him get away with murdering Mandy. And I'm not going to let him get away with hurting me.

I just don't know what I'm going to do. Yet.

So for now I just want to get to know more about this pig.

Tonight they're going low-brow. I've followed Strand to a very nice, old hotel on Randolph, west of his usual haunts on Michigan Avenue. It's a lovely remnant of old Chicago with a really elegant lobby, but it's several pegs down the price scale from the elite digs they've been shacking up in.

I follow him from a half block or so behind. Once he ducks in the door of the hotel, I speed up. He always goes directly to the elevators, so why spend any more time than necessary out in the deep freeze?

I enter the lobby behind several businessmen and take a quick look to make sure Strand isn't in the reception area. He isn't. I don't see him by the elevators, either. The great man is probably already getting it on with Mrs. CEO.

Beyond the reception area, the lobby widens and narrows in a series of sitting rooms, all clad in wood paneling and furnished with old highback chairs and overstuffed sofas. There is a bar, and a waitstaff delivers quaffs throughout the lobby. I love the elegance and latter-day gentility of this place. I haven't been in here in years, and never as Bobbi. It's cold outside. I decide to stay for a drink, for old time's sake.

I settle in an old chair at the edge of the room, well away from the bar and the elevators. I try to be obscure. It is dim in here, and sitting on the perimeter of the room, I do not stand out.

A waitress comes to take my order. As she draws close, she makes me and she does one of those double takes people do with their eyes—she looks, looks away, looks, looks away, and finally establishes eye contact with me.

"Good evening. Ma'am," she says. She is a little uncertain with the "ma'am" part but handles it. The hotel sees plenty of gays and even the occasional trans person in the course of a month; it's in the middle of the theater district and theater draws the GLBT community like money draws Republicans. She hands me a small menu and recites tonight's drink and appetizer specials. "What can I bring you?" she asks.

I order a glass of wine, no food, and watch her whisper something to another waitress and the bartender when she goes to fill my order. I pay with cash when she brings my order, but wait with the tip until I leave. She'll probably think I'm going to stiff her, so she'll leave me alone. That suits me perfectly. I could use a little alone time right now.

For bar wine, this one isn't bad. I swirl it in my mouth and savor the taste and recall another time, maybe five years ago, when I sat in this lobby and stayed in this hotel for a weekend with a very nice man. He was from a small town in Iowa, married, kids, apple pie. He came to Chicago on business a couple times a year and stayed over on Friday and Saturday night to imbibe in the cultural benefits of the big city: mainly, a male bed partner and a play.

We met in a bar. He was actually looking for a male prostitute he had met before and we just started talking by chance. We hit it off and he asked me if I'd be his theater date the next night. It ended up being one of the most fun weekends of my gay life and I had the feeling it was like that for him, too. I never saw him again, but I've often wondered how things worked out for him.

At the edge of my vision I see a figure approaching. I glance over. My heart freezes. It's Strand. What the hell? Faster than I can inhale he sweeps into the chair next to me, his jaw clenched, his eyes narrowed.

"Bobbi, my goodness what a small world, isn't it?" His voice is dripping with sarcasm. He doesn't wait for me to answer. "What are the odds that we would see each other right here, tonight? My, my. I would love to find out what you've been up to, but I have to run. Let's plan to get together soon, though, okay? Let's plan on having a *smashing* good time."

He slaps his thigh hard when he says "smashing." I wince. The sound conjures up visions of flesh splattering in my dreams. My heart seizes.

"Let's plan to do that very soon. Very, very soon." He smiles that cold smile of his, all shark teeth and snake eyes. He is gone before I can utter a word.

He was trying to be menacing and it worked. I'm frozen in place, numb with dread. He is beyond angry. He means to beat me, maybe kill me. Whenever he feels like it.

We have entered into a whole new realm.

* * *

HE ENTERS THE ELEVATOR shaking with rage. The tranny thing, the boy with tits, has the gall to be following him! Stupid cockroach!

On the ride to her floor he gets his rage under control and considers what the tranny is trying to accomplish. Revenge, but how? Maybe by feeding the gay rumor mill with stories about him and Martha. The GLBT community's rumor mill is an underground unto itself, rife with juicy news about sexual transgressions of the rich and famous. Reaching everywhere, boardrooms, city hall, barbershops. Everywhere. He begins to seethe again. It would never get in the papers but the buzz would be embarrassing for Martha. It could end her marriage. And it could cost him the account.

Stupid cockroach!

He stops at the door of her room. 'Stupid dead cockroach,' he thinks. He returns to the elevator, and then to the lobby, looking for a stupid tranny boy with tits to scare the shit out of. The really fun stuff will come later, but this will be a good appetizer. The beast is hereby in ascension.

* * *

AFTER MY ENCOUNTER WITH Strand yesterday, I had nightmare after nightmare. I would recall his dead eyes as he deliberately hurt me. I watched as he killed Mandy, his face a mask that never registers an emotion. I dreamt he waited for me in my apartment, behind the door, and jumped me as I came in; in that nightmare he was going to kill me by stripping skin off my body until I finally died.

There were others, many others. I woke up with raccoon eyes from lack of sleep. I tried to reduce the puffiness with cold slices of cucumber, then a hemorrhoid ointment, then I tried to hide it with makeup. I was only half successful. Several people have asked me if I'm okay today. They didn't say I look like crap, but I'm sure their concern was based on me looking like last week's oatmeal.

I had half a dozen customers today—not great, but for a slow Tuesday, not too bad. Especially considering where I was a couple months ago when I had some Tuesdays without a single customer, not even a walk-in.

Better still, four of today's customers were repeats. They knew they were coming to see an oversized transsexual hairdresser and they had already made their peace with it. It was interesting how that changes things. We just jumped right into the service, then into small talk. There wasn't any of the tension about me being trans and them trying to deal with that.

It was boring. Pleasantly boring. I look forward to the time when all my days will be like that and I'm just another hairdresser trying to make people look their best.

I'm heading straight home tonight. After last night's scare, I'm dropping the private-eye stuff. Tonight will be a well-cooked meal—soup, salad, and a sautéed whitefish filet with a touch of lemon, maybe some chopped green onions, a dash of pepper.

As I start up the stairs to my apartment I'm trying to decide whether or not to substitute a baked potato for the soup. I notice something outside my door. Halfway up the stairs I can see that it is a bouquet of flowers. Alarms go off in my head. Flowers are part of Strand's language. The thought makes me shiver. I slowly ascend the stairs, hoping they're from Marilee. Or maybe Ray. Wouldn't it be nice if they were from Officer Phil…with maybe an invitation to dinner and a night at the theater? Yeah, dream on.

They are yellow roses, a dozen of them. In the dead of winter. I fish out the card and open it. My heart stops.

It reads: *I have a big surprise for you!* No signature.

None needed.

I automatically look over my shoulder, as if the bastard were waiting to fly at me with a knife as soon as I read the card. Nothing.

I ascend the stairs to the top floor to make sure he's not lurking. My heart is pounding. It's dark and I'm scared. There's no chance he's still here, but if I don't prove it to myself I'll spend the night cowering in fear about it. There is nothing at the top of the stairs except the doors to the two third-floor apartments. I walk all the way back down to the ground floor. As I step out on the porch I pull the flowers out of the wrapping and fling them onto the front lawn.

I say a short, silent prayer over them. *Eat shit and die, Strand.*

* * *

HE WATCHES FROM HIS CAR, *parked across the street from the tranny's building. His lights are off, but he doesn't bother to slouch down. He doesn't care if the tranny sees him or not.*

The tranny bursts onto the porch from inside the building, still wearing the silly coat it walked home in. Anger is etched on its mannish face. It flings the roses toward the curb, the blossoms separating in mid-air and fanning across the icy grass. He smiles. The bitch's anger pleases him. It's not just anger, it's fear, too. He can smell it from here. Delicious.

January

STRAND PROMISED TO COME CALLING almost a month ago and he hasn't made good on it yet. I think the weather is holding him back, though I know he hasn't dropped the matter.

We haven't been above freezing in a week. We've had highs in the single digits, with wind chills below zero at night. Usually when it's this cold, it's also clear. But we've had overcast skies and a six-inch mini-blizzard, and several light snowfalls. The snow doesn't melt because it's so cold. The stuff on the street turns to a frozen slush during the day because of the road salt, but it doesn't actually melt. The slush clogs curbs and gutters and loose snow blows into your face wherever you walk. If you don't wear tall boots, when you step off the curb the slush seeps into your shoes and you are in for a bad day.

If you do wear boots, the salt-laden slush turns them to junk in a few days. You can try buying crappy boots for the sacrifice, but they just fail faster than expensive ones. You really can't beat Mother Nature, not in the Chicago winter.

On the street, we look like a city of mummies. People wrap scarves around their necks and the lower parts of their faces. When the wind is whistling up the streets, people wrap the scarves up over their noses and pull hats to just above their eyes.

The one positive part of this is that, on the street, no one can tell I'm trans. And it's too cold to give a damn anyway.

Most of my friends and customers are at their annual breaking point with Chicago's winter weather. They talk of Florida, California, tropical islands.

Me, I take solace in hot meals and steaming baths, good books, offbeat programs on public radio. And not being killed by Strand. Earlier this week I was Officer Phil's companion for a stage play at a neighborhood theater. No, he's not interested in me. Alas. He likes to attend social events in the community with members of the community. He spreads it around—always someone different. The play was awful, but I had a wonderful time getting ready for it and Phil was a very thoughtful escort. And the experience gave me material for many nights of erotic dreams. Yes, I still have a crush on Officer

Phil. I may always have a crush on Officer Phil.

I am thinking of myself as a woman more and more now. I have dreams about making love as a woman, what it would be like to be with a man. I have those dreams about making love with women, too. About what it would be like to make love with a woman as a woman.

Bisexuality is another of my abominations against all that is Puritan and hypocritical in America, and I should be ashamed of myself. I'm not though. In fact, a lot of us trans people who go through all the rejection that comes with transitioning get to a point where loving someone and being loved back is more important than minutiae like gender.

Whatever. What's significant is that I see myself as a transwoman now. My memories of Bob Logan, strapping six-footer with rippling muscles and Marlboro Man looks, are pretty much gone.

But I also realize I'm not ever going to pass for a genetic woman and, to be honest, I don't feel like one. To many of my transsexual sisters who grew up hating everything about being male, their life's goal is to look, act, and talk like a genetic woman. And to be accepted by genetic women as a woman.

I'm coming to realize that there are anomalies in my transsexual makeup. A lot of them. I never minded being a boy as a child, even though I would have preferred to have long hair and wear dresses. I mostly preferred boy's games to girl's games and I had friends in both genders.

When I started going through puberty I got much more interested in girls, both as a boy and as a transsexual. As my female classmates grew breasts and started wearing tight sweaters and short skirts, I found it hard to think about anything else. It was very confusing. On the one hand, I wanted to have sex with half the girls in my Junior High. I got erections in almost every class from gazing at the girls. On the other hand, I also wanted to have cute hair and perky breasts and boys getting erections by just looking at me.

I think that's a good definition of *conundrum*.

Like so many trans youth of that era, I didn't know the name for the disease I had, but I knew it wasn't safe to talk about, or to act out. So I did what I was supposed to do. I spent the first four years of puberty trying to get laid, and the next ten or so after that trying to decide if I liked it.

Well, let me clarify that. I did like it. It was better than being horny. But I was thinking I'd like it better if I was the one on the bottom. Back in those days, no one talked about transsexuals, so I assumed I was gay. After a few years as a gay man, I finally realized the main thing I liked about being gay was it allowed me to be effeminate. I wasn't attracted to men any more than I was to women.

When I started cross-dressing and got active in the TransGender Alliance, things started coming into focus. The first thing was learning that gender identity and sexual preference are two completely different things. One of my mentors used to say, "gender is who you are, sex is who you love."

Of course, even knowing that much, it took years to think of myself as a transsexual. I couldn't tell you why, really. I suppose it's because transsexual isn't something anyone wants to be. It's way off the map of accepted behavior in our society. If someone hates you for it, it's okay because you are not really human. If someone is nice to you, it's because they're a saintly person, not because you are human and deserve to be treated well. It's a tough road to travel and the only ones to complete the journey are those who have no other choice.

I thought when I finally came to think of myself as a transsexual that there would be this door-opening clarity in my life at last, a blast of bright light and certainty. But that's not how it works. Not for me, anyway. There's always the nagging doubt about whether I really am a transsexual, and even after you cross that bridge, there's the question of what kind of transwoman you are. Will you go all the way with GRS, or will you be a non-op transsexual, a permanent she-male, in the unkind jargon of our times? If you are a non-op, will you be a full-time female in your presentation, or will you spend part of your time in male mode?

Over the years, I've found that I just prefer to dress and act like a woman, and that's really what pushed me to transition. I don't know if that's a good reason or not, and neither does anyone else.

As for Strand, I hoped we had reached a sort of unwritten truce after the flowers on my doorstep. I quit following him. Message delivered. I hoped that would be the end of it. But there have been several occasions when I felt like I was being watched. On the street. In a store. At a café. I couldn't actually see someone staring at me, but the feeling was very real. Too real to ignore. So I used spy-novel techniques to see if I could spot someone following me. I'd stop suddenly to look in a store window, or pretend to change my mind about something and walk back to a store I had just passed. Or just go into a shop, go out the alley exit and circle around. I'm now sure there are two different men who follow me on different occasions. It figures. The work is too low and cold for Strand right now.

They are both middle-aged, white men who dress in common clothes. One wears a tan coat, blue stocking cap, blue jeans and work boots.

The other one is a squat, powerful-looking man who looks like a laborer—blue pea coat, Levis, boots, shaved head, no hat. I didn't see either man's face.

They aren't following me because I'm cute or because they want to go for walks in sub-zero temperatures. Which means they're doing it for someone else. They're doing it for Strand.

* * *

MY APPOINTMENT BOOK has been improving, thanks to my leafleting and my rebirth as a creative stylist who doesn't apologize for being who she is. My comeback started with weekdays, especially around the lunch hours and in the evenings, right after work. That's when the commuters schedule. I've even come in really early a few times to do a client who had an important event scheduled for the day. It isn't the money that motivates me—it's that they really appreciate it. It keeps them coming back and gives them a reason to talk about me with their friends, so it's good business, too. But the big thing is how much they appreciate it.

My Saturdays have been building too, and this is the best one I've had since I came out as a transwoman. I had a full book this morning, from eight to noon, and everyone showed up on time.

Now I'm working on the best gig ever. A young Pakistani-American woman chose me to do her wedding updo today. I was shocked that she even let me audition for the work. She came a few weeks ago for a trial updo. I had never seen her before. She got my name from one of my clients and added me to a list of hairdressers to trial with. I had always thought Muslims had the same low opinion of trans people that fundamentalist Christians do, so I didn't really think I had a shot. But I had plenty of time for her that day and I love doing updos, especially with beautiful hair like hers. I'd do them for free, just because the process and the end result totally and completely light up my soul and make my senses tingle. It's the most beautiful art there is.

She was a very sweet girl once we got past her shyness. We talked for fifteen or twenty minutes to start. I didn't even touch her hair. I asked her about the wedding ceremony, the events of the day, and what she needed from her hair that day in practical terms—would she be outdoors much?

After we got to know each other a little, I even asked if she would want to take it down before or after she and her husband consummated their marriage. She smiled and said she hadn't thought about it. We both blushed. I explained that some updos have dozens of hairpins in them and take forever to take down, while others can be done with just a few pins. She thought fewer might be better. A girl after my own heart.

Once we got through the preliminaries we spent another ten minutes talking about updo shapes and heights. By then she was really enjoying herself. She had already decided about me: she had given me the right to ask anything of her, and in so doing, had given herself the right to say anything in response. Not that she was ever anything but ladylike, but she completely enjoyed going through a repertoire of looks with me that ranged from coquettish to gutter tramp. I doubt if she had ever before been so unreserved with a stranger about her hidden self, the self that always wonders what you'd look like in a tiny leather mini skirt, a skin-tight T-top that just covers the nipples, stiletto heels and hair out to here.

Oh my, how I can identify with that!

I ended up doing a breathtaking one-off updo that combined lots of teasing with a simple braiding technique. Honestly, I've never seen such a fantastic do, even if it was my own work. It had body and height and was so sexy it smoldered. At the same time, the twists of the braid gave it an elegant, feminine touch. Most of all, it set off her features perfectly, calling attention to her beautiful dark eyes and her perfect oval-shaped face and her full, sexy lips.

As I looked at her in the mirror, part of me was thinking that she might have a place in my erotic dreams, even though there wasn't a chance in the world that she would choose me for the wedding day do.

Surprise, surprise. She did pick me, and over her regular hairdresser at a very exclusive North Shore salon, and a Pakistani hairdresser favored by many brides in her community. I will never have the courage to ask her if this choice means Allah is okay with transsexuals, but that doesn't matter anyway. What matters is, she's okay with me and doing her hair is the highlight of my month. Maybe my year.

I have been working on her for two hours. She wanted perfection and was willing to pay for it, so we are making a full afternoon of the event. Other members of her wedding party are getting their hair done by my colleagues, which is boosting my popularity in the salon quite a lot. Her friends take turns sitting in the chair next to mine to talk with her. They speak in Urdu, but the friends make frequent furtive glances at me and she frequently looks at her image in the mirror, with smiles accompanying both events, so I know her hair and probably her weird hairdresser are a main topic of conversation. And they like what they see, at least with the hair.

Me too.

Usually, we have updo customers wash and condition their own hair before coming in, otherwise, the process just takes too long, but for this client, I started with a shampoo and blow-dry to make sure the hair is perfect—moisturized, sealed, slow-dried, no frizz, plenty of body, optimum texture. Then hot rollers, teasing, smoothing and braiding. Then the details. Then the mounting of her tiara. Then more details.

She has long, medium-coarse hair and a lot of it. It is wavy with some tendency to frizz, so it takes forever to dry. On the other hand, after a careful blow dry it's almost perfect for what I'm doing since it holds a curl well and has the lovely natural shine of youth. The only mild imperfection is her hairline, which, like many, has lots of squiggly little hairs sticking out and the hairline itself does not follow the oval shape of her face.

I keep the front of her 'do' soft and a little puffy to absorb most of the fine hairs, and to help me contour the hairline. I snip a few fine hairs and even pull a few others.

As I do the final spray and mount her tiara, her friends and most of the salon staff gather round. Applause breaks out as she stands up shyly. The applause is for her, but it is for me too. I'm glowing so hard I could melt. God, life can be so sweet!

* * *

ONE THING ABOUT BEING trans, you're never far from a fall.

I was so giddy after my updo experience I decided to walk home and enjoy the moment, the cold be damned. I'm now huddled in a booth in a coffee shop about six blocks from my apartment. My coat is still on, my hands surround a steaming cup of hot chocolate.

A group of teens in a booth on the other side of the room are laughing and pointing at me. One of them, a girl, a cheerleader type, stopped at my booth a few minutes ago on her way to the bathroom. "Are you a guy or what?" she asks, giggling. It's a rhetorical question, a put-down, though she pauses for a moment as if waiting to hear my response. She has a pixie face, her chin cutely narrow, long healthy hair worn down and straight, grayish blue eyes, cute body. Cute, and also sexy. Queen of the hop, especially in high school. She laughs gaily, tosses her hair, and continues on her way.

Shortly after she returns to her booth, one of the guys comes by on the same journey. Homecoming hero good looks. Private school swagger—white kids who go to public schools in this city tend to be less arrogant. "Fucking queen," he said.

A man of few words.

I wish I could say these taunts don't hurt, but they do. My giddy high is gone. My feelings of warmth and joy have been shunted aside. My eyes are moist but I refuse to give them the satisfaction of seeing me cry.

In moments like this, I am like my trans sisters. I can't understand why people take delight in making others feel bad. A moment ago I was a human being in a state of rejoice because I had done something nice for someone else, because I had done something artistic and creative. Now I am just a clown. A queen. An outcast.

I should leave, but I came in here to get warm. Besides, I won't give them the satisfaction of running me off, even though they have already ruined my day.

As I sip my hot chocolate I wonder if these kids are wholesome religious types who are in the process of growing up to be sanctimonious hypocrites, like their parents probably are. Life is sacred, as long as we're talking about someone else's pregnant teenage daughter, as long as we don't have to pay anything to support the unwanted child, as long as we can still depend on our professional army to kill unseen rabble we think might be a threat to our safety and our sacred right to get fat in front of television.

But this is stupid of me. Young people, even really nice ones, can be very cruel at times. I was. I clearly recall a moment in college when a friend of mine and I laughed and snickered our way through an entire group lunch just because everything a very effeminate gay male student said seemed funny to us. Yes, consider the irony. Not only would I become such a person myself, I was to go even further and become a woman. Or try to.

No, this incident is not about them as much as it is about me. I am weird. I don't belong. I just have to live with that.

* * *

FOR THE LIFE OF ME, I don't know why I agreed to do this.

I'm in a queue waiting to enter the Cadillac Theater. I am shivering. It's not the cold, it's the situation. I feel conspicuous in this milling crowd of theater-goers. Most are nicely dressed, some sumptuously so. I've done my best to get in the spirit. I'm wearing a sexy black suit that has a long skirt and a waist-length coat that rises in a wide V. The coat works with a layering white teddy to display some cleavage. I'm wearing black hose, 2-inch heels and a tiny white, faux-fur-lined coat that falls just above my waist.

My shivering is interrupted by a man's arm coming around my back. His hand grasps my upper arm and he pulls my body into his.

The arm belongs to Ray, the father of the transgendered child, Laurie.

He called the same night I had been humiliated in the coffee shop, wanting to know if I would go to a musical with him at the Cadillac.

I love the Cadillac. It is a grand old theater and one I went to in my youth when it was a movie palace with a different name. I also love theater. All kinds. Drama, musicals, you name it.

But no, I said, I didn't think I could make it. Just too much going on in my life right now.

Oh, said Ray. He sounded disappointed. "I got the feeling you liked me when we talked last month," he said. "I know I like you. I was hoping we could get to know each other a little more. I promise you, I'm a gentleman. I will treat you well. I'm polite…"

I explained that I did like him, that I thought he was a very nice man with a good heart. But, I said, I had a nasty incident in a coffee shop recently and I just don't feel like being in public right now.

He brought up the bicycle analogy, getting back on, and all that. I wasn't swayed. Then he said that if something happened, I wouldn't be alone. He'd be there too.

You know what? He would be there. That's what occurred to me at that moment. Ray was the kind of person who would be there with you, no matter what. So I agreed. I still didn't want to go out, but he was right—even about the bicycle analogy. If I'm going to be a transwoman, I have to be one every day. Period.

So here I am in the crowded lobby of the Cadillac Theater with a man's arm around me. He is a big man. Ray is all of 6-4, which is why I get to wear heels. And he's something over 250 pounds, a soft, teddy-bear look that I find quite attractive, now that I take the time to consider him socially.

You'd think two large people like us would attract a lot of attention in a crowded room like this, but we don't. People take passing notice of us, and I draw some double takes, but no one stares or points. This is the theater, after all. Some of the congregated masses are gay. Plus, the place is crowded, the crowd is buzzing and moving. Nothing stands out but the general confusion. I relax. It feels good to have his arm around me.

We move with the crowd into the seating area and wend our way to our seats. Ray has chosen well. We are in the middle of the third row of the first balcony. We won't stand out. We won't have to constantly stand up to let others move by us to their seats.

It is warm in the theater thanks to the heat generated by hundreds of bodies. I am relaxed and drowsy. The syncopated rhythms of the show have a narcotic affect on me.

The milling of the crowd around us wakens me. It is intermission. I have been sleeping soundly, my head resting on Ray's shoulder. As I sit up he looks at me, a gentle smile on his face. "Usually my dates don't fall asleep until I start talking about myself," he says.

I am embarrassed and begin apologizing profusely. "No need," he says. "I'm glad you're comfortable enough with me to doze off. I'm flattered." I wrap my arms around one of his and hug him. "Thank you," I say, as we begin working our way out to the lobby.

As I join the endless queue for the ladies room, I listen for objections to rise from the women in front of and behind me. I hear none, though a couple of women in front have glanced back at me several times. They have made me, but don't seem particularly concerned. Just curious.

I can handle curious.

Inside the ladies room I attract more glances, mainly when I wash my hands and check my makeup. These are just the "oh-you're-trans" glances. There isn't time for comments or questions. The intermission is short, the lines are long, and if you want to get to your seat before the second act curtain you have to keep moving.

Ray is waiting as I emerge from the ladies room. He hands me a plastic glass of champagne and offers me his arm. I lace mine through it and we stroll leisurely through the crowd. God, this is nice. I actually feel like a woman on a date.

I stay awake through the entire second act, wondering if I should invite

Ray up when he takes me home, wondering if he would make a pass at me, wondering what I would do if he did.

We have dessert and an after-dinner drink at a café near the theater and talk. Ray talks about dealing with his new daughter, and his ex-wife, and his business. He owns a print shop and competes with the big chains by providing better service, higher quality, total reliability.

He asks me about transitioning, about what I did before, how I got into hair.

The time flies by. At midnight he says he has to call it a night, he has a full day in the shop tomorrow. So do I. On the cab ride to my place I invite him up. He declines. Same reason. I understand. He says he's had a great time and asks if I'd be willing to do this again. I answer by putting my arms around him and kissing him. I don't know if this turns him on as much as it does me, but I can hardly breathe when the cab stops at the curb and we unclench.

"Oh yes," I exhale. I leave the cab before he can collect himself. My legs feel rubbery and my body is on fire.

As I make my way on shaky legs to the door of my apartment I wonder if this is the real thing or if I'm just so horny from months of abstinence—with one notable and much-regretted lapse—that anyone would turn me on.

* * *

February

ROBERTA IS ON A LONG RIFF about transgender assertiveness and I'm having a hard time staying awake. The other girls are getting restive, too, though I seem to be the only one on the edge of slumber.

Roberta is the facilitator of the Alliance's monthly transsexual support group. I started coming to meetings again last summer when I started seeing Roberta privately for my transition. I don't find the meetings particularly helpful or interesting. The people who tend to dominate the conversation use the forum as a place to vent, and the frustrations they ramble on about are as familiar to me as my fingers and toes, which tonight are polished a bright red—my nails, that is. I almost never use bright red for nail polish or lipstick. I just don't look feminine enough to pull it off. Why tonight? I guess I'm just feeling more girly than usual. I have my hair up in a messy twist with dangling curls here and there and dangling earrings that match my large black and gold necklace. I'm wearing a low-cut silk blouse with a form-fitting skirt that stops well above the knees, black hose and medium-heeled half-boots. I'm a little old for this look, but sometimes a girl just has to have fun.

My private sessions with Roberta are once a month. She's tried to get me to come in more often, but money is tight and, like I said, I'm not that sold on the therapist/patient relationship. Once a month has value because she can see changes in me and we can talk about them.

Meanwhile, I come to the support group as a sort of compromise with her, but also because the surgery is becoming real to me. It has been an abstraction for as long as I've even thought about transitioning, but lately, I find myself planning on it. I've circled a date on my calendar, I've set aside savings and I've chosen the surgeon. I have even figured out what weeks I will have to be gone from the salon while I recover.

Roberta is a transwoman herself. She is very tall—an inch taller than me. After she told me she was trans I could see it in her, but not before. She is one of those women who is attractive without being beautiful. She's very slim, and wears tasteful clothing in subdued colors. She moves, sits, and stands gracefully.

She has a soft voice. Her shoulder-length hair is curly and prone to frizz, but it's feminine and the simplicity of her style works very well with the rest of her.

She is giving us a pep talk on being assertive. Not in-your-face assertive like Cecelia, but get out of the closet, stay out of the closet, be proud of who you are assertive. This lecture was precipitated by a girl who sobbed her way through a narrative about attending a family dinner as her feminine self. I guess she expected some degree of acceptance since she had told her family she was trans and what that meant. But they weren't ready for dear Abby, not in a dress and makeup. They never are. Her father took one look at her, said "Jesus Christ!" and left the room; he never came back. Her brother and his wife wouldn't talk to her or even look at her. Her mother cried. Her sister asked if this was really necessary.

Roberta is a little like the teacher in the old movie *The Prime of Miss Jean Brodie*. She is demanding that we stick up for our right to be ourselves. She and I have danced round and round this topic for months. She's right, to a point. I think of her when humiliating experiences make me want to stay indoors and avoid the public.

But there's this other reality, too. The other reality is that there are quite a few people who will never accept a transsexual as a woman. That includes lots of parents and siblings. If you look like me, it also includes large numbers of people you meet or just pass on the street. Some are outright bigots, but most are regular people who just can't handle it. We carry a stigma about us that is hard for others to get past.

I realized this once and for all when I saw a television show featuring a group of really gorgeous, extremely successful transwomen. I had always thought if a trans person could look that good and accomplish so much, they'd be accepted completely as women. Why not? They are more attractive, smarter and more accomplished than the vast majority of genetic women. Turns out, there's always something. Each of them had been successful in their careers and had no trouble turning heads as beautiful women when they walked through a crowd. But to a woman they felt their love lives were hollow. They had no problem getting laid, of course. The difficult thing, the maybe impossible thing, was finding a committed, loving relationship. "As soon as I tell him I'm trans, it's over," one said. They all agreed. They told different stories to illustrate their points. Sometimes it ended right there. Sometimes it ended by degrees. He didn't want to take her home to mom and family. He didn't want to go to out as much. The relationship gets stale. The "maybe we should see other people" session comes along.

I knew it would be like that for me before I heard those women, but hearing them drove the point home. I will never have an intimate, long-term lover, not a male one, anyway. I will have breasts and a vagina, I'll wear nice clothes, I'll have beautiful hair, I'll think of myself as a woman, but many others won't think of me that way. I'll get laid as often as I want by male adventurers, I might even have friends who fuck me when we're both horny. But I'll never be loved as a woman.

And I have decided to accept that. It's not everything I want in life, but it's the best I can have. I don't want to spend my life pretending to be a man, not when I can spend it trying to be a woman.

***

THE MEETING ENDS mercifully at ten p.m. and I join a group of girls heading for the El station. We travel together into the city, ignoring the stares of the train's night-riders, a motley collection of students, janitors, gangstas and the odd regular person. They leave us alone. Everyone just wants to get where they're going, except maybe one or two punks. But we are too many for them to mess with. And trannies aren't good marks for theft since most of us live close to the poverty line.

When we get to the Loop we go our separate ways. I take the Red Line north, drawing mild interest from the half-dozen or so riders on my car. I get off at Belmont. It's further from my apartment than Addison, but on support-group nights I like to stop at a diner near the Belmont stop and take a few minutes to think about things over a cup of tea.

I take a surreptitious glance around as I exit the train to see if anyone seems to be following me. It's something I've always done, even when I was a man. This is the city.

No one else gets off my car. Two kids get off the car in front of mine and run lightly to the exit, disappearing before I've taken my fifth step. It is silent on the subway platform except for the click of my heels. Below the raised platform, Boystown twinkles quietly to the east, its eclectic cafes and clubs still beckoning at ten-thirty on a Tuesday night in mid-winter. Sidewalk traffic on Belmont is sparse. Plumes of vapors rise from the mouths of a couple vigorously walking and talking. Single figures move swiftly east and west, muffled and hunched to ward off the cold. On a summer night at this hour, Belmont would be teeming with street life, but the icy fangs of February have pushed people indoors.

I descend to street level in a darkened staircase, its lights sacrificed to vandals. Near the street level, the sky comes into view, unblemished by ambient light. The moon fills my vision, full and fat, set off by hundreds of tiny stars. The sight stops me dead. I gape in awe, my mind suddenly filled with romantic notions. It would be so nice to be holding hands with someone special just now, to share this moment.

The sound of feet scraping on stairs behind me interrupts my reverie. I turn, startled. All I see is a glimpse of a retreating shape shuffling up the stairs. Heavy footfalls, like work boots would make. Dark on dark. A shadow. Probably male. Where did he come from? The platform was empty when I got to the exit. Why is he going back up?

I'm spooked. I descend the last few stairs as fast as I can in heels and walk briskly toward the café. It's probably nothing, but I feel like the man might be following me. Why? Because he moves so furtively. Because I didn't see him get off the train when I got off and I didn't see him on the platform. Weird. I want to get where people are.

As I cross Wilton to the café I glance back. Nothing. I relax a little. On the street, it's not likely anyone will mess with me. I wonder how big he is. I try to remember what he looked like in my fragmented glimpse of him. Work boots. Blue jeans. A light colored coat, maybe tan.

The tan coat rings a frightening bell in my memory. One of the men I thought was following me a few weeks ago wore a tan coat and a blue stocking cap. Of course, thousands of men wear tan coats and blue stocking caps in Chicago during the winter. I'm not even sure this man's coat was tan and I didn't see a hat. It's nothing.

I relax and enjoy the clear, chill air and the glowing warmth of the Belmont Avenue lights. It's like being in an idyllic Christmas card scene. With no one looking, I let my hips roll as I walk, one hand swinging girlishly, the other holding the purse strap slung from my shoulder. I don't let myself be girly in public very often, but at this time and place it feels good.

Clarke's is an upscale bar and grill with a pleasant ambience. Great breakfasts, sinful burgers, inspired beer and wine list, rich selection of teas. It sits on the southwest border of Boystown, a place where Lakeview's straight yuppies mingle with gays and lesbians and transpeople. In Lincoln Park it would be pretentious and pricey, but in Boystown it's just comfortable.

The place is quiet tonight, a smattering of customers, some reading, some in quiet conversations. Plenty of open tables. People straggle in and out. As I sip my tea I find myself thinking warm, personal thoughts. How nice it was to go out with Ray. How much I look forward to dinner with him this weekend. I wonder what it will be like to have my surgery and to be making this walk with nothing between my legs. I wonder if I have any fun clients coming in tomorrow. My mind jitterbugs from one fleeting thought to another. I am enjoying this immensely. I feel alive with anticipation.

The cozy quiet overcomes my sense of time. When the waiter checks on me it's close to midnight. Much too late for a working girl who will be on her feet all day tomorrow.

Outside I pause briefly, debating what route to take. I usually take Wilton, a battered side street that goes north next to the El tracks for a long, ugly block, then turns into an alley that wends its way under the tracks. This late at night, it's creepy enough to be a set for a horror movie or a Hitchcock thriller. Its single virtue is it cuts ten minutes off my walk home.

I take a long look around, especially at the El station. Nothing moving. I opt for the shorter route. The one advantage to being a big muscular girl is that people don't mess with me.

I start down Wilton, working on my girly walk. I try to get more swing in my hips by centering my steps, like a fashion model. I hear footsteps behind me and blush. Some dog-walker got an eyeful of me trying to be girly tonight. Fodder for a water cooler story tomorrow. I glance back to see who has witnessed my folly. It's a man in a tan coat and a blue stocking cap, blue jeans and work boots.

My skin breaks out in a thousand pinpricks of panic: It's the guy. The guy who was following me before. And he's walking briskly.

Alarm bells jangle in my head. I turn quickly and pick up my pace, looking for someone, anyone, out on the street. Someone parking on the curb, maybe. A dog walker. Someone to call out to. There is no one. Like a living nightmare, there is nothing moving on the street. I glance back. He is gaining on me. It feels like he's pursuing me. I break from a fast walk to a high-heeled trot.

Mid-block, I reach an alley. As I glance into the dark, hoping to see an apartment dweller coming or going, a man darts out of the shadows. He is moving fast. Really fast. He is on me almost as quickly as I can comprehend what is happening. There is something menacing about his approach. And there's something wrong with his face. I realize with horror he is wearing a nylon stocking over his face. He means to harm me. Another step and he is on me. I shoot a straight right hand at him but it is slow and awkward, hindered by my tight-fitting coat and my teetering balance on high heels. He parries it easily. My mind clicks forward. I start to swing my left hand, thumb first, at his eye.

Before I can move my arm someone grabs me from behind and cups a hand over my mouth. I can't see him, but it has to be Tan Coat. In front of me is Bluto, a thick, brutish looking white man. The mask distorts his features, but I sense a heavy five o'clock shadow to go with his nylon-flattened nose. A nasty looking mug. This is going to get ugly.

My world goes black. One of them cups a large, gloved hand over my mouth. His arm covers my eyes. They push and drag me into the alley. My feet go out from under me. One is holding my legs, the other has my torso. They carry me like a rug, running. One sniggers quietly. Five steps. Ten. They stop. My feet hit the ground. They throw me against a wall like a rag doll. I struggle to my feet, trying to get air in my lungs so I can scream for help. Bluto grabs the zipper of my coat. I knee him hard in the balls. Tan Coat grabs me from behind. I try to resist but my heels make it impossible to get leverage. Bluto grunts and lurches back half a step, then brings an overhand right to my face. I see his eyes just before the blow lands. He wears a look of determination, but no particular emotion. Then his meaty fist lands, smashing my nose and lips. I see stars. I lose control of my legs. Tan Coat holds me up.

"Hey lift his arms up a minute," he calls to Bluto. Referring to me as a male is an intentional insult, but I have bigger problems.

Bluto lifts my arms over my head. They are like jelly. I want to resist but my body has shut down. I want to smash his windpipe with a good shot to the throat. I want to kill them both but I can't get my nervous system and my muscles to react.

As Bluto holds my arms, Tan Coat lifts the bottom of my jacket over my head, inside out. It's like a handcuff and a blindfold. They laugh. It's very funny to them. One of them throws me on something that feels like a packing crate. I land on my front, my face slapping against the flexing wood of the crate, sending more waves of pain through my body. They grab my legs at the knees and yank me backwards. When they let go, my knees and toes drop to the pavement. My torso is flat on the crate, my arms held over my head by my coat. I hear a belt buckle being loosened and one of them sniggers.

Two hands jerk my skirt up over my hips and rip down my panty hose. Something hard enters my anus. He thrusts roughly, big strokes. Pain shoots through my body. This isn't sex for the man on top. I'm being brutalized. I can feel tender skin ripping. Oh God, I think, please don't let me get AIDS! Oh God, please let this be a broomstick he is using.

The sniggers continue. When one finishes, the other mounts me. When he is done they pick me up and throw me against a wall. My head hits hard, knocking me almost senseless. Pain flares from all parts of my body. My jacket is still over my head. My skirt is on my waist. My panties are around my knees. More sniggers, joined by a high-pitched chuckle.

"Be careful who you piss off, you fucking freak," one says in a low voice. He hits me in the stomach with all his strength. I fall.

The receding sniggers tell me the two have left.

For a while all I can do is cry. I sob in terror and in anger, in wretched helplessness. I don't know how long.

Finally, I will myself to ease my jacket down, then I struggle to my feet. There are fluids running down my legs. I can smell urine and excrement. I lost control of my bowels during the rape. My anus feels swollen and it aches. My insides ache, too. My stomach feels like a broken bone. I feel pain with every movement.

I find tissues in my purse and try to clean up. Even in the dull green glow of a distant streetlight I can see that the tissue is covered with blood as well as excrement and urine. My brain dully registers the fact I see no semen. Maybe they used condoms.

I am sobbing reflexively, but I wipe the fluids off before they drip into my boots, then I lower my skirt. If I had a gun right now, I don't know if I would use it on myself or try to chase down my assailants. I am seething with anger. I'm angry with them for what they have done to me. But I'm angry with me for being such a pathetic human being. For being a victim. Part of me feels like a village idiot, a man in makeup and a skirt who just got the ass reaming he deserved for being so pathetic.

I don't have a gun. All I have is a house key, which I now put in my fist like a small knife. If those bastards try me again I will blind one of them. I swear I will.

Sobbing, I try to walk from the alley like a lady, even though I feel like human garbage. My home is four blocks and a lifetime from here. Each step hurts. The hurt is everywhere. My rectum. My ribs. My stomach. And my face, from Bluto's punch. My lips are swollen so badly I can see part of my upper lip when I look down. My nose is broken. I stop twice to see if blood is dripping from my ripped anus. It isn't, but the feeling persists.

As I walk I think. Should I report the rape? To what end? A physical exam. Official sympathy from a bureaucrat. No semen for a DNA test, not that they'd go that far anyway. What kind of description do I give? Bluto, an ugly mug in a mask, sniggers a lot. Tan Coat has a blue hat, like a million other Chicago men.

Even if I could make one of them, the grim reality of my situation is, he'd beat the rap. His word against a tranny. Who would you believe? Who would care?

Why did this happen? I wonder. It was planned. Someone waited for me at the El station. Someone else waited for me in an alley on my way home. They knew I'd be in those places after ten o'clock on a Tuesday night. They didn't pick me out of a crowd. They were waiting for me.

Why?

Be careful who you piss off you fucking freak. The attacker's words come back to me now.

And then I know. I know who called this tune. I know the miserable psychopathic mother-fucking bastard who put these thugs on me.

I will have my revenge, John Strand. I swear it.

It will be painful and bloody. I swear it.

It will be humiliating. And it will be final.

You have my word on it you animal.

* * *

IN THE END, I go to the Emergency Room and the doc there instantly deduces that I've been raped, calls in the cops, and I end up having to go through the rape drill. It's like being raped again, since there's no hope of apprehending the rapists. The female cop makes a show of sympathy, but it isn't heartfelt. She's thinking in the back of her mind that I was asking for it, a man in a mini skirt flashing cleavage, wearing a messy updo.

We all go through the motions. They pretend to care, I pretend to think they care. No, I didn't know my assailants. No, I can't identify them. They wore masks. No, I haven't broken up with anyone or stiffed a john.

It takes all night, but I get through the cop stuff and get some medical attention. The nurse regards me like an alien but tends to me. The doctor is completely indifferent. My lips are sewn up and the swelling is starting to recede, thanks to ice packs. My nose has been reset so it is straight. My rectum has been swabbed and cleaned and stitched. The good news is, no semen residue, so there's a very good chance I won't get AIDS out of this. The bad news is, I'm going to be tender and swollen there for a while, and there is a risk of infection.

At eight o'clock in the morning. I call Roger at the salon and tell him what happened, that I won't be in for a few days, maybe a week, because it will be that long before my face won't scare people. He is aghast and sympathetic. He wants to do something. Just don't fire me, I tell him. He's already doing the best thing anyone can do for me—he's thinking of me as another human being, a worthwhile member of society. Imagine that.

At ten I get a call from Cecelia. The salon had called to cancel her Thursday makeup appointment. The girl was very murky on why.

"Are you okay, Bobbi?" she asks in her no-nonsense voice. As in, don't bullshit me.

I want to say yes and get rid of her, but somehow as I try to form the words I erupt in an uncontrollable crying jag. Every time I try to talk I cry again. I manage to squeak out a "No," then I hang up. I can't talk. I'm a total mess. I am unwanted by the world I live in. I do not want to go out into it. I don't want to be seen. I can't stand the thought of being ridiculed again. Or beaten. Or raped. I don't want anyone's sympathy.

All I really want to do is kill Strand and then myself. But I won't go until I get that inhuman bastard.

* * *

ANDIVE IS THE PERFECT FOIL, he thinks, as the man describes the alley scene. A pro bono client, two-time loser with a penchant for ultra-violent sex.

He's the only one between Andive and two or three decades in a dark cell. Andive's freedom depends on his loyalty. And even if Andive tried to betray him, the man is such a scumbag his word would mean nothing in court. No DA in the state would be stupid enough to build a case around Andive's testimony.

Life always works out for the planners.

He makes Andive relate the alley scene again and again, pushing him for more details each time. Andive is embellishing a little now, he can tell. Still, it makes his dick hard when Andive describes the tranny squealing as he sticks his cock in her ass. And he likes the part about Norcross grabbing and twisting her tiny balls when they're done with her. And the hits, the deep smacking sound they made when they slugged her afterwards.

"The only real downer," says Andive, "is the place smelled like shit when we were done. She crapped all over when Norcross hit her that lick. Fuckin' disgusting queer!"

He could smell the shit, the urine, the blood. He could hear the tranny crying and mewling. It was intoxicating.

"I wish I could have been there," he thinks. "But my day will come."

* * *

MY SOLITUDE LASTS exactly twenty minutes, which is how long it takes Cecelia to get from her place to mine. I don't answer her knock, but she doesn't let that stop her. She pounds on the door and shouts my name, not caring what the neighbors think. Or anyone else for that matter.

I give up and open the door. Her hands fly to her face and her eyes get wide as saucers.

"Good Lord, Bobbi!" she exclaims. "What has happened to you?"

I hold up my hand for silence and close the door then move painfully back to my living room and lay on the couch. My butt is too sore to sit on.

"I was beaten and raped last night," I said.

"My God!" she exclaims. "Where? What happened?"

It's like going through the rape interview again. I have to hand it to Cecelia, though. She thinks of everything, even details the cops didn't have on their sheets. For twenty minutes we go through every excruciating detail. I don't want to, but Cecelia is relentless.

At one point she asks me what they smelled like.

I look at her like she's crazy. "What can you be thinking, Cecelia?"

She opens her mouth to lecture me but stops, mouth agape, looks at me, and laughs. We both laugh, she more demonstrably than I since my lips are stitched and swollen.

"Good girl," she says. "I know a little about this stuff. I know how you're feeling. Someone has tried to dehumanize you in the most humiliating way possible. It makes you feel like human waste. You want to die."

Cecelia lets her words hang in the air for a moment.

"It will pass."

I glance at her. She nods her head slightly in the affirmative, as if to say, really.

She wants me in counseling immediately. She pries Marilee's number out of me and calls her while I listen. She sets up a meeting for this afternoon. Marilee will come here. She goes to the kitchen and makes a lunch, lecturing constantly from the other room.

Have I talked to Officer Phil? No. Let's call him now. No. Why not? Because he never solves anything. We go back and forth.

"Here's the truth of the matter, Cecelia," I say when I just can't stand the topic any more. "I didn't see my attackers. I can't identify them. If you brought them in here right now with two other guys and gave me a gun I wouldn't know who to shoot."

"Well, honey," says Cecelia, "If we could get it down to four I'd just shoot them all."

We laugh again. Tranny humor. A little bit male, a little bit female.

But I'm not cheered. I'm focused. From the moment those bastards debased me, my life has taken a new direction. I will not have a life of my own until I wreak my revenge on John Strand.

As Cecelia prattles on, I tune her out to consider whether she is someone I can use as an ally in my war with Strand. For some reason, I keep thinking no. She's a good friend, devoted, fearless and all that, but for some reason I just can't let her know what I'm thinking.

When Cecelia leaves, I tell her I'd appreciate her confidence in this matter. I really don't feel like talking about it for the next two months with everyone I see.

Ten minutes after she leaves, Officer Phil stops by. A sympathy call. He read the report and feels just terrible. They're looking but I didn't really give them much to go on.

Well, no shit, Phil, I think to myself. I was busy getting my face bashed in and my ass reamed.

Have I thought of any other details? he asks.

Well, no, Officer Phil. I've been working on silly things like when I'm going to be able to work again, or when I can have a bowel movement without bleeding, or how many more times those two will get to shove me into an alley before Chicago's finest blunder onto them and, oh wow, intercede. Possibly even make an arrest or two. This I actually say. All of it.

Phil drops his gaze and nods his head in understanding. "I'm sorry, Bobbi," he says. "We all are. If you think of something—anything—let me know."

For a split second I thought about telling him about Strand, but the thought perishes in an instant. If they wouldn't investigate him in a murder, they surely wouldn't in a rape that didn't even directly involve him, not even by accusation. Plus, Phil is a very nice guy and really hot, but he's no Sherlock Holmes. And his colleagues in the department aren't as nice or as hot and they don't solve crimes against trannies either.

Officer Phil is experienced, though, and knows when to leave. He departs quickly.

I rest for another hour then my phone starts ringing—and doesn't stop for the rest of the day. At least a dozen of my friends from TransGender Alliance call to express horror and sympathy. Cecelia's confidentiality must have lasted from the time she left my door to the time her feet hit the sidewalk outside

That's why I can't enlist her help in my revenge. She would never be able to shut up about it. Plus, as I think about it, I realize that Cecelia has a conscience. For all her bravado, she doesn't break laws. For all her tough talk, she'd never have the anger or decadence to cut a man's balls off. I do. I will. This is my promise to myself. Before I kill Strand, I will cut off his balls.

Marilee arrives. She fusses over my bruised body, making ice packs for the tender places, kissing me softly on the cheek and hugging me carefully. I tell her about the attack, how it happened, what it felt like. It feels good to unload to someone who actually cares. Tears run down her face as I talk. When I stop, I can see the anger in her face. She asks if there was anything familiar about the two attackers. Did they seem to act in concert?

Good point, Marilee. That's exactly what I'm thinking. They knew I went to the monthly meeting in Oak Park, what El line I take, what stop, and how I walk home. One must have tailed me on the train, or maybe just at the station platform, then called the other guy, who was driving the van. Idly, I wonder if they had it all set up for a previous month and something came up—an untimely truck delivery in the alley, maybe, or bad weather, or a squad car coming down the Wilton as I crossed the mouth of the alley.

"How badly did they hurt you?" Marilee is asking. She doesn't mean my face.

"It hurts a lot," I answer. "They wanted to hurt me and they did. So I have a lot of bruising and ripped tissues. I bleed when I defecate and will for some time they told me. But they didn't think I'd need surgery."

She asks about AIDS and I tell her about the absence of semen.

As we talk I wonder what kind of men they were. They weren't just thugs, or tranny bashers. They were cruel men who could get aroused at the thought of raping someone they thought of as a man. It was an act of abuse. Dominance. A violent release for them. They aren't hit men or paid goons. More like kindred spirits in Strand's perverted world. Strand goes for transwomen with an ounce of eroticism and a pound of hate and loathing. His buddies are cut from the same cloth. It amazes me that they could get physically aroused in those circumstances, but I have to remember, for these kinds of people, it isn't sex. It's domination. Prison sex.

I don't mention Strand to Marilee. She wouldn't be able to handle it. She'd think it was her sin for confiding in me in the first place. And she'd never be able to live with my revenge on Strand. I'm not sure I can either, but I can't live if I let him get away with it either.

Marilee stays for two hours, spending part of her time answering the phone for me. She leaves when Emily arrives. Em brings dinner from a fine Boystown café that does French-Chinese fusion cuisine. They don't do takeout, Emily explains, but the owners are suckers for a good story and she told them mine.

Emily stays until seven, when I assure her I'm fine. Tomorrow, someone else from TGA will bring lunch, and someone else, dinner, she says. They're going to get me to the weekend then I have to come out and face the world.

"You'll have friends waiting to hold your hand," Emily says, smiling as she steps out the door. I don't let her see my tears. How is it that we humans can be so incredibly good to each other, and also so incredibly bad?

* * *

"HAVE YOU REMEMBERED anything else about your assault?" It's the rape specialist who interviewed me at the hospital three nights ago after the ER doc deduced I had been raped.

She is middle-aged, about 5-7, short hair worn in a simple one-length blunt

cut and bangs that fall nearly an inch above her eyes. Practical, but the affect is
very severe. Her face is pointy and somewhat narrow despite puffy deposits of
middle-age spread in her cheeks and jowls. She has a cop's body—sturdy, strong,
overweight. She looks tough and mean. She has no bedside manner, either.

"One guy looked like Bluto wearing a nylon stocking over his head," I
recount. "He was a white guy with Mediterranean skin. He had a dark beard
growth, a shaved head, thick hairy forearms. The other guy wore a tan trench
coat and a navy blue stocking cap. I never saw him. One of them chuckled a
lot—I think the stocking cap guy. Bluto sniggered."

I shrug. Nothing new. And the rape sergeant doesn't really care anyway. Her
voice and posture clearly convey that this is pro-forma, something she's doing
because Officer Phil is pushing the agenda. Phil observes with full interest.

The rape sergeant looks at me with barely hidden disgust, the way genetic
women who find transwomen repulsive do. I remember this look from the
initial interview. Eyes that look at me but not at my eyes. Mouth that bites out
words and casts them in my direction. A flat, bureaucratic voice, sighs implied
at the end of each phrase and sentence.

She clears her throat. "Do you prefer to be called Mr. or Ms.?"

I am wearing women's jeans, a woman's top, a woman's hairdo. I'm wearing
women's boots with 2-inch heels. I have C-cup breasts. I'm not in full makeup
because of my cuts and bruises, but even with the dab of blush and light eye
makeup I indulged in, I am more feminine in my presentation than the officer
is. She is deliberately insulting me.

"Bite me, Sergeant," I say. My voice is at a conversational level of volume,
but it cracks with anger. "You don't want to be here and I don't want you here.
Go do something else."

A flush comes to her cheeks. Her mouth tightens. She's pissed. She's
also inhibited by Phil's presence. It wouldn't be good for her to say what she's
thinking in the presence of a viable witness.

"Well," she says, haughty and defensive, "if you don't help us we can't help
you."

"Sergeant, have you ever solved a case involving the rape of a transsexual?"
I let my own hostility creep into my voice.

"We're not here to talk about me…"

I cut her off. "That's what I thought. You have the same regard for my kind
as the rapists do. You're worthless to us."

Her face goes full red. She's ready to blow and I'm ready to strike the match that will do it. Officer Phil stands and jumps between us.

"Ladies! Ladies! Let's calm down," he says. "This isn't getting us anywhere."

"It can't get us anywhere," I answer. "This nasty bitch thinks I got what I deserved, and so do all of her colleagues except maybe you!" Tears trickle down my cheeks. The tears anger me, but the rape sergeant is even angrier.

"You loudmouth pervert!" she yells back. "You make me sick. You sick fucks get all dolled up like two-dollar whores then come whining to us when some guy jumps you. You make me sick!"

She slams her file shut and leaves the room.

Phil sighs and sits down.

"You aren't helping me, Bobbi," he says.

I blot up my tears and pull out my powder to fix my makeup. "Officer Phil," I say, "Let's face it. You're the only cop on this force that gives a damn one way or another about me or any other transwoman out there. And you are a street cop, not an investigator. The people who are supposed to investigate these things think a transsexual getting raped is like a mobster getting murdered. It's a crime with a happy ending. You guys never solve transgender crimes. Not rapes. Not murders. Not theft. I appreciate what you're trying to do, but I have to tell you, this was like getting raped again. That nasty hag wanted to puke as soon as she saw me. If she was a guy she'd be a tranny basher herself.

"Let it go, Phil. You can't help me and your department won't. It's over. I've learned a lesson. Be prepared!"

"I don't like the sound of that, Bobbi" he says. "Don't be planning anything stupid."

"Like what?" I ask. "Like putting a bullet in the head of the next son of a bitch who tries to rape me? I've got news for you, honey. I don't care what the so-called law thinks. This isn't going to happen to me again. Not ever!"

I'm crying again. Perfect. A six-foot transwoman with stitches in her lips, bruising on her nose, and tear marks on her makeup. The perfect clown.

We stand in unison and I start heading for the door. Phil puts a comforting hand on my shoulder.

"I'm sorry, Bobbi," he says. "I'm sorry you were raped, and I'm sorry we don't instill more confidence in you. I'm going to do everything I can, including getting a new case officer assigned."

I nod. If I tried to talk I'd just break down in sobs. He's a nice guy and earnest, but he couldn't make a jaywalking charge stick. As for the department as a whole, well, they don't all hate us, but we're at the bottom of the pyramid of their priorities. In a city with lots of rapes and murders, the ones involving trans victims only get solved if the perpetrator is standing over the victim picking his nose when the cops arrive. He drives me back to my apartment in silence.

I'm on my own. But I knew that. I came with Phil today because I needed to get out of the apartment, needed to show my battered face in public and live with the results. What better place than a police station, where they see everything everyday anyway. Even Rape Sergeant Bitch wasn't a surprise to me. What surprised me was how little patience I had with her. And how callous I'm becoming to the opinions of people like her.

This says something about me, but I'm not sure what. Perhaps this is the assertiveness Roberta preaches. Whatever, I'm sick of being the recipient of crap from other people. I'm going to get in some licks myself.

* * *

"HOW CAN YOU LIVE like this, Bobbi?" Roger is spending part of his day off from the salon looking in on me. He brought his partner, Robert, to install a television set, complete with illegal satellite service. It's cute and considerate of them, but there's a problem.

I don't want it.

"I'm not going to support 200 channels of right-wing television stations," I explain.

"They aren't all political," Roger says. "Most of them aren't."

"There are only two kinds of stations on cable," I say. "The ones that take advantage of weak minds and turn them into right-wing Nazis, and the ones that create weak minds with bad programs and blizzards of commercials. I'd rather read and listen to the radio."

Roger and Robert glance at my pathetically beaten portable radio, then at each other. They smile. It looks like I got it from a garbage can, and I did. What the heck, it gets public radio. That's all I need.

We go back and forth. It's fun. At noon, Robert goes out to pick up some lunch for us. Roger brings me up to date on the salon news. The salon is doing well. My customers have mostly re-booked for next week with the warning that I will still have some scars to show for my ordeal. The official word is that I was mugged and beaten.

I thank Roger for that bit of discretion. Rape leaves a stain on the images of genetic women, it would be ten times worse for me.

Those who didn't rebook all took appointments with other stylists in the salon. Roger is impressed and thinks I should be too. I don't have the busiest book in the salon by a long shot, but my people obviously like the experience they have with me and the shop.

I appreciate the good news. Maybe I won't have to dip into my surgery fund after all. When I first thought I'd be out for a month because of the broken ribs, I drew up a financial plan. It was grim. I'd have to live on money I have been setting aside for my sex change operation. It hasn't been easy to accumulate this money. A little comes from my regular earnings at the salon, and the rest comes from my private customers. None of it comes in big chunks. It was depressing to realize that in addition to the physical and mental damage done by the goons, their work was also going to prolong my time in she-male limbo.

The cheeriest part of Roger's visit is his assessment of my appearance.

"You look pretty good, Bobbi," he says, after a long once-over.

I smirk, a look of disbelief on my face.

"No, really," he says. "You have some cuts and bruises that anyone would notice, but you aren't disfigured. You look like Bobbi and your injuries aren't going to put off any customers."

He is sincere, and he knows what he's talking about. I couldn't be happier if Brad Pitt had just told me I was the most beautiful girl in the world.

"I think whenever you're physically and mentally ready, you should come back to work," Roger says. "So, how are you doing physically and mentally?"

Actually, I'm doing pretty well. My ribs hurt like hell if I turn wrong or breathe too hard, but I did an updo on a mannequin this morning and found that I could move easily through the work. Just for fun, I mimed a haircut, then a set of foil highlights. Same deal. No problem.

My rectum is healing. I'm not getting blood in my stools any more, and I can sit and walk with just mild discomfort.

Mentally. Well, mentally it's more complex than that. The part of me I show to Roger is the part that is dying to get back into the salon. God how I miss doing hair. I miss the smell of the place. I miss the theater of my colleagues' sexy clothing and creative styles and getup. I miss the customers, the conversation, and the gossip. I miss helping people feel good about themselves. And I miss getting all girlied up to go to work.

Roger is delighted. We agree that I'll be in Monday morning. They have booked me for half days all week—half, mornings, the other half, afternoons and early evenings. Roger wants to know if I'm sure I can do it. I'm sure. Just as sure as I am that the person who did this to me will be punished.

And that's the other side of my mental state. I am homicidal. Not generally homicidal, just absolutely and completely focused on Strand. No matter how good I feel, no matter where I am in my transition, I will settle things with Strand. That will not change, not until the deed is done.

Robert returns as we finish our business talk. He brings sushi for all and a stereo for me. A stereo! Robert is a contractor and an electronics whiz. He does reconstructions and remodeling and he's very successful. Still, I'm speechless when he shows up with a very sophisticated sound system and sets to installing it. I try to object, but both partners shush me up. It is a spare system and if I don't like it they'll remove it but I have to give it a month.

How about that?

* * *

RAY OUTLASTS MY objections and pays me a visit a week after our cancelled date. He brings a bottle of wine, and takeout Chinese, plus several classical music CDs to run on my fancy new sound system.

About midway through Brahms and my second helping of Moo Shoo Pork, I tell him that I wasn't just beaten up, I was raped too. It just comes out. Ray is very easy to talk to. Maybe the nicest and most sympathetic man I've ever known. Kind of a male version of Marilee.

"It appears they used condoms," I tell him. "I don't have any signs of STDs, but that's no guarantee. Neither is the absence of semen. A lot of rapists don't actually orgasm, I'm told. They're just in it for the blood and meanness of it."

Ray nods sympathetically.

"I'm just telling you in case you were ever thinking of, you know..." I struggle to say it, goodness knows why. I'm certainly no blushing virgin.

He looks at me blankly for a minute, then recognition clicks in. "Oh. Oh!" he says. "Okay. Well, thanks." He's a little nonplused, stammering for words to say. "Let's not worry about that right now. Let's get you better."

Good answer. I don't want to think about sex right now and I don't want to talk about it. In fact, I think I brought it up just now to invite him to walk out the door and not come back. I'd rather get the bad news now than later. Plus, if he dumped me now I wouldn't have to worry about whether or not my libido will ever come back. I'd hate to string along a nice guy if there was no hope.

Oh, hell. Like Cecelia says, I worry too much.

* * *

NO ONE RUSHES UP to gush over me or anything on my first day back, but everyone greets me and a couple stylists give me hugs.

Roger comes out of his office to give me a paternal hug and a warm welcome. He makes a show of examining my face and pronouncing me beautiful. I'm not beautiful of course, but I'm trying to feel beautiful, in a defiant sort of way. I'm wearing a short skirt, black hose, black heels, and a low-cut black top that shows plenty of cleavage and the top of my lacy black bra. My hair is up in a loose updo. I'm wearing red nail polish and red lipstick. I'm doing my best to recreate my appearance on the night I was raped. I feel like I need to face down all the phobias that were produced by that experience. This is one. I have the right to try to look sexy if I want to. I'm not going to let the rapists take that from me, too.

My first client is a referral. She knows about me from another customer. Her original appointment had to be rescheduled because of my recovery, but she went along with it, thank goodness.

"I'm so glad you could get me in today," she says. She asks about my scrapes and bruises. I reiterate the mugging story. "I hope it's not related to your, uh…" she struggles to find the right word.

"No." I say.

She tells me how she heard about me, that she first noticed how cute her friend's cut was, then she was blown away by the color I did on her a month ago and I immediately remember who her friend must be. We talk about that as I cut her hair. This is a get-acquainted visit. She doesn't say so, but we both understand it. If she likes me and my work and the salon, she'll be back for something fancier in the future. For now, it's a trim, but the trim needs to give her a subtly different look than she had before.

Her hair is a medium-length bob, the perfect cut for a middle-aged professional woman.

The old Bobby—the male one—would have just given her a trim or he would have spent another ten minutes trying to get her to agree with his ideas for improving the cut. The trans Bobbi has learned to just do it. If it's really a good idea, ninety percent of the time the customer will be elated and will come back again, and that's twice as good as I did the other way.

As I work she asks me questions about what it's like to be a transsexual. She is polite but very curious. I change the subject after a while to find out about her. She's divorced, one child, great job, lousy social life, house in the suburbs.

Her words fuel my vision for her cut. I add layers and sculpt the front so the sides taper away to her ears. The layers give her more movement. The opened front takes years off her face and shows off her nice eyes and bone structure.

She is very happy. She lays a big tip on me and books a color appointment for a month from now. I am even happier. God it's good to be back doing hair! And what a wonderful first client.

The morning goes well. I have only thirty minutes open from nine to two p.m.

My last client is a character test. I've been curious all morning to see how this is going to go. She's the same lady who flew off the handle the first day I worked as a woman. *"My God, Bobbi! You have boobs!"* I'll never forget her saying that, or how stupid I felt.

I always knew you were light in the loafers, but this! This!

Now I can't wait to find out why she came back.

I ask the assistant to seat her for me so I can sneak a quick trip to the bathroom. When I come back I come around the chair in front of her to say hello and shake hands. She smiles as I do so, and her eyes pass over all of me, from my teased, red-streaked permed hair to my swollen cleavage to my mini-skirted legs to my sexy heels.

"Very cute, Bobbi" she says after her visual tour of my body. "You look very cute. I'm still having a hard time with this, but I have to hand it to you, you do a lot with what you've got, honey."

I take this to mean that she still views me as a freak, but an acceptable one, not a monster. It's a start. Later, she says she came back because no one can do her hair the way I do.

Well, she's a nasty, vulgar, opinionated jerk, but she's my jerk.

* * *

PEOPLE ARE STARING AT ME. They look away when my gaze turns in their direction, but no matter where I turn, some of the people in this crowded gym are looking at me.

I feel like a hippopotamus in a tutu.

My doctor suggested that I start working out with a personal trainer who does physical therapy, partly just to get my body working again after the trauma of being raped and beaten, and partly for my general health.

"Bobbi," he said, "you're middle aged, you're changing genders. You've lost muscle mass and you don't have much tone. You're in a business that's hard on the body—carpal tunnel, bad backs, bad knees, bad hips, you name it. You need to learn some exercises for toning and stretching. You should do some weight lifting, too, to strengthen your frame and your bones. It will help your recovery, and it will help you for the rest of your life."

I fought it. Maybe I could find a book and work out at home? No. Maybe I could get in-home instruction? Yeah, an hour for what I make in a day. Maybe I could put it off until after my transition. I could, but it would be stupid.

So here I am in a crowded North Side gym that also serves as a meat market for the twenty- and thirty-something straight crowd. It's a Thursday lunch hour slot. Most of the people in the gym are young professionals, getting in a mid-day workout and looking for social prospects. Many of them are attractive people, in good shape and working to stay that way. The aerobics area is evenly split between men and women. The free weights and machines are predominately male populated and I sense that most of them are straight.

I don't think many of them have ever seen a transsexual before. Not from the way they variously glance and stare at me.

Kevin, my trainer, demands that I ignore the others. "We have work to do," he tells me, over and over again.

I try to focus on his instruction and the exercises, but it's hard. I am self conscious to the point that I'm on the verge of a nervous breakdown. And it didn't just start when I came in the gym. I spent hours thinking about what I would wear and shopping for the outfit—it's just a black tank top, sport bra and gray sweat pants—then about where I would change. No way could I shower in a public place! The thought of the stir I would create in the women's shower room was the stuff of nightmares for me. How could I get in the session and still get to work in a timely manner?

But in the end I am more serious about my health than I am about my inhibitions, and I call Kevin. He at least has worked with a couple other transsexuals and wasn't the least bit hesitant about taking me as a client. He was also familiar with the body changes we go through and had an exercise regimen that worked pretty well, he said.

The big drawback was that he only works out of one gym in the city, a north Loop emporium that caters to corporate workers during the day and upwardly mobile in-crowders at night. Definitely not a tranny magnet.

We start with some warm ups. A few minutes on the treadmill, light stretching, a few minutes of modified step-aerobics. My breasts seem to jiggle like melons. This is completely irrational—I'm not that big to begin with, and I'm wearing a firm sports bra. Really, it would be hard for anyone to tell I'm a woman except for my hair and makeup.

But I feel conspicuous about everything. I fear that all the physical movements will cause my penis and scrotum to shift outward, giving me a male bulge—and giving my many onlookers something to laugh about. This is almost as irrational as my jiggling breasts fear; my male organ has shrunk so much from my months of hormones it couldn't create a noticeable bulge unless it was fully erect. Still, like an amputee who senses the presence of a limb that's no longer there, my tiny she-male penis still feels like Bob's member as I exercise.

My fears and inhibitions make me focus all the harder on Kevin's instruction. My form is perfect on everything. Stretching. Lunges. Curls. Presses. I'm working light weights—10, 12, 15 pound dumbbells, lots of reps, short breaks between sets. Abs, back, torso. Balance. Aerobics. Finish with stretches.

I'm grateful it was only a forty-five-minute session. A full hour would have killed me.

Kevin finishes by taking me through the routine verbally. I need to do this at least three times a week, he says. I should do aerobics once or twice a week, too, he says, but not until the soreness is gone from my ribs. He recommends several classes.

"Come on, Kevin," I say. "What do you think is going to happen when I walk into a women's aerobic class?"

"What do you think is going to happen?" he asks.

"I think the instructor is going to gag and half the class is going to leave," I say. "This is Yuppyville here. Home of white bread and Republicanism."

"You're a wuss, Bobbi," he says. "When you come to the gym, it's all about you. What you can do for yourself. You don't look around to see who's watching. You get to work and do what needs to be done. No one will mess with you. The classes are for anyone and everyone. Men, women. Gay, straight. We have people who are a hundred pounds overweight in those classes. We've had amputees and cripples. How do you think those people feel when they start? But nobody hassles them. Mostly the other people in the gym are impressed that they're taking care of themselves.

"This isn't about what other people think, Bobbi. It's about what you DO. What you do for yourself."

Good pep talk. We make an appointment for the same time next week. I take out a three month membership, promising myself I will come Saturday after work and Tuesday before work for stretching and weights, and Monday for aerobics. Monday will be the acid test because I'll have to come in the evening after work. Rush hour in the meat market.

* * *

MY AFTERNOON HAS BEEN slow since the usual lunch-time rush. I have cleaned all my tools and gone over my workstation like a cleaning machine. Everything sparkles, even the base of my chair. The whole salon is quiet. Just one customer in a chair, and two stylists in back.

Roger calls me into his office. Our supplier rep is there, the one who sells us our main line of color and hair care products. He's an okay guy. Short, stocky build, fortyish, good-looking guy. He has always been nice enough to me, even though he works hard at projecting himself as a straight guy. I was openly gay when we met and I think he was trying to make sure I didn't mistake him for a kindred spirit. I've only seen him a couple times since I started transitioning and those were just in passing. Not even enough time to complain about the weather.

"Bobbi, you know Steve," Roger says as I enter the office. It's a tiny space with just enough room for two chairs on the other side of Roger's desk. Steve stands as I walk in and holds out a hand.

"Hi, Bobbi." He smiles a salesman's smile.

I return the greeting and shake his hand. He glances at my hand and wrist for a minute. I'm wearing several rings on that hand and a black leather wrist band studded with silver ornaments. It goes with my black jeans and black top.

"You're certainly going through a lot of changes these days, aren't you," he says as we all sit down. In my peripheral vision I notice that he looks down my top as I bend into my chair. I wonder what he thought about what he saw. I'm not wearing a bra today.

"Yes," I say, smiling. "Big changes. Thanks for noticing."

I don't know why I said that last part, but I'm glad I did. You can be too serious about this stuff.

He nods and smiles.

Roger picks up a brochure on his desk and clears his throat. "Bobbi, Steve was just telling me that SuperGlam is looking for some local hairdressers to work their exhibit at the hair show next month. They want a colorist and an up-do artist, among others. They'll work with SuperGlam's platform artists doing three shows a day. I nominated you."

I'm speechless for a second. My boss has just told me I'm his best hairdresser, in so many words. This is a very big deal. Plus, the SuperGlam platform shows at the Chicago Beauty Show are high theater. Everyone goes to them, partly for their sheer theatricality, and partly because SuperGlam is on the leading edge of new styles and techniques.

"Thank you," I finally blurt out.

"Would you like to audition with them next Wednesday?" Steve asks. "It's in the morning. They'll have models there and you'll be asked to do a color and an updo. You'll need to bring your tools, but they'll supply everything else."

Obviously, they've been talking about this. Wednesdays I come in at noon. No conflict. No lost billing time. No rescheduling of clients.

"I'd love to," I say. It's not something I have to think about. I'd reschedule the First Lady to get a shot at doing platform work at the Chicago Beauty Show.

The audition is in a suburban salon near a commuter train station. I don't get compensated for auditioning, but if they pick me I get a nice daily fee and lots of digital photos and film clips showing me working on the SuperGlam stage. That's gold in my business. The more we talk, the more enthusiastic I get.

"Okay, any questions?" Steve asks, closing the meeting.

"Well, just the obvious one, I guess," I say. "Do you think they'd really consider a transsexual for this gig?"

"Yes I do," he says. "If you're good enough, they'll pick you. Come on, Bobbi! It's a hair show, not a football game. You'd add to the atmosphere."

I can see his point. Some of the platform work at beauty shows is very far out—dos in geometric shapes that rise several feet above the model's head, backcombing demos that create huge beehives of hair, colors that blow your eyeballs out of their sockets. And in the crowd you see wild clothes, wild hair, wild colors, and gay partners holding hands. It's civilized, but wild.

So yeah. There are times when being a colorful freak can work for you.

* * *

THIS IS MY SECOND SOLO workout in the gym. I have an audience, but it's very small and I don't think they find me very interesting. I'm not wearing makeup and I have my hair in a ponytail. I'm wearing all gray sweats and between my baggy T-shirt and tight athletic bra, I look androgynous and boring.

I do ten minutes of light aerobics, ten minutes of stretching, twenty minutes of weights, and ten minutes of more intense aerobics. I finish by walking on the little track on the perimeter of the gym to cool down for five minutes, then my final stretching.

While I'm doing my last stretching sequence, I notice a man standing at the edge of the stretching area, watching me. He seems brutishly masculine, almost as wide as he is tall, hairy, super thick musculature, a mean looking fat face with squinty eyes. My worst nightmare is about to happen. I brace for the humiliation as I attempt to exit the stretching area. He steps toward me. He is about 5-9, maybe 5-10. He has to weigh at least 250 pounds. He looks like an Olympic weightlifter. "Are you Bobbi?" he asks. He sounds and looks like an Ernest Borgnine on steroids.

I could be cagey, but that would just forestall the inevitable. "Yes," I reply. I focus on his thin, nasty lips, waiting for the sneer to form, and the vile words to follow.

He steps forward and extends his hand. "Thomas," he says.

I stare at his hand, then his face. Then it dawns on me, he's introducing himself. I reach out with my right hand somewhat tenuously. "Bobbi," I say. His hand feels like a huge slab of beef. I'm sure my effete, fingertip handshake inspires disgust in him, but really, even if I still remembered how to do a male handshake I wouldn't have been able to get much squeeze into his big, hard hand.

"Your trainer, Kevin, is a friend of mine. He said you were worried about getting hassled here," Thomas says. I nod. I can't think of anything to say.

"Well, this is a pretty friendly gym," he says. "I don't think you'll have any problems. But if you do, let me know. I'll take care of it."

I try to think of what to say. Of all the possible things that might have happened when this large, ogre-like man presented himself, this is the one I would never have guessed.

"Thank you," I finally utter. Before I can stop myself, I add, "That is so sweet!"

Well, it is sweet, but I feel like I just praised a horse for its cologne. I kick myself for being so femme. This can only offend a macho guy like Thomas. But he breaks into a wide smile.

"I'm not as nasty as I look," he says.

Point taken. Of all the people who should know better than to judge someone by their looks, I should be a leader in the field.

"You don't look nasty," I lie. "You look…strong."

"Good one!" he says. "If you'd called me handsome I would have never trusted anything else you said." He beams for a minute. "So, what do you do when you aren't pumping iron?" he asks.

"I'm your classic gay hairdresser," I say. "Except instead of being gay I'm trans." He doesn't seem to mind my effete diction and I'm feeling more comfortable talking to him.

"How about you?" I ask.

"Believe it or not, I'm an RN. A registered nurse," he clarifies.

I'm sure I gape, just like those disbelieving souls who gawk at me. "I'll bet they love you in the psych ward," I say, wishing immediately that I hadn't. It's just that I once dated a nurse in my Bob days and she had terrifying tales to tell of her stint in a psych hospital. Strength might save lives there.

"That's there for me any time," Thomas says. "But my heart is more in emergency care, or surgical recovery. I actually did children for awhile, but it was too heartbreaking."

The vision of this massive, Neanderthal-like man crying over a suffering child plays all over the movie screen in my mind. First, unimaginable, then, unimaginably touching. We chat like old friends. I have to cut it short to get to work.

"I wish you had longer hair," I say. "I'd love to get you in my chair so we can keep talking."

"We should have coffee some time," he says. I agree. He gives me his gym schedule, a widely variable sequence of morning, noon and evening sessions—the curse of the shift worker. I will adjust my schedule so my workouts coincide with his.

* * *

IT'S HARD TO SAY HOW my audition is going.

Platform gigs demand that you work fast, lightning fast, with great technical proficiency and theatrical flair. A lot of hairdressers can do the speed and technical proficiency, but not so many have stage presence or the ability to produce the over-the-top glam styles that look good on stage.

Those qualities aren't absolutely necessary for the colorist role I'm auditioning for. Whoever they pick will do the work while the big name star stylist—the one people pay to see—does the talk. Still, they use these roles to develop new platform artists. It's necessary. Platform artists tend to burn out after awhile. It's brutally hard work—high pressure, time constrained, and you work in front of sophisticated audiences that see every tiny misstep you make. Plus, most of them work full time as hairdressers in a salon on top of their show gigs. One of my favorite showmen told me he worked a hundred hours in weeks when he had shows because he still ran a full book at home.

Why do they do it? Really, I think most of them just love doing hair, like all of us, and they love having an audience. But the practical reason is, you build a fantastic reputation. Depending on their home market, top-rated platform artists might get $100 or maybe even $200 for the same haircut for which I charge $60.

My color exercise goes pretty well. They give me a unique foiling pattern to follow, and ten minutes to do it. The trick is to memorize the pattern and don't stop to look at it after you start. If you do, you won't come close to ten minutes. You end up using the diagram as a crutch, stopping constantly to refer to it. I tried to memorize it as if it's a piece of art, with the foils like chevrons used to create a geometric design on the head. When I transfer the design to the model's head, I do it artistically, adapting it.

I finish in just under eleven minutes—good enough, since we all know I'll get faster when I get more familiar with the pattern. My color coverage appears perfect to me—no runs or bleeds on uncolored hair, no uncolored splotches on the colored hair, no big gaps at the roots. The pattern looks right and the color falls beautifully. If that wasn't the pattern, it should have been.

They don't tell me how I did and I don't see anyone else's work.

The updo exercise is much more challenging. At my station are two SuperGlam hair care products that I am to use to create a large, sexy updo in thirty minutes. They want to see lots of backcombing for volume and a style with motion and class.

Well, motion and class are very much subject to personal taste, and when it comes to hair, what's beautiful to some is butt ugly to others. So you just have to be who you are and do what you believe in.

My model has shoulder-length, light brown hair with a few highlights in it. The hair is fine textured with just the tiniest hint of wave and there's a lot of it. The texture is a bitch to work with for a big-hair up-do. It will resist holding the backcombing, it will take forever to curl with a hot iron and it won't hold up very long.

As I regard my model and think over the different updo designs I've used, I keep coming back to the bridal updo I did in January for my Pakistani-American client. When they give me the start signal, I go for it.

I cut corners on time in my curling iron work by focusing on the first few inches of the hair; the rest just gets loose curling. Then I section out the pieces for a two-strand braid and alternately tease and spray them until they rise like curved horns from the model's head. I do not spare the hair spray. I use it like so much cement, to lock in the teasing. Her comb-out is going to take a long time and a lot of care.

After I do the sectioning and teasing I go back over her head, carefully brushing smooth the outer surface of each section and arc it into the braid.

It isn't really a braid. The model's hair is too short to braid when it's teased like this. So I pin the tip of each strand in place. I'm done in twenty-eight minutes and use the last two minutes just to primp and spray and fuss over the geometry of the do.

I don't know what the judges think, but I think it's so sexy I can hardly breathe. God, how I'd love to get an updo like this myself for a night on the town, maybe in a slinky black dress and three-inch heels.

Just like in the color audition, they tell me thanks, we'll call you, and I'm out the door. I have no idea what they really think, or if they'll call at all.

Well, that's show biz.

* * *

March

T.S. ELIOT CALLED April the cruelest month, I guess because of its variability wherever he was living when he wrote that. That was one of the few things old T.S. wrote that I understand, and I disagree with it.

In Chicago, March is the cruelest month. It comes in like the proverbial lion and goes out the same way. The only lamb in our March is served hot in an upscale Greek restaurant. March is the part of a Chicago winter where the rain is colder than the snow, when howling winds make ambient temperatures academic, when any given day can bring any kind of weather—or all kinds.

My work with Kevin has made me a fitness nut so I walk to and from work even in this crappy weather. I walk briskly in athletic shoes and carry my glam shoes in a shoulder bag that doubles as a purse.

I'm dodging puddles on my way to the salon, wrapped in a trenchcoat over a hooded sweatshirt. My hair is down in scraggly curls, still wet from the shower, so I wear the hood over it. It turns out the women's locker room at my gym has private shower stalls, so my lack of perfect female body parts goes unnoticed. Which removes one phobia from my list, even though there are many more to go.

When I get to the salon, I hurry to the employee bathroom. I say good morning to everyone I see. They return the greeting. Most do it with a smile. The two ladies who find me disgusting don't go so far as to smile, but one nods and the other emits a non-committal "morning" to me. This is all fine with me. I'm really happy here again. My colleagues don't love me but they don't dislike me either, except for maybe the two puritans. What I get from all of them, including the puritans, is a sort of tacit acceptance. I'm just Bobbi, a hairdresser. If I need help, they'll provide it. If they need my help, they'll ask for it.

My role in the little personal conversations has diminished somewhat since I began openly transitioning. Not because they tune me out, but because I don't have much to contribute. When we talk about boyfriends and girlfriends, husbands and wives, children, parents, relatives, I can only listen. I'm not married, I don't have a lover, and my family disowned me long ago. So I ask a few questions and do a lot of listening.

I have mentioned my dates with Ray a few times. This seems like safe ground since it's not a sexual relationship. I don't share with them any personal stuff, just how nice the concert was, or the movie, or the restaurant. Only my shrink Roberta and my friend and shrink Marilee know what I think and what I feel. And even they don't know everything.

What they do know is, my body is healing rapidly. I don't know if I'll ever become a blithe spirit in this world. But I feel good and I enjoy my life. I still have nightmares about the rape, and sometimes about my "date" with Strand. And I have nightmares that are based on those experiences but move off in fictional directions. In some, I am killed or just brutalized. Bones are broken. Foreign objects shoved up my vagina or my rectum. In others, I do the beating and killing. When I speak of my dreams to Roberta and Marilee, I share the emotions, but I never identify Strand. That is my secret.

These dreams are all troubling, even the ones in which I have my revenge. I don't sleep well. But my body and mind seem to have adjusted. I have lots of energy during the day. I get off on doing hair. I usually have a fun night or two each week with friends. I'm back to full time at work and my billings are decent. I have quite a few new clients coming in. I hope to be back to my peak by summer.

I've even shared with both Roberta and Marilee that I'm getting really horny again. For a long time after the rape, I just couldn't think about sex. It's not that I associated sex with rape. I just wasn't interested.

That's changing. I even dream about sex some nights now. I still have the nightmares too, but I also dream about sex. It isn't Jane Austen material. It's sex, not love. But it's fun, not mean. Mostly it's with men, but sometimes with women. And I am always a woman.

Roberta thinks this last point is important. She thinks I'm beginning to accept myself as a woman now, and as I progress I will be much less self-conscious about how others see me. I wish I could be as certain. Those doubts still nag at me almost everywhere I go.

* * *

MARILEE AND I ARE IN her home office, door closed. We're friends, but this is a counseling session, full force.

It started out as just coffee talk between two girlfriends. I told her about the hair show audition and my new workout schedule and a little gossip from the salon. She told me about a couple of new clients—no names, of course—and a romantic weekend with hubby. She asked about my love life, and I told her everything is still on hold until I transition, or decide not to.

"You still have doubts, then?" she asked.

"I still have options, more like," I said. "I think of it as a certainty. I will be scheduling the surgery as soon as Roberta gives me the go-ahead. I think of myself as a woman. I dream of myself as a woman. I love my body. I love my clothes. But you know, until it's actually done, I have the option of backing out."

We spar over this for a while. My point is simply that lots of girls back out at the end. To make the final journey to womanhood, you have to be castrated, then the surgeon crafts a vagina for you from the spare parts. It amazed me the first time I met a transwoman who just couldn't do that. She lived successfully as a woman, preferred life as a woman, but just couldn't take the final step. As it happens, she has plenty of company. Some girls can't face castration, some can't afford it, some just don't need to go that far to achieve an inner peace.

"Are you hedging because you have issues with the rape?" she asked. That put her in full shrink mode. I am an unwilling patient, but I love her and I don't want to offend her. I try to brush the issue aside. No, the rape didn't change my gender identity. I was raped as a man, after all, or a she-male at best, I point out.

"Bobbi," she says, "when you think about the rape now, what do you think?"

I look at her, confused. "I remember it. I remember how menacing they were, how brutal. I remember getting hit and feeling blood and swelling. I remember having my skirt lifted and having them shove their cocks in my ass. I remember being left in a puddle of blood and the stink of my own shit to die in an alley. Is that what you mean? Did you think it would go away?"

"No," she says. "I wanted to make sure you are still dealing with it."

"Dealing with it?" I echo. "If I could find those two goons I could deal with it. Since I can't, I just have to suck eggs."

"What would you do if you found the two rapists?" she asks.

Talking about the rape has tapped a rage deep inside me. Now it is intruding on my most precious friendship, causing my friend for the first time to become my shrink. The thought of that makes me even madder. I know I should censor my response, but I don't.

"If I could find the people responsible for my rape and beating I would find a way to kill them. Very slowly. I would make sure they were still alive when I cut off their penises, and still alive later when I cut off their balls."

"You have a lot of anger, Bobbi."

I make an exacerbated face, like a teenager. "Marilee, I was raped! Does anyone just walk away from that with no anger?"

"Of course not," she says, gently. "Have you thought about castrating them before?"

"Pretty much every time I think about the incident," I answer.

She brushes an imaginary speck of dust off her lap. "How do you feel about other men?" she asks. "Do you want to castrate them too?"

"Of course not," I answer.

We go into what I think of as a shrink cycle. She presses me on the issue. Am I abstaining from sex because men and/or male organs disgust me? No. Do I fantasize about sex with men? Yes. Do I like it? Yes. What do I see in my fantasies? I try to pass off romance-novel generalizations, but she pushes me to be graphic. When I finally relent, I hold nothing back. I know my fantasies are different than a genetic woman's fantasies. Mine are the product of both male and female urges. My sex dreams are often raunchy. I describe them in a non-stop monologue, like a rebellious adolescent. Go ahead, hate me, I'm thinking. I tell her that my sex dreams include lovemaking with other women. Angry as I am, I hope she doesn't ask me who the women are. I'm not sure if I can lie right now, but if I tell the truth I fear I'll lose a friend and a shrink in the same breath.

She doesn't. She smiles. "Good. I'm glad you still have lustful feelings," she says. "That's important, and it's a good thing."

She allows a moment of silence to hang in the air.

"The next step is forgiveness," she says.

I look at her with incredulity. "You must be kidding," I say. "I would never forgive those monsters for what they did. I can't imagine that anyone would."

"Of course not," she says. She smiles her loving mom smile at me. "I'm talking more about forgiving life for insulting you so personally and so violently. Some people let experiences like this define their lives. They never recover. Every day from that point on, they are the person who got raped in the winter of Oh-nine. They never go back to being Susie, the homemaker, or Ellen, the violinist, or whatever."

"But they must go back to their jobs," I respond.

"They do, but Susie doesn't think of herself as a homemaker any more, she thinks of herself as Susie the homemaker who was raped and had her life ruined by the experience," Marilee says. "My point is that you have a choice. You can acknowledge traumatic events in your life and keep on living, or you can let those events dictate how you live your life and how you feel about life."

She waits for me to respond. "I understand the words," I say finally, "but I'm not sure I get what you mean."

Marilee stands and walks to her bookshelf. She selects a book and hands it to me. It's *The Count of Monte Cristo.* "Have you read it?" she asks.

"Yes," I answer. "In high school. And I saw the Richard Chamberlain movie back in the eighties."

"What's the storyline?"

I give her a stream of conscience answer. An innocent man betrayed. Lost years in prison. Escape, great wealth, revenge. It is a classic story of revenge, I summarize.

"Is it?" Marilee asks.

"Of course it is," I answer. "He destroys the villains who took so much from him."

"Indeed," says Marilee, "But what did that cost him?"

The answer hits hard. He loses his second chance with the love of his life by failing to extend mercy to her husband. I nod to Marilee, tears forming in my eyes.

"Hate is destructive," she says.

I nod again, a chilling thought passing through my mind: if I knew who my rapists were, I would stop at nothing to take my revenge. Even understanding the Count's tragedy, I would repeat it. Such is the power of hate.

* * *

WHAT A STRANGE DAY this has been.

It started with a morning phone call from Ray.

"Is everything okay?" I asked.

"Oh yeah," he said. "I just need to talk to you about something."

I asked if we could meet after work, and we began dancing around each other's schedules. Finally he asked if he could just stop by in half an hour. I agreed.

When he arrived I was still undressed. I threw on a robe and answered the door. We exchanged greetings and I seated him in the living room while I ran into the bedroom and put on clothes. We talked through the door. Business was good for both of us. The weather was crappy. When I finished dressing I sat him next to my makeup table and started working on the war paint.

"So, what brings you to my boudoir?" I asked.

He paused. I already knew what was coming. "Well, I need to let you know about something that's going on in my life," he said. "We've gotten pretty close and I've had a great time with you…" He stopped, looking for words.

"But…" I said, helping him out. I know what's coming.

He smiled thankfully and nodded. "But, well, with all the stuff my ex and I have been through since our daughter came out…well, Bobbi, she asked me if we could try again and I didn't have the heart to say no."

"I'm so glad for you," I said. "Ray, I hope it works out. You are a very wonderful man and you deserve all the best. Thank you for being so considerate of me."

He didn't understand the last part, but in my world, guys don't do this business face-to-face. The good guys call you, but mostly the guy just disappears.

We chatted for a few more minutes before he left. I would still be his hairdresser. He would recommend me to his wife and his daughter, too.

I was mildly disappointed. I was definitely interested in Ray, but we had done a good job of keeping the relationship on a friendly level, so the letdown wasn't like stepping off a cliff.

My spirits were buoyed when I got a call on my break from the SuperGlam people to tell me I am on their show team. I'll be doing an updo in one stage presentation and doing updo demos in their exhibit. I was thrilled and scared at the same time. It suddenly hit me that if something goes wrong, the fact that I am a large, ugly transsexual trying to look like a woman is going to magnify it.

Now I'm sitting here in a coffee shop across the street from the Gender Alliance meeting place. Cecelia is wailing at Officer Phil who is making a courtesy call on the Alliance tonight. The poor guy arrived early and ducked into this place for a quick coffee—and encountered us.

Cecelia is seething about the lack of police protection for the trans community. Her first words to Phil after he sat down in our booth were a demand for an update on the thugs who raped me. Phil told her, nicely I thought, that they had no leads. It was true and Cecelia already knew that, but she is in a venting mood, and vent she does.

"Let's see," says Cecelia. "There was the girl beaten up in back of the Baton a year ago. There was the murder of Mandy last May. We had cars vandalized at the Alliance meeting in December, and two animals beat and raped Bobbi in February. What do these things have in common? They all involve crimes against transgendered people in Chicago and none of them have been solved.

"What does that tell us, Phil?" Cecelia asks. It's a rhetorical question. She doesn't even pause for air. "It tells us that it's open season on us in Chicago. That the Chicago PD doesn't give a damn about the trans community. What do we need to do to survive, Phil? Do we need to form our own vigilante committee?"

Real concern shows on Phil's face. He tries to respond but Cecelia is on a roll. She's also getting loud. Many of the patrons of the place are now watching us.

"We're not going to just wait to be raped and beaten and killed, you know," Cecelia says. "Tell your superiors, if the cops don't start protecting us, we're going to protect ourselves."

She repeats this point several times, along with the history of unsolved crimes against trans people. When she finally stops, Phil is statesmanlike.

"We clear the same percentage of crimes against the trans community as we do any other group," he says. "The fact is, the unsolved cases are just like Bobbi's. No obvious suspects. No identifications, not even good descriptions of the assailant."

Cecelia is unusually belligerent tonight, even for her. She snaps back, "I know for a fact your investigators heard from several people that Mandy was doing rough sex trysts with John Strand. I know for a fact that your investigators got chapter and verse about what a mean motherfucker he is. So where's the indictment? Nowhere, that's where. He's too powerful. No investigation. No charges. It was just a tranny, so who really cares in the Chicago PD?"

Phil's face flushes. It's the first time I've seen him show any sign of anger. "You're wrong, Cecelia," he says. "You're very, very wrong. We investigated every lead, turned over every stone. I'm not going to get into the specifics of the case with you, but we've done everything possible to find the murderer. So far, we don't have a case against anyone, but it's still an open investigation."

Cecelia sneers. The waitress comes by and asks if we want anything else. It breaks the tension somewhat. I announce that it's time to get to the meeting and we prepare to leave.

Part of me sympathizes with Officer Phil. It's true. The unsolved crimes against trans people tend to be cases like mine. The thug or thugs prey on a transgendered person who is alone somewhere. No witnesses. They wear masks. No descriptions.

But part of me says Cecelia is dead right, at least about Mandy and Strand. It feels like the law enforcement protects the rich and powerful and just doesn't do squat for the weak and vulnerable.

When I think of that, I don't get as agitated as Cecelia. I don't feel the urge to rant and rave and beat on the table. But when I think of Strand getting away with murder, the memory of his unblinking shark eyes comes clearly into focus, and I can feel him grab my breast and squeeze, and I see his eyes take pleasure in my pain and I can see his disgust at my tears. And that makes me seethe! But unlike Cecelia, I'm not interested in venting. I don't want to talk about it. I want to see the expression in those dead eyes when his nose is crushed, his kneecaps broken, his manhood cut off. I want to run a sharp knife from his sternum to his crotch and pull his intestines out and watch him watch wolves eat them.

As I see these things happening to Strand in my imagination, I feel a sense of...what? Shame? Disappointment in myself? Shock at my own violence? Marilee is right, I know it. Hate is corrosive. I need to get over this to get on with my life. But I don't see how I can get on with my life until I settle up with Strand. Until then, he owns me. He's in every view I have of my self-worth.

He kills Mandy. He has me raped. Then he walks free with not so much as an interview with the cops. He's revered by politicians and newspaper editors and police brass. He can do anything he wants. Me, I'm just a freak. He can have me removed from this earth tomorrow and get away with it. Oh, Cecelia will rant, and Officer Phil will wring his hands, and a few of my friends will mourn my passing, but Strand will still walk tall with the big shots in the St. Patrick's Day parade. He'll still make millions and live the good life. Killing me is just swatting a fly. There is no law protecting transsexuals from Strand.

Which simply means, we have to do it ourselves. Well, actually, I have to do it myself. I keep coming back to that.

* * *

I AM SWEATING LIKE A PIG. Swatches of hair have pulled free from my ponytail and flop in sopping strands around my head. My baggy T-shirt is completely soaked and clings to my body like a stinking second skin, belying my androgynous cover by graphically outlining my cleavage.

Ordinarily, I'd be self conscious about this. But at this moment I couldn't care less. I am kicking and punching a bag held by my kickboxing partner. I have no idea who he is or what he looks like. We exchanged names a while ago, but as soon as I started attacking, all I could see was Strand. I have been attacking in a savage rage at every opportunity since then. When the instructor whistles for us to stop, I do. But I only half listen to him while the other half of me recalls what it felt like to connect with various parts of Strand's body.

I get off a strong kick, follow with a hard jab then plow my shoulder into the bag knocking my partner off balance. I kick viciously and he topples over. In my fighting rage I want to continue the attack, but check myself just in time. I realize where I am and that the young man scrambling angrily to his feet isn't Strand. The instructor's whistle blows, but most of the students have already stopped to stare at me.

"Everything okay over there?" the instructor asks. There is tension in the air.

"My fault. I'm sorry," I say. "I got carried away." I face my partner. "Really, I'm really sorry. Please don't hold it against me," I say. He accepts my outstretched hand, but his face says he has no interest in being my kickboxing partner. I can't blame him. Bad enough he got knocked on his butt, but by a fairy, to boot. I would have had a hard time with that back in my Bob days, too.

After class, Thomas approaches with a small grin on his face. "Bobbi, Bobbi, you are a killer out there, girl!"

I sweep a glob of hair from my eye and try to smile. Thomas has no idea how true his observation is.

As I prepare to leave, the instructor issues a few innocuous words of counsel, as in, don't beat the crap out of other students, okay? I nod. He glances at my chest as he leaves. He couldn't help himself and he tries not to be obvious about it. It's okay. It's a lot for someone outside the trans community to take in.

We go to Thomas' place and pick up Chinese food on the way. It's just a few blocks from the gym and I can use his shower. My maidenhood will be safe. Thomas is gay and lives with his lover and one other roommate.

We have his place to ourselves. His partner is working tonight and the other roommate is out on the town. After my shower I don Thomas' bathrobe, wrap my hair in a towel and join him for dinner. We make small talk as we eat. He tells me I look very feminine in my bath garb. He bets I have lots of male suitors. I tell him about my ban on sex, and why. He seems genuinely surprised. 'Just say no' isn't a widely practiced policy in our little neck of the woods.

Thomas serves beer with our dinner. Not my beverage of choice, but I take one to be polite and for some reason it tastes delicious. I have another. Perhaps because of my dehydrated condition, I feel a buzz and a tingle. Good thing Thomas is gay, I think, I'm starting to find him attractive. Even though he looks mean and tough, he is one of the nicest, gentlest people I know. Instinctively, I trust him completely.

"So what was the deal with the kicking dummy today?" he asks. "You looked like you wanted to do someone in."

I try to dodge the question. "I was just working out some anger I have toward someone I used to know," I say.

Thomas doesn't let me off the hook. He gestures "come on" with his hands and says, "Let's hear it. Boyfriend did you bad?"

"Not a boyfriend," I say. "And it was worse than bad."

"Is this where your cuts came from?"

I nod yes. I'm healed now, but there are other kinds of scars.

"I'd like you to tell me about it, Bobbi," he says. "I'm not just being nosy. I care about stuff like this."

"Why?" I ask. I'm starting to tear up just thinking about what happened to me.

Thomas smiles and holds up a finger. "Uh-uh-uh," he says, "I'll tell you mine if you'll tell me yours."

I dab my eyes with a tissue. "Okay, but you don't get to see my vagina."

He laughs. He tells the story of his drunken father beating him and his mother. When he got drunk. When he got mad. Whenever he felt like it. Thomas grew up with fear and loathing for his father and doubts about his own worth. He wet his bed well into junior high. And with the arrival of puberty, he became aware of his lust for other males, another thing to be ashamed of.

He channeled his fear and anger into sports—wrestling, boxing, and finally weight lifting. It was a good cover for a boy who wanted to kiss other boys. Even if someone had figured him out as queer, by the age of sixteen he was too tough and strong to mess with.

His father seemed to sense this and backed off on the abuse when Thomas was around. Until that fateful day when the old man found one of Thomas' books about homosexuality in the house. The old man began taunting him, called him a pussy and cocksucker, screamed insults at him. Then he made the mistake of pushing him. Thomas was just a high school junior, but he finally stood up to his father. He beat him bloody in a short, one-sided fight that was a mismatch from the start. When it was over, Thomas sent the old man on his way, never to be seen or heard from again. He cared for his mother until she died a few years ago. She was an ineffectual, sad creature who never acknowledged that her son was gay. He's always had a thing about protecting women and children from thugs and bullies. My kind of guy.

I tell him about being raped and beaten. He unconsciously makes fists as I tell my story. We're both wishing he had been there at the time.

"And you have no idea who the guys were?" he asks when I'm done.

"None."

He thinks for a minute. "It seems so orchestrated," he says. "I mean, how is it one guy was on the El platform and the other guy was four or five blocks away in an alley? Did you ever think about that?"

I nod yes. He gestures with his hands again, keep talking.

"I think they were hired to hurt me," I say. "There's a very bad man out there who likes to beat up transwomen, and I think he's even killed one. Maybe more.

"I was trying to learn more about him and I think I got too close."

"Who is this guy?" Thomas asks.

"Let's not get into that right now," I say.

Thomas looks at me questioningly, gestures with his hands again.

"I think I'm going to have to settle this myself and the less you know, the less damage you can do to me if someone questions you about it later," I explain.

Thomas' eyes widen. "Good God, Bobbi!"

"Yes." I agree.

"What happens if he gets you first?" Thomas asks.

"Probably he gets away with it," I say. "It's happened before."

"Bobbi, promise me you'll leave his name in a document that comes to me if something happens to you," says Thomas.

"I don't want you or anyone else involved in this," I say.

"I am involved," says Thomas. "Promise me or I'll keep bugging you to find out who he is."

"Okay," I say. Inside, I'm thinking that if a man like Thomas ever proposed to me, I'd have to say yes.

* * *

ROBERTA IS STARING AT ME with her dark eyes. Her expression is amazingly complex. It's solemn and soft at the same time. Like a mother, or like a very serious older sister watching a young sibling struggle with something.

Her question hangs in the air: "What makes you think you're ready for gender reassignment surgery?"

A rush of different thoughts flashes through my mind spontaneously. They are not answers, but they are reactions.

Because I don't like having a penis there...because I want a vagina... because that part of me just doesn't feel right any more.

Conversely, I don't think I am ready. How would I know I was ready? Aren't you supposed to tell me?

Aloud, I say, "I don't know what makes you ready. I know I think of myself as a woman. I never think of myself as a man, even though I'm aware of being in between. I know I love dressing as a woman, wearing makeup. I love having breasts and I'd really love it if someone would feel me up. And I want to have a vagina. I want to be rid of this penis and scrotum. I want to be able to cross my legs comfortably. I want to make love as a woman." My voice trails off. I don't want to get graphic, though I'm sure Roberta has been exactly where I am.

"Do you think those thoughts and desires make you a woman?" she asks.

If I were a man I would find Roberta powerfully exotic. She is slim and feminine and has that feline seriousness about her and a certain distance from everything. She's wearing an elegant gray wool skirt below the knees and a matching suit coat with a conservative white blouse and a simple pearl necklace and pearl earrings. She could be a Radcliffe grad.

By contrast, I must look like a trollop. I've come directly from the salon, so I have on sexy heels, tight jeans and a low-cut top that shows some cleavage. My hair is teased up in a messy big-hair do.

I know most transwomen tend to get to where Roberta is as time goes on. I'm not there yet.

"Look," I say. I hate these shrink games, even if I love the shrink. "I know you're going to stomp all over me with new insight, but yes, I think these thoughts and desires are why I am becoming a woman. I'm sure there are many other, much less fun things that make up a woman and that I am sorely lacking in them, but I'm prepared to live with that.

"In fact," I say, "I've concluded that I won't ever be a woman like a genetic woman is a woman. I think no matter how completely I evolve, I will see the world as a transwoman, as someone who lived half her life as male, then changed genders.

"I don't think others will ever accept me as a woman," I continue. "I'm always going to look different, my voice is never going to be womanly. Nobody is ever going to ask me to marry them. But I'm going to enjoy my life anyway. I'm going to love getting laid, even if I have to hire men to bed me. And I'll always love the clothes, the hair, and the rest of it.

"I know this isn't the right answer, but it's the answer. I'm not a man. This is what I am. And I want a vagina to go with it."

A small smile plays at Roberta's lips. "Very good, Bobbi!" she says.

"That's the right answer?" I say with incredulity.

"There's no right or wrong answer," she says. "It's about knowing who you are and what motivates you. You are doing splendidly in that regard. No big surprise. You are a very thoughtful person."

I glow under the praise. Roberta is very thrifty with her compliments.

"And I'd like to correct you on one thing," she adds. "You are very womanly. It's inside you. What we need to keep working on is letting it come out and express itself."

"Does this mean you are going to recommend me for GRS?" I ask. I confess, I'm getting restless. If she'd sign off today I'd try to have it done next week.

"It means you'll get to make the decision yourself when we finish the year," she answers. She goes on about state of mind, mental preparedness, and self-acceptance.

* * *

WHAT A HIGH! Hundreds of people are applauding us enthusiastically. The emcee of our updo show has just asked the crowd if they liked what they saw.

As the applause dies down, he thanks each of the on-stage performers individually. With each name, a different platform artist raises his or her hand, smiles and bows to the crowd. The applause picks up each time. I'm the third name. I smile and bow, blushing like a schoolgirl. The applause seems even louder than for the other performers. As I straighten from my bow I look out on the audience. It might be true. The audience is loud and boisterously enthusiastic. Some are standing. There are a few whistles. Realistically, this is pretty much how they reacted to the other stylists, but for someone who just didn't want to be ridiculed, this is an unbelievable surprise. My heart is beating as though I've just crossed the finish line after running a marathon. My model is standing next to me. She is beyond stunning: tall, beautiful, seductively clad in a tight ball gown, and wearing the tall, sexy updo that I created. That's what the applause is for, but in a way, people are accepting me, too.

This must be what narcotics are like. Even as the applause wanes and the emcee directs the audience to someone else, I feel beautiful and sexy and accepted. I also feel like I'm a really talented hairdresser, with something worthwhile to share with the world. I have value.

It is my final stage appearance at the hair show. Suddenly I can't recall a single moment of the hours of self doubt and overwhelming anxiety that have marked the past week of my life, and especially the past few days. The shows have gone well, but until now, the end of each practice and each live show was muted by the knowledge that there would be a chance to fail on a grand scale at the next show.

Not now. There is no next show. As I realize that, I feel a great wave of regret. What will occupy my life now?

But my emptiness is short-lived. As the audience gives the star of our show a standing ovation, models and hairdressers leave the stage. When the applause dies down, we circulate to the front of the stage to meet with the adoring public. A milling throng envelopes us. Most are women, all are hairdressers. They peer closely at the models' hair. My model actually sits so that they can inspect my work. Most of the hairdressers want to talk to Evelyn, the star of our show and the most amazing dresser of formal hair I have ever seen. Having her coach me has been an education worth more to me than a PhD from Harvard. She works magic, curling and backcombing hair, and shaping it into forms that are both artistic and beauty-enhancing. And she imparts her wisdom generously, even to the strange-looking transwoman. Especially to the strange-looking transwoman. She told me I looked beautiful working on stage and that I had great talent. It wasn't the old showbiz BS, either. She meant it. I melted, of course. Every time I look at her or think of that moment, I get weak knees and rapid heartbeat. She probably doesn't even know how precious her acceptance and encouragement are to me, and I'm not sure I could find the words to say so. Not here and now.

As people move from my model to Evelyn's circle, some of them pause to share their praise with me. A few ask technique questions. A group of four wander over to me from Evelyn's throng. Their leader is a fiftyish woman with icy-blond hair cut in a sassy punk style that hairdressers of all ages seem to be able to pull off. She has a big smile, no inhibitions at all.

"So," she says, "We were wondering if you're transgendered." It's a statement, not a question, but she is expecting an answer. The two women with her blush at her bluntness, but they are eager to hear my response. The male, a slender young man projecting his gayness with an earring in his right ear and his youth with tattoos and gangsta clothing, looks somewhat embarrassed, but he's waiting for my answer, too.

"Yes I am," I respond. There is a moment of awkward silence.

"Well, how is that for you?" she asks. I look at her quizzically. She laughs. "You know, how are your clients with that? And the other stylists?"

"Oh, that's a complex picture, I'm afraid," I respond. I like her. She's curious, not judgmental. "I lost a lot of clients at first, but business has been coming back. I'm lucky. My boss stuck with me and I work in a city that's pretty accepting."

She keeps smiling. She can't think of anything to say.

"Where are you from?" I ask. That gets things rolling. They're from Iowa. She's Judy, the wild-child colorist. Carol is the owner, a pretty woman in her forties who can't quit staring at me. Betty is the other woman. Bob is their newest staff member. He's struggling to get a client base. They think he's having acceptance problems because he's gay. I look at him as we talk. He's wearing Levis with holes in them, a baggy T-shirt and a baggy flannel over it, black canvas athletic shoes, untied. Tattoos on both forearms and on his neck. I don't say it, but it seems to me no one would get to the gay part because he looks like a slob. That act could be a tough sell in Boystown, the most accepting place on earth.

Judy wants to ask more questions, but other people mill into our circle and the Iowans drift away after awhile, Judy not quite ready to ask the penis question in the presence of others.

I migrate to a conference room where the SuperGlam creative director,

Dennis, is having a short meeting with the demo staff and crew. Dennis is very Hollywood in his remarks, drenching us all in an unending flow of superlatives. He is pumped about how good the shows have been, and he manages to praise everyone, from the support people to the models and stars.

I'm still giddy when the meeting ends and we go our separate ways. As I pack my tools I try to decide how to go home—cab, El, walk? I feel a warm feminine glow. I feel sexy. These feelings don't come around all that often and I have an urge to bask in them. I'll cab up to the north Loop area, I decide, and walk from there, maybe do some shopping, stop for coffee, whatever.

Dennis catches me as I'm putting on my coat. He swings behind me like a leading man, grasps the coat's collar, and helps me put it on. He is as close to God as anyone in the hair business so I'm on the verge of wetting my pants.

"Bobbi," he says, "We haven't had a chance to really talk. These shows get crazy." He gestures manically. "But I just wanted to tell you, you were great out there. Evelyn thinks you're a genius and I think you have fantastic charisma." Peeing in my pants isn't a figure of speech any more. I'm so excited my bladder feels like it's going to burst. I can't think of suitable words to say, but that's okay. Dennis isn't here to listen to me gush. He goes on about my work and my stage presence.

"Anyway, here's the thing," he says. "We may have a position open up on our regular show staff in the next few months. It would mean doing hair shows in New York, LA, Las Vegas and Miami, plus a half-dozen academy gigs around the country. The money is good, but I have to warn you, the pace is wicked. Think you'd be interested?"

This is like asking a junkie if she wants another fix. "Yes!" I exclaim, nodding my head. I haven't been on this kind of an ego high in…well, ever. My entire soul is on fire. My cheeks hurt from smiling so much.

"Good," he says. "No promises right now, you understand, but I'll be in touch." With that he wraps his arms around me, administers one of those show-biz faux hugs, and moves on to the next person before I can say a word.

* * *

JUST WHEN I THINK life can't get any better, I roll into the salon and find a copy of the Chicago *Tribune* on my station. It is opened to page ten where a red crayon circles a large photo showing my updo model from yesterday and me in the background. She looks stunning. More than stunning. She looks sexier than a retouched nude in a men's magazine. I actually look okay, too—I look like a transwoman, but kind of cute. Neither of us is identified by name, but the short article says this updo at the SuperGlam stand was one of the highlights of the international hair show. Now there's something to wet your pants over!

I bet SuperGlam loves that publicity. I do, and I'm not even named. Before I even take off my coat I run down the block to the newsstand and pick up four more copies.

I needn't have bothered. Roger has already contacted the paper to make arrangements for reprints. We're going to do a mailing!

* * *

HE'S SIPPING COFFEE and scanning the morning Tribune, *part of his daily ritual. He is a speed reader, capable of consuming a page of information in seconds and applying it creatively days or weeks later. He reads the news and business sections of the* Trib *in the time it takes the average peon to read a page or two of sports news.*

It's part of what makes him so powerful.

His scanning stops abruptly at a photo on page 10. It shows a beautiful woman with a fancy hairdo. But that's not what stops him. In the background stands that tranny. The manly one. Looking smug. Recovered. She probably doesn't even remember Andive and his buddy in the alley, he thinks. She looks like she's having the best time of her life, all smiles and cleavage.

He studies the photo. There are people around them. The caption says it's from the beauty show. The stupid bitch has gone and won a prize or something.

His rage flares. She is a thing! People should see her in an alley with a cock up her ass and a puddle of shit under her. That's what she is. Not some fashion queen. The sight of her makes him feel ill. He wants to hit her, beat her senseless, hear her cry. Watch her die.

He struggles for self-control. People are so stupid.

Time to put this trash in its place.

* * *

I AM LOUNGING ON THE COUCH in Thomas' apartment wearing a pink robe with a dark pink fluffy collar. It is a gift from Thomas and his partner and manages to be both snuggly and sexy at the same time. I love it, even though pink isn't my color. I have just finished showering and my body is completely limp. I'm not quite as maniacal in kickboxing class as I was in the beginning, but I still work at it like a madwoman.

Thomas comes into the living room with steaming plates of pasta and sauce for both of us. His is packed with meat, nourishment for his huge muscles. Mine is vegetarian, just what a girl needs to stay healthy and slim. It's working. Since I've been running and working out I've lost several more pounds.

We make small talk for a while. I am distracted. The thought of my body changes gets me back to Strand. How will I defend myself against him and his thugs when I'm losing body mass and strength every day?

"What's bugging you, Beautiful?" Thomas picks up on my mood.

"When I got home last night there was a doll hanging from my doorknob. There was a string around its neck, like a noose. And it had a big nail sticking in its butt. No note or anything, but I know who sent it. It's the guy who had me raped.

"That's just the kind of game he likes to play," I say. "He likes everyone to know he's smarter and stronger than anyone else. He's telling me that he's coming for me. And he's enjoying it."

Thomas shakes his head in dismay.

"Thomas," I say, breaking the silence, "You've seen me work out and you've seen my kickboxing class. What do you think my chances are of taking out a 200-pound man in good shape if he was running at me with bad intentions."

"Oh my," says Thomas. "What do you mean by *take out?*"

"Ideally, to kill him," I say. "But I'd settle for disabling him."

Thomas thinks about it for awhile. "To be honest," he says, "the odds aren't great. It would take a perfect shot at the perfect time and if he moved his head even a little you'd have a better chance of hurting yourself than hurting him."

"That's what I was thinking," I say. We lapse into silence again.

"How would you handle it?" I ask, staring at him. "Let's say there's a 300-pound homicidal maniac who's after you. That would be like me taking on a 200-pounder. He's all muscle, and mean. He's bigger, faster and stronger than you are and he wants to hurt you. What do you do?"

Thomas puzzles over this for a while. "The problem with using a gun or mace is, if you hit him with it before he hits you, a court of law will see it as you assaulting him. If you wait for him to hit you, you probably won't be able to resist his strength.

"So…," Thomas says pensively, drawing out the 'o.' "Personally, I'd go with a preemptive attack. A surprise. Gun, mace, baseball bat. Those might work. But I think I'd use chemistry. I'd get an animal tranquilizer or a very fast-working muscle relaxer, something like that. I'd load it in a hypodermic needle and deliver it like I was slapping him on the back or something. By the time he realized I gave him a shot he'd be feeling the effects of it. In a few seconds, all I have to worry about is how to handle his limp body. Three hundred pounds is a lot for one man to handle."

Indeed. But I'm thinking that I might be able to handle a 200-pound man. And Strand might not even be that heavy.

"How would you get a tranquilizer?" I ask.

Thomas shrugs. "Maybe off the Internet. But that's awfully risky. I guess I'd find a black marketer who handles stuff like that."

"How do you find someone like that?"

"It's an ugly business," says Thomas. "You have to know someone who knows someone who knows someone, you know what I mean?" I nod. He continues, "I really hate that stuff. I hate those people. But if you need that for your safety, I'll get it for you."

"Thank you." I say it softly, my voice husky with emotion. I've never had a friend who would take that kind of risk on my behalf.

One of my many quandaries as I thought about transitioning all those months ago was whether or not I could ever fall in love as a girl. I was thinking of love as something else, but I have my answer. I can fall in love. I love Thomas because he is so noble and worthy. If he were into me, whatever I am, I would love to be his partner or wife. I love Marilee, too. If she were into women and into me, I'd set up house with her in a heartbeat.

These loves are different than the love I felt as a man. As a man, the sexual attraction came first then later maybe you find the person to be the other things you want. As a woman—or a she-male if you don't credit me for womanhood—it starts with loving the person. The sexual interest comes later and it's not the important thing.

Oh, I still feel pangs of outright lust. Quite regularly. With strangers as well as those I love. I don't know if that will ever go away, but maybe there will be love, too.

* * *

THIS HAS BEEN THE craziest week in my hairdressing career. It started first thing Monday morning when one of our hairdressers didn't show up for work. Her roommate called in to say Roxie had overdosed over the weekend and as soon as she gets out of the hospital she's going into rehab.

It turns out Roxie is a junkie. I don't know who else knew, but I certainly didn't. She has always been nice to me and good with customers, and she's a very good hairdresser. I felt a desperate sickness in the pit of my stomach hearing about her habit. I hope she makes it all the way back. When Roger makes the announcement he tells us we'll all be picking up some of Roxie's clients until she gets back.

The next day, one of the prudes who think I'm a pervert announced that she was pregnant. This was not a happy announcement for her. Trudy often talks about how she has pledged her life to Jesus Christ and actually tapes televangelist shows and slings moral judgments from the scriptures around like arrows in an Indian raid. She is pregnant with no husband in sight. She spills the news to us in an impromptu gathering in the break room. She rattles off the words like she is reciting the pledge of allegiance. She's ashamed and humiliated. She put herself in a compromising position. She has only herself to blame. She will ask for forgiveness for the rest of her life. Life is sacred so she will carry the baby to term and raise it the best she can. She asks for support and love from all of us.

She never looks at me during this recitation. Maybe she's thinking God will forgive her for getting knocked up as long as she doesn't socialize with trannies. Not my most humanitarian thought of the day, I guess.

Later, during my lunch break, two stylists were discussing the news. One of them said Trudy was all Jesus and sunshine by day, but a wild child by night. It wasn't a case of the boyfriend backing out, it's more that she can't even guess which stud struck gold.

It would really infuriate her to know that I feel sorry for her, but I do. I think a lot of religious zealots are people who are trying to overcome deep, painful issues in their lives. I feel for them, even though I think the religiosity makes them worse.

As for being a Rush Street slut, well, hairdresser gossip is sometimes long on drama and short on facts. Either way, she has my sympathy. We trannies know all about humiliation.

One of Roxie's clients that Trudy was supposed to do came in Wednesday looking like a street person. Her hair was matted and tangled, and glistened with an oily glaze. She smelled like cigarettes and grime and that was from four or five feet away. She wore designer clothes, but they were wrinkled and unkempt.

Trudy almost fainted when the client sat in her chair. She excused herself and ran back to the break room, nearly hysterical. She was riding a really awful streak of bad luck—I was the only stylist in the room.

"Bobbi, Bobbi," she sobbed. "Can you help me? Can you help me please?" She tells me about the client, the stink that makes her ready to vomit. The filth. Maybe the woman is a junkie too, like Roxie. She fears she'll pick up a disease that will hurt her baby.

Could I do the client?

Trudy has always regarded me like the proverbial turd in a punchbowl. I used to sometimes dream about having a moment like this when I might humiliate her as certainly as she has me many times. When the time came, though, all I could see was a broken-hearted girl whose world was flying apart and who was scared out of her wits by everything.

"Of course," I said. I sat her down at the table and got her a glass of water. "I'll take care of it," I said, and left.

The client's name was Cleo. I told her that Trudy was pregnant and having morning sickness issues, and that I'd do her service today—no charge, because of the confusion. Cleo looked dubious. She was trying to decide if she was desperate enough to have a transsexual do her hair.

I'm really good, I told her. Very definitely in Roxie's class. In the end, Cleo came over to my station. Normally I move the hair into different shapes and inspect the scalp during a consultation, but that would have been pointless with Cleo and it seemed to me there was a chance of infection by touching that ugly, stinking mass on her head. Trudy hadn't been exaggerating. Cleo reeked.

So I caped her, whisked her off to the shampoo bowl, and scrubbed her down with a clarifying shampoo. Three shampoos! Each one involving rigorous scrubbing of hair and scalp. Ordinarily, we use the clarifying shampoo on customers with very oily hair, but just on the first shampoo. We go with something milder on the second because the clarifying formulation is really strong. I had never done a third shampoo until that day. I felt like the health of her hair was a distant consideration after my own survival and maybe that of everyone else she encounters in life.

"Do you usually do three shampoos?" she asks as I apply the conditioner.

"Not usually," I said. "Your hair and scalp were pretty oily and I wanted to make sure we got you balanced." I thought the reference to "balance" was especially brilliant.

"I know. I'm sorry," she said. "I have really oily hair and I forget to wash it sometimes."

I asked her when she had last washed it. She couldn't actually remember. Probably four or five days ago, she guessed. My guess would have been a full week, including a day or two of swimming in a sewage ditch. She knew it was out of control, that's why she came in even though Roxie wasn't here. I asked her how she knew Roxie, thinking maybe they hit some shooting galleries together. But no, Cleo just came in here one day on her lunch hour and drew Roxie. Roxie did nice work and was fun to talk to.

I would love to give her a hip, avant-garde cut, but she clearly does not care for her hair and the cut would be wasted on her. I decide to trim her bob and give it some asymmetrical pieces. She'll at least look good when she leaves the salon.

As I work I ask her how often she normally washes her hair. "I'm terrible about that," she says. "I don't know why. I just hate to shower and wash my hair." Once she starts talking about it she just keeps going. She doesn't know if it's a phobia or if it's just that she gets so into her work. She's a certifiable workaholic, fifteen to eighteen hours a day. Weekends too, but she takes the work home. At first she laughs about it, but later, the raw emotions come out. Her marriage is failing. Her husband isn't interested in her any more. She expects him to ask for a divorce any day now.

"Why not just come in here two or three times a week?" I suggest. "Come in on your lunch hour. We'll have the assistant give you a shampoo and blow dry. You'll love it. It won't take much time and it's a lot cheaper than a divorce."

She laughs a little, but my message is a serious one. She's a pretty nice looking lady when she cleans up. Thirtyish. A cute body just a shade on the chunky side but with nice boobs and decent legs. Nice face with full lips that could be pouty. Pretty eyes. If we could trade bodies I'd do it in a heartbeat.

That's the saddest part of the service. She's a nice lady, vulnerable, with some kind of psychological disorder. The solution to the part of her problem we can all see is easily solvable. But I know she isn't going to solve it. For some reason I won't ever understand, she can't change what she's doing. The divorce is inevitable. I wonder what the rest of her life will be like. She thanks me profusely at the end of the service and says she'll think about my shampoo idea. She will, but she won't do it.

How sad.

At the end of the day, my crazy week goes completely insane.

As I'm straightening up my workstation, the receptionist comes back with a bouquet of flowers.

"Bobbi!" she says, "Are you holding out on us? Who's the new guy?"

"I'm sure I don't know," I say, as I receive the bundle. I place it on my table and peel back wrapping paper to find the card. My heart stops when I read it.

"Bobbi, we miss you and can't wait to see you again. All of us this time— Curly, Moe and Larry."

I get the reference. Thug #1, Thug #2, and Strand. This was meant to scare the crap out of me. And it's working.

The receptionist says something else but I don't answer. I can't. I can't draw breath to make words. She leaves.

Strand is getting very close. He is the cat and I am the mouse between his paws. He will play with me for as long as it's fun, then he will devour me.

I wonder if they will be waiting for me somewhere on my way home from work. I can see them pulling me into an alley, beating me, six arms and fists flailing, crushing my nose and teeth and cheek bones, then shoving their cocks in my ass, then other things. I am sweating and shaking. I sit in my chair and take deep breaths for a while. When I feel able to talk, I call Thomas.

He escorts me home. I show him the card that came with the flowers. "I can't ignore this anymore," I tell Thomas.

"Can you help me get the kind of tranquilizer we talked about?" I ask.

Thomas nods. "I'll need some time, so be careful." He gives me his schedule so I can call him for escort service. He'll also get me some pepper spray.

What kind of world do I live in?

* * *

I DON'T KNOW WHEN they are following me and when they aren't. I see them once in a while, a glimpse here and there. I'm careful about where I go and when, but otherwise, I want them following me. And I want them cocky and arrogant.

Today I have walked casually from the salon to a wig and costume shop.

Inside, I make a show of trying on several drag queen wigs—big, oversexed things in different shades of blond. I do it in full view of the shop's big display windows, primping and posing shamelessly. While I'm trying them on a sales woman waits on me.

"This is just for fun," I tell her. "What I really want to look at are mustaches, beards, side burns and a man's short hair wig."

Her eyebrows arch. "Having second thoughts?" She says it playfully.

"A kinky partner," I answer.

"Kinky's good," she says.

She brings a selection of facial hair to a private room. We go through everything looking at color, texture, and length. I make my purchase and tip her grandly. When I step out of the store anyone who bothered to notice me would assume I'm carrying a wig in my Global Wigs bag.

But what's in the bag is a man everyone thinks is dead. Bob Logan, or someone who looks a little like him, is coming back to life for a little while.

* * *

IT IS EERIE LOOKING into the mirror seeing vague traces of my male self in the strange image that appears there.

Wearing a male wig and male clothing but without costume facial hair, I look like an effete man, maybe even a woman in drag. How ironic is that? It's a bit of a shock to realize how much I have changed in the long months of my transition. My skin is utterly smooth, my beard long since gone in a blaze of electrolysis and hormones. My eyebrows are thinner than a man's, and shaped to help create the illusion of rounder, wider, more feminine eyes. My face has narrowed slightly, from weight loss I suppose, and my lashes seem longer.

I start by applying eyebrows, a slightly bushy set. Instantly, I look much more masculine, though I still look more like Bobbi than Bob. I add sideburns that extend about halfway down my ears. I look like a pretty boy gone country and western. Goofy, but not many people would recognize Bobbi in there.

When I put on the van dyke beard, I am completely transformed. A man looks back at me. Ordinarily, the sight would sicken me. This is not who I am. But today, this is work. And it's working. Under close scrutiny, the skin is too smooth where it isn't covered by facial hair, but no one will study me that hard.

I don the gray businessman's suit I picked up at the resale shop by the

Center. I look like an English professor. When I add the trench coat I look like an English professor getting ready to go for a stroll in Hyde Park—London's Hyde Park, in fact. For kicks, I complete the look by selecting a black umbrella with a hooked handle from my closet; I brandish it like a cane as I walk.

At eleven o'clock I peek out my door to make sure no one is coming, then glide down the stairs. My male shoes feel awful—heavy and stiff and they look incredibly ugly to me. But the show must go on. I slip out the back door and take a walkway to the alley then move out to the street; if Larry, Moe or Curly is watching my front door, they won't see me. If they see me a half block from the place they won't recognize me. No way.

My Sunday outing lasts about two hours. I work on walking in a more masculine manner. Again, I find myself hating the exercise. I miss my prissy walk. I don't want to be a boy.

I stop for coffee, again for a newspaper, again for breakfast. Then I do a little shopping. No one recognizes me in the coffee shop or the restaurant, two places I occasion in my real-life Bobbi mode. I pass better as a man than I do as a woman, though I still attract a few double takes as I make my way around town. It's my voice and my gestures. I've been working on the voice for a long time, so that's kind of a compliment. The gestures. Well, that's just me. Male or female, I'm femmie. I just feel better that way. Still, I try to subdue both the voice and the gestures and keep telling myself that this is only temporary.

I really don't like being perceived as a man by others, even though they accept me. At some point, I realize how profound this is. All these months I have feared the strange mix of surprise, hostility and astonishment I get from others as Bobbi, the transwoman. Now, in my little male charade I discover that their acceptance is not nearly as important to me as being me.

What a strange way to learn such an important lesson.

I smile as I stroll. I feel almost reborn. I know who I am. All I have to do is survive long enough to enjoy that certainty.

Just that.

***

April

THIS IS THE ULTIMATE April Fool's joke, except April first was yesterday and my client isn't here as a joke. My knees feel like rubber, my jaw must surely be scraping the ground.

A moment ago I pranced into the salon from the break room and stood behind the client in my chair, evaluating her scalp and the length and texture of her hair. I used to introduce myself first, but this small act of arrogance has been very successful for me in establishing my authority in the hairdresser/client relationship. It helps get the new client's mind off the fact that I look a little odd and lets her know that I am a hairdressing star, at least, in my own opinion.

Nice hair, I thought. Medium-fine texture, moderate wave, nice highlights. Healthy, well cared for. I look up into the mirror as I start moving the hair around in relation to her face. That's when the air went out of my world.

B. Richards wasn't a new client. B. Richards is Betsy Richards, the former Betsy Logan, wife of Bob Logan, the former me. My ex-wife is sitting in my chair.

She notes my reaction and her smile freezes. "Was this a bad idea...?" She starts to say Bob then catches herself. "Bobbi." She finishes.

I grope for words. "No," I say, finally. "It's just a surprise."

"I saw your picture in the paper the other day and I thought, you know, this would be fun for both of us," she says. "Is it that I'm remarried?"

"No, no, not at all," I say, regaining my composure. "I'm happy for you. I was happy for you when we met for lunch."

She looks at me dubiously.

"Really, Betsy," I say. "I don't have many manly thoughts any more. I feel more like your sister than your ex."

She beams. As she smiles, her eyes appraise me, from top to bottom. I can almost read her mind as she takes in the spiral-permed auburn hair with red and blond highlights, half up, the hip eye makeup and heavy jewelry, the cleavage, the tight short skirt with fishnet hose, the platform heels.

"You look…" she pauses, "…really nice, Bobbi." She means it. "It's very weird for me to say that. It's very weird to think it. I have to forget who you were before and just see you as you are now. I never thought my husband would someday look good in a mini skirt and heels. Is that all you?" She gestures to her own breasts which are cloaked in conservative business clothes but still the focal point of a youthful, fit, and wonderfully proportioned body.

"Yes," I say. We talk boobs for a moment. She guesses I'm at least a C-cup. I tell her I'm getting close to a D. She asks what it's like to "go through the change" and we both laugh at her choice of words. Painful, I tell her, and exhilarating.

I realize we have used ten minutes of her appointment time to chat and quickly move back behind the chair. I resume positioning her hair this way and that around her face, then trying different levels of volume on the sides and top.

"What were you thinking of today, Betsy?" I ask.

"Just a trim," she says. "To be honest, I just wanted an excuse to see you again."

"I'm flattered," I respond. I lead her back to the shampoo bowl, waving the assistant off. As I work on her, I say, "Just in case you hadn't thought about it, whoever is doing your hair is very good. The color is great, the hair is healthy, and the cut is very precise. A hairdresser this good is worthy of your loyalty, so my feelings won't be hurt if you don't reschedule."

"That's very generous," she says. "Actually, he's moving. And so am I."

"Really?" I say. I feel like she's leading up to something.

"He and his partner are moving to Washington, DC. The partner landed a job in a law firm there. Jonas is choosing between salon offers."

"What about you? Where are you moving?" I ask after I get her back in my chair and begin the service.

"Well," she says, shifting slightly in the chair. "I'm not moving moving. I'm just not going to be coming downtown to work anymore. Bobbi, I'm pregnant. I'll work a few more months, then I'm going to be a stay-at-home mom for a while."

I smile widely. "I'm so glad for you, Betsy." I bend and hug her. A real hug. "I'm so glad," I repeat.

"Thank you," she says. After a pause, she says, "Are you sure?"

I come around in front of her so we can look directly at one another. "I am completely sure. One of the things I worry about is that you may have wasted too much time with me. I'm so sorry for that, Betsy. I just didn't know who I was."

She puts her hand on my wrist. "It wasn't a waste. We loved each other." Tears come to her eyes. "I think we still love each other."

I nod. I'm getting misty too.

"It's not that I don't love Jerry," she says, sniffling, "I do, very much. But you were my first love and sometimes I wish you were the father."

Tears flow freely for both of us. "That's sweet, Betsy," I say when I get my voice back, "but honestly, I'd rather be the mom."

We laugh, but it's true. I have fantasized about being pregnant and about raising a child as a mom. It is a pleasant vision, but one I try to avoid. Science hasn't blessed transsexual women with the ability to reproduce. Why pine for something that isn't possible?

I work fast to finish the cut, letting the conversation taper off. As I check my work, she catches my eye in the mirror. "So, are you, you know...like, all woman now?" she asks.

"No, not yet," I reply. "But I'm getting close. It looks like I might be ready for GRS this summer."

"GRS?" she asks.

"Gender reassignment surgery," I answer. "Vagina day."

"Isn't it hard to think about that?" she asks. "You know, having it cut off?"

"A couple of years ago I wasn't so sure," I tell her, "but I'm at a point now where I can't wait. That's just not me. I'm a girl. I want a girl's body."

Our conversation is stifled by the noise of the blow dryer as I finish the service, but Betsy scribbles her home address and home and cell phone numbers on the back of her business card and hands it to me when I finish.

"Will you have lunch with me before I retire to mommyhood?" she asks.

"I wouldn't miss it for anything."

"And can I book a cut and color with you?"

"You don't need to ask," I say. "Just don't make me cry so much, okay?"

She smiles, tears up, and sniffles. Me too. For a moment I feel the old pang. I stand outside myself and watch my hulking form next to my ex-wife, a towering she-male next to a beautiful woman. My reality and my fantasy.

But the image fades almost instantly. I hug Betsy. A full body hug between two women. I love her and I know she loves me. We are sisters in a very special way. I will be her child's aunt and I will love them both with a passion that is new in my life. Because I'm finally me. This is who I am.

* * *

COMING OUT CAN BE MURDER

FOR REASONS I WILL never understand, people here expect April to be a season of sunshine and daffodils, of blue skies, warm breezes, and calm waters on Lake Michigan.

I'm considering this irony as I walk into the teeth of winds gusting up to thirty miles per hour, maybe more. I'm leaning forward like a ski jumper going downhill just to keep from getting blown backward.

The ambient temperature is in the mid-forties, but it feels much colder thanks to the wind and overcast skies and wet air. Yesterday was sunny, sixtyish, with gentle breezes.

Pedestrians are in real danger of being impaled by umbrellas blowing inside out, or just dismantling altogether. It's funny in a Three Stooges kind of way to see some commodity trader in a thousand-dollar suit and four hundred dollar trench coat have his umbrella collapse, exposing his expensive threads to the vicissitudes of our nasty weather.

But the highest comedy of all is watching slight women try to wield umbrellas in these winds. Seriously, they can be blown about like plastic grocery store bags. I know, it isn't really funny, especially if it's happening to you or someone you love. But it looks comical.

Although I have done a great job of losing weight and thinning down, I have enough body mass to deal with the winds, albeit in a staggering sort of way. My problem is staying warm. I have very little body fat and I make vanity compromises. I'm a hairdresser. I have to. And today I'm taking it further. Today is a special day.

Instead of a winter coat, I'm wearing a very stylish spring coat just because it makes me look trim and feminine. The wind is blowing through the fabric as if it weren't there and underneath the coat I'm wearing a stylish but thin blouse, no bra, and a short skirt.

It's hard to tell what part of my anatomy is coldest. My lips and nose are numb, but my ears are aching they are so cold, and I can hardly feel my toes. I did stop to stuff my hair under a cute beret, but it does nothing for my ears. And my toes are a sacrifice to the shoe gods who made me wear open-toed sandals today.

Ordinarily, I would make a few concessions to reality. I would don a sweater and maybe a windbreaker. I'd change into boots and wear thick socks with them. I'd wear a stocking cap or wrap a long scarf around my head and ears.

But today is a special day. It is Tuesday evening, and tonight I'm celebrating my Tuesday night tail. Every Tuesday for the past four weeks, I have glimpsed a man following me home from the El station. The first time I spotted him I started hyperventilating with fear. Good God, I thought, this can't be happening again!

When I got over my shock I faced the reality that my rapists were getting ready for another event. I've been careful on Tuesday nights to spot them even as they follow me. The prey stalking the hunter stalking the prey.

It won't be so easy for them this time.

I saw the man in the blue stocking cap and tan coat as I got off the El tonight. Sometimes it's the other guy, but it's always one or the other of them. And tonight we're taking a special stroll, Blue Hat and I.

Three blocks from the El station and I reach Rape Alley. Instead of darting to the other side of the street as I have previously, I duck into the alley and press myself against the building wall, out of the wind. I make a show of letting my trench coat fall open as if the belt had come untied. If Blue Hat is looking, I make sure he gets an eyeful. I bend down to fix the strap on one of my sandals, letting my blouse-top open to expose my bare breasts. My beret comes off, allowing my spiral curls to burst out. Before I replace the beret and re-tie my coat, I shake out and primp my hair. I don't know if this is rousing Blue Hat's angry rapist instincts or not, but it's the best I can do.

I take a deep breath and enter the alley. I go into an exaggerated femme walk, hips swaying, short steps, one hand held out to the side, the other swinging in rhythm to the sound of my heels on the asphalt surface. The alley is riddled with potholes and cracks and I pick my way through them like a helpless virgin, holding my arms out for balance, stopping to carefully step across a crack. To catch a predator, dear old dad once told me, you need bait that looks attractive and vulnerable. He was talking about fish, but I think it will work with a shit-heel predator like Blue Hat, too. I look like an easy victim, easy enough to take all by himself.

The alley is dark and completely deserted. The nearest street lamp is out. The only sounds are the muted noises of passing vehicles out on the street and my own footsteps. Three buildings into the alley I pass by the recessed area in which I was raped and beaten a few months ago. A large, hulking form stands in the shadows. Thank god! I don't know who he is, but Thomas promised he'd be there. My heart races and my breathing gets short. This is the stupidest thing I've ever done.

I keep walking. I want to see if Blue Hat is following me. I want to stop and turn to find out with an urgent desperation. But I don't. I keep swishing down the alley, hips rolling, arms out, a tranny slut looking for a good time.

Half way down the alley I hear a short yelp followed instantly by the sound of a heavy blow meeting flesh and bone. Sure proof that Blue Hat did follow me into the alley. A moment later, I hear it again, more of a grunt this time, as another blow strikes home. I don't pause to watch or listen. I keep moving to the end of the alley then turn north, drop the hooker walk, and go home.

In my wake, a former rapist and would-be repeat offender is lying in a heap, the victim of an attack himself. He hasn't been raped, but he has other problems. I don't know what they are exactly, but I'm betting on broken bones. Whatever it is, Blue Hat isn't going to be following me again. Not alone, anyway.

No, I don't feel good about it. This isn't a choice I'm making. People are waging war on me and I don't have the money or the connections to employ the law to defend myself. Whoever the brute was in the alley, he just delivered a message to Mr. Blue Hat that the law never would, and the cost to me is about what a downtown lawyer would charge to shake my hand, hear my story and tell me my chances of winning aren't good.

I don't want a war. In my heart, I am a sissy. I want to do hair. I want to wear girlie clothes and go shopping and have my surgery. I want to make love as a woman, to be aroused as a woman, to have a woman's orgasm. I want to stroll along the lakefront in the summer in shorts and tank top with Marilee or Cecelia, sipping iced coffee. I want to be a platform artist at hair shows making other girls beautiful and sexy. I'd love to be an aunt to Betsy's baby.

But more importantly, I don't want to be a victim. I will be goddamned if I will wait for these thugs to hurt me again. I'm not kidding myself. Strand may end up killing me anyway, but I'm not going to go willingly. And I won't make it easy for him.

* * *

I LOOK OUT MY PEEPHOLE to see who's knocking. It's Officer Phil in his CPD blues and another man wearing a suit. The suit looks like a cop, too. I yell through the door for them to give me a moment, then slip on a robe. It's late in the morning and I should be wearing more than underwear, but

Wednesday mornings are leisure time for me. I don't go into the salon until one. So I had a nice breakfast, and a leisurely bath and coffee. I had just started doing my nails when Phil and his friend came calling.

I open the door and fold my arms across my middle. "Hi Phil."

"Hi Bobbi," he says. "This is Detective Wilkins. We'd like to talk to you for a minute. Can we come in?"

"Of course," I say, and step back into the apartment so they can enter. They move past me at the entry to the living room. Detective Wilkins is a middle-aged black man, heavy-set, strong looking. He has not taken his eyes off me from the time I opened the door. I'm sure he's seen trannies around the station—hookers and junkies and so forth—but I'm thinking he hasn't really had any human contact with one of us. He's too curious. Right on cue, as he edges past me into the living room his gaze drops to my chest. *Are they real?* he's wondering.

They sit on my couch. I offer them refreshments but they decline. I get a glass of water for myself and sit on one of the stuffed chairs facing the couch, crossing my legs tightly. Definitely not a good audience for a beaver shot.

"Bobbi, we are looking for people who know anything about an assault that occurred last night in the same place you were assaulted in February," Officer Phil says after I sit down. "Do you know anything about that?"

I react quizzically. "No. Nothing," I say. "Was it another transwoman?"

Detective Wilkins flashes a grimace. Phil keeps doing the talking. "Actually," he says, "the victim was a white male fitting the description you gave of one of your attackers."

"Description?" I ask. "What description?"

"He was wearing a tan coat and a blue stocking cap," says Phil. "We're wondering if it's the same guy."

I shrug. "I never saw the face of either guy. I'll be glad to take a look at him, but I don't see much chance it will help."

"Did you have anything to do with this, Bobbi?" he asks, straight out.

I am taken aback. "I'm sorry?"

He repeats the question. Detective Wilkins has a smirk on his face and that angers me.

"Are you asking me if I beat up a rapist last night?" I exclaim. "Me? *Me?* I'm a fairy, Phil. A hairdresser. A transsexual. Can you honestly picture me as a mugger?"

The anger in my voice is real. These bumbling idiots wouldn't walk across the street to investigate the rape and beating of me, but the thought that I might have wreaked revenge on my assaulter has them concerned about public safety. I'm seething.

So is Detective Wilkins.

"We think he was set up," Wilkins says in a low voice. His face is etched in anger. "We have a report there was a woman in the alley about the same time the victim was beaten. We think maybe he was lured in there by someone with an axe to grind."

His voice is very menacing. He's trying to scare me into confessing all. He has picked the wrong transwoman at the wrong time.

"It wasn't me, Detective," I respond. "I don't beat up men. Or women. And I can't help saying it would be nice if Chicago's finest were half so concerned when a transgendered person gets beat up. But when that happens all you can say is there are thousands of men in Chicago with blue hats and tan coats."

"Let me tell you something," he says. "We know what went down in that alley. We know you set it up. And we're going to prove it. We're giving you a courtesy call right now for your own good. If you tell us what happened it'll go better for you. But you keep playing games with us and we'll make you wish you were never born. We're talking a felony assault. That's real jail time. Think about how it's going to be doing time as a she-male."

He stops and stares expectantly, eyebrows raised. I'm supposed to talk. To acquiesce, like a good little tranny.

"I am doing time as a she-male, Detective," I answer quietly. "I'm not getting fucked in the ass every night, but I have to endure many other indignities, including fewer rights under the law than other people get. Right now, I'd like you to take your vile threats and your intimidating presence out of my home. If I ever see you again it will be with legal counsel at my side.

"Now please, leave."

Wilkins is internalizing his anger. It must be hell to play bad cop and get shot down by a transsexual hairdresser. Phil shrugs and shakes his head slightly, feigning regret.

"I wish you wouldn't leave it this way, Bobbi," he says. "We're on your side. Really. You don't know what you're getting into here. You hire a guy, you start something. Your victim has friends who come looking for you. Maybe the guy you hired blackmails you someday. Maybe he decides to beat you up too. It works that way sometimes. You're a lot safer letting the law handle it."

"I'm still waiting for the law to handle it," I say. "When I was raped your rape sergeant thought it was my fault. When a guy you think is one of my rapists gets beat up, you think it's my fault. Well, I'm just a tranny hairdresser, but I think there's a pattern here and it really doesn't seem to be working in my favor."

"You're a real smart ass!" Wilkins shakes a finger in my face, his body taut with rage. It's not a show. He really hates trannies. Me in particular. "Don't come whining to us when this guy's friends come looking for you. You're on your own!"

"Indeed," I say, as I open the door for them to leave. "Something we can agree upon at last."

As their heavy footsteps descend the stairs, I close the door and lean against it, raising my hands to my face. What have I done? I'm shaky and suddenly cold. The law is against me. The lawbreakers are against me. This is crazy! I go into full panic mode for a moment. Part of me wants to call them back and come clean. Instead I sit down and take deep breaths until the shaking and panic subside. I can come clean any time I want.

After a moment of calm I think it through again. If I confess I will be convicted of something, I'll ruin Thomas' life because he arranged for the muscle, and I'm still a sitting duck for Strand and any thugs he wants to hire. No, there are no options now. Now we just play out the story.

* * *

HE TOOK THE CALL out of curiosity. Andive couldn't possibly have a wife, could he? No, Grace Andive was his mother. That was a hard concept too. Jack was in the hospital with many broken bones. He had been mugged in an alley on the North Side and wanted his mom to let Mr. Strand know.

As soon as he hung up Strand contacted Andive's skulking buddy, Curtis. Another thug with a violent sheet and a special thing for queers. Strand had never met the man. Andive was his only contact and Andive swore never to tell Curtis or anyone else about him. He hadn't. Curtis had no idea who Strand was when he called for a meeting...and Strand didn't tell him. Just set up a meeting in a bar and asked him what went down in the alley.

And now he's listening with mounting fury as Curtis tells him what Andive had managed to say through his wired jaw and miles of bandages.

"He never saw it coming," Curtis is saying. "One minute he's following the faggot, and the next minute someone whacks him with a baseball bat. He thinks the first shot broke his ribs, but his face is smashed and his kneecaps are busted and some fingers on one hand were smashed. He's a mess..."

Jesus Christ! Strand swears silently. The man in front of him is a hulking moron and he's simpering worse than a tranny. And he hasn't even been harmed. He hides his disgust and keeps listening, trying to rein in his rage. He already knows who set up the beating.

"Some of his bones aren't just broken," the man says. "They're shattered. And the poor guy doesn't have insurance."

Strand waves his hand. "That will be seen to. Tell me what you two were doing before that happened. How did he end up in that alley?"

The moron tries to think. "We've been following that tranny for a while. Andive would take a night and I'd take the next one. We'd do three nights a week, sometimes four. He told me we were charting patterns. He said we were going to have another party with her. We just needed to find the right place."

Curtis shows him some of his notes. A list of places she stopped, trains she took, streets she walked, the times. The search for a pattern. At first, not much of one, Curtis says. Every day was different. Different time leaving the shop, different destinations, different times getting home. Some nights she goes out, some nights she doesn't. But lately, Tuesdays had a pattern. She left work around eight, took the same route home. It looked good.

"I was careful, but Andive didn't give a shit if the queer saw him or not," says Curtis. "Like, how much trouble can a fuckin' queen be, right? Shit!" Curtis' chin quivers.

Inwardly, Strand sneers. A thug with the heart of a sparrow. Definitely no help here, he thinks. He tells Curtis to go home and lay low for a long, long time. "Don't talk about this to anyone, understand?" says Strand.

The man nods.

"I mean no one!" he says again ominously. "The people I represent are everywhere and if you say anything, they'll know. And what happened to Andive will seem like amateur hour compared to what they'll do to you. Capiche?" He throws in the Italian word just to intimidate the idiot.

Curtis nods. Strand dismisses him with a hand gesture. As the man slinks away, Strand orders another drink and thinks. His initial rage is turning to pleasure. It's time for the A-team to step in.

"Bobbi, Bobbi," he sighs to himself, picturing the tranny in his mind. "You're too smart for a couple of strong-arm morons, but you have no idea what you are up against now." He smiles. He recalls how easy it was to seduce the tranny, how much she loved being mounted.

It was time to erase this thing that had the temerity to stalk him. It didn't seem like much of a challenge, really, even though she had managed to dispatch one of his thugs.

It needs to be done soon. He'd have to check his calendar, but maybe this weekend. Otherwise, next weekend. Talk about your Saturday night special!

* * *

THE TREMBLING THAT HAS been with me much of the day has quieted. I am curled up next to Thomas on his couch. His arm is around me. I feel secure in Thomas' arms and in his presence. I think that's what's so seductive about him.

I fill him in on my little police visit. He fills me in, too. He verifies the rumor Cecelia passed on, the one going around the trans community. My back-alley Romeo suffered a broken jaw and missing teeth from the first stroke of the bat, then a broken kneecap and a broken shin from the next two strokes, then broken ribs and brutally swollen and sore testicles. No wonder the cops were so agitated.

"Strand is going to do something big really soon," I say. The shaky feeling is starting to come back. "He must be raving mad. The biggest charm he finds in us trannies is how weak we are. We're so compliant. Beat us. Shake us. Rape us. We just keep coming back for more.

"Except now some tranny skag has gone and put one of his goons in the hospital. For a guy who loves power and has to have total control, that's like getting peed on. I don't have much time."

Thomas nods. "I think you're right. What's our next move?"

"Our next move is to get you out of the picture so you don't get splashed with whatever happens next," I say.

He starts to object, but I wave him off. "Believe me, there's no other way. Just one thing before you go, can you get me the tranquilizer? Like, tomorrow?"

Thomas nods. "I should have picked it up today. You'll have it by lunch tomorrow, special delivery."

"And it can't be traced to you, right?"

"I don't see how. I'm using a go-between who's buying from a dealer who got it from the source, whoever or whatever that is," says Thomas. "The only thing we have to worry about is that it's the real stuff."

"Do you expect them to screw us?" I ask.

Thomas shrugs. "I don't expect it," he says, "But you know how it goes. Maybe the source backs out at the last minute. Does he give us sugar water and take the money or does he tell us up front? These people aren't boy scouts."

"So I'd better have a backup plan if the tranquilizer doesn't work, huh?" I say, thinking out loud.

Thomas nods. "At least one," he says. He argues for making him and maybe a friend part of Plan B, but I won't have it. Nobody is going to go to jail for helping me.

I'll keep thinking about alternatives if the tranquilizer fails, but right now I only see two—run like crazy so I can fight again other day, or just duke it out with him and hope I can slip in a self-defense technique before he gets me.

The assertive alternative isn't working for me. In my private moments, I try to visualize my shot to his windpipe landing, but I keep seeing him parry it easily, laughing at what a weak sissy I am. I try to gouge his eyes with my thumbs, but he easily pushes my hands away, my body weak from months of hormones. This vision is prejudiced by my guilt about sacrificing my maleness to be a woman, but it is also based on reality. I'm not as big and strong as Strand.

Thomas' partner rolls in. He doesn't know about this drama and it's better to keep it that way, so we drop the subject. We make small talk until I get up to go home. Thomas puts on a coat and kisses his partner goodbye. He is walking me home. Sort of. I don't want him to be seen with me. I don't want him to be implicated in whatever I do to deal with Strand. So I walk and he follows.

It has become very cloak-and-dagger. We use different routes routinely now. We leave his flat by way of the alley. I've never seen a tail when I'm coming and going from Thomas' place, so I'm pretty sure Strand's goons don't know about Thomas. And that's an advantage I'd like to maintain.

* * *

DECADES HAVE PASSED faster than this miserable night. I have been beside myself with anxiety all day. This is the day I settle things with Strand. Of course, this was much easier to contemplate a week ago, or even a few days ago when all I could think about was that bastard maiming me.

The closer I get to the appointed time the more doubts I have. I can't see any way the plan will work. All I can see is how it will fail. The many ways it can fail. It is just incredibly farfetched, now that I seriously think about executing it.

And even if everything else works, I don't think I can kill Strand. As rewarding as it felt in my dreams to watch the life ooze from his evil body, now all I see is a helpless human being and I don't see how I can bring myself to kill him. And if I do kill him, I don't see how I can live with that memory, that realization about myself, for the rest of my life.

I've never been a fighter. I've had maybe three physical altercations in my life. The last one was in junior high and it was with my best friend. Tempers flared, we started swinging wild haymakers at each other until we were both too weary to take another swing. Then we made up and that was the end of my fighting career. His too, I bet.

As I try to quell my anxieties I also have to deal with my well-intentioned friends.

Four of us are having a private group session with Roberta at her apartment. I should have known it was a setup when it turned out that Cecelia, Katrina and another friend of mine, Grace, were the other members of the group.

The subject of the group session is me, and what a miserable excuse for a woman I am. They are taking turns ripping me for my shortcomings.

For Katrina and Grace, the theme keeps coming back to my self-consciousness and my preoccupation with how I look. The favored mien among male-to-female transsexuals is an attitude of haughty indifference to what those around you think. Just hold your head high and press on—regardless.

That approach does work better than anything else, at least in this me-first society that America has become. Our citizens respect ego and arrogance a lot more than they respect humility and sincerity. Still, that's just not me. At least, not until recently. Now, I seem to have simply grown tired of caring what other people think. Although it would be nice to have people to think well of me, I no longer have the energy to give a damn when they don't.

My friends haven't really seen much of that in me yet. It's too recent. I could argue with them, but they would just see it as a dodge. So I let them yammer on.

After beating that subject into the ground they start on my male-like appearance tonight. I'm wearing unisex jeans, a boy shirt, a sports bra that flattens my chest, and a baggy coat. My face is devoid of makeup, not even mascara or lip gloss. I'm not wearing any jewelry, not even a ring. I still have long, curly hair and a feminine presentation, but the overall affect is androgynous.

I will become much more masculine looking later, not that any of them will see it. In one of my coat pockets is my boy wig; in another, a bag holding my glue-on facial hair and the adhesive. In another pocket is the syringe with the animal tranquilizer that Thomas got me. I'm going to switch to male mode later tonight. I've already scouted the restaurant; it has a one-person men's room with a locking door. I don't want to risk going home to change and maybe picking up a tail from one of Strand's thugs or just being seen by a nosy neighbor.

My friends see something else in my sudden androgyny. Grace accuses me of being in denial; Katrina thinks I'm going through a dyke phase. I don't confirm or deny, I just say I'm expressing myself and that I also express myself frequently as a girly girl.

Cecelia has always given me grief about my self-consciousness and doubts, but she doesn't say much about these things tonight. After Katrina and Grace get tired of beating me up, Roberta asks Cecelia if she has anything to add.

"I think Bobbi's assertiveness will take care of itself," says Cecelia. "She has great role models..." she gestures to the assembled group, including herself, "... and she has an ego. It's coming out slowly but surely. I think she's come a long way in the past year."

I smile at the unexpected praise.

"But I'm actually much more worried about something else with Bobbi, something new," says Cecelia. "Since you were raped, you've been withdrawing from the rest of us. You're getting secretive. That's not good, Bobbi. For what we're doing, changing genders, we all need a village. We need a support structure. You have one. Use it."

"What are you talking about, Cecelia?" I ask.

"You know what I'm talking about," she says. "We never see you anymore. You're taking karate classes and lifting weights and running, and when you aren't doing that you're working. We were just starting to wonder what happened with you and all of a sudden Officer Phil comes sniffing around wanting to know about some thug who got beat up right where you were raped.

"Bobbi, I don't know if you're into something heavy or this is just circumstantial, but you need to keep in touch with the community. There will still be times when no one else can provide the kind of support we provide. Because we've been there.

"But I don't see the trust from you and it worries me. I don't hear you talking about things with me or anyone else. I see you withdrawn, and that's dangerous."

The others are on me like jackals on a wounded fawn. They restate the points made by Cecelia many times, adding only anxiety to the discussion.

Roberta remains her solemn, quiet self through all this. She knows more than the others, but not the whole story. Not even close. I can't tell them what's afoot. I pledge to do better. I explain that I've made some new friends, along with getting into an intensive fitness program. I thank them for caring and weep a little as I hug each of them. It isn't an act. I hate not being able to share with them what I'm doing and why. But this can't be shared. If I succeed, they share a lifetime of guilt, either because they give me up to the police, or because they don't. Anything I share is a curse.

This is a ride I have to take myself.

When the session mercifully ends, Cecelia and Roberta want to hit a bar. I try to decline, but Cecelia is way ahead of me.

"Come on, Bobbi," she says. "You're off tomorrow morning. You can sleep until noon if you want."

I agree to just one drink. The truth is, I just don't want to be around anyone I know right now. I know what I have to do tonight and my nerves are on fire. I'm jumpy and moody. I have doubts and overwhelming fears. I barely made it through the group session without the others recognizing how distracted I am. The last thing I want is another hour or two of exposure to my friends.

I resolve to focus on my friends and what they say for one full hour. I will bury my plan, my fears, and my doubts in a corner of my mind, until my polite hour of congeniality is up.

* * *

MY CONVERSION TO a goateed male bon vivant goes flawlessly. I have a drink at Guisseppe's bar around nine-thirty. Guisseppi's is a nice Italian restaurant in Boystown, and nine-thirty is a quiet time in the bar area. I drink alone at a small table. After twenty minutes or so, I drop my tab and a $10 bill on the bar then step into the men's room. No one notices. I am just one more male face in Boystown, maybe a bit effeminate looking, but not enough to matter. The bartender doesn't even look away from the sporting event on television when I leave my check and make for the bathroom. It's all standard operating procedure.

Inside, I slide my breast squasher over the sports bra for an almost flat chest. I glue on the sideburns, mustache and beard, then put a hair net over my head hair and slip on the male wig. I take the precaution of pinning it in three places. I finish by relieving myself. By force of habit, I sit to pee. I wash my hands, check myself in the mirror one more time, and leave. The entire exercise takes maybe ten minutes—about what someone experiencing a little gastric distress might need.

No one notices me emerge from the men's room, and no one notices me leave. The only customer in the bar has his back to me, and the bartender is still watching television.

As I leave, I'm working on my walk, concentrating on keeping my hips and butt stable, my hands and arms close to my body, taking longer strides. In my mind I'm singing the refrain from *"Walk Like a Man."* It doesn't actually help, but I like the song.

So begins my night of club hopping. I have several hours to kill before Strand will show at his club. It has taken me weeks to get his pattern down.

I move from club to bar to club, staying thirty or forty minutes at each stop. I order designer water or Virgin Marys in each place. The bartenders and wait staffs see plenty of this, especially in men my age. Lots of yesterday's party animals start drying out in middle age—or die young.

My stomach feels as if it is eating itself. My anxiety is so high I want to scream at the top of my lungs to relieve the pressure in my head. I try not to think about what's coming up, but it's impossible to think about anything else. I'm in the middle of a mental nightmare when the first guy hits on me. In my vision, Strand is bound and gagged and hanging by his arms, his feet not quite touching the floor, his dead fish eyes looking at me without expression while I try to convince myself to slit his throat or run the knife into his heart.

When my would-be admirer puts his hand on my shoulder I jump as if shot. Romeo is startled too then sees my abashed reaction and smiles.

"Sorry," I say, "I was a million miles away."

"I get it," he says. "Do you want company?"

He looks like he'd be good enough company, an earnest man with a friendly face, probably in his early forties. Short hair with a receding hairline, dress slacks, a crisp blue shirt, and a suede blazer. He looks intelligent, whatever that looks like. And he looks like a nice man. But gay Bobby is long gone, and this isn't the time, anyway.

I shake him off, nicely.

The other passes are less tempting. The men aren't as cute or as nice, and their overtures are crude. One younger guy, very drunk, throws his arm around my waist and says, "My place is just a block from here. What do you say we get it on!"

I turn down his kind offer with an amused smile and he stumbles off to proposition someone else, or maybe drink himself into a stupor.

I'm in a kind of Alice in Wonderland state, where nothing is quite real. I long for the simplicity of the days when I thought I was a gay man. Nobody wanted to beat me up. Nobody stared at me in stores and restaurants. Nobody jumped me in alleys to rape me. Granted, intimacy was hard to find, but it's going to be even harder as a transwoman.

But the reality is, I'm not actually a gay man. I'm a transwoman. And someone is trying to hurt me. And no one can help me but me.

The bars and clubs go in and out of focus. The people are like Mad Hatters and White Rabbits, caricatures of life in a world spinning out of control. I begin to feel ill. Just after one o'clock in the morning I break out in a profuse sweat and feel my stomach rising. I almost walk into the women's room, saved by a woman coming out as I near the door. I remember suddenly that I'm in male drag and make for the men's room next door. I go into a stall, lock the door, and throw up. I heave until nothing is left in my system, then sit on the stool, waiting for the world to stop whirling. I still feel sick to my stomach, but there is nothing left to vomit.

I hear two men at the sinks. One makes a reference to a "hearty party boy"—me, obviously—and they both laugh. I wait to come out of the stall until they are long gone and there are no other voices. I wash my hands, splash water into my mouth to rinse, then onto my face and towel myself off.

I can't do this, I realize again, for maybe the hundredth time tonight. It's just not in me. Even if I had the emotional strength to see it through, I don't have the physical strength. I feel weak. The vomiting has robbed my joints of strength, and months of hormones have reduced my natural strength to almost nothing. I'm not a woman and I'm not a man. I am looked upon as a freak wherever I go. Some people think I'm a nice freak, and some think I'd be fun to fuck, but really, I don't fit in this world. That's why Strand can kill me any time he wants and get away with it.

As I think about it, I think maybe that's the solution. Just let Strand kill me. I'm sure it will be painful and humiliating, but at least it will be over.

I leave the club and walk the streets for a while, considering all this. The cool air clears my head. I'm still jittery. I still feel weak and inadequate. I'd still be happy to die tonight and get it over with. But I make the turn for Skyscrapers anyway.

* * *

I STEP INTO SKYSCRAPERS for the first time since my little tryst with Strand last fall. The thought of the place has made me sick ever since. I go in the front door this time.

It's Thursday night and the hard-partying set is in attendance. Young t-girls are in abundance. Big hair, big breasts, lots of skin. I can't tell which are hookers and which are just expressing themselves. There are genetic women in the crowd, too. Lots of them come to gay and trans bars to dance. A few are hookers, and some are just hoping to get laid by Mr. Right. The men are mostly younger and mostly hetero or bi. Some come to gawk at the t-girls, and some come to experience sex with them. The young ones stand at the bar and stare openly, trying to get a girl to return the glance, to indicate an interest. The older ones mostly sit, but they, too, try to get the attention of the scantily clad women passing by constantly. There is a smattering of gay men here, too. They can dance here without getting hit on.

The place is famous for druggies and sex. I never liked it. I always felt like I was swimming in a sea of wasted lives when I was in here, even before Strand came along. It's where the desperate engage in acts of self-defilement. It's depressing. I wish I could leave and never return, but I can't. I have a mission to accomplish and I won't ever get this far again. I know it. I may back out, but not yet.

***

AFTER FORTY-FIVE MINUTES of mutely observing the dancers and hustlers and sex-hungry throngs, my cue to act comes up.

A skinny t-girl with Barbie-Doll hair and a super-low-cut blouse barely covering the nipples of her bulbous breasts opens her cell phone and holds it to her white-blond hair. She looks to be all of eighteen, but the extensive work on her body suggests someone at least in their mid-twenties. The breasts are at least part plastic, her lips are too full and don't smile quite right, her cheekbones seem artificially high, the skin around her eyes has been stretched to make a masculine face look feminine. It works. It should. She's wearing tens of thousands of dollars of plastic surgery, not to mention her investment in female plumbing.

I can't hear her. The place is so loud I wouldn't be able to hear her if we were side by side. But it's not hard to interpret her conversation, even from twenty feet away. She smiles, says something, listens, smiles again, her lips reading "Okay." She is Strand's new tranny squeeze and the Great One has just beckoned her. She gaily flits to the coat check. I follow and move past her as she waits for her coat. I exit the club, make two lefts and walk down the block into the shadows, looking for Strand's car. I know the pattern.

His car is parallel-parked near the end of the block, in the shadows. The engine and the lights are off. He is almost invisible. I spot him only because I know his car and I'm looking for it, and because I've seen how he plays this game.

I'm halfway down the block when the girlfriend turns the corner, her stiletto heels tapping out echoes as she starts down the sidewalk. I stay on the other side of the street, well out of the range of Strand's mirror view. I put on disposable gloves as I walk—the kind I wear for doing color. We'll be doing red tonight, I think.

The girlfriend can see me in the distance, but to her I'm just a local boy going home. As I near Strand's car, I drift out of the streetlight toward the porch of a brownstone and nestle into the shadow of a tree. I'm sure Strand is completely unaware of me. My heart is pounding and I'm gasping for air as if I've just run a four-minute mile. I can feel perspiration on my face and beads of it trickling down my back.

The girlfriend is still a hundred feet or so away when he spots her in his mirror and starts the car. I hear the door locks click open, see the brake lights come on. This is my cue. My anxiety hits heart attack levels. Really, as hard as I breathe I feel like I'm suffocating. I need to dash across the street, open the driver's door, subdue Strand and push him to the other side of the car, then drive off before his girlfriend is close enough to identify me.

But I can't move. My need for oxygen is so severe I drop on all fours and suck in air like an asthmatic. One leg cramps severely. My heart feels like it will burst. I can hear the girl's footsteps change speed as she approaches the car. I look up when I hear the door open. I am furious with myself. My time has come and gone. I can no longer get to Strand without being seen. I feel tears of fury and frustration form in my eyes.

"Hi sailor, looking for a really good fuck?" she says, loud enough for me to hear across the street, over my own near-death rasps. Not a good move if you want to curry favor with Mr. Secretive.

The interior light of the car gives me a theatrical view of what happens next. Strand lunges across the passenger seat, grabs her arm and yanks her violently into the car. Her head strikes the door frame and I hear her short cry of pain. The door is still open when she turns to Strand, one hand on her head, tears coming from her eyes, her mouth forming the words "What's wrong?"

Barely has she formed the last word when Strand's fist strikes a vicious blow flush in the middle of her face. The sight and sound of it is sickening. I know exactly how that feels—the shock, the numbness, and the pain. The humiliation. I can see splotches of blood on her face, the look of distress and hurt.

Love, Strand style.

The distraction curbs my anxiety attack. Fear and doubt give way to seething anger. In a rage I stand, wheezing, shaking, but mobile, not sure what to do. I want to attack, but I can't have a witness.

Strand's rage settles the matter. He slaps her across the face with the back of his hand so hard I can hear it like a gunshot. Her head swivels violently, like a rag doll. She struggles to get out of the car and he tries to grab her arm and pull her back in.

I dash for the driver's door in a limping sprint, trying to ignore the leg cramp, pulling the needle out, the cap off. As I near the door, the girl twists out of Strand's grasp and sprawls on the grass by the curb. She is sobbing, but not screaming. She has no voice to scream. It is a casualty of shock. She is scrabbling on her hands and knees, her ass hanging out of her tiny skirt, her purse strewn beside her, looped to her wrist. She is trying to find her feet so she can run.

As I reach for the door handle Strand flings the door open to get out of the car. He registers a shock of his own when my body fills his view, an intrusion he could not have imagined. I am operating on instinct now. The world is moving in slow motion. I see Strand's eyebrows arch in surprise and his mouth make a small puckered "O." His arms begin to move into a defensive posture but it's too late. By the time the first nerve synapse triggers the first hint of movement in his hands and arms, I stick my thumb in his eye. He brings both hands to his face and cowers. I drive the needle into the side of his neck and squeeze the plunger. His arms move another five or six inches, then his jaw drops and he gapes at me as his body melts into a limp pile and sags back onto the driver's seat.

We're now in the dream I envisioned when I planned this, Strand in a stupor in the driver's seat. Part of me is stunned at this reality, but mostly I'm acting out the vision just like I saw it. On automatic pilot. No second thoughts. No doubts. Just do it. I roll him over the console, onto the passenger side. As I push his butt and legs over the obstruction, his head and shoulders drop to the floor in front of the seat. I reach across him and pull the passenger door shut, then pull away. The girl is halfway to the corner, in a stumbling, staggering run punctuated with broken-hearted sobs. She hasn't seen me. I doubt she has seen anything since he bashed her in the face. She has no idea that her assaulter has now become a victim himself.

I drive a zigzag course for several minutes to see if anyone is following me. I force myself to ignore the seat belt warning that repeats itself after short pauses. It reminds me that I have an unbelted kidnap victim in my car.

My heart is racing. I am panting and sweating. My senses are taking in every sound, every sight, every moving thing. I want terribly to put the gas pedal to the floor and be gone from here. But I make myself focus. I make myself keep the car at the speed limit. I take stock of the situation.

It occurs to me that Strand may suffocate the way he is positioned and even a minor fender bender would snap his neck, a much easier death than I have planned for him. I stop on a quiet street and adjust him so he's sitting up in the passenger seat, seat belt on, and continue on my way.

When I was fantasizing about taking my revenge on Strand, I envisioned all kinds of ways to kill him and places to do it. In the weeks after my rape, I favored torture, with him hanging from something, me cutting off his penis, later his scrotum, and still later opening his abdomen and showing him his own entrails. That was an angry fantasy. I don't think I'm capable of that sort of torture, but the killing part of my plan is murky even now. He will know who is killing him, and why. The rest I'll kind of make up as I go along.

My favorite location for his death was the alley where I was raped, but that isn't practical for many reasons. I had thought about trying to find an abandoned warehouse or maybe an unoccupied house somewhere. I once went for a hike in a forest preserve, scoping out places I might use. The safest and smartest thing would have been to just kill him with the needle and leave him in his car somewhere. But that would have just been murder. I want more. I need more.

In the end, I decided on using his place. Not his multi-million-dollar condo in the sky—there would be too much security to overcome there. No, I am headed for his other place, his love nest.

I know where his apartment is, but I'm temporarily disoriented from my zigzag driving. Panic begins to overtake me as I imagine him coming to while I'm still trying to get my bearings. I breathe deeply, once, twice, five times. At last, Milwaukee Avenue comes into view. I am minutes from his special apartment.

I pull into the alley behind his building and kill the car lights. I find a garage door opener in the glove box; when I press it, one of the two garage doors in front of me rises. I pull into the garage and close the door. I flip on the overhead lights before the opener light goes dim. I pull two lengths of nylon cord from my pocket and tie his hands and ankles. I stuff a rag in his mouth and tie a length of cord around his head to hold it in place. Then I go through his pockets. I find a key ring with what looks like house keys on it.

I turn off the garage light and cross silently to the building's two back doors. One opens to a staircase going up. I choose the other one. When I followed Strand to this place, I didn't dare follow him into the alley, but I watched from the street and marked where I saw the lights go on. This building, first floor.

I still don't know if he has an alarm. There's no way to find out but to enter, so that's my plan. If I trip an alarm, I just leave him there and try to disappear.

I try three keys before I find one that works. I open the door and step into a hall that leads to a kitchen. No alarm panel that I can see. I check the front door. No alarm. I wait and listen. No alarm. No noise. The place seems deserted. A few plates and glasses in the cupboards, a few beers in the refrigerator, a bottle of wine on the counter. A few place settings and utensils in a kitchen drawer. Curtains drawn on every window. A cold, lonely place. As a love nest it's like sex in a casket.

Hauling in Strand is exhausting. He's a fit six-footer, maybe 180 pounds. Maybe more. It would have been hard for Bob Logan. For Bobbi it's nearly impossible. I hoist him on my shoulder and my knees buckle. I right myself, then stagger one laborious, lurching step, teeter, balance, then another step. It seems to take forever but I finally reel across the threshold and haul his limp body into the living room.

I lock the door and conduct a quick tour of the place. Two bedrooms, two baths, living room, kitchen with eat-in space. The rooms are big, with high ceilings. It's an old building that probably had an expensive makeover in the eighties or nineties.

The larger bedroom is fully decked out, the only room in the house that looks like it's used much. It has a four-poster bed with nice linens, night stands on both sides with clock radios and reading lights, two chests of drawers, an easy chair and footstool in one corner, area rugs, and a walk-in closet. One of the chests is completely devoted to sex toys—dildos in a variety of sizes, chains, a velvet whip, restraint devices, soft ropes, a box of condoms, several lubricants, body oils. I don't have time for a full inventory. I'm fighting panic and anxiety with every breath I take. But before I close the last drawer, I grab a section of rope.

As I look for a place to hang Strand—by the hands, not the neck—he begins to stir. Panic sets in. My pulse races and I start panting. I can feel beads of sweat trickling down my face, my back. I worry that I will have a total panic attack, like on the street. That makes it worse. I breathe deeply.

I have about ten feet of strong nylon cord and a heavy lag eye screw in my pocket. My plan was to sink the screw into a cross beam in the ceiling and hang him from it. In my days as Bob the home handyman I was handy enough to know it could be done, but the chance of me finding the beam on the first try is worse than awful. My backup plan is to lay him out on the floor and tie off his arms above his head to a door knob or something, and his feet to something else. But I'd rather have him hanging vertically.

I force myself to breathe deeply and slowly as I go in the kitchen. I need an implement—maybe a standard table knife—to put in the eye of the screw to sink it in the ceiling. His silverware is flimsy. I check the other drawers and cupboards in the kitchen. Luck! There is a small plastic tool case under the sink with wrenches and pliers and several screwdrivers. I pry the biggest screwdriver out of its molded slot and go back in the living room.

Strand moans. The clock is ticking. I look for a likely place to sink the lag eye screw, trying to guess where the cross beams run in the ceiling. My gaze stops on the doorway that separates the living room from the kitchen. Of course! The framing would support a man's weight. I slide a kitchen chair to the threshold and use the screwdriver to punch a hole through the dry wall. It's messy and louder than I'd like, but fast. In seconds I have a hole above the two-by-four framing. I run Strand's bondage-game rope through the hole, then sit him in a chair underneath it. I run the long rope between his hands and partly boost, partly hoist him upright. When I finish, he is dangling from the arch, his feet just touching the floor. He'll be able to relieve the pressure on his wrists and shoulder sockets by standing on his feet, but he won't ever be comfortable.

I check my watch. It's nearing three o'clock in the morning. Strand and I have two hours left together. Five o'clock in the morning is the best time for me to leave. It's dark and early enough that neighbors probably won't see me, and anywhere else I'm seen I'm just an early shift worker.

I position a chair in front of him and sit down at last, exhausted, nervous.

Until now, I have been focused on my work, on executing a plan. I focused on each step, blocking out everything else. It helped keep the panic under control. I have been amazingly proficient. As I sit here I realize with awe and dread that I have done this with the ruthless efficiency of a professional killer.

Having time to consider all this is not good for my mental state. Doubts cascade into my consciousness. I'm not a killer. I'm not even a fighter. I don't even engage in nasty conversations. What am I doing here? How can I walk away from this without killing him?

I begin planning how I will leave before Strand sees me. I could just leave him dangling. Someone will find him eventually. He'll be pissed but he won't know who to blame.

It's an attractive fantasy, but a fantasy none the less. He would keep stalking me. He won't stop until he kills me. Or I kill him. Would I rather be the one getting killed? Being the killer is so ugly. So messy. Or I can still leave and take my chances with the police.

The thought evaporates. No. I will not be the victim. Somehow I have to find the strength to do the unthinkable, right here, tonight.

Strand is mumbling and shaking his head. I look at him to see how close to consciousness he is. I try not to see him as a human being. I want to look at him and see him beating Mandy to death. I want to see his fists pounding her skull and ribs to a broken pulp. I want to see his cold fish eyes as he squeezes my breast until I cry. I want to envision him as he tells his thugs to beat and rape me. I want to look at him and feel my anus being violated, I want to feel that pain and see him laughing as his buddies tell him how it was, butt-fucking the tranny.

But what I see is a human face. I can see that he is feeling pain. His eye is swollen and red from my thumb. I can feel the unbearable ache in his shoulders. I see his hands turning white from lack of blood circulation. I want out of here. This is not where I belong. This is not me. I'm a hairdresser. A sissy. I want to be giving some crabby old lady a perm. I want to be a girl. I want to wear makeup and get my nails done. I don't want to hurt anyone.

And I don't want to have to live with the memory of hurting someone.

I hold my head and try to turn off the torrent of thoughts.

Strand reaches consciousness. He groans in pain and looks around slowly, not understanding. I stop crying and watch, mesmerized. The man whose last conscious act was beating the shit out of a t-girl is waking up dangling from the ceiling of his own love nest. What a mind-fuck that must be.

At last his sweeping gaze stops and comes to rest on me. He has trouble focusing because of the swollen eye. He blinks repeatedly. After a while, a sort of recognition kicks in. He is a prisoner. I am familiar to him. He takes in my tears, my feminine sitting posture. He sneers contemptuously. He thinks tears are a sign of weakness. Stupid man. Stupid, arrogant man. His sneer recharges my determination.

I stand and walk to him. He stares at me, his eyes glaring with hatred and sheer rage. He makes angry noises muffled beyond recognition by the gag. I wait for him to stop.

"Welcome to our last date, Strand," I say. My voice is the final clue as to who I am. He roars into his gag, almost no sound coming out. His rage is terrifying. A psychopath out of his mind with anger, all directed at me. Trussed as he is, I can feel him ripping my arms from my body, tearing my flesh from its bones.

I take a short breath and bring my hands to my face in horror. He sees my doubt and lashes out with his feet to kick me. I dodge him easily. All those hours of kickboxing lessons and conditioning make it child's play.

My horror gives way to reflexive action. I strike him with a karate jab flush in the solar plexus. It is a hard punch, with perfect leverage and timing. My knuckles penetrate well into his diaphragm. All the breath leaves his body and he gasps for air. His face turns red. He wets himself.

"Strand, you're pissing yourself," I say. "How does that make you feel?" His viciousness angers me. I can't resist a little taunting.

As he struggles for air I run another rope around his feet and up his back, then tie it around his neck. He can still kick if he wants to, but his range is very limited and each attempt will leave his shoulder sockets supporting all his body weight. "Kick all you want now, Killer," I say.

When his breathing becomes normal again he locks my eyes in a stare down. His lips naturally curl back into a sneer.

"You really can't control yourself, can you?" His viciousness helps me focus. This is about him, not me. "You have such incredible hate for me, for Mandy, for that girl you beat up in your car. What is it with you, Strand? Is it trannies you hate? Or everyone? Are you a psycho gay like John Wayne Gacy? Or just a mean motherfucker who figures he can do whatever he wants?

"That's what I think it is, Strand. You're a mean motherfucker and you're just going to keep beating and killing people until someone stops you. That's why we're here, Strand. I'm going to stop you."

I try to keep my voice steady and strong, but I waver a little at the end. Enough to remind Strand that I'm a simpering transsexual, not a real person.

He sneers audibly then tries to shriek again. He jumps and pulls with great strength, trying to free himself or pull down the beam. The noise alarms me. I punch him in the solar plexus again. As he gasps for air, I tighten the line connecting his feet to his neck. If he jumps again the noose will close off his windpipe.

"After you had those goons rape me I dreamed about this moment. A lot. My best dream was cutting off your cock and your balls and letting you watch me play with them while you bled to death."

More anger, maybe laced with the first pangs of fear. More gyrations, but no jumping. He is a very strong man, I realize. I'm a little worried about the crossbeam and rope holding up. I check my watch. It's three-twenty. I don't think I can last until five and I'm not sure the bonds will last that long either. So I must kill him now. Or not.

I move out of his line of sight and into the kitchen. I have a folding knife in my pocket. It has a sharp, three-inch blade, which is plenty. But I'd rather use something here. In the silverware drawer I find a stainless steel carving knife.

Back in the living room Strand looks worried. Through a series of grunts and sideward nods of his head, he communicates a conciliatory message. As in, cut me down. Let's just be friends.

He's right about me. I'm a pussy and I'm not really capable of doing the rest of this. If he had started this way, I might have fallen for it. But he didn't start this way. He is just working through the sociopath's bag of tricks. He started with the real Strand, the animal who despises everyone, especially me. His act is playing on a continuous loop in the theater of my mind. Every time I think I can't go forward with this, the movie tells me I can't go back.

"Sorry, Strand," I say. "There's no turning back now." I turn to face him, the knife in my hand. His eyes widen a little. I'm surprised. He's actually afraid.

He grunts and gestures some more.

"When I thought this up, I kept thinking of torturing you, or at least abusing you the way you abused Mandy and me and God knows who else," I say. I put the point of the knife against his crotch. His eyes show animal fear.

"But you're in luck, there," I say. "I have no stomach for torture. Or killing. I want to kill you even less than you want to die. Really. Isn't that the hell of it, though? I just don't have a choice anymore, so neither do you."

He interrupts me with more noises. He's encouraging my humanitarian instincts.

"No," I say, slowly shaking my head from side to side. "If I let you go, you'd just keep killing people, starting with me." He interrupts with more grunts and movements. More urgent now.

"I'm sorry. I'm really very, very sorry." I walk behind him. I put his house keys and car keys back in his pocket and pat him on the back.

"Goodbye Strand," I say. He thrashes wildly, trying to kick me, his weight swinging from the beam above. He connects, but there is no power in the blow. I step back and let him gyrate until he has no strength left. I focus. There is nothing in the world but what I have to do next. I block out all other thoughts except for the need to execute John Strand. A single movement. Nothing else in the world. No conscience. No morality. No law. Just one simple action.

He finally stops moving, sags, and breathes deeply. Before he can exhale I reach in front of him and put the blade of the knife to his throat with my right hand and place my left hand against his back for leverage. In the same instant, I slice the knife across his throat and deep, pulling with all my strength. Hard. Fast. Before I think about it and change my mind. Before he even knows what's happening and can start kicking and twisting again.

Blood spurts out in revolting torrents. He makes gurgling, bubbling sounds that penetrate into my very soul. I choke back the urge to vomit. His body spasms. Again, I choke back the urge to vomit.

In a few seconds it's all over. For him, anyway. For me, it is the beginning. For the rest of my life I will have to live with the knowledge that I'm a murderer. It is a curse. But I knew that going in. I focus my entire being on what to do next, squeezing the desire to panic and cry hysterically into a distant compartment of my brain. His body goes still. He dangles limply from the cross beam. Careful to avoid the blood, I check his pulse. There is none. I wait five more minutes and check his pulse again. None. He's dead.

I leave the knife on the floor, near his feet. Try not to notice the sickening mix of drywall powder and blood. The urge to vomit comes again. This time I run into the bathroom and puke into the toilet for several minutes. Empty my stomach. Dry heave as if to empty my conscience.

When it's over I wash my gloved hands in the sink, wipe down the toilet, triple flush. I check all the rooms to see if I have left anything behind. I inventory my clothing. I try to control my breathing. I try to dam up the panic that is everywhere. My senses are exploding. Lights and colors are blinding, the smell of blood cloys at my lungs, punishing me for breathing.

I sit for several minutes, trying to calm myself, thinking through my plan. What's left? I have all my clothing. The bathroom is clean. The knife and screwdriver are in the living room. My unused folding knife is in my pocket. There is no sign of me here. Other than Strand's dead body which I cannot look at. There are no fingerprints to wipe down. I've been wearing gloves since I left the club.

Heart pounding, mouth dry, I turn off the lights and leave by the back door, locking it as I go. There's no going back now.

The chill spring air helps revive me. For two blocks, I concentrate on walking and try to get my breathing back to normal. I'm a party animal returning home after a late date. I walk briskly, but not in a panic. I remember to put my hands in my pockets and walk like a man. I walk south on Milwaukee for a while, then east, trying to focus on what I have to do. Trying not to think about what I have done. Refusing to think about what awaits me when Strand's body is found.

Two miles from Strand's love nest, I drop my gloves in a public garbage can. A mile later I stop in a crowded bar and use the bathroom. When I emerge, I'm just another reveler who shouldn't be driving home. I hail a cab and get out a few blocks from my building. I walk the rest of the way, sliding in through the alley and the back door. There is no one on the street to see me, no lights on in the building.

In the safety of my own apartment, when the door closes behind me, the enormity of what I've done, the evil, violent, savage act I have committed hits me like a tidal wave. I lose the power to stand. I melt to the floor, my back against the door. Sobs come in great retches, my voice screams out in a tortured whisper. "Murderer! Cold blooded murderer!" I planned every step, every detail and carried out a murder like a hit man.

I can hear Strand gurgling and rasping. I can see him pleading for his life. I see his face, unencumbered by the gag, a kindly, warm expression. Handsome. Friendly. What have I done? Did I imagine the evil in him? I wonder. Am I crazy? Am I a threat to those around me? I put my head between my knees and sob. I should have tried to get to know him. Find out why he was so mean. This is crazy, I know, but I can't help myself.

Eventually, the urge to vomit comes again. I open the toilet seat and dry heave until my stomach aches. Afterwards, I rinse my mouth and see my image in the mirror. Facial hair. Male wig. I am revolted by it. I pull off the disguise, putting the facial hair and male wig in a bag so I can dispose of them in the salon where a little more hair won't be noticed. I put the boy clothing in two other bags that will be dropped off at two different charities. I go in my bedroom and put on my girly pajamas, then brush my teeth and brush out my hair. It helps. I'm still a murderer, but at least I'm Bobbi again.

* * *

AMAZING. I ACTUALLY slept for several hours last night. I thought I might never have a natural sleep again. In fact, I planned to ask Roberta to help me get a sleeping pill prescription at my appointment tomorrow.

Despite the sleep, there is an unreality to my world as I get up and go through my morning rituals. I am a murderer. I slit the throat of another person. The fine vibration of the knife blade slicing through cartilage echoes in the nerves and muscles of my right hand. My hand can still feel the knife handle, the pressure. I can see the back of his neck, his head tilted upward in supplication. Can see the blood spurt from his throat like water from a garden hose.

The sights and sounds of that act are fresh in my mind and even when I turn them off, there is a surreal quality to everything.

The silence in my apartment is deafening, but the thought of playing something on the stereo nauseates me. I seem to move in slow motion. The sound of the water running from the tap is like giant waves crashing on a rocky shore.

My body feels shaky. Things I hold in my hand feel like they will fall from my grasp. My knees are weak. I feel dizzy and the room whirls every time I stand or turn around. I wonder if I will pass out when I walk down stairs. I wonder if my anxiety will produce a heart attack, or maybe a stroke. I know it won't, but I think about it more wishfully than with dread. It would be an easy resolution to something I'm not sure I can handle.

I make coffee out of rote habit. It smells awful. The thought of food is repulsive.

As I dress I wonder if I left behind any incriminating evidence at Strand's apartment. Strangely, I don't fear this. There is no room in my consciousness for worry about a trial and jail. I can't get past my own condemnation for what I've done. And yet, when I make myself think rationally about it, I can't think of a better alternative I had.

Putting on makeup and doing my hair helps.

* * *

"WHY DO YOU THINK you're having trouble sleeping?" Roberta asks.

She's really smart and perceptive, but this was very predictable so I'm ready to steer our discussion far away from last night.

"A big part of it is needing to have a vagina," I say. "I'm at a point where I can't stand having this penis any more. It's uncomfortable and it's preventing me from having a sex life. I'm so horny I can hardly stand it. Every night I dream about making love with someone." It's mostly true. I feel that way about my genitalia now. Of course, my sleeping problems stem from a different source. I'm a murderer. I left a dead body hanging to rot in a North Side apartment.

My subterfuge works. She asks me questions about my sex life, my desires. Interest in both men and women is fairly common she says. She asks who my fantasy partners are, how many, how often. I respond honestly.

"Why do you think this is coming up now?" she asks.

"I think it's because I'm ready. It's time. My doubts are gone. This is who I am and I'm tired of being trapped in the old body."

"But is this just to relieve horniness? Couldn't you go out and find a lover?" she asks.

"Of course I could," I say. "But that wouldn't change anything. I'm a woman. I will never, ever present as a man again. I will never be a man again. And I'm just tired of being between genders."

Tears begin to flow. They are honest tears and I've meant what I said. Seeing Bob in the mirror yesterday was hideous, and not just because of the murder. That isn't me. If I had to go back to dressing and acting like a man, life would not be worth living.

After a long moment, Roberta asks, "What kind of woman will you be, Bobbi?"

"A transwoman, Roberta," I answer. "One who feels like a woman inside and has some of the physical characteristics of a woman. But people around me will know I am trans. Some will hate me for it, some won't. I wasn't born in a woman's body and I don't think I'll ever be like people who grew up as women. That's okay. I can't define myself by what I'm not. I'm what I am. A transwoman. I'm ready for whatever comes. This is who I am. Period."

We spend the rest of the session talking about transwomen and genetic women. Roberta isn't crazy about my willingness to differentiate between the two, and to categorize myself as less than a woman woman. Transsexual women are like that. Most of them pursue a goal of total acceptance, complete immersion. Most believe they are every bit as womanly as a genetic woman. I probably would too if I was 5-5 and 120 pounds and could wear an off-the-rack size 4 or 6. But I can't. I'm six feet tall with wide shoulders and a male's bone structure. I can be pretty, I can be effeminate, and I can even be sexy, but very few people will see me as a genetic woman.

I can deal just fine with that, I tell Roberta. What I can't handle is having this penis between my legs. It started out as a cover story, to justify sleeping pills. But as we talk about it, I know it's true.

* * *

I GET TO THE SALON just a few minutes before my first appointment, half running the last block. I huff and puff through the waiting area and back to the break room. I empty my bag of hair in the garbage can the assistants use to dump their sweepings in. I dig deep in the can with one hand and place my bundle in the middle, then cover it again. I wash my hands and run back into the salon.

The receptionist is on the phone. She catches my eye and points to the waiting room. I nod. Yes, I'll get the client myself. I check the appointment list on my station. Lilly. A new client.

The waiting area is packed. We're busy today. Every head looks up when I enter the room. You don't see obvious transwomen every day, and I suppose I have an especially wild look today, having spent the night kidnapping and murdering someone.

"Lilly?" I call out.

A nice looking middle-aged professional woman stands, a smile on her face. "You must be Bobbi," she says.

"I am," I reply, leading her to my chair.

"I've heard so much about you!" she says.

One of her co-workers is a client, a prize from my days and nights of handing out pamphlets. Back when I was an innocent transwoman, fearing only rejection from my fellow man. This thought passes quickly. We are doing hair here. This is what I do. I focus, both on Lilly and on her hair.

The day flies by. I am booked solid. My colleagues are busy too. Business has been picking up, and not just from the change of season. My little promotions last winter have brought in some new business, and we're getting good word of mouth buzz, too. I think having a transsexual in our midst might be helping business more than hurting it, even for the other stylists. Either way, being busy is the perfect tonic for me. I shut out the mental torture, the guilt, the worry. I just do hair.

At seven my last client is done. I clean up my station and walk into the night. It's raining, but the night air is warm and there is no wind to fight.

I'm walking home. I need the exercise. I'm blowing off the gym for a few days but I need the exhaustion that comes from a brisk walk after a long day on my feet. That's the only way I'll manage to sleep. Roberta's psychiatrist colleague has called in a sleeping-pill prescription for me, and I'll pick it up on the way home. But I prefer not to use narcotics. We'll see.

Halfway home, I stop at a deli for soup and a half sandwich. I'm not hungry, but I haven't eaten in 24 hours except for some crackers and juice one of the girls at the salon gave me. I know I need some calories.

The deli girl gawks at me but I'm too tired to give a damn. Funny, my indifference seems to make her indifferent too. How about that.

I don't look behind me on my way home tonight, nor will I for many nights to come. Thomas or one of his friends will shadow me for a while to see if the thugs come back. He doesn't know about last night's episode, though he certainly knew it was coming. It's nice not to have to watch my back any more. I just don't want to pull any of these good people into jail with me if the cover blows off this thing.

By the time I get home I've managed to focus on my heels clicking on the pavement, and moving my hips and arms in a feminine fashion. It feels so good! God how I want this for the rest of my life. Just let me walk free and feel like a woman.

* * *

NEWS OF STRAND'S DEATH hit the media yesterday, four days after the murder. He had been missed at work Monday morning, but no one knew about his love nest so he was just a missing person until the cleaning lady stopped in Tuesday and saw a dead body hanging from a beam at the entrance to the living room.

The discovery came early enough to make the evening television news, and it rated front page coverage in the newspapers this morning. Details about the murder are sparse. Investigators think the apartment was a love nest. Sex paraphernalia including S/M tools were found on site. The neighbors never saw anyone there, though the folks upstairs sometimes heard late night visitors arrive. Etcetera. There are no immediate suspects, but police are thought to be seeking persons of interest who were romantically linked to Strand.

There is a lot more information available on Strand himself and the media is intrigued with it, especially the way it contrasts with his tawdry end. Rich. Powerful. Hugely successful. Brilliant attorney. Skilled networker. Influential friend to the mayor, the governor and many other Illinois politicians. Man about town. Constantly seen with beautiful women. Popular, garrulous. The profiles make him seem like a cross between Cary Grant and a civic leader, with a dash of weird sex thrown in.

I thought this moment, when I would be following coverage of my horrible act, would drive me to a nervous breakdown. I thought it would fill me with fear that the police investigation would lead to me. I thought that I would find sleep impossible as I worried about going to jail.

Reality is oddly different. My tension peaked before his body was found. Along with guilt and self-loathing at what I had done, I was stalked by the fear that the murder had been discovered almost immediately and the police were keeping a lid on it while they investigated a trail of clues that lead to me.

It was almost a relief to finally hear they had found the body. I am less relieved about their seeming lack of leads. Who knows what games are being played? As much as I might fear the clues lead to me, I fear even more that they will lead to the arrest and prosecution of an innocent person. What do I do then?

Through it all, I'm managing to sleep a little every night, without drugs. I'm still wired, to be sure. Sleep is brief and restless. My appetite is still off, but I'm coping. Every night as I go to bed my mind is invaded with scenes from the murder. I can feel things I felt at the time, especially the knife slicing through Strand's throat. I can see the blood gush out, hear the gurgling, feel the vomit start to rise in my throat. I remember his gestures of innocence just before I killed him. I can't keep my mind from conjuring up the conversation we might have had, me probing to find out why he became what he was, him telling me about his abusive childhood, crying, cleansing his soul. Emerging from the apartment alive, a changed man who would honor trannies for the rest of his life. Silly. Ridiculous. Irrational.

I go through this torture for a while, then I force myself to go through the events that led to that murderous moment. I remember these events but I can't feel them like I do the murder. I make myself see them. Mandy being brutally beaten to death. Strand hurting me for no reason other than to make me feel bad. The threats. The rape. More threats.

That helps me live with it. I won't ever be righteous about what I did. I should have gone to the police and taken my chances. In my darkest hours now, it seems so clear that the police would have handled it. They would have protected me. They would have reinvestigated Strand for Mandy's murder.

But in my lucid moments, I come back to my original premise: If I had come forward with my accusations, I would have been humiliated, publically ridiculed and probably beaten to death myself.

I go through this thought process every night and sometimes once or twice during the day, too. It doesn't make me feel good, but it makes me feel as though I'm still a person, not a psychotic murderer. It helps me live with myself, and that lets me sleep a little.

My father's final homily on the Vietnam War was that life isn't fair or unfair, it just happens. So you can end up in a situation where no matter what you do, it's wrong. You take hostile fire from a village. You know if you return fire you'll kill some innocents. If you don't, the snipers will pick your guys off with impunity. "Me," he said, "I take them out. I get screwed either way, but at least if I survive I get to find out what's on the other side of the court martial."

I never thought of my father has having profound thoughts until this mess evolved. Now I think back on his words often. I wonder what he would have thought if he could have witnessed this, his disgusting fag offspring taking out a monster. I wonder if he would feel connected to me, in some way.

* * *

CECELIA HAS BEEN CALLING since the Strand story hit last night's news. I dodged her calls last night, but my phone is ringing again. It's nine o'clock. I leave for work in an hour. I don't need caller ID to know it's Cecelia. I answer on the fourth ring.

"Have you heard the news?" she asks. No greeting, no self-identification. Cecelia gets right to the point.

"About your friend Strand?" I ask.

"MY friend!" she answers. "You're the one who thought he was so hot. Anyway, the psychotic bastard is dead. Long live his murderer!"

She is exultant. I wish I could feel so good about it, and I would if it weren't for the fact that I am the murderer. It's a hard thing to realize. The burden of this deed presses on all my senses. I will never experience sheer joy again because this weight impinges on everything.

"Well," she says, "aren't you going to say anything? I thought you'd be as happy as I am."

By not speaking I've made her suspicious.

"I'd be a happier if he had been brought to justice for murdering Mandy," I say. "But yes, it's nice to know he's off the streets. Have you heard anything about the investigation? Do we know who did it?"

This gets her going. Cecelia loves to dish the dirt. The few facts that are known about the case are on TV she says, but the rumor mills in the police department and at the courthouse are buzzing. He's had several girlfriends in the past year, some of them at the same time. One was married, a high-powered corporate executive. And of course Cecelia had tried again to make them aware of his connection to Mandy and the trans community.

That makes me swallow. I had hoped his connection to our world would be ignored, a rumor with no foundation, the ultimate insulation for me. No one knew about our one-night stand, so I don't expect any investigation to get to me anyway, but just the same, it would be nicer if they stayed in the straight world with their probe.

I have trouble staying focused on Cecelia's gossip. It's not the thought of being found and convicted that distracts me. It is the sense of loss. I lost my innocence in all of this. Not my virginity. What I mourn is the loss of my naiveté. Will I ever again be able to feel the first rays of morning light on my face and dream of beautiful things? Of a gentle lover, a perfect hairdo, Marilee's soft smile?

Cecelia is irritated with my lack of communication. "Am I boring you, Bobbi?" she asks sharply.

"No, honey," I say with a sigh. "I'm just distracted. I have to get ready for work. I'm running late. Can we continue this later?"

She agrees, but it's clear I've ruined her morning.

* * *

AS MUCH AS I LOVE doing hair, this day seemed to last forever. I had a cancellation and a no-show, which never helps. Any time I spend sitting around is time spent in guilt and depression. But even the clients who came in were somehow boring today. Everyone seemed to be in a snappy, edgy mood. No one was elated with their service.

A couple of them acted disappointed. It's the eternal frustration for hairdressers. The lady comes in wanting a new look, but you can only do so much with short, straight hair, especially if the client won't let you get into color or texture. So she leaves disappointed, looking like she did when she came in.

As her hairdresser, you try not to let it get to you. But it does. I live for the customer who walks out of the salon on air, feeling like she's been reborn with the work I've done on her. When someone leaves disappointed, I take it personally. I'm sad and I'm disappointed in myself.

It's especially hard now, with the specter of Strand's murder hanging over me. That realization has weighed heavily on my heart and mind all day, and it's getting worse with every step I take now. I'm walking north on Clark Street in a neighborhood favored by lesbians, though like all of the GLBT neighborhoods on the North side, it draws lots of gays and straight people too. I turn into a really cute neighborhood café. Sitting on a stool at a raised table in the corner is Officer Phil. He smiles and waves when I enter. I smile and wave back.

We exchange greetings and I peel off my light spring coat and hang it on the back of my stool. As I hoist myself up on the tall seat, I glance at Phil's face. For a moment his eyes seem to be popping out of his head, and he blushes a beet red. I have inadvertently given him a total boob flash struggling onto my stool. He struggles to regain control of his outward appearance, consciously looking away from my chest.

"Sorry," I say. "Would it be better if I kept my coat on?"

He accepts my question as a rhetorical quip and simply smiles.

I'm dressed like a slut today. Rebellion I guess. My feelings about the murder and who I am and what I did are very complex and very fluid. When I finally got around to dressing this morning I just had this unstoppable urge to express my femininity. Sometimes that comes out in a conservative flowing long skirt and peasant blouse, sometime in a mini skirt and net hose. Today it came out in streetwalker garb—a low-cut lacy top, no bra, skin-tight black pants, stiletto heels, hair in a high twist with dangling strands of curls at my temples. And I just started my meeting with Officer Phil by flashing him. Great form.

We do how-are-you small talk until the waiter takes our orders. Coffee for Phil, water for me. A great day for the restaurant business.

"So," I say as the waiter leaves. "I'm wondering if you called me here to propose marriage or what?" Officer Phil laughs, maybe blushes a little.

I don't know what has gotten into me. This is not like me, but it feels right. He's way too somber and, beneath my veneer, so am I. Let's laugh a little.

"I'm sorry about my outfit" I say. "If I had known you'd be calling today I would have worn something more presentable to work and I wouldn't be embarrassing you like this."

He smiles. "No problem, Bobbi. You look great." He pauses for a moment. "I'm just asking around to see if anyone knows anything about John Strand, the guy who was found murdered yesterday. Cecelia claims he was involved with Mandy Marvin and we have some reports he might have dated some other trans women from time to time. What can you tell me about him?"

I straighten my posture and strike a thoughtful pose, gazing into the distance. "Well, Cecelia introduced me to him once and I've seen him around a couple of times, but not with anyone from the community. Cecelia said he hooked up with a t-girl or two, but I can't honestly say I ever saw that." I kind of shrug as if to say I'm sorry.

"Does this mean I have to pay for my own drink?" I ask.

Officer Phil chuckles politely and shakes his head no.

"I understand Cecelia wasn't the only one who thought he was seeing Mandy," says Phil. He says it conversationally, but it's a question.

"I've heard that, too," I say. "That's been all over the community since Mandy was murdered. I don't know if it's true or not, but I hear the talk so much I sort of assume it's true."

"But you don't have personal knowledge they were dating?" Phil asks.

"No," I answer.

"You and Mandy were good friends," he says. "A lot of people told me that during the investigation. Didn't she tell you anything about her love life?"

"Not a lot," I say. "We weren't really close friends. I was her hairdresser and I adored her and we talked a lot when I did her hair. But we didn't have a lot in common. You know, different ages, different crowds…"

"She was a party girl, I remember everyone saying," says Phil, coaxing me to talk more.

"Yes she was," I agree. "She was into the club scene. The girl could dance and party 'til dawn."

"Was she a hooker, Bobbi?" he asks.

I pause for a moment before answering. "She turned tricks for money, like a lot of the young ones. That's probably how she paid for her surgery. But she told me she was getting out of the trade months before she was murdered. She was a good kid."

Phil nods, as if in agreement. "What about her and John Strand?"

Small alarm bells are ringing in my mind. I have already answered this question, and quite plausibly.

"Like I said, I never saw them together. Mandy told me she had a new lover, but she never said his name and she never introduced me to anyone as her lover or her special friend or anything like that."

"Do you think anyone in the trans community would be capable of killing Strand as revenge for Mandy Marvin's murder?" He has an earnest look on his face.

I respond in disbelief. "I can't think of anything less likely than that," I say. "We're all in various stages of castration. We can be mean and petty and irrational, but transwomen are almost never violent. You tell me—when was the last time a transwoman was charged with a violent crime in Chicago?"

He accepts this as a rhetorical question. We both know that transwomen have never been charged with murder in Chicago. Robbery, yes. Prostitution, oh yes. The occasional misdemeanor assault charge coming out of a domestic violence situation. But transwomen just aren't violent people. Other than me.

We sip our drinks in silence.

"The other thing I wanted to talk to you about is the State Attorney's victim assistance unit. I didn't know this, but Cook County actually has a victim assistance person who specializes in GLBT crimes."

I stare at him blankly.

"This has to do with when you were raped, Bobbi," he says. "There's a person in the State Attorney's office who should have gotten your case report and who can help you push the case along. For some reason, she never saw the paperwork on your case."

"And you're surprised by this?" I say. "Your rape sergeant probably puked on the report every time she thought about talking to a dirty transsexual. Anyway, it's over. Life goes on."

"It's not over until you give the system a chance to work," says Phil. "There are only two places in the country that have advocates who specialize in GLBT crimes. We're serious about protecting your safety and your rights, but you have to meet us half way."

"What do you want me to do?" I ask. But with a growing dread, I already know the answer.

"I want you to meet with her and see if between you two we can't get your rape investigation reopened." Phil hands me a business card.

A week ago, I would have jumped on this. Not with a lot of enthusiasm and certainly not with the expectation anything would come of it, but just to give the system a chance. Now, the worst thing that could happen would be for the system to work, for the new investigation to lead to the thugs, then to Strand, then right to my door.

I glance at the card and slip it into my purse.

"Promise me you'll call her," says Officer Phil.

"I'll try, but I make no promises," I answer. I allow a little anger to show through. "This is pretty late in the game Phil. I've already been through the abuse your rape sergeant doled out, and all the hurt and pain, the feelings of uselessness, the contempt from polite society. I got past it on my own and I'm doing okay.

"The other thing is, I've got a lot on my plate. I'm going to be working as a platform artist at a hair show in New York next month, and I'm getting ready for my operation. The big one."

It's true. Roberta has cleared me for gender reassignment surgery this summer, so I'm getting ready to set the date. I've also scheduled a consultation with a plastic surgeon to see about feminizing my appearance before and after. And on top of all that, SuperGlam wants me to work on stage in their presentation at the New York hair show. Somewhere in all the gloom and despair in my life, some part of me is rejoicing at this honor.

Phil takes my angst well. He gives me a five minute pep talk on why I should call and all the good things that can come from it. I'm actually feeling a little guilty when we finish. The GLBT advocate has been trying to reach out to the trans community for several years, it turns out. I could help her cross the bridge and maybe no one would ever have to murder a shit heel like Strand again. Or maybe I would just put myself in jail.

* * *

May

IT HAS BEEN A WEEK since Strand's murder first made the headlines. It has been a miserable week. Sleep is still hard to come by and when I do sleep, it's only in short bursts. I have very little appetite. Workouts are a chore. Even work at the salon is a struggle. Most of my clients don't notice it, since I've always been more of a listener than a talker. But my mind wanders while I work, even when the client is talking. And even though my work is technically good, it lacks flare. When the client wants a bob, she gets a bob. When she wants a highlights retouch, that's what she gets. The creative urge to do more, to add a spiff here and there, is just missing. I wish it weren't so. I miss that feeling when creative juices are flowing, and I miss that combination of surprise and delight that so many clients expressed when I was really on my game.

I'm hoping desperately that this part of me is not a casualty of the Strand murder too.

There is still a constant war going on in my head. On one side is the knowledge that I murdered a helpless man in cold blood. With that vision of myself comes shame and regret, and a slide show in my memory of images of Strand hanging in his living room. I remember every word we exchanged, every thought I had. I remember the last moment I considered not killing him. I remember the knife slicing through his throat. I remember the spurt of blood. I remember the vision of his body sagging above a puddle of blood on the floor. *I did that!* I think.

The other side in the war is the cold, hard, rational rebuttal to the guilt. *I had no other choice.* The cops would never believe me, and even if they did, there was no proof. Maybe I could have gotten a protection order. Not likely, given Strand's stature in the community and the lack of evidence I had of intimidation. But even if I had, that would have only provoked him. And he had already shown that he didn't have to be present to make his point. His thugs would have just done his dirty work for him while he was dining with a priest and a judge somewhere.

But there's a small voice inside me that's saying I didn't give the law a chance. That I wanted to kill him all along. That otherwise I would have opened up to someone like maybe Officer Phil about the incidents that led up to my rape.

And there's yet another voice that screams *Bullshit!* This voice erupts as I picture telling my story to a cop or a prosecutor. *Yeah, I had a date with this rich, powerful guy who seduced me and later squeezed my breast really hard and made me cry. I made him for the one who murdered a friend of mine, mainly because of the look in his eyes when he said it wasn't him. No, I never personally saw them together, but lots of people in the community said they were a package. I followed him for a while to see if he was going to beat up any more trannies, but he caught me and had me raped by two guys I never saw.*

It sounds ridiculous when I think of it that way. So ridiculous I start to wonder if Strand really did beat and kill Mandy. Did I kill a man who never murdered anyone, who just had bad manners and a mean disposition? It reminds me of a televised rape trial I watched some years ago. Halfway through the trial, it was clear that no rape had been committed, that the two people had consensual sex, during and after which the guy treated the woman shabbily. It was debasing for her, but not rape, not in the legal sense of the word.

What if Strand's only misstep was treating me badly after sex? What if the two goons were acting on their own?

But their words come back to me.

Be careful who you piss off next time.

They were working for Strand. They had no other reason to follow me. If they wanted to rape a transwoman they could have picked hundreds who were younger and cuter than me, and smaller.

And so it goes, a constant run of contrasting images and thoughts flashing through my consciousness. It is exhausting. I wonder if being constantly stalked by Strand's goons might have been better. Or if the stalking and harrassment might have ended with the beating of the last goon who followed me. If this murder was all for naught.

This unending cycle of doubt and guilt saps all my energy. I have thought several times that death would have been better, that maybe before it's over, I'll consider suicide.

Oddly enough, what keeps me going is not wanting the bullies and bigots to win. The thought of people reading my obituary in the paper and thinking, *there goes another tranny misfit*, is too humiliating. As long as I'm alive and doing hair, even people who hate me or hate trans people have to at least acknowledge my existence on this Earth. It's my planet too. I've killed to stay here and I'll be damned if I'm going to be bullied out.

Such is my frame of mind as I head up the walk to Marilee's house. It is a strange sensation to realize it was almost exactly a year ago that I came here for the cop party. It was my first appearance as a woman with a group of straight people in a social setting. It's breathtaking to think how much things have changed since then.

As I ring the bell I realize what a beautiful day it is. Birds are chirping, trees are budding. Spring flowers are in full bloom. Lawns are green and the grass is tall. Spring is erupting all over and I'm just noticing it for the first time. I need to live better than this!

Marilee sees me in. We take our usual places at her kitchen table, sipping coffee, making girl talk. I tell her about my last session with Roberta, and my preparations for surgery. She gets me up to date on her husband and kids, a new (nameless) male client who has a fetish for high heels but not for cross-dressing, her garden. The conversation starts to wane.

"Bobbi," she says in that sort of pensive tone women use just before they hit you with something big, "Something isn't right with you. I can feel it. You look tired. You don't have your usual energy and enthusiasm. And you're holding something back. I don't know what it is, but I can just feel it. What's going on?"

God but this woman is perceptive. What do I say? I open my mouth but can't find words. As I search for the right thing to say I realize there is no right thing to say and there never will be and I break into tears. I cannot control this outpouring of grief. I sob and sob and sob. Marilee pulls her chair next to mine and puts her arms around me. I rest my forehead on her shoulder and continue crying.

When my crying subsides from hysterical levels, she rubs my back with one hand and holds me close with the other. It feels so good. She is the mother Bobbi never had. Her arms are warm. Her heart is good. Her breath is soft on my face. I feel loved and protected.

"Tell me about it, Bobbi," she says in that soft mom's voice. "You need to let it out. It's eating you up. Tell me."

I wrap my arms around her and hug back. "I can't Marilee. It's my curse, not yours. I can't let it be yours."

She pets my head. "Bobbi, I've been hearing people's darkest thoughts for years. It won't destroy me. Tell me about it."

"I can't. I can't," I say. "It's too awful. It's too…too…" Words fail me.

"Too what, Bobbi?" she says gently. "Talk to me. Go ahead. You'll feel better."

"I betrayed you. You'll never trust me again. You'll never forgive yourself. You'll never forgive me." The sobbing starts again. "Marilee, I love you more than anyone in the world. I can't lose you. Not you too."

She hugs me tighter and lets me cry for a while. When I calm down she takes my shoulders in her hands and straightens me up so we can look at each other eye to eye.

"Does this have to do with John Strand, Bobbi?" she asks. Her tone is motherly, but firm. I can't lie to her. I nod my head yes.

She stands up and takes my hand.

"My office, right now," she says. She is very businesslike.

I stand and follow her on shaky legs. In her office she seats me on the couch and takes her shrink chair.

"Do you have a credit card or checkbook with you?" she asks. I nod yes. "Give me one or the other," she says. "You just became my patient. The fee is $30. Our first session started 20 minutes ago, okay?"

I nod. We take care of the financial transaction. She gives me a personal history form to fill out later, but before I leave.

"Okay," she says. "Everything we say is protected by the patient-doctor relationship. Tell me everything. Everything. Even if it takes all day." I start to argue but she shushes me with an outstretched hand. "Everything!" she commands.

I have no tears left to cry, so I cover my eyes with my hands for a minute, then start.

"I killed him," I blurt out. It's not the beginning, but it's the first thing she needs to know. "The fact that I could do that, that I did do that, is almost more than I can bear. Maybe it will be more than I can bear. The fact that he's gone from this earth isn't troubling at all."

Then I start at the beginning. Hearing the news about Mandy's murder, deducing that this was the event that had so shaken Marilee a year ago. Picking up the trans community gossip on Strand. Meeting him. Having sex with him. Being physically hurt and intimidated. Following him. Getting caught. His overt threats. The people following me. The rape, undoubtedly perpetrated by the same goons he had following me. The taunting flowers. More tails. Getting one goon beaten up. The sense that he would kill me soon. Not wanting to be a victim. Not trusting the legal system. Planning his murder for weeks. Executing the plan. Executing Strand. The aftermath.

I try to give her the Cliff's Notes version of things several times, but she makes me go through everything in detail.

When I finish, Marilee's eyes are moist. She has been brushing away the occasional tear since I told her how it felt to be abused by the bastard after sex.

"Well," she says, "We have a lot to talk about." The sadness in her voice sets off alarm bells. My god, I realize, Strand wasn't her patient! I killed an innocent man.

I interrupt her. "Was he the guy?"

She looks at me with those large soft eyes, so sad, for the longest time. My heart sinks. At last she nods her head.

"Yes," she says. "Yes, Bobbi. He was the guy. That much at least I can take off your shoulders.

"And yes, I still love you. I'll always love you. You are my daughter and my friend and you have a good, good heart, Bobbi."

We stand and embrace and cry in each others' arms. I have never loved anyone so much.

* * *

I HAVE STROLLED home the several miles from Marilee's house. It's like floating on a cloud because of the relief I feel. But it's a dark cloud. No amount of relief will ever undo what I've done. Still, compared to where I was, my spirit is light. She loves me. Marilee loves me like a daughter. She forgives me for murdering Strand. This makes me feel human, somehow.

My walk home has given me time to realize how deeply it hurt when my father disowned me and my mother just followed him mutely into the haze. I never cried, never cursed, never looked back. I thought I got away clean.

But I didn't. It's one thing when your lover leaves you, or when a friend becomes alienated. Those things cause hurt and anger, but in the end, they're just people you met. There will be others. But when your parents reject you, when they can't stand the sight of you and your only sin is being who you are, it's the ultimate rejection. They can't replace you and you can't replace them.

Marilee isn't my mom, I know that. But having an older friend who loves me unconditionally and thinks I'm a special person—that's so much more than I ever expected from life. I'm so thankful. I feel so fine.

I savor the feeling as I turn down the street to my apartment building, but almost immediately I see the unmarked police car in front. I'm not naïve. They aren't here to see the neighbors and they don't want a haircut either.

As I turn up the walk to my porch I hear two doors open and close. At the door I glance back. Detective Hardcase is walking briskly toward me, another plain-clothes guy I've never seen before in tow.

When he reaches the bottom of the stairs to the front door he flashes his badge. "Robert Logan, I'm Detective Allan Wilkins of the Chicago PD and this is Detective Harold Johnson. We'd like a word with you."

I close the door, still standing on the porch. Calling me Robert is a deliberate attempt to intimidate me. It also shows he's done his homework. I haven't legally changed my name yet. "Okay, fire away."

"Can we come in?"

"Last time you were in my apartment you threatened me and treated me like dirt. No," I say, watching him get tense in the face, "I don't think I want to see you in a private place."

"We can be back with a warrant in thirty minutes." Always the bully.

"Suit yourself," I answer. "Are you going to do that or are we going to talk?"

"What do you know about the murder of John Strand?"

"What I've read in the papers and heard on the news," I answer.

"Did you know him?" Hardcase is loud as he asks questions. His face is inches from my face. I can smell his breath, which reeks.

"I've met him and I've seen him a few times since then."

"Seen him? You dated him?" It's really not a question so much as a statement, a conclusion.

"No," I say. "I encountered him. Once at a party, another time in a bar in the theater district. And I cut his hair once, I think."

"So you never dated?"

"No."

"You're sure?" Again, it's not a question. It's a challenge. Like there's something else coming.

"I'm sure." But I'm not, of course. I'm wondering if they've found some proof that Strand and I were more than casual acquaintances.

"Be very, very sure," says Hardcase. "We've got someone who says you two were an item."

I will myself to remain silent. Hardcase waits me out, waits for me to crack and start jabbering. I don't.

"We're running down all kinds of leads," he says. "Phone calls he made and received, emails, credit card charges, everything. If we find out you've been holding out on us it will go hard for you."

He's bluffing. We both know it. No one has told them I dated Strand. But it's not a total bluff. They could find some connection to me in the paper trail. The flowers, maybe. I make a snap decision.

"I'm sure it will," I answer. "Anything else?"

"What do you know about Strand being involved with a hooker named Mandy Marvin?"

"I know that was the hot rumor in the trans community when Mandy was murdered," I answer. "I don't know that to be a fact. I never saw them together."

"Did you know this Marvin?"

"Yes," I answer. "I did her hair. We were friendly but not close friends. She didn't tell me who she was dating." Exactly what I told Officer Phil.

"Dating?" Hardcase spits out the word with equal parts disbelief and contempt.

"Yes, she dated men, even when she was a hooker." I look Hardcase in the eye. "A lot of young transsexuals do both, you know. They use prostitution to get the money they need for their transitions, but inside they're just like young women everywhere. They want to fall in love, get married, live happily ever after."

Hardcase snorts contemptuously. He closes his notepad. "We'll get back to you. You're not planning on leaving town any time soon, right?"

"I'll be heading for New York in a couple of weeks for a hair show," I answer.

"Check with us first," Hardcase says.

"Sure. Just send me the court order," I reply. It's not confidence I feel. It's rebellion. I really have a thing about being bullied. Jesus, I killed a man about it.

Wilkins glowers at me then nods slowly, knowingly. "Let's see how cocky you are when we throw you in a cell with bunch of butt-fucking niggers from the south side." Wilkins is black himself, so he uses the guttural racial reference to strike terror in my prissy white heart.

He flashes an ugly smile in my face. "Did I mention we found hair and skin follicles in that apartment? The lab is doing a workup right now."

He turns and leaves, the other cop following.

"We'll be back." It's a threat.

I feel a wave of terror pass over me. My heart almost stops. Could I have left strands of my own hair in Strand's apartment? Wearing a wig? Could the wig hairs be traced to me? I wonder if there are wig hairs still in my apartment.

As I climb the stairs to my apartment, I realize with certainty that there must be traces of wig hairs in my place—along with traces of hair from dozens of clients, maybe hundreds. Human hairs. Synthetics.

Halfway up the stairs I realize there isn't enough time or money to collect and analyze all the hair and skin cell samples in my apartment, much less match them to samples from Strand's place. Hardcase was running a bluff. And not even because he thought a degenerate fag like me had killed Strand. He did it just to fuck with my mind because I'm a degenerate fag and he can get away with it.

My fear turns to anger. I've had it with people feeling like they can be rude and mean to me just because I look funny to them, or because they think I'm morally inferior. I'm sick of being bullied. I'm sick of bigotry.

Inside my apartment, I nuke a frozen dinner and inventory the contents of my purse. I find it. The business card for the GLBT advocate in the Cook County State Attorney's office. I call her direct dial number and get her voicemail.

"Hi," I say, "My name is Bobbi Logan. I'm a pre-op transsexual. I live in the Boystown area. I've just had a visit from a police detective who threatened to put me in a cell with a bunch of quote butt-fucking niggers unquote. I gave him no reason to treat me like that. I answered all his questions. I feel intimidated and threatened by this individual. Are you someone who can help me with this matter?" I leave my work and home phone numbers.

If I haven't learned anything else as a transsexual, it is a reaffirmation of the first thing you learn as a child playing dodge ball: ducking alone isn't enough. You have to fire back now and then or no one will respect you.

Least of all, myself.

My next call is to Cecelia. Yes, Detective Hardcase tried getting in her face, too. Yes, she'll get me the name of a good attorney from her attorney. No, she didn't know about the LGBT advocate in the State Attorney's office. Yes, she'll make the call and she'll pass the number on to the other girls.

It feels good to fire back. This time, anyway.

* * *

ONE OF THE CONDITIONS Marilee laid down was that I had to tell all to Roberta because Roberta is my counselor. "She can't do her job if you hold out on her," Marilee scolded me.

Roberta's normally placid demeanor evaporates as I confess. Her jaw drops, mouth opens, her eyes widen, a hand comes to her lips. I've never seen her react like this. It scares me.

"Bobbi!" she gasps. "You? You could do something like this?"

"It was easier to do than to live with, if that helps," I say.

She shakes her head.

"Who have you told about this?"

"Just Marilee. I didn't want to tell anyone. I didn't want anyone else to have to deal with the guilt. Yesterday, it just came out during a chat. She registered me as a patient then made me promise to tell you. And she'd like you to call her."

Roberta is frozen in place, chest heaving, her hand still at her lips as if holding back something. She isn't looking at me, isn't talking.

I'm unsettled. Roberta has been a counselor for a long time and I know she's dealt with all kinds of situations. For her to be so upset over this has me feeling like a monster.

"He was stalking me, Roberta," I say. "I didn't have a choice other than to die myself or get raped again. I'm not dangerous."

She nods. "I know, Bobbi. Give me a minute."

We struggle through the hour. She recovers her poise to ask most of the questions Marilee asked, to hear my answers without expressing horror. We will talk again tomorrow. She's still my counselor. But I don't think she'll ever see me the same way again.

Who would?

* * *

OFFICER PHIL CALLS my cell at four-fifteen. I stop breathing as I read his name on my caller ID. Only a handful of people have my cell phone number, and he's not one of them. Good God!

"That wasn't the smartest thing you ever did, Bobbi," he says. No hi, no introduction. He must be getting lessons from Cecelia.

"How did you get this number?" I shoot back.

"I'm a cop."

"This number isn't listed. Anywhere. How did you get it?" There's an edge to my voice. I can feel perspiration dotting my brow.

"It doesn't matter. You have bigger problems anyway."

"What are you talking about?" I'm on my way to the gym. I look up and down the street to see if a squadron of police cars is closing in to bust me.

"Complaining about Wilkins. He's been taken off the Strand case and he's angry. He has a long memory. Plus it makes us wonder about you."

"What are you wondering?" My relief is palpable.

"We want to know what you have to hide." For the first time there is real menace in Officer Phil's voice.

"That makes me wonder if you're all a bunch of bigots," I fire back. I can feel my face flushing with anger. "I answered every stupid question. He treated me like slime. He called me by my male name, he called me a fruitcake and my friend a hooker. He threatened to have me quote butt-fucked by a bunch of niggers, unquote, his words. If you think I should take that from him or you or anyone else you can forget it."

"I'm just telling you as a friend to be careful," says Phil.

"Thank you, Officer," I say. "I'll just share with you that I'm not in a mood to be careful and neither is anyone else in the community. We're pissed off that Chicago's finest stand around and scratch their balls when we get beat up or murdered, and now when some straight rich guy gets it you want to accuse one of us. Wake up Phil. In the history of Chicago no trans person has ever killed anyone. You're just a bunch of bullies and bigots and we aren't going to take it anymore.

"And Phil, I don't know what you think you're pulling here, but you know and I know I'm not the only one who complained. I know at least six other girls did too, and if you keep this crap up it's going to be dozens. And if going to the State Attorney's office doesn't get you off our backs we'll go to the papers.

"So here's my friendly advice to you Officer Phil, stop with the intimidation."

He's silent for a minute. "Okay, Bobbie, I've done what I can," he says and hangs up. The sign off was supposed to leave me in doubt, but his words were hollow. The new detective on the case won't be wasting time in Boystown on the Strand murder.

And frankly, even if they somehow prove I did it, I wouldn't back down on this stuff anyway. I'm sick of being treated like a freak and a lesser human being.

* * *

MY ANGER MUST SHOW. No one wants to be my kickboxing partner tonight. The instructor has to hold my kicking dummy. I attack with newfound relish. After a week of languishing in guilt and doubt, I come to class with as much fury as I had in the beginning.

It feels surprisingly good. Rejuvenating. This must be why bigots and bullies almost universally gravitate toward righteous anger. It helps you live with the truth about yourself by putting the focus on someone or something else.

Yes, thanks to Officer Phil, I may actually get a good night's sleep tonight.

I catch a glimpse of Thomas after my class. As I stop at a drinking fountain I can see him in the free-weight area. He winks but doesn't wave. I give him a small smile. We've put our friendship on hold for a few more months. I don't want the police finding a connection between me and someone strong enough to beat up a thug, not while they're sniffing around the trans community in the Strand murder investigation.

I miss Thomas. I miss having that kind of friend.

* * *

MY PASSION IS COMING back. We're nearing the end of May and I seem to have put the image of myself as a cold-blooded murderer in a separate compartment in my mind. I know it's there. I pass the door to the compartment every day, many times every day. I know what's inside. But I don't go in very often and wallow in it. I make note of it and keep moving on.

My passion for hair came back first. I can even tell you the exact time it came rushing back. It was a couple of weeks ago. Things had been getting a little better for me mentally and emotionally anyway, and I had this nasty old lady come in for a new style. She bitched about everything. Her hair. The salon. Her life. Having a transsexual do her hair. Chicago being taken over by blacks and foreign-speaking Mexicans, Chinese, Indians, and so on.

I tuned her out and worked in silence. I didn't really want her to come back, but I also didn't want to be distracted by her jabbering. She was one of those ladies who, even in her mid-seventies, had beautiful thick hair in an elegant silver-gray color. Even though I had no use for her as a person, her hair was special and I fell in love with it as soon as I touched it.

I gave her a gorgeous bob, one of the best I've ever done. Precise, stylish. With a sassy angle moving forward, like a young movie star. It worked. She looked like a socialite heiress who still enjoys a good romp in bed, maybe with a youthful lover. I actually forgot for a moment what a nasty person she was. She did too. She actually smiled and said she loved it.

Maybe she'll come back, maybe not. Angry people like her are really unpredictable. But from that time on, I have been back in the groove, enjoying my work, enjoying my customers.

This weekend has been a passion extravaganza. I'm in New York at the biggest hair show in the U.S. SuperGlam upped my deal. Not only am I on stage twice a day for their big shows, I also spend two hours a day at their exhibit doing updos on the floor where visiting hairdressers can cluster around and ask questions.

This has been the greatest gig ever.

My backcombing technique has gotten much better from all the coaching I've gotten from Evelyn and the hours of practice I've put in. I pull a lot of people into the booth. People see my "after" models posing in the area and see me turn a strand of flat, straight, limp hair into a puff in the blink of an eye and they are hooked. Getting straight, fine, healthy hair to hold a tease is one of the biggest challenges in hairdressing.

A few stop in to see what gender I am. I am tall and broad-shouldered, but I'm working in a hot mini dress, fish net stockings, black platform sandals, and a revealing T-top. The gender mystery deepens when they hear my voice. I'm using a microphone and a single-amp speaker that's just loud enough for my corner of the exhibit, and passersby catch a few syllables. Like my shoulders and my size, my voice doesn't ring true. Some stop and watch, because even in New York transwomen as obvious as me are rarely seen in public. Some walk away faster, for the same reason.

The ones who stay are fun. We have a running banter. They ask me where I'm from, how I got the idea for this or that style, how I lock in the backcombing, how I do my backcombing technique, what kind of customers I have in my own salon, do I dress like this for work, are my colleagues okay with me being trans, how often do I do updos, what do I charge.

The time flies by.

As I finish my last show and start packing my tools, one of the ladies from the crowd lingers and approaches. I recognize her. She's tall, maybe 5-9 or 5-10 in flats, a trifle heavy but with a sexy bosom and a pretty face. She has short dark hair worn in a spiky fringe. It sets off a round face with full lips, pretty eyes, and a devilish smile.

"I loved watching you work," she says, extending a hand for a handshake, "I'm Jen and I have one more question."

I smile and shake her hand. She asked several questions while I worked. I remember liking her for her interest and animation. "I enjoyed your questions," I say.

"So who's going to do your updo and get you out on the town tonight?" she asks. Her smile is warm and suggestive. I think she's making a pass.

"Poor me," I say. "Everyone has already gone out to play."

"Can I take a shot at it?" she asks.

"I'd be flattered."

"One condition," says Jen. "Afterward you let me take you to dinner."

Wow, twist my arm. In this city a hot dog and fries costs you a house and a firstborn. I smile and agree, and sit in the styling chair. Jen goes to work with my tools.

* * *

WE MAKE QUITE an entrance at a Soho restaurant. Me in a radical-chic updo formed from masses of curls and grand puffs of teased hair. I'm in a cocktail dress; it's black, form-fitting and stops a few inches above the knee— Fifth Avenue sexy, even on me.

Jen did a costume change, too. She's wearing a suit that is masculine but somehow projects her femininity at the same time. We are an odd couple, she being butch and me being girly-girly in a lumberjack kind of way.

This being New York, we drew lots of stares. New Yorkers are uninhibited about these things. Jen enjoys the attention, she tells me. She dressed for it.

Jen is from Indianapolis. She's in her mid-thirties. She tried marriage. She's had girlfriends and boyfriends. One of her girlfriends became a boyfriend while they were together. She has decided she is indifferent about sexuality, and she's getting that way with gender identity too. I tell her about the "gender queer" kids in Chicago—they often mix male and female appearances. One young bearded man I knew would go out on the town in mostly male attire except for a female top and breast forms. One of my customers is a young woman who sometimes wears male clothing and adopts male mannerisms, but still looks like a woman. "Do you prefer to be referred to as a female or a male?" I asked her the first time we met. "Either," she said. "Or both."

Jen thinks this is cool.

After dinner she takes me to a lesbian bar. We draw lots of stares here, too. Especially me. Interesting. In a gay male bar, I am usually ignored. Mainstream gays like their men more in the cowboy/athlete mode. The lesbians I've known have been polite enough, and some of them have partnered up with my transsexual sisters, but not until the sister has fully transitioned and feminized.

So the stares are probably about us as a couple. You don't see our combination very often.

We talk about doing hair, people we've dated. She asks me lots of questions about transitioning. She's astonished at how much I've invested in electrolysis. At one point, I confess my morbid fear of having large hairy breasts whereupon Jen impishly reaches inside my dress and feels me up.

"It worked," she says. "You feel great."

I smile and blush profusely. I'm wildly aroused.

"Ohhhh, you liked that!" she says. I nod. "Me too, sweetie," she says. She kisses me on the lips, a long soft kiss. Her lips are plump and warm. She puts her tongue in my mouth. I suck on it gently. She murmurs something and we hug.

When I regain my composure, I tell her about my abstinence pact. She thinks about this for a moment. "Are you afraid if we have sex that you'll want to be a man again?"

"No. My gender isn't an issue any more. I'm a woman," I say. "If you make love to me, you'll be making love to a woman no matter what body parts I have. But I'd like to have all the right ones."

Jen nods. "Okay. I understand. I'll wait." She pauses. "But we can still neck and pet, right?"

I nod. The anticipation of her warm flesh on mine has robbed me of the power of speech.

* * *

June

IT IS ONE OF THOSE EVENINGS we get in Chicago that you don't get anywhere else. Oh, you can get the same weather in California or Florida, but it doesn't feel as good there because you haven't paid for it with a long winter.

You can get the same feeling about the weather in Indianapolis or Milwaukee, but you don't get the ambience. Nothing against any of those cities, but not even New York has Chicago's combination of architectural majesty, beautiful beaches, hip urbanity, and an arcane touch of Midwestern innocence.

I'm walking home from the salon. I inhale the evening air and feel like I'm walking in a dream. It is good to be alive. It's good to *feel* alive. I feel the vibrations of life all around me, from the throngs of people moving about on their way to restaurants and clubs and goodness knows what else, to the traffic, the buildings, the sidewalk art, the light clouds etched in the dimming light of the skies.

This is a milestone moment. The end of something before the beginning of something else. Like New Year's Eve. This is my last evening in Chicago as a pre-op transsexual, a woman with a penis. Tomorrow, I will board an airplane to Colorado and in three days I will have my male parts removed and I will finally have my vagina. I know this sounds grizzly to you, but it will be a fantastic relief for me. As my transition has progressed, as I've become more absorbed in living my life and less worried about how others see me, my male appendage has become increasingly bothersome. A nagging sore in my consciousness that constantly reminds me I am not whole yet.

I am forewarned that I will be in great pain and discomfort, and that I will not feel at all ecstatic about having this vagina. Not for many days.

No matter. I'm getting it done. I am giddy with the knowledge that I am at last getting it done. As for the pain, well, it's just physical pain. It subsides after awhile. When I think of pain, I think of my father's disgust, his open contempt for who I actually am. I think of my mother abandoning me because my father said to. I think of all the nasty, cutting remarks people have sent my way because I'm different.

I think, too, of pleasuring a man and having him despise me for it. I think of being raped and beaten and left in an alley like garbage.

And yes, I think about what I did to Strand. I think about the months of dithering about what to do, and the weeks of actively planning to kill him, the shame I felt at savoring the idea of it. I think about that night, how I almost didn't do it, how Strand treated that poor t-girl. I think about what he looked like and what he said when he reached consciousness. Most of all, I still remember everything about the kill. Positioning myself behind him, feeling the knife slice through skin and flesh, severing his carotid artery, seeing blood spurt on the floor, watching his body do the death shake.

That movie still plays in the theater of my mind. Not every day. Not any more. But several times a week, anyway. I sleep through the night now, but I don't sleep like the innocent. I never will again. I bear the burden of knowing who I am and what I'm capable of doing. I have it within me to slit a man's throat and watch him die.

That's not WHO I am. But it's part of who I am now, and it will always be a part of who I am. Bobbi Logan: passionate hairdresser, transsexual woman, loving friend to many, murderer of John Strand, himself a murderer.

So whatever physical pain awaits me I readily accept.

Every once in awhile I hear about Wilkins interviewing someone in the community, working on his own time to get a lead on Strand's murder. It's a reminder that the police might someday blunder onto a trail that leads to me, and that I would then be incarcerated for the rest of my life. It isn't likely. John Strand was a secretive man with a lot to hide. None of the facts they've uncovered about him seem to lead anywhere. They don't even know about the poor girl he smashed around on the last night of his vile life. In fact, the rumors about him and Mandy are the only connection the police have between him and trans world, and Cecelia is making life miserable for them on that score.

If they do bust me, at least I'll get locked away as a woman. That was the deciding factor with Roberta giving me the okay to go ahead with gender reassignment surgery. When we finally sat down and talked about the murder, she wanted me to put off GRS while I came to terms with what I had done.

I begged her to let me go to a more intense counseling schedule instead. Because if I got busted before my surgery, a life sentence for me in a male prison would be the most painful possible death sentence, much worse than Strand's end.

She pondered this for a week, then told me in her quiet, dignified way that she would agree to an accelerated counseling schedule. She held me to it, too. The sessions were three times a week at first, then two, and they were painful. We revisited every moment of my conflict with Strand, every emotion I felt, even the finest details about the sexual escapade with him.

Ever the pragmatist, Roberta wanted me not only to understand what I did, but also to consider alternatives I could have explored—to the murder, to the secrecy, to everything. Most of all, she said, I needed to come to grips with what I had done. I needed to be able to put that information in a place where I would never forget it, but where it didn't affect everything I do, every thought I have.

I'm getting there.

Hillary Clinton was right. It takes a village. And not just to nurture kids, to nurture everyone.

The community is what has pulled me through. I've been hugged by Marilee more in the last six weeks than my own mother hugged me in my life. Cecelia calls me every day. Ray comes in every four weeks for a haircut and to get us caught up on each others' lives. Betsy calls several times a week to see how I'm holding up as my time draws nigh. She wants to meet me at the airport when I come home and drive me to my apartment.

Today at the salon, Roger and the girls got me a cake and had a champagne toast for me in the mid-afternoon. A year ago, I was an embarrassment to most of them. Today, they were celebrating my imminent sex change and talking about it openly with their clients. I have kissed and hugged every one of them. Even Trudy, my religious colleague. Some of them even had tears as we embraced.

Yes, I know none of them is aware of the fact that I murdered someone, but I think if they knew the whole story they might be able to forgive me for even that trespass, even Trudy, just as they have forgiven me for being a transsexual.

Of all the things that have happened to me in the past year, Trudy's transformation is one of the most remarkable. I never would have guessed that this person who was so angry and judgmental toward me would become my friend. I think it shocks her, too. And I know it makes her feel good, just like it does me.

Thomas has called a few times, too. He takes the precaution of using a disposable cell phone to make the call. We'll restart our open friendship in the fall, we've decided. That will give him time to forgive me for having my penis cut off (a standing joke between us). I think his partner will find it a little easier to have me around then, too. I'm no threat for Thomas' affections as a woman, not that I was as a she-male either.

Somewhere in all of this I gradually came to realize that I love this place, this time, these people. This is where I learned to accept myself. Bobbi, a strange-looking woman who used to be a man, who has this weird girly-girl streak, who loves to do hair, who killed someone once. After that, loving the people around me was easy. Some of them loved me before I loved myself.

I think you know I'm not talking about romantic love here. I'm talking about the kind of love that bonds people together as they deal with life's endless contingencies and surprises. I include Roger, my boss, in that circle. He stood by me when it really didn't make good sense to stand by me. He doesn't know it yet, but he's getting paid back. Today I called SuperGlam to turn down a full-time gig in their New York facility doing demos all over the country and even Europe. It would have set me up for life, big money, prestige, a big name. I could have charged $150 for haircuts the rest of my working life.

But you know, I'm doing okay here financially. My business is growing and I'm helping the salon grow, too. It makes me feel, I don't know, valuable. Worthy. Like I'm someone.

And in the end, I just couldn't leave my friends and my community. I wouldn't be the same person someplace else. I could never say goodbye to Cecelia. Or Roberta. Or Roger. Certainly not to Marilee. I want to be a doting aunt to Betsy's child. I want to see how things turn out with Ray and his wife and their trans-child. I want to be here this summer when Jen comes up from Indy for a visit, and I want to visit her down there.

I want to fall in love someday. I want to share a life with someone who can handle what I am and who I am. I can do that anywhere I guess, but I need to do it here. This is who I am. This is where I make my stand.

AUTHOR'S NOTES

COMING OUT CAN BE MURDER

SINCE MY GREATEST HOPE in publishing this book is to increase public acceptance and understanding of transgender people, a few words about the use of the term "tranny" are in order.

In the transgender world, "tranny" is a pejorative word, much reviled by most transsexuals as an expression derived from smut websites.

I have made it part of the vocabulary of the book's villains, and I have also allowed some transgender characters to use the word in certain situations. For example, when our heroine Bobbi thinks about how trans-phobes see her, she sometimes uses the word "tranny."

The expression "tranny chaser" is doubly pejorative, using an ugly word with another to create an expression that marginalizes men who are attracted to male-to-female transgenders. While some men who are attracted to transwomen are "creepy" (a word often used in the same phrase as "tranny chaser"), most men who socialize with transwomen simply accept us as people; romantic relationships sometimes evolve as a result.

I encourage you in your dealings with transgender people to avoid the use of these pejoratives, and to be sensitive to the gender-defining pronouns you use in your communications. For example, someone dressed in women's clothing and bearing a female name will prefer to be referred to as "she" or "her."

SEXUAL PREFERENCE and gender identity are two different aspects of human development. Most of the trans women I know lived as hetero men until they came to grips with their transgender identities, and even most of those who transitioned to female still preferred intimacy with women. I chose to have Bobbi experiment with a gay lifestyle before discovering her transsexual identity; this isn't an especially common path among transsexuals, but it happens and I liked it for my story.

Similarly, I chose to make Bobbi a bi-sexual transwoman, attracted to individuals in both genders, because in her journey, rife as it is in rejection and abuse, intimacy is ultimately about the person, not the gender or race or political allegiance.

PLEASE NOTE THAT the Chicago Police Department has programs and initiatives to sensitize their personnel to transgender people and their issues. Compared to police departments elsewhere in the U.S.—or the world, for that matter—Chicago PD probably rates at or near the top when it comes to treatment of trans people. That, of course, does not mean that all crimes against trans people—or any other group—get solved. In *Coming Out Can Be Murder*, the negative comments about police work stem from community frustration over an unsolvable crime—one with no witnesses and virtually no physical evidence.

I READ JOHN GRISHAM'S *Street Lawyer* on my way to a convention many years ago. By the time I got off the airplane, my attitude toward homeless people had changed dramatically—hopefully forever.

Through his words and storytelling, I learned to consider the homeless I encountered as people. I established eye contact instead of pretending they weren't there, I said hello, and I answered if they asked me a question. If they were selling something, I listened and either bought or declined courteously. If they were looking for a handout, I gave or said I couldn't, if that was the case.

I discovered that homeless people have human qualities I can relate to, just like nearly everyone else. My life is better for having reached this realization.

My greatest ambition is that this story does the same thing for you and how you relate to transgender men and women. It's so easy. Just say 'hi.' Ask what's new or how they are. Smile. Wave.

We have more in common than you think, starting with the fact that all of us are here for a short walk on a small planet. Let's make the most of it.

~Renee James

CPSIA information can be obtained at www.ICGtesting.com
Printed in the USA
LVOW120336170512

281987LV00004B/2/P

9 781935 766285